ASCENSION

St. Martin's Paperbacks Titles by
Caris Roane

ASCENSION

BURNING SKIES

WINGS OF FIRE

ASCENSION

CARIS ROANE

St. Martin's Paperbacks

This is a work of fiction. All of the characters, organizations, and events portrayed in this novel are either products of the author's imagination or are used fictitiously.

ASCENSION

Copyright © 2010 by Caris Roane.

For information address St. Martin's Press, 175 Fifth Avenue, New York, NY 10010.

ISBN: 978-0-312-53371-7

Printed in the United States of America

St. Martin's Paperbacks edition / January 2011

St. Martin's Paperbacks are published by St. Martin's Press, 175 Fifth Avenue, New York, NY 10010.

10 9 8 7 6 5 4 3 2

ACKNOWLEDGMENTS

My deepest gratitude to my agent, Jennifer Schober, who worked one very fine miracle on behalf of *Ascension*.

To my editor and sister-in-enthusiasm, Rose Hilliard, who loves the world of books and storytelling almost as much I do. Okay . . . as much.

My thanks to Danielle Fiorella, who created an amazing cover that exceeded all expectations.

To Laurie Henderson and Laura Jorstad, who blew me away with the careful and considerate production of this book. The copyediting was outstanding.

Thanks to the marketing team of Anne Marie Tallberg, Brittney Kleinfelter, and Eileen Rothschild, who have worked to put this book in the hands of the readers.

And finally, many thanks to Matthew Shear and Jen Enderlin, who said *yes*. Now there's a powerful word.

I have loved being part of this team.

Vampire.
A most sacred mantle lost to the desecration of those
who partake of dying blood.
Vampire.
Keep thyself pure.

—*Collected Proverbs,* Beatrice of Fourth

CHAPTER 1

Kerrick stood by the bar at the Blood and Bite, looking for
a woman, the right woman, the one who would keep his head
straight, the one he *craved.* His thighs twitched, heavy muscles he'd worked hard an hour ago, muscles demanding relief.
Hunger lived in him now, deep, begging, fierce. He was a
vampire and a warrior. He needed what he needed.

Yet something had changed and now he *craved.*

What he *craved,* however, he couldn't have.

He'd taken vows.

His gaze slid around the south Phoenix club, into the
many dark corners, the deep padded booths covered in red
velvet, past the flashing strobes meant to disguise the various dark deeds that brought mortal women in droves to the
vampire joint. The bar had the only real light, enhanced by
a tall mirror behind a landscape of hundreds of gem-like
bottles. The rest of the club slid to darkness all around the
edges.

Vibrant moans punctuated the noise of the club and made his thighs twitch all over again.

Still, what he needed wasn't here, wasn't the fuck anywhere. He'd awakened a few hours ago with a hum in his chest that wouldn't go away, a need unfulfilled and now screaming. It wasn't just sex but sex was what called to him as an opener, a place to begin. He hunted with his groin but couldn't find *her*. Not here. He wasn't even looking. He couldn't look. He'd taken vows, goddammit.

"You listening?"

Kerrick shot his gaze to Thorne. "Shit. Sorry. No."

"What the hell is the matter with you tonight?" Thorne, the leader of the Warriors of the Blood, sat on a stool next to him nursing a tumbler of Ketel One.

Kerrick leaned his hips against the bar and turned to scan the dance floor. Loud sexy music pumped through the dark club. Shadows passed back and forth, women giggling, men chasing as they had from the beginning of time. He shook his head. "You ever had an itch you couldn't scratch?" He heard Thorne suck in a deep breath then exhale like he'd been breathing water.

"Sure. Every night of my life."

Kerrick palmed the back of his neck and rubbed. The muscles were tight, but then they'd been tight for a few centuries. How long had he been here? Twelve. Yeah, his muscles had been tight for twelve centuries. What would it be like to have the strain worked out of every muscle?

He turned in the direction of the barkeep then tapped his glass on the counter. Sam Finch, owner of the Blood and Bite, drew close with a bottle of Maker's and refilled the tumbler with two fingers of liquid gold.

Kerrick nodded his thanks then threw back the whiskey. He was used to the burn as he swallowed. He let the fire eat up his throat. He breathed in the vapors, felt his veins melt a little, yet no relief. Never relief, just a slight unwinding. "Where's Medichi?"

"I told you," Thorne said. His voice always sounded like he'd roughed it up with some coarse-grade sandpaper. "I sent him to Awatukee. Everyone's out already. Again, what the hell is with you?"

Kerrick scowled. "Shit." The rest of the warriors had received their assignments for the first round of battling, but—like every night for a warrior—anything could happen and usually did. "I've got this uneasy sense that all hell is about to break loose. And it isn't even a full moon." Kerrick tapped the bar once more. Sam refilled. He always took care of the warriors, staying close. "That will be Endelle."

"*What* will be Endelle?" Thorne's phone buzzed. He flipped Kerrick off then slashed the small flat card to his ear. "Give." He nodded and let loose a bunch of *yes, ma'am*s for the next minute.

Kerrick shifted hips and torso, his gaze locked on Thorne. The brother's hazel eyes were red-rimmed and not from weeping—too much Ketel One and no reason to put the bottle down. Thorne kept his fingers around the tumbler, stroking his thumb up and down the cold glass. He was Endelle's numero uno, and Endelle answered to no one. She headed the main peacekeeping force in their world, and the warriors were hers to command. She was also a stick of dynamite, lit, ready to go off.

Kerrick drew in another deep breath. His gaze drifted to the dance floor. A wicked beat had the ladies gyrating and the men putting their hands everywhere. A few fangs pierced necks, which forced Kerrick to take another deep breath. He should get out there and get some relief. Blood would help. So would getting inside a woman. Yet how long would the buzz last? These days, not even two minutes, so what was the point?

Besides, what he needed wasn't swinging her hips on a dance floor and what he needed he'd vowed never to take again. What he needed was a scent meant only for him, a myth, a woman who could fill all the deep gorges of his heart. And even if he found her, he was bound, hands together, ankles lashed, mouth gagged, heart blocked by a steel cage of guilt. So . . . shit.

He slung back the Maker's and tapped the bar again. Sam was once more at his elbow.

"Yes, ma'am." Thorne slugged Kerrick's thigh and caught his attention. He looked up at Kerrick but kept speaking into the phone. "Sure you don't want someone else? That particular warrior needs some R and R. In fact, I think he ought to be pulled for the night." He drew the phone away from his ear and winced. Kerrick could hear the shouting; the words were the same set he used when he was just a little pissed off. He smiled and sipped. Endelle had lost her subtlety a few millennia ago.

Endelle. Bitch-on-wheels, yet he'd die for her. She was what kept their world from sinking beneath the enemy's boot and Kerrick served her, they all did. The Warriors of the Blood loved her, hated her, goddamn respected her.

"Yes, ma'am." Thorne's head bobbed, and more *yes-sum*s followed. Finally he thumbed his phone and replaced it in an upper slit of his black leather kilt. He wore battle gear and would soon head out like the rest of them. "You've got an assignment."

"Now, that's what I'm talkin' about." He needed his sword in one hand and his dagger in the other. Battling always helped, always took some of the strain from his neck. He stood upright, ready for action. Thorne just looked at him.

"What?" Kerrick snapped.

"It might be a woman."

Kerrick shook his head. "She wants me to protect a mortal female? What the fuck? You know the vow I took and so does Endelle. I don't guard females."

Thorne met his gaze head-on, no blinking.

"Shit." Kerrick dug in his heels, lowered his chin. He split his resonance. "Not gonna do it." He'd taken a vow and the hell he'd overturn it just because Her Supremeness willed it so.

"Endelle *requested* you on this one, no one else. She never pushes me about assignments so she must have her reasons. Besides, she didn't have any details. She saw something in her meditations, which as you know do not always pan out."

"I'm better off battling. With the mood I'm in, I could crush skulls with my bare hands tonight." His biceps flexed and quivered, a thoroughbred at the gate.

"Sorry. She wants you."

The song ended abruptly and Kerrick's voice boomed the length of the building: "Fuck you."

All conversation, from one end of the club to the other, got knocked off track for about three long seconds. Kerrick glanced around and anyone looking his direction immediately looked away. Warriors weren't known for their sweet tempers.

Thorne rose from his seat, his hazel eyes hard as steel. He met Kerrick's gaze dead-on. "You don't have a choice."

"The hell I don't and *that* would be Jeannie."

"Jeannie?" Thorne cried. "What the hell are you talking about?" His phone buzzed, and he flipped Kerrick off again as he drew the card to his ear. "Give," he barked. "Oh. Hey, Jeannie. Sorry. What's up?"

Jeannie worked at Central Command. All the night's assignments flowed from Central straight to Thorne. Central mapped the entire metro Phoenix area and knew exactly where the enemy operated and where the warriors needed to be. Kerrick narrowed his eyes, his fingers flexed around his tumbler. He imagined his sword in one hand, dagger in the other. His heart rate increased.

"Got it," Thorne said. He returned his phone to the same pocket and let another juicy set of obscenities fly. "Okay. You've got a reprieve. Four pretty-boys active in a downtown alley. You know the drill."

"Four," Kerrick murmured, nodding. He almost smiled. He clapped Thorne on the shoulder. "Thank you," he said. "But please just get me the hell out of this other bullshit assignment."

* * *

Alison Wells sat in her office, perched on the edge of her cream-colored wing chair, the therapist's chair, her Black-Berry clamped to her ear. The last thing she wanted to do was have a conversation with her sister about her love life, but for some reason Joy was pressing her to start dating again.

Taking a deep breath, Alison said, "I think you're forgetting that the last man who made love to me ended up in the emergency room . . . bleeding . . . and *unconscious*." She gripped her phone hard, painful memories crowding her head.

"Not so loud," Joy cried. "I have *regular* eardrums, remember?"

"And I'm telling you that I don't want to talk about my ex. I closed this chapter on my life the same night I rode to the hospital and nothing, *nothing,* will cause me to open it again."

"Lissy, it's been three years. Maybe things have changed. Maybe some of those *special abilities* of yours have calmed down a little. Maybe you could find some huge bodybuilder who could handle all your power. I mean . . . really. You should try again. *Really.*"

Alison sighed as a familiar longing filled up her chest until she could hardly breathe. Why couldn't she have been more like Joy, even a little bit, Joy the younger sister, the normal sister, the sister with the gorgeous husband and nine-month-old adorable baby boy?

They were like night and day. Joy with her curly brown hair and dark eyes who resembled their father, while Alison with her straight blond hair and blue eyes took after Mom. The only thing she shared in common with her sister was her height. At six-foot apiece, they'd both been teased all through middle school and well into high school.

Joy had made the best of it and took up cheerleading.

Alison had known her height for what it was, one more thing that set her apart from everyone else.

Her gaze skated over the empty wall unit opposite as well as the pictureless walls. She had sold the furniture a week ago to the therapist taking over most of her practice. Other than the foot-high unity statue sitting in the center of the coffee table, her office was a desert, as dry as the air outside, as lifeless.

Her gaze shifted to the alabaster carving, and a silent curse worked her tongue. The last remnant of her eight-year stint in private practice was that aggravating statue. She smoothed back hair already pulled into a tight twist. If only her sister hadn't called to discuss her love life, maybe she wouldn't feel quite so ready to scream.

"Please, Lissy," Joy said in a voice that sent a warning chill straight down her spine. "I really, *really* think you should try again."

All the breath left Alison's body as she stared at the alabaster family. She thought of her nephew whom she loved more than she had ever thought possible, one of her links to normalcy as Aunt Lissy.

Her heart fractured then broke into a million pieces.

This couldn't be happening, this truth, which Joy's desperate tone had finally unveiled, the reason for her phone call.

Oh. No.

At last she drew breath. She took several. "Joy," she whispered. Her heart thumped through a couple of questionable beats.

"Yes?" Nothing more than a squeak this time.

Dear sister. Dear *normal* sister. "How far along are you? Six weeks? Eight?"

"Did you just read my mind? You're not supposed to, remember? You just broke Mom's rule."

"I didn't read your mind. I wouldn't, not without your permission." Another breath, another effort to calm her unsteady heart. She needed the truth, but she didn't want to hear it. "It's just that you haven't brought up my love life in, oh, let's see, three years. *Really.* So how far along are you?" She didn't want to know. *Joy, please don't say it.*

A heavy sigh followed. "Two months, one week. I just didn't know how to tell you."

Alison used her free hand to white-knuckle the armrest of the chair. "And you thought I'd be upset?" Dammit, her eyes burned like she'd just rubbed them with chili peppers. *Upset* didn't begin to describe what she felt. *Upset* would have been a lazy walk on the beach.

She squeezed her eyes shut and bent over, folding up like a taco to keep everything inside from spilling out. She had only one wish: that the world would end right now.

A second child. A husband, a home, little T. J., and now another baby on the way.

"Of course you'll be upset," Joy said. Her cadence had slowed down. "You think I haven't noticed how anytime we're together you pick T. J. up and don't give him back until we've loaded the car? Even then I have to pry him out of your arms."

"Saw that, did you?"

"Oh, Lissy, I know how you look at Ryan and me. Do you suppose for even one second I don't get how much your heart's broken? What kind of sister do you think I am?"

Alison could have sworn she'd been more careful, more circumspect, but maybe that was like a ripe tomato trying not to be red. She should have known her sister would see through her. "I'll be all right." She swiped at damp cheeks.

"Like hell. I'm so sorry, Lissy." A soft sigh, then, "Maybe you could—"

"Please don't," she cried. "Not another word. Please." She squeezed her eyes shut as she pulled herself together. "I have an idea. Why don't we just forget about me for a moment." She arched up from her hinged position and forced herself to be a good sister. "I want to hear every single detail about this new life, so tell me everything. When did you find out?" More tears tracked her cheeks.

The tenor of her sister's voice returned to the usual soft wind-chime treble as she rattled off all her symptoms, travails, and excitement. She had to pee too much already, her hemorrhoids were a bitch—and she wasn't even three months along, thank you very much—and she had the worst time just staying awake. But oh, God, she could hardly wait until she felt the first movement of life, the fluttering deep inside, the certainty a new baby was on the way.

Alison listened and made every appropriate ooh and aah even though she pressed a hand to her chest the whole time. Her gaze became fixed to the heavy-as-hell alabaster statue, sculpted to show the images of father, mother, and child, a symbol of internal unity, the exact representation of the goal of therapy. She had thought herself so clever at the time buying it.

"I have to wear maternity pants already . . . ," Joy rattled on, a car on a salt flat gaining speed.

Alison stood up and rounded the coffee table. She positioned herself opposite the window then looked down to stare at the alabaster figures once more. She had loved everything about the sculpture until her sister's first child had come into the world. Then the meaning had changed, shifted, taken on razor-sharp edges, which kept slicing Alison up.

"We've already been talking about names. Ryan really wants a girl . . ."

Alison's mind drifted over her own peculiar struggles. She had been born with a bizarre assortment of weird abilities that made it impossible to get close to a man; strange extrasensory "gifts" that didn't always have a controlled end, especially if she was caught up in a moment of, well, increasing passion.

A vow of celibacy had followed the trip to the emergency room, an absolute requirement given her *oh-so-special* abilities.

But this, Joy getting to live out her life in the usual manner, had set coals to the bottom of Alison's feet.

"We're looking at cribs tomorrow and Ryan wants to get one of those double strollers . . ."

She leaned over the table and assessed the exact point of balance required to palm the heavy statue in one hand. She'd be able to now since she'd been working out hard for the past six months, running, weight lifting, stair-stepping, Spinning.

How nice in this moment to be so strong.

She wrapped one hand around the statue then lifted. She hefted the family to shoulder height then arched her wrist slowly to support the statue in her hand. She pressed it a couple of times. Up, down. Up, down.

"You're still coming to Mom and Dad's, right?" Joy asked.

"Absolutely," she said, forcing the enthusiasm, but it was like pushing raw potatoes through a sieve. "Mom would kill me if I didn't show."

Three days from now. She would need every second between to gain perspective, to remind herself of all the good things of her life, to be able to be around her sister and not be overcome by either jealousy or despair.

Goddammit.

"So, Mom said you already have an idea for your dissertation. You must be thrilled about starting school again. You've always wanted to go back."

Alison couldn't listen anymore, couldn't respond in a happy voice one more time. Yes, she was going back to school, and yes, part of her was excited, but Joy had the life Alison wanted, the normal life with love, a good man, babies. No, she couldn't utter one more positive word.

She decided to lie and spoke in a hushed voice. "Listen, Joy, my last client just arrived so I'd better go."

"Oh, yeah, of course. See you at Mom and Dad's."

"You bet."

"Love you."

"Love you more."

Alison pressed the little red button then tossed her cell sideways onto the cushion of the wing chair. She kept her gaze fixed on the four-by-eight window. Her eyes burned all over again and her throat constricted.

Her last client wouldn't arrive for a little while yet.

She had time . . . to get her head straight.

She flexed her powerful right arm. Oh, but she shouldn't do this. She really shouldn't. She had been a responsible tenant in the medical building for the past eight years. This could be classified as insane.

Despite her calm reasoning, she pivoted to stand with her left shoulder facing the window. She drew her right arm back. She even lifted her left knee for more stability and strength, like a Diamondback pitcher. Then, without allowing her thoughts to muddle the moment, she aimed the statue at the long plate-glass window above the green chenille sofa and threw with all her might.

The shattering glass sounded like heaven and for a split second, she could actually smile. The moment dragged out in slow motion until reality struck and she realized exactly what she had done. Without thinking, she reached out and snatched a pocket of time, slowing the forward movement of the shattered window until time stopped.

What?

What?

All the glass froze in place. Even the unity statue floated three feet beyond the sill.

She looked down at her hand, palm up, fingers curled in. She felt the pull on her entire arm as though a large rubber band had stretched out and grabbed hold of some distant invisible object then held tight.

She shook her head, astonished.

Alison Wells . . . human . . . held *time* in her hand.

How was this possible?

How were *any* of her special abilities possible? From the time she was a little girl, she could perform amazing preternatural feats, but to what purpose? Her powers simply made no sense in her world. She had no use for them, no way to exhibit them without being shipped to Area 51 and studied as a science project.

Beyond that, what was the point, ever, of being able to seize a little pocket of time and hold it in your hand?

Once Kerrick prepared for battle, he called Central and got a fold, a quick dematerialization, to the downtown Phoenix alley. The journey between lasted a rough second, maybe two, a dark ride through nether-space, a blanking-out then sudden hard awareness, a blinding rush of adrenaline followed by a blast of endorphins. To arrive was to be prepared . . . for anything.

Kerrick was one of the most powerful warriors on Second Earth. However, he had a flaw, which still chapped his hide. He couldn't fold himself to another location. He had to get an assist every time from either Central or one of his warrior brothers, even Endelle on occasion.

As his feet hit asphalt, he dropped slowly into a crouch because there they were. His gaze followed the pale, blue-tinged creatures as they emerged laughing from the left T of the alley—death vampires.

God, they were beautiful, part of the lure to bring mortals within their grasp, within their thrall. They were the mythical yet very real creatures of darkness that hunted victims at night to hide the faint bluish cast to their skin. The *undead.* Oh, they breathed, their hearts beat, but the basic belief in right and wrong had long since been shoveled into the ground and eaten by worms. Any remnant of humanity had gotten buried in the addiction to dying blood, a hunger worse than heroin, nicotine, Jack Daniel's, and meth all put together.

Kerrick stretched his preternatural vision and saw the blood smeared over thickened fangs, lips, cheeks, and chins, a red trophy of the hunt. Three of them. Where was the fourth?

The sun was barely set, still dusk, and these three bastards had no doubt just killed a mortal apiece. They were giddy, twirling in circles, shoving at each other like drunken buddies coming out of a bar at two in the morning. The alley, with chain link on one side and the ass-end of a worn-out strip center on the other, didn't provide anonymity for the denizens of Second Earth, which meant these bastards didn't give a fuck if they were seen.

Christ.

They were also in their most dangerous state. Power flowed through those veins right now, steroid-like, ripe with death. These vampires would be juiced and feeling no pain.

Good thing he was here. Only a handful of warriors were big enough, strong enough, fast enough to deal with these assholes, and he was one of them. Besides, more than any other night he could remember in a long time, he needed this fight. His muscles ached to move, to fly, and yes, to kill.

Something was on the wind. Something big. He could feel it.

He flexed his right arm, heavy with muscle and built up every day to support the weight of his sword. Using his mind, he folded the goddamn fine-looking forged metal into his hand from a secured weapons locker in the basement of his home. God, he loved the feel of it, the grip wrapped with leather to fit his fingers, the wicked weight, the balance. This was his sword, bonded only to him. The edges were as sharp as samurai steel, a double-edged carbon-steel blade meant for destruction.

His wing-locks began to thrum, preparing for battle, a vibration that went into his groin and tightened his balls. He wore flight gear, sturdy black sandals strapped all the way to the knees with shin guards, a thick black leather kilt, and a heavy studded harness, also black leather, buckled down at the waist, running straight up his chest, over his shoulders, and down his spine to allow for his wings. In the front a slot in the harness held a dagger at the exact angle necessary for his left reach. On each wrist he wore a studded black leather guard.

He withdrew the dagger now and started flipping the weapon end-over-end, catching the handle each time, setting the throw in rhythm to the slam of his adrenaline-soaked heart. He'd had his weapons a long time. They were his closest friends and he only traded them in for new ones when there just wasn't much metal left to polish or sharpen.

A sword in his right hand. A razor-like dagger flipping in his left. Life got no better than this.

With a thought, he swelled the muscles of his back and his wings began to come, flying through the locks, an orgasm of movement that flooded his body with a surge of male strength. Pleasure whipped through his thighs down to his feet then upward through his groin, his abs, his shoulders and arms.

His wings unfurled, easing into their massive height, another reason he could fight these bastards—Warriors of the Blood had god-like wings, fit for battle.

Good. Life was good.

His gaze hadn't wavered a diamond cut from his prey. He could have lifted into the air, swooped, then severed each head before a second had passed. No, he wanted these night-feeders to pay for the lives they'd robbed, to know at least a moment of terror before their carbon-based DNA returned to Mother Earth, any dimension. As the Creator was his witness, he'd always make them pay.

A fourth death vamp came around the corner zipping his cargoes and grinning, his skin so pale and edged with blue that he looked translucent in the dim alley light.

One of the bastards caught sight of Kerrick and alerted the others. As a group they turned in his direction.

Game time.

He smiled as wings sprouted from each of the vamps, feathers all in black and none of the spans as large as his. Swords flashed into hands, folded from underground bunkers where the night-feeders lived during the day.

He created a powerful mist, which would keep what needed to happen well away from the eyes or ears of any nearby mortal. Mist, when present, worked on the mind to create confusion. The average mortal, or even ascender for that matter, would simply fail to register anything covered in mist.

He swept his wings in a single brisk downward thrust then shot straight up into the air to float about thirty feet above. He waited, wings wafting, heart calm, strong, steady, certain. He flipped his dagger again. Flip. Flip. Flip. Catch. The gentle touch of his fingers to the dagger hilt a deadly, lethal pressure ready for release. The forefinger of his right hand stroked the crossguard of his sword.

The charge came, two from the left, two from the right,

rising into the air, a coordinated squadron complete with battle cries. He moved with his singular gift—speed. He became a blur and sliced in crisscross patterns until he severed a wing and a body fell. He caught one death vamp high on the torso and took the head as well as the shoulder and part of a wing.

Two on the ground.

Two to go.

The latter were more skilled, well trained, but he let loose the dagger and caught the left vamp in the throat. A spiral of wings ensued as the pretty-boy lost control. Meanwhile the remaining vamp, high on power from the drain, clanged steel. Kerrick's arm reverberated from the shock, yet oh how good it felt. He allowed the vamp to show his skills as he met each flap of his adversary's wings, thrust of feet, fall of his sword arm.

He drew the battle out, wanting the practice, wanting to sustain the chemicals now racing in his blood and feeding his brain with a whole lot of feel-good.

With a flurry the death vamp came at him, a roar in his throat. Kerrick caught his sword in an upswing, threw his arm in a circle in order to catch his opponent's arm, then flipped the sword out of the death vamp's grasp. The force of the blow and the sudden lack of sword weight sent his opponent flipping over twice before his wings caught air.

But it was too late.

Kerrick flew at him, drew his knees up, then planted both feet on the death vamp's chest, thrusting him backward toward the ground. He drew his wings in close, all the way to half mount, following fast as he locked stares. His adversary's wings slowed him but gravity pulled Kerrick in tight. He lifted his arms then plunged. His sword pierced his enemy's abdomen just below the sternum. A cry filled the air.

Half a second before the pretty-boy hit the asphalt Kerrick spread his wings and eased the last few feet back to earth.

Breathing hard, he paused to draw in his wings swiftly

through his wing-locks. Once he was settled, his muscles thinning to normal, he retrieved his dagger still stuck in the flesh of the second opponent. He wiped the blade, two swipes on the kilt. He folded the dagger, another quick dematerialization this time of steel, back to his weapons locker.

He finished the job quickly, severing the rest of those beautiful heads. Dying blood altered even the features, enabling every death vamp to lull the next mortal into a sense of awe and therefore safety before the fangs took the jugular. The skin, with its hint of blue, was . . . *exquisite,* especially at night—and that was exactly the point, to stun the victim with unnatural beauty.

He scouted the area for more sign of the enemy, but nothing returned to him except the distant rumble of a Harley engine. As he started to regain his breath, he folded his sword back to the locker.

He spread more mist far and wide, drew his phone from his pocket, then thumbed it once. He took another deep breath and stood upright. Sweat poured. He could smell the blood of his adversaries on his skin and on the leather of his weapons harness and kilt. Looking down, blood spattered even his sandals and bare toes.

"Central."

"Hey, Jeannie," he said, catching his breath. "Four to pick up. Make it quick."

"It's not even a quarter after six, barely dark."

"No shit."

She sighed. "I guess this is going to be one of those nights and it isn't even a full moon. Okay. Locked on. Cover your peepers." Kerrick closed his eyes. A flash of bright light took away the bodies, the debris, even the blood on the ground.

He made his way to the top of the alley and felt his chest tighten. This was the part of his job he loathed. Drained and dead mortals always gave him the shakes. The T of the alley dead-ended about fifty feet to his left. Decrepit apartments sat opposite in a low-slung row, bars across all the first-story windows.

He moved fast until he saw who had been chosen to feed the death vamps' addiction and what had been done to them. Then his feet slowed as though he slogged through mud.

Only one adult among them. Christ. He'd had a whole lot of years to get used to the carnage, but this was off the rails.

He swallowed bile.

A mother lay at an awkward angle, drained, her back broken. Two young boys to her left, necks ravaged from the feeding. However, the worst was on her right, a young teenage girl with her small skirt pushed up around her waist and her legs split wide, her white thighs covered in blood. He fell to his knees, lifted his face and arms to the darkening sky, then let out a roar.

A familiar agony swamped his chest, a misery that lived in him now, dictating the progress of each night, tearing up his soul. He drew the girl's legs together and pulled her skirt down. "You have been avenged," he whispered. "May your journey to the arms of the Creator be swift, and may you know peace."

Peace.

What would that be like? He never slept through the night. None of the warriors did. He awoke to terrible images, and these would likely torture him more than once in the coming weeks.

He withdrew his phone again, thumbed, ordered the uptake. He closed his eyes and saw the flash of light.

Once the job was done, he spoke into his phone. "Jeannie, fold me back to the basement. Now."

"You got it."

He felt the vibration.

Once in his dwelling, in the dark cavernous room below his house, he dropped prone to the cement floor then stretched his arms straight out. He had no outlet for the pain he felt, for the fury. All he could do was this: take a moment to grieve, then reaffirm his vows of continual vengeance, of living his solitary existence, of devoted service to Endelle as a Guardian of Ascension.

Why take a vow,
When all vows are broken?

—*Collected Proverbs,* Beatrice of Fourth

CHAPTER 2

Alison stared at her fingers, still held in an upward claw-like position. She kept testing the pull on her arm. She wasn't even certain how long she'd been standing there, mystified by what she had done.

Sweet Jesus.

A pocket of time.

Surely she had just passed all the bounds of nature now.

So what did that make her? Like she didn't know—a freak, a one-woman sideshow.

She glanced at the shattered window, at the shards of glass, lit up by the nearby parking-lot light standard, a glittering glass rain suspended two stories above the earth. So exactly how long had she been standing here, frozen in place, stunned by the enormity of what she had done, *of what she was still doing*?

She looked once more at all the splintered glass, just sparkling away, unmoving, a visual poem suspended in time.

A lump formed in her throat about the size of her car, and not the little Nova, but the super-sized Hummer. Her eyes felt chili pepper hot all over again. She just didn't understand who she was. How could she be doing this, standing in her empty-shelved office, her hand outstretched, her fingers cupped, a piece of time held within? Where did all this preternatural ability come from? And what possible purpose could it ever serve?

The unity family hung by the sheer strength of her powers just three feet or so beyond the windowsill, heads aimed at the asphalt parking lot as though diving into a pool.

She drew her arm back slowly and felt the hard pull on her muscles. Time retreated for her, a lethargic reversal. The statue came back to her followed by the glass fragments, all returned in perfect accord to re-form an unblemished window. She had never tried out any of these skills before, stasis of objects, retrieval of time pockets.

The statue now sat in her palm, and she released her hold on infinity. She felt a strange quick vibration around her that drifted away, ripples in a pond. In the distance a sonic boom sounded, action–reaction.

She settled the statue once more on the coffee table then returned to sit in the wing chair. Energy sang through her nerves and caused the little hairs on both arms to stand upright. She trembled.

She took a deep breath then another. She straightened her shoulders. What a strange evening this had become—her sister pregnant, her heart crushed all over again, and now a couple of new powers.

Perfect.

When she felt hysteria rising, like a geyser in her chest, she put a hand over her mouth and drew in a long deep breath through her nose. She closed her eyes and forced herself to relax.

She had a client coming soon, in the next ten minutes or so, her last client. She needed to hold it together just a little longer, then she could go home and have a meltdown if she wanted. Right now, she needed to be professional.

Okay. She relaxed and put both hands out in front of her as though holding the world at bay. She breathed.

She heard a siren in the distance, not unusual around such a large medical complex. The hospital was just a mile down the road.

Her heart rate slowed down. She could breathe better.

So she wasn't normal, who was? So her soul had this strange new gaping wound because her sister was having her second child? So she had a problem she would never be able to solve in this lifetime, on this planet? So did millions of people. Why should she be any different even if she was *so very different*? She wasn't starving. She had a good profession and a house she owned. She had a family who *loved* her with a capital *L*. Yeah, she had some serious losses she was grappling with, but who didn't in this hard-edged, unfair, and at times *brutal* world?

She nodded to herself several times and shored up her determination. She sealed up the deep wound then set her mind on her future, a most excellent future.

She nodded.

Okay.

When his phone buzzed against his abdomen through the pocket in his kilt, Kerrick finally rose from the cement floor in his basement. This was just the first wave of fighting. He needed to get cleaned up and moving. Unless, of course, Endelle still wanted him on guard-dog duty.

He extended his senses, as he had in the bar, and reached for the caller's identity. Thorne was on the com but the hell he was going to answer his phone right now. Endelle was going to have to find someone else to serve as the woman's guardian. Thorne could do it himself, or any of the other warrior brothers. Serving as a guardian to a female would make him vulnerable and he took pains never to be in that position, so yeah, his brothers could pick up the slack.

As he headed to the shower, he folded off his blood-spattered kilt and weapons harness, his heavy warrior sandals, leather wrist guards, and sweat-soaked briefs. He let the garments drop to the cold cement floor in a trail behind him.

Once in the bathroom he turned the lever on full force and let the water heat up.

He reached both hands to the back of his neck, popped the leather *cadroen*, the ritual clasp worn by all the warriors, and released his hair. He set the clasp on the sink, the last of several that his wife of many decades ago had worked with her own hands. He touched the intricate, embroidered strap, rolling it over to look at the attached miniature carved dagger made from rhinoceros tusk, which secured the piece together.

Memories of his wife flew through his mind, of her small nimble hands, her love of the needle and colorful silk floss. She had made several *cadroen* for him during the ten short years they were together. This was the last of them. Decades of making war would wear out even the toughest pieces of leather.

He turned around then stepped inside what was essentially a car wash of a shower. He moved in a slow circle, letting all eight powerful heads wash away the remnants of the recent battle.

His phone buzzed again, stupid fucking preternatural hearing.

As before, he extended his senses. Thorne again. He sighed. He needed one more minute to clear his head before he engaged the next round.

He ended up in front of the main nozzle, set at seven and a half feet with a punishing angled spray. He planted both hands on the smooth cold tile and let the hot water pound the back of his neck and work the muscles all across his shoulders. His long hair separated and slid forward to form a wall on either side of his face. Blood and sweat swirled down the drain. He didn't usually come apart after a kill, but Christ, those kids.

Something had changed in his world. Children had been off limits for centuries. Now the death vamps sucked as they pleased, inflicted pain as they pleased, took innocence as they pleased.

His brain cramped. The muscles around his eyes squeezed tight. He breathed in the damp air, flared his nostrils, then tried to shut his brain down. He failed.

Goddammit. He had reached an impasse, this no-man's-land of vows and vengeance from which he could not retreat. His chest felt like he'd strapped on a boulder then carried the damn thing around day and night.

He concentrated on the water beating against his skin. He sucked in air and forced himself to breathe, in and out, in and out. He calmed himself the hell down. He rubbed his left pec and winced at the agony burning beneath that had nothing to do with musculature.

Unfortunately his hearing was too evolved and the phone buzzed again, a relentless fly in his warrior's world.

Thorne again.

Too. Fucking. Bad.

He shut the water off and toweled himself dry. He wrapped the towel around his waist. He brushed out his hair in hard pulls with a stiff-bristled brush. He'd take these few minutes, goddammit. He looked at the *cadroen* but refused to pick it up. He'd go unbound the rest of the night, a little piece of rebellion, to hell with rules and tradition.

He moved to his weapons locker and mentally opened the steel reinforced cabinet. He drew the double doors wide. His blooded sword and dagger lay parallel and waiting, right where he'd sent them from the alley. Using soft cloths, he wiped both weapons clean of the blood then folded the cloths to the laundry. By morning, after the night's work was over, he'd oil and tend his weapons.

He lived in the basement of his mansion on Scottsdale Two. He'd shaped loose living quarters from the long narrow underground room: a place for his bed, workout equipment, a locked weapons locker. He'd even spent a fortune building an after-the-fact expansive bathroom, one that fit his large warrior body and occasionally even his wings.

His phone buzzed yet again. Not Thorne this time. He crossed to his kilt still heaped on the cement floor then retrieved the phone. "Yeah, Jeannie."

"Thank God," she whispered. "We're in deep shit. Endelle has been yelling at Carla for the last ten minutes because Thorne couldn't reach you. We have a sitch in Paradise Valley and she wants you on it. Now. You with me?"

Kerrick drew in a deep breath. "Is Thorne with Endelle?" This couldn't be happening.

"Yep. He said to say you didn't have a choice on this one."

Kerrick pulled his phone away from his ear and released a violent string of obscenities. When he could speak in a normal voice again, he said, "Give me the deets."

"Thorne wants to patch in."

"Fine."

Thorne's deep, rough voice hit his ears. "We don't really know what's going on. You may or may not have to guard the woman. Right now there's just a pretty-boy off the grid."

"So why does Endelle have her panties in a wad?"

"She said we'll know more once you take care of our off-campus head case."

Kerrick breathed hard through his nose. Okay. He could take care of the death vamp. After which, if there happened to be a mortal woman in need of protection, Thorne could work that out. "I'm on it."

He could sense his brother's relief. Endelle must have had him by the nuts on this one, but why?

"I'm going to hand you back to Jeannie. She'll give you the whats and wheres."

"Hey, Kerrick," Jeannie began, "you'll be going to a medical complex in Paradise Valley. The pretty-boy's at full-mount. Call when you're ready."

"Thanks, Jeannie." He thumbed his phone.

He dropped the towel, folded on clean battle gear, then tucked his phone into the pocket at the waist of the kilt. With a dismissive wave of his hand, he sent the old gear directly to the laundry room.

And the war against the death vamps just kept on rolling.

Whatever.

As he adjusted his harness, he brought his dagger into his hand then secured it once more into the front slot. He hated the fact that his personal weakness, his inability to dematerialize, would force him to call Jeannie so that Central could do a fold to Paradise Valley One.

Goddammit.

Aw, hell. He'd been a caged beast for at least the past two centuries, a lion roaring for some kind of release.

And tonight . . . well, tonight, for whatever reason, every nerve in his body was on fire. After he took care of the off-campus head case, he'd head back to the Blood and Bite. He needed to suck back a few Maker's, maybe get laid. Yeah, a few fingers of whiskey and he definitely could use a little horizontal R&R with some jugular action thrown in.

Maybe then . . . Christ, maybe then he'd feel normal.

Alison opened her eyes as yet another siren sounded down the street, drew closer, then ceased, which made at least three in the past ten minutes or so. Apparently, someone's patient required serious emergency medical care.

She still sat in her wing chair, drawing in one breath after another, trying to calm down, trying to let her rational brain make sense of recent events. A walk might help, even just around her office.

She was about to get up and stretch her legs when she heard the door open. She shifted in the chair to look over her shoulder. Her last client had arrived, Darian Greaves.

"Alison," he said. "Our last appointment. I must say I feel quite sad."

He always looked like he'd walked straight out of *Good-fellas*. Despite the fact that he lived in warm, casual Phoenix, he never wore anything but a very fine wool suit to her office, all in black today, including the tailored shirt. For contrast, a yellow silk tie slashed a perfect line down his muscular chest. He looked like an oversized stinging insect covered in Hugo Boss.

He was quite beautiful, his bald head perfectly shaped,

smooth and tan, his black eyebrows thick and manicured, his dark eyes large, round in appearance, almost child-like. On his right pinkie he wore a black onyx ring. He had only one flaw—his left hand was misshapen, and because of the way the fingers curved, she thought there might have been some nerve damage along the way.

Over the past year of his therapy, his first and only year as far as she knew, he'd remained a locked-down mystery, especially since he was the only client whose mind she'd been unable to penetrate no matter how hard she tried. An anomaly. She didn't often reach into a client's mind. With Darian, however, she could not even skim the surface of his thoughts, let alone penetrate the depth of his psyche. *Why* had been the question she had been unable to answer.

He was the victim of monstrous childhood abuse, physical and sexual, all at the hands of a foster father. Even though he had been candid about his troubled past, there had been no significant progress, almost as though he recited his woes from behind a twelve-foot-thick cement wall. If he were at all serious about recovery, he would require a decade or two of therapy, nothing less. One thing she knew for certain: She could not be that therapist. In her opinion, he needed a hard-core psychiatrist and a lot of medication.

She glanced at the clock again. As always, he had arrived precisely on time, not a minute past six thirty. He couldn't leave his corporation—his *army* as he liked to call the rank and file of Greaves Enterprises—one second sooner. He was very fond of punctuality.

"I don't suppose I can talk you out of graduate school," he said, rounding her chair and heading to the soft green chenille couch. She held her breath. He smelled so strangely of lemons tinged with . . . what? Turpentine? Now, that was also an anomaly. With his sophisticated appearance, he should have smelled, at the very least, of Obsession.

"How sad to see all the empty shelves," he observed, as he paused in front of the wall unit. He shook his head slightly. After a moment, he turned then headed the rest of the distance to the couch. He sat down, smoothing his coat as he went. He crossed his legs at the knee, so formal, so gentleman-like.

He settled his gaze on her, but she found she had nothing to say to him. After the conversation with Joy and after holding a piece of time in her hand, somehow her mind had become a complete blank.

"Are you unwell?" he asked, his eyes narrowing.

Alison once again took deep breaths. Thoughts of Joy drifted through her mind as well as the shattered window and reversal of time. Everything seemed to be changing. Even her dreams in the last two weeks had become charged with strange and unusual images, some frightening, some intriguing.

Joy, a reversal of time, strange dreams.

Darian with finely tailored wool suits, a psychotic mind, and no Obsession.

She leaned back. "Why did you ever seek me out, Darian? To be quite honest, I don't believe I've helped you at all this last year."

He lifted an arched brow and smiled. He even chuckled. "Straight to the point. I always liked that about you. As for the past twelve months, you are right, I wasn't interested in therapy, just in you. I wanted to get to know you. As it happens, I'd like you to forget all about graduate school and come to work for me."

What was wrong with his voice? It sounded strange, as though his resonance had split not once but several times. She felt an odd pressure within her head. She squeezed her eyes shut and blocked the sensation. The pressure eased as quickly as it had begun. She opened her eyes.

"Incredible," he murmured, his gaze fixed on her.

"What is incredible?"

"You, of course. I want you to tell me you will consider working for me."

She shook her head. The suggestion stunned her. "I hope I don't offend you, but I'm fully committed to therapy as a profession. I simply have no desire to enter the business world." She so didn't want him to press her further.

"Working for me would involve much more than the usual exchange of goods and services. I believe I could keep you challenged, content, and I would certainly make it worth your while."

How could she tell him she would never in a million years work for him, not for all the money in the world. "I'm sorry," she said firmly. "The answer must be no."

His dark gaze commanded her. She found she could not look away from him. What had he said? Would she consider working for him?

The next moment he was in front of her on his knees. *On his knees.* He had hold of her arm and rubbed the inside of her wrist, the tender place over her veins. He stroked her skin back and forth. "Say yes," he whispered, his voice still carrying a strange resonance. Why didn't she fear him? He was large and muscular, powerful, the sort of man you imagined on black op missions deep in some Third World jungle. She had felt this from the beginning, his complete and utter lethal presence.

She should have feared his proximity. Fear would have been normal, but all her instincts were held in some kind of stasis.

"I will give you anything you desire," he said. "I have great wealth at my disposal. Say you will come to me, align with me, work side by side with me. Say it and *I will give you the world.*"

He would give her the world.

She didn't want the world, she wanted what Joy had, and he most definitely could not give her that.

Yet somehow she leaned toward him, drawn in, unafraid. Her pulse sped up as he stroked her wrist. Desire of a distinct sexual nature descended on her, a gentle rain on her skin. Was he *seducing* her?

"You're feeling it, aren't you? Say yes, Alison. We would be magnificent together." The split resonance drifted over her, beckoning her. She wanted to say yes.

Her breaths came in quick little puffs. Her eyelids felt heavy. This wasn't right. But she couldn't seem to help herself.

She breathed in, meaning to draw more of his heady seductiveness inside her, but the smell of him, lemons and turpentine, shocked her senses. She turned her face away and squeezed her eyes shut. Her mind cleared and she pressed her back and shoulders into the chair. "I'm sorry, Darian. I have no wish to work with you now or ever. You could offer half a dozen worlds and I would still refuse."

She shivered then felt Darian's breath on her neck. He chuckled softly. "Half a dozen," he murmured. "You have no idea how poetic your choice of words is, how perfect, how portentous, and I feel in you, I sense in you, a complete negation of my proposal. Again, I feel very sad as though I am losing a friend, perhaps the only true friend I have ever had. What a pity." Did he just graze her throat with his teeth? Yet she couldn't seem to move.

He released her wrist and, as though he had never been close to her at all, he once more sat on the sofa and again crossed his legs at the knee.

"I'm sorry, Darian." Her mind felt a little strange. Had he just knelt in front of her? The memory seemed vague now, indistinct, like a dream.

"This is most unfortunate," he said, "and I, too, am very sorry. I want you to understand and to remember my regret. I know we must go our separate ways, that much I believe was clear to me from the beginning, but I truly, truly wished it otherwise."

For the smallest moment, her heart softened toward him. She believed he was sincere. She had never seen regret on his face before. However, she saw it now. Had she misjudged him in some way?

The front door of her office suite slammed open and a second later one of the dental hygienists from the group next door appeared in the doorway. She was a tall, lovely redhead, her skin freckled and fair, yet two clownish spots had popped out on her cheeks.

Alison stood up. "What is it?"

The young woman glanced from her to Darian then back. "I'm sorry to disturb you, but one of Kelsing's dental patients has been killed right on the sidewalk." She threw a shaking hand behind her.

"You mean in an accident? Hit by a car?"

She shook her head back and forth. "No. Her throat. Torn open. Mangled. Here in the courtyard. The police have already taped the area off and an ambulance just pulled up. Thought you should know. I've already told everyone else in this wing."

"Thank you," Alison whispered as the woman turned and ran out. She glanced at Darian. She had some obligation to finish the hour with him. On the other hand, what was the point? Still, she waited for him to choose.

He rose to his feet, a half smile on his lips, sadness in his eyes. He gestured with an arm extended toward the door. "Well, I think we ought to see what all the fuss is about, don't you? Perhaps the report has been exaggerated."

Kerrick felt the vibration as Central folded him to the outskirts of the medical complex in Paradise Valley.

The moment he felt asphalt beneath his heavy strapped sandals, he sent a wall of mist before and behind. He wanted to get this motherfucker then get the hell out. He'd let Thorne deal with whatever mortal female was causing Endelle to throw a bitch-fit.

Just as he prepared to fold his sword into his hand, he stayed the thought.

Something was wrong.

He scanned the area and cursed. Why hadn't Jeannie told him that the circus had already come to town? The parking lot was full of emergency vehicles and they'd been here a while, longer than his time in the shower. One length of yellow crime scene tape extended into a group of uniforms, though he wasn't able to see the source from his position.

He slid his phone from his pocket and thumbed.

"Central. How we doin'?"

"Jeannie, what the hell is going on? There's already a cavalcade of medical and law enforcement vehicles here."

"I don't know what to say." A flurry of taps followed. "I'm not getting anything."

"Shit." There was only one reason Central's network hadn't picked up this mess—Greaves was here. Holy shit. "Okay. Do you see any mist trails?"

"There are a few minor ones around the death vamp, and yours, of course. I'm seeing a dull area to the west of you about twenty yards away. Do you see a Ramada or something?"

"Nope, but the party's right there."

"Holy shit," Jeannie cried. "Has to be the Commander. Even you can't do mist like that, and you do it better than anyone."

"Gotta be Greaves. Stay close."

"You got it." He heard more tapping.

He dropped low. He could see the victim from where he crouched. She was stretched out on the sidewalk, a woman whose curly black hair was just visible from beneath a white sheet. All around her, red stained the cement. His heart sank into his gut. She'd been drained in public long before sunset. And now he had a circus to manage.

What the hell was the Commander doing at a medical complex? Which begged the question, why had the death vamp shown up here as well?

He rose up then walked a good twenty yards to the west. He kept his mist tight. Any mortal looking in his direction would experience confusion of mind and fail to see him.

A host of onlookers surrounded the scene, lining the cement stairs and gathering in pockets across a two-story courtyard catwalk to watch the doings. In front of the catwalk, the death vamp floated about eight feet off the ground and turned in a lazy circle, euphoria on his face, blood on his mouth. His black wings, at full-mount, obscured a number of the onlookers from view.

Kerrick thumbed his phone then brought it to his ear again. "Found our head case. Big wings, too, which means he's been around a few centuries. He's twirling between two sets of stairs, enjoying one helluva high from the drain. At least he had enough sense to mist the area first." Kerrick could see a faint web-like structure around the death vamp, but his powers of penetration far surpassed the pretty-boy's ability to create the mind-bewildering substance.

"In addition to the death vamp's signature, there are two strong grid signatures nearby as well."

"Two?" he cried.

"One is probably the Commander," Jeannie said. "And the other?"

"Who the hell knows?" He lowered his phone but stayed on the line.

The whole situation bugged the shit out of him. The only directive the Commander's army honored was the law of absolute secrecy. However, the gore he'd cleaned up earlier, as well as the woman now on the sidewalk, had been left for anyone to see. So either Greaves's army was getting sloppy or they no longer had orders to do cleanup. One way or the other, the war was becoming a whole new kind of nightmare.

He did a quick scan of all the individuals present, from the police officers and emergency techs, to the spectators near the crime scene, to the various huddled groups all up the stairs, until on the catwalk above the courtyard he found a blond female whose gaze was fixed not on the white sheet and black curls but on the spinning death vampire. Everyone else was focused on the crime scene.

Holy hell.

By every natural law, she shouldn't have been able to see the death vamp, but her face had a wind-blasted expression so he knew she wasn't looking at a goddamn maypole. Yet how was that even possible, and what did it mean?

The death vamp hid part of her from view. Kerrick strengthened his mist and moved to his right. When he saw her fully, time slowed, thickened, then stopped, a hard slam on the brakes.

His lips parted to allow for more air. A sense of knowing flowed through his mind, his body, a wide erotic river. The mortal was as familiar to him as blood down his throat, though he had no idea who she was. She was at least six feet tall, blond, blue-eyed, an elegant figure, although those were just a group of stats. He *knew* her.

His body set up a dedicated hum. Even his wing-locks vibrated. How did he know her? He searched his memories. Nothing came forward. The same river of knowing once more flowed through him, like he'd already *been* inside her in every possible way or that somehow he knew he would soon *be* with her. Holy shit. The small of his back tightened and he began to grow hard.

Okay. This was way the hell off target.

He pulled himself together and focused on the situation. Something was really wrong.

He moved a few paces again to his right in order to complete his scan of those catwalk spectators that the twirling head case still blocked from view.

Holy motherfucker, so it was true. Commander Greaves stood right next to the mortal as calm as you please and even inclined his head to Kerrick in a slight bow of recognition. Naturally, Greaves could see through his mist. Holy shit. Holy hell. What the fuck was going on? What was the Commander doing with this mortal female? No wonder Endelle was freaking out.

Must be an ascension in progress, yet everything he was looking at was completely without precedent.

Despite his shock, however, he needed to prepare for battle.

He drew in a deep breath and felt the familiar vibration through the muscles of his back, the sweet thrum that preceded the powering of his wings through his wing-locks. He let them fly. He let them extend to their full height and breadth. He stretched them and held them at the farthest reaches of full mount until his head swirled with endorphins and a fighting sheen of sweat flowed over the entire surface of his skin. He wanted Greaves reminded of the extent of his powers, that he wasn't an ordinary warrior, and that if he wanted to go head-to-head, Kerrick was goddamn ready, right here, right now, this place, this time. Bring-it-the-fuck-on.

The Commander, however, merely inclined his head again, acknowledging the presentation of his wings as a threat. Then he turned to the female and said something—so, yeah, he knew her. Afterward, he simply departed, leaving in the opposite direction, away from the crowd lining the stairs. No flash, no spectacle, this man, this vampire, just infinite maneuvering and plotting, the bastard.

Kerrick jerked his phone back up to his ear. "Jeannie?"

"Yeah? Trouble?"

"I need to know if one of the two signatures just fell off the grid."

A pause, followed by a series of taps.

"Yep. Vanished. Is that a good thing?"

"Very. That was Commander Greaves."

Jeannie whistled. "Holy shit."

"Ditto. Now tell me, is the other signature still marking your screen?"

"Yep, though the reading is a little skewed."

"I'm not surprised. I think the second signature belongs to a mortal."

"Are you shitting me?"

"Nope."

"I've never heard of such a thing."

"Me, neither."

"So have we got a vampire-in-the-making or what? Can you see what's in her head, see if she's been called to sport a pair of fangs?"

"Give me a second."

Kerrick reached out toward her with his senses and tried to drive into the female's mind, but damn she had shields, like walls of granite.

He stared at the woman and frowned. Who the hell was this female? She was tall for a mortal and wore her hair pulled back in a severe twist at the back of her head—she kept herself in control. He got that. She was in fact beautiful, with large blue eyes, full sensual lips, a straight nose, and in that split second as he looked at her, a third strange kind of recognition rocketed though his body and his hormones shot into outer space. Goddammit, he was attracted to her like falling apples to gravity. His groin burned. What the hell?

His wings rippled in anticipation, tightened and shimmied as though the future had suddenly reached back and grabbed the present by the balls. His groin lit on fire again and his eyelids felt weighted and heavy. The muscles of his thighs jumped and his biceps flexed. The woman had power. Shit, that was such a turn-on. Making love to this woman would be like entering a hurricane of sensation.

He wanted her. Now. He wanted her beneath him. He wanted inside her and pumping hard.

What the fuck?

For a moment he drew his wings to half-mount, bent over at the waist, planted his hands on his knees, and forced himself to take one deep breath after another. For all his vows, he suddenly knew temptation, deep, soul-searing temptation. A hyphenate from the ancient language came to mind, *breh-hedden*. Mate-bonding. The kind he believed was just a myth, yet here he was out of his mind with need and desire. Was it possible?

He closed his eyes and shut his brain down in a hurry. This shit was so not going to happen. Besides, with a death vamp still hanging in the air, he needed to focus. He had a job to do. He sucked more air into his lungs.

When he calmed down, he rose up then did a quick scan. He profiled the female's powers—so many—telepathy, empathy, hand-pulse, and she could dematerialize. No mortal had ever ascended with the ability to fold . . . except one . . . Endelle. No wonder the Commander seemed to have staked some kind of claim on her. *Holy, holy shit.*

Endelle must have known, and right now he felt like he'd been suckered into something. He shook his head, back and forth, a strong negation. None of this mattered, not what he was experiencing, not Endelle's scheming, nothing. He had a vow to keep and he would keep it.

A little calmer, he brought his phone to his ear. "I can't tell what's going on with the female because I can't punch into her head."

"What?" she cried. "You can get into anybody's head."

"Not hers." His voice was rough, like he'd swallowed a box of tacks. "At least not from this position."

"Then what do we do with her?" Jeannie asked. She sounded as shocked out as he felt.

"You know the rules."

"Yeah, yeah. No interference. Blah-blah-blah."

"Amen to that. I'll just have to get rid of the death vamp and we'll see what happens over the next forty-eight hours. You'd better let Endelle know what's doing. Tell her Greaves was here as well and tell her about the strength of the woman's signature. I'll know more later."

"I'm on it."

He thumbed his phone and once more returned it to the tight narrow pocket of his kilt.

He summoned a different kind of deep breath and shifted his gaze to the pretty-boy.

Time to take care of business.

Who can comprehend the lure of the breh-hedden,
except those caught in its teeth?

—*Collected Proverbs,* Beatrice of Fourth

CHAPTER 3

Alison released a deep sigh that Darian had finally left
since she couldn't comprehend what she was seeing. A hallucination, maybe?

A winged creature drifted slowly in a circle about ten
feet away from her. He was very beautiful, extraordinarily
so. His dark brown hair was long, well past his shoulders.
He was muscled like a bodybuilder and wore only black
cargoes, no shoes, no shirt. He sported a massive pair of
glossy black wings, the feathers barely moving but keeping
him both aloft and spinning very slowly. His chin and chest
were streaked with blood, his feet—oh, God—at least two
yards off the ground. His eyes were closed and he looked
euphoric, like a drug addict who'd just taken a hit of his
favorite supply.

His strange twirling reminded her of something from a
film heavy on the CGI side. In fact, the whole courtyard
had the appearance of a movie set, dozens of people

crammed at the far end of the catwalk and down the stairs, all chattering quietly, hands covering mouths, and a host of emergency vehicles and corresponding personnel. The center of attention was a body stretched out on the cement, surrounded by yellow tape, the view blocked by several officers, thank God. Given the blood on the creature's body, she could only presume he'd killed her, the way a fictional vampire would kill his prey.

So what exactly was this *thing* with the porcelain skin that hung in the air without any apparent cable support? Was she really seeing him? Did he exist? A psychopath who had somehow strapped wings onto his back—without straps? And how did he pull off the float-and-spin?

She shook her head in complete disbelief. She blinked several times. She glanced at the spectators to see their reactions to this strange creature, but no one—not one person— was looking at him, thus confirming her suspicion that she was hallucinating.

She moved close to the railing and stared down at him. A familiar gripping sensation pulled at her heart, a longing she couldn't explain, a yearning that had tormented her for the past few weeks, but surely not for this monster?

"Al-is-on" emerged in a singsong cadence from the creature's mouth. "I'm ready for you."

He spoke her name?

She formed a thought and let it fly from her mind: *Why can no one see you?*

The fanged freak stopped twirling, plunged toward the cement, then stopped to float suspended in the air just inches above the ground. His wings undulated slowly. He turned his back to her as he looked around at the spectators then came into profile as his gaze skipped from face to face all up the stairs. Yet no one looked at him. So yeah, maybe he existed only in her head. She'd seen *A Beautiful Mind* and she'd read a number of case histories on schizophrenia during the course of her studies.

His wings fluttered and his body shifted a little more as

his gaze worked over the small knots of onlookers all across the landing until he found her.

He met her gaze and smiled. His shoulders relaxed.

Alison, he said, his lips unmoving. *So, my sister was right and you are here after all.*

Telepathy. He was able to communicate with her telepathically.

A pair of fangs—*fangs*—descended, thick white incisors against perfect lips. Red tinted the grooves between his teeth.

Fangs?

Wings?

Blood?

Her mind shifted around and around. The word *vampire* once more tumbled through her brain, end-over-end-over-end, leaving her dizzy.

A slow, perfectly executed downward sweep of the creature's glossy black wings sent him floating upward. He rose toward her and once more conversed with her telepathically, his dark gaze fixed to hers. *I am here to take your powers so that I can destroy what is evil in our world. Your blood belongs to me now.*

As his words reverberated through her head, her ankles filled slowly with cement. She tried to move but couldn't. He wanted to take her blood?

Nausea rippled through her stomach, as though her body knew things her mind couldn't yet comprehend.

Who are you? she sent. The movement of his wings caused the leaves of the surrounding ficus trees to flutter as if a breeze filled the outdoor courtyard. *Why can I see you when no one else can?*

He ignored her questions and aloud said, "I must have your blood."

She shook her head. Her chest grew tight. How was it possible after all this time, after all these years of hopelessness, after three decades of living trapped with powers that made no sense in the normal human realm, she would have to meet a terrible winged being, maybe even a vampire, who might actually share her abilities, but who had only killing on his mind? Why couldn't she have met a good guy?

When he reached the catwalk, however, her nerves settled down. He was incredibly *beautiful,* so pleasing to the eye. Did she really need to be frightened of such a creature?

He settled his hands on the railing and smiled, a lovely smile. He drew his wings back and flipped his legs over the side. He landed easily and bore down on her, a wall of thick exquisitely shaped muscles, a fluttering of glossy feathers, a show of fangs. As the blood on his chest came into view, however, her mind sharpened and her instincts fired up.

Yes. She should be frightened.

For the entire duration of her adult life, Alison had never, *never* engaged in a dematerialization in plain view of other people. It was one of her rules, an important rule, one that had for years helped her to feel like she had a place in the world, that all her exceptional and useless gifts could exist side by side with *normal.*

But this monster had already made his intention clear, and right now this rule would have to go. Hallucination or not, and though she felt completely freaked out at vanishing in front of God and everyone, she pictured the courtyard below and moved herself there with a thought followed by a brief vibration of blood and bone.

Kerrick's head swam as he watched the mortal female fold from the catwalk to a position not three yards away, her back to him as she gazed up at the now stunned death vamp. Kerrick had been ready to intervene, his wings thrumming, when the pretty-boy explained his mission. His words alone, his professed purpose, had forced Kerrick to pause—a death vamp ready to destroy that which was evil? Did he actually mean the Commander?

But then the woman folded. He knew it was possible because he'd read her powers. However, since he still couldn't fold, he was mesmerized, and not a hair of her tight blond twist out of place.

He looked her up and down from behind.

She wore black pants, short-heeled shoes, and a light green silk top fitted to her body. She looked elegant and controlled, like she kept herself wound up into a comfortable knot, just like her hair. He so got that. She had probably spent most of her life holding back, trying not to freak everybody else out because of *who she was*. Yeah, he really got that.

His nostrils flared and a sudden scent of lavender hijacked his brain. Damn he was dizzy! He rubbed the center of his chest over his heart. The scent gave him a rush, the way he sometimes felt after throwing back half a dozen shots of Maker's in quick succession. Yeah, like that. Damn. The surface of his skin felt hot and he *craved*. This was what he needed, what had been calling to him since he'd awakened with that weird hum in his chest. He took a step forward and sucked in more of the lavender scent. Holy shit, the scent was *her*. Addiction swept through his body, sudden, hard, complete.

He wanted the lavender on his lips and down his throat. He wanted her body beneath his. He wanted her back arching, her hips meeting his. He wanted to be inside her mind. Damn . . . he wanted her blood.

Holy hell. He backed up and shook his head. He ordered his mind . . . his body . . . *again*. He forced himself to think rational thoughts, like he had a job to do and this was a mere mortal and he had sworn off getting involved with a woman so long as he remained a Warrior of the Blood.

Movement on the catwalk brought his gaze slashing back to the business at hand. The head case now stood on top of the railing, black wings flapping slowly. He sustained his balance with the practice of centuries.

Time to get this over with. He released the densest part of his mist in order to reveal himself to the woman.

He closed the distance then clapped his hands on her arms. "Don't move," he commanded.

Her head snapped in his direction as he spun her toward him. He repositioned his hands so that she faced him now, but he still had hold of her.

Goddammit, time thickened once more. He had never seen eyes like hers, light blue, rimmed in gold, exquisite. His body lit up again, a torch whipped by the wind, flames shooting everywhere. He probably should let go of her arms, but he sure as hell didn't want to.

His gaze fell to parted lips and a possessive split-resonant growl formed in his throat.

"Who are you?" she asked, her voice a hoarse whisper. "Are you going to kill me?"

He shook his head. "I'm here to protect you." Other thoughts scrambled his head. *I will always protect you. I was born to protect you. I will serve as your* guardian, *now and forever.*

Breh-hedden shot through his head once more.

Hell, no. Not gonna happen. Fucking . . . hell . . . no.

"You were born to protect me?" she asked, her eyes wide, her brow crinkled. "What are you? And what do you mean by guardian and that 'bray' something?"

"You just read my thoughts even though my shields are in place?" Holy shit! The woman could get into his head, engage his mind, *read his mind,* an ability that went way beyond telepathy. He knew of only one woman on Second Earth capable of doing that . . . Endelle. Jesus. The woman before him had so much fucking power.

Her lips parted, her gaze shifted back and forth from his face to his right wing, to his left wing, to his weapons harness, then down to his kilt and his heavy gladiator-like sandals. "What are you?" she repeated, her voice dropping to a whisper.

He drew in a deep breath and somehow found the power to release her arms. "Will you stay put while I deal with the death vamp?"

She looked him up and down. She blinked several times. He felt her mind pressing against his, and he let her dip in. She staggered slightly but after a moment withdrew, relaxed, then nodded. "Death vamp? As in death vampire?" she asked.

How confused she must be right now. "Yes, and I need

you to stay right where you are so you won't get hurt. Will
you do as I say while I take care of the winged creature on
the railing?"

She glanced at the waiting death vamp and nodded.
"Yes," she said, her voice breathless. "Okay. Yes." She swallowed hard.

He moved past her, drawing his wings aside to avoid
striking her. He ignored the scent of lavender, which now
assaulted him like a cyclone.

He stood several feet in front of her, blocking the death
vamp's view of her. He extended his wings to either side as
far as he could, another protective move, his gaze fixed on
the enemy.

His quarry scowled and rose into the air, his gaze
searching.

"Come down," Kerrick called out.

"Warrior, leave us," the death vamp cried. He rose higher
still until he could see the woman, then he smiled.

"Come down and face me," Kerrick commanded. He
folded his identified sword into his right fist once more, the
wrapped leather soothing against his palm. He drew the dagger from the harness.

"I won't fight you. I'm not here for that," the death vamp
cried out. "I need the woman's blood."

"Well, you can't have it."

"You don't understand, Warrior Kerrick. I can destroy
Commander Greaves if I take her blood. My sister, a very
powerful Seer, told me about a mortal, Alison Wells, the
woman behind you, who would be here today, this evening.
She would have all the power I needed to do what must be
done. You and I both want the same thing. Step aside and
let me take her blood."

As Kerrick faced the death vamp, however, he had only
one recourse. "Tonight, unfortunately, I stand between you
and the woman. You'll have to face me instead, just as you
are." When the death vamp would not shift his gaze away
from the female, the one he had called Alison, Kerrick split
his resonance and thundered, "Look at me!"

Only then did the head case tear his attention away from her. He met Kerrick's gaze and cried out, "Wouldn't this mortal be worth the sacrifice to see the Commander dead?"

"We don't trade on the lives of mortals." Kerrick knew this wasn't going to be simple. He needed the death vamp to attack, but the pretty-boy was fixed on the woman and the last thing he wanted was to end up chasing the bastard through the air.

Thorne returned to the Blood and Bite in one foul mood.

Endelle had thrown a bitch-fit about Kerrick's ingratitude, insubordinate attitude, and all-around bullheadedness, then offered Thorne a ten-minute lecture on how he needed to get control of his warrior brothers.

What-the-fuck-ever.

He had nodded and said all the right things, the whole time wondering how soon he could get back into the field. Given her mood, however, he doubted he'd be doing much else for a while except watching the damn clock.

Endelle was keeping him close tonight, a duty he detested. Unfortunately, her displeasure about Kerrick's fuck-off attitude was only half the picture. The other half drew his nuts up so close to his body, he could feel the short hairs.

She'd told him flat-out she was recalling Marcus, effective immediately.

Holy shit. Marcus. *Marcus.* Former Warrior of the Blood who had made a permanent jump to Mortal Earth the night Kerrick's wife and kids had died.

God help us all.

"I need a drink, Sam."

"You got it, *jefe.*"

Fuck.

Marcus.

Shit.

Endelle might as well call the brothers together and toss a lit grenade in their direction. Of course the warriors could use Marcus's muscle as well as his four millennia of experience, but shit . . . Marcus?

He released a heavy sigh, the one born of way too many meetings with Her Supremeness. He perched on his favorite stool, the one at the end of the bar that let him keep a constant watch on the entire room, the rows of red-velvet-covered booths, the dance floor, the dark hallway leading to the bathrooms, and of course everyone else seated at the bar. He settled his left elbow on the polished wood, his right knee jutting out into the room, then leveled his stare at Sam.

"Back so soon, *jefe*?" Sam asked. He spoke in his bar-booming voice since the music thumped and loud conversation rattled the length of the club. He threw the towel over his shoulder, popped a tumbler on the bar with his left hand, then poured a decent amount of icy Ketel One with the other.

Thorne stared at the glass and felt the ease start even before he took his first sip. Sam resumed his glass-polishing duty and had the great good wisdom to keep his trap shut. Thorne wasn't surprised. Samuel Finch, owner of the vampire nightspot, had shrewd eyes, the kind that looked, grabbed a swift impression, made a judgment, which all led him to keep his trap shut.

The warriors were in for a shitstorm. Looked like a major ascension was in progress, a female, which no doubt had Greaves sporting a raging hard-on, the bastard. Of course, he'd try to get to the ascendiate first, to turn her if he could. If he couldn't—goddammit—he'd send his minions to kill her. He often wondered just how much self-control it required for Greaves to restrain his killing instincts. Of course, by law he couldn't harm either an ascendiate or an ascender outright, nor could Endelle attack Greaves's army—death vampire or otherwise. Yet how many times had he wished Endelle could cut loose and end this war. Unfortunately, if either Endelle or Darian started slaying outright, it was the same as launching a nuclear weapon. The only possible end would be vast destruction, which of course benefited no one.

He scrubbed a hand down his face and threw back the Ketel.

The result was that Endelle worked her ass off night and day to keep two worlds from sinking beneath the Commander's ambitions, which was why he'd give his life for her, *bitch* notwithstanding.

Her efforts, however, weren't cutting it, and every night the Commander shipped more death vampires in from around the goddamn globe. Last night Thorne had battled three Russian death vamps who spoke to him in words that sounded like ice skates cutting across a frozen pond. He'd made them dead but they'd been three fierce motherfuckers.

Something had to break in Endelle's direction soon. Greaves seemed miles ahead of Endelle's organization, and not just in manpower; the asshole had a workable plan and he was workin' his plan. He spent the majority of his time coaxing High Administrators from all over the world to join his forces. When he got enough of them on his side and when his army, a combination of regular soldiers and death vampires, swelled to just the right proportion, well, it didn't take a genius to figure out what would happen next.

In the meantime, it was up to the Warriors of the Blood to keep the number of death vampires in check. Only Thorne's elite group had the preternatural power as well as the pure physical strength to slay death vamps night after night, usually battling alone and usually battling three or more of the pretty-boys at the same time.

There was another policing unit, of course, the regular Militia Warriors. These squads served Second Earth all over the globe and, like the Warriors of the Blood, worked to keep death vampires in check. However, it usually took at least four Militia Warriors to bring down one death vampire—and even then casualties were heavy.

The Militia Warriors had training camps and received regular instruction from the Warriors of the Blood, although in recent months, given the activity at the various Phoenix Borderlands, what training the warriors could offer to the camps had dwindled to a trickle.

Bottom line? Endelle's administration was officially up shit creek.

Okay, so maybe Endelle was right. Maybe Marcus was necessary.

Who was he kidding? Marcus should have been recalled fifteen years ago when the first of the High Administrators had defected, the proverbial handwriting on the wall. But holy shit, his brother warriors were not going to be happy, especially Kerrick. Goddammit, Kerrick would have a seizure the moment he saw the sonofabitch. When Kerrick's wife had died, Marcus had said things to him no man should ever say to another man.

His gaze shifted to Sam, who wiped more glasses, all of which already sparkled like diamonds. He arranged them in neat tidy rows, adjusting for eighth-of-an-inch discrepancies. He polished all the bottles as well, a kaleidoscope of ambers and blues, melons and greens against the mirrored wall. He tidied and swept. The man had pride.

Another bartender, Sam's nephew, served drinks up and down the bar, but Sam stuck close to Thorne. If a Warrior of the Blood was present, Sam served him personally. He had for over a century now.

Thorne tapped his glass on the counter. Sam moved forward then poured the Ketel again.

"You might as well tell me," Sam said, a soft shout above the music.

Thorne's gaze snapped to his. He scowled. He shifted his knee into the bar then formed a protective triangle with his hands around the tumbler. With his right thumb he rubbed the deeply grooved scar running down the inside of his left wrist, an old cut that extended almost to the center of his hand. Sam drew close, turning an ear toward him.

"Nothin' to tell." Shit, his voice sounded more gravelly than ever. Too many nights not sleeping.

Sam snorted. "You were with Endelle. There's always something to tell. You're bleeding from the stripes on your back."

Thorne wanted to laugh at the image, but couldn't. He dropped his gaze. He lifted the tumbler once more to his lips. A heavy sigh swept out of his parched throat, and he soothed it with a long solid slide of vodka. He let the burn float back up. He no longer winced. He hadn't winced for years. He'd made a pact with Ketel and they'd both kept it . . . diligently.

Something dug at the back of his mind. What was it Kerrick had said? An itch he couldn't scratch? Damn straight he had an itch.

Thorne met Sam's gaze again. "She's bringing Marcus back."

Sam dropped the glass in his hand then swooped with preternatural vampire speed and caught it before it hit the floor. "Holy shit," he muttered as he rose upright. His head waggled back and forth. He was a small man with a barrel chest. His shoulders were broad and he had no hips. He wore suspenders because there wasn't a belt capable of holding up his pants. "Things are so bad, *jefe*? I thought she said she'd only bring him back if he sucked the black off the bottom of her stilettos."

Thorne shrugged but then what the hell else could he do? The decision was already made.

He had only one response right now—he tapped the bar again.

His phone buzzed as Sam refilled his glass. He glanced at the message. He smiled. "Luken just texted," he called out. "He took six down and he's headed in."

Sam let out a whoop. "Six. That Luken. He's one powerful warrior."

Thorne nodded. Luken was the peacekeeper of the bunch, and with Marcus heading toward Second later tonight, Luken's ability to keep the brotherhood on an even keel would be put to the test.

"All the warriors in later?"

"Within the hour."

Alison stood with her arms wrapped around her stomach, no less than six feet away at any given time from the winged man called Kerrick, Warrior Kerrick. Over the past ten minutes he had made his intention clear—he meant to protect her. What had he called himself, her guardian? He had reiterated, about a dozen times, that the death vamp wouldn't be taking her blood tonight. What did any of this mean?

Right now her head was spinning and because of all the adrenaline in her system, her arms and legs shook like she had a chill. Was she looking at her death, right here, right now?

Despite the number of times the death vamp shifted his position, however, Warrior Kerrick had kept his powerful winged body between her and the beautiful pale-skinned creature still on the railing.

She understood the warrior's tactic: to bring the killer in close, rather than risk becoming separated from her, which would leave her vulnerable to attack.

Oh, God. Was this even happening? She shifted her arms tighter around her abdomen. The shakes swept through her once more. Okay. She had to get control of these sensations. She refused to look at the black-winged creature any longer. She focused instead on . . . Kerrick. Yes, his name was Kerrick . . . Warrior Kerrick.

She drew in a deep breath. Better.

As much as she might question the reality of the situation, she had to admit that if this was still part of an elaborate hallucination, she had one fine imagination.

The warrior's skin was a rich golden color, in marked contrast with the pale death vamp. He wore a black leather kilt and a harness, which ran down the center of his back between his wings. On his feet were gladiator-like sandals. He looked made for war, an ancient kind of war, a war conducted in the desert.

The argument between Kerrick and the killer continued, always with the warrior's refusal to negotiate. The death vamp often flew away from the railing to make a pass or two and look at Alison, but he never failed to return to the refuge of the two-story catwalk perch, a standoff that afforded her the chance to continue her appraisal of her would-be guardian.

She couldn't fathom either the magnificence of the wings, taller than his height by several feet, or the intricately muscled back that supported them. The feathers were a very pure white in contrast with the killer's glossy black pair. She wanted to move forward and touch them, to see how they did what they did. Was the structure hard or soft, and how could wings of this size emerge just from his back? On the other hand, how could she do half the things she could do—read minds, send hand-blasts of inexplicable power, dematerialize, capture pockets of time in order to reassemble smashed windows?

The man, the warrior, stood at least six-six and every exposed part of his body bore heavy, ripped muscles. He had thick wavy black hair, which appeared to be damp, flowing away from his face to his shoulders and a few inches beyond. Every muscle in his body had been honed, probably from years of this kind of police or military service, or whatever it was he did.

She glanced from him to the death vampire. The creature with the black wings resembled the mythical vampire—he was beautiful in a way that mesmerized, and he used his fangs to drink people to death. In contrast, Kerrick was nothing like the popular freakish, emaciated images. No, he was all man, warrior, and incredibly built. Not the stuff of night-feeding vampire legend at all. He was so much more than that—moral, protective, a self-proclaimed guardian.

She had touched his mind.

He. Was. Honorable.

The longings she had felt earlier returned in full measure and intensified, crushing her heart. She bent over slightly. She worked to catch her breath. What was this deep internal sensation, this yearning? And why did it possess her so profoundly in this moment?

A shiver stole across her shoulders and she straightened. What had Joy told her not an hour ago, to go out and find a bodybuilder, that maybe such a man could handle her array of abilities? Could this man—warrior-vampire-guardian, whatever he was—could this man take all she could give?

She struggled to breathe, and a peculiar humming vibrated strangely through her body. Her lips felt swollen and her skin tingled . . . everywhere. Desire, forbidden for years, descended deep into her abdomen. Oh, God, she actually clenched as pure sexual need wept from her.

The winged warrior straightened suddenly. He turned back to her, his eyes almost crazed. He pointed his sword at her. *You must stop that now.* Funny how she knew he meant her desire for him.

She nodded several times then gasped as the killer launched from the railing. For a painful second she feared she might have just cost the winged warrior his life. And how typical would that be?

To her surprise, Kerrick simply turned and, in a blur of motion so fast as to be imperceptible, launched himself at his opponent.

In the next moment the airspace between the second and third stories of the complex became a vortex of spinning, writhing wings, clashing swords, and feral grunts.

She watched, astonished at the quick brutal movements. Within a matter of seconds, however, stillness hit the air. The black-winged body shuddered and fell to earth. Hard.

With a gasp Alison moved toward the creature, wanting to offer her help, but blood poured from a deep wound in his chest and flowed onto the cement. Her stomach churned. She covered her mouth. There was no way he could survive.

His head was cradled in a nest of broken black wings, and he lifted a hand toward her. He was so beautiful.

You must come to us. You must help us end this war.

What war? she sent. She received no answer. His eyes closed as his body shook uncontrollably. A moment later, he fell still.

Kerrick floated down beside her. He began drawing his wings into his body. She shifted and watched as one by one the feathers began to narrow to incredibly fine points and disappear into the rolling landscape of his back. Was it her imagination, or did his muscles thin out and reconfigure to a more normal masculine shape as well?

She blinked several times. Her head felt full of clouds.

Wings? A sword battle in midair?

She reverted her attention to the death vampire at her feet. She shook her head, stunned.

Death vampire?

Was any of this real?

She forced herself to breathe. She felt light-headed, unsteady on her feet. She opened her lungs, drew air. Her left arm was still wrapped tightly about her stomach but her right hand now covered her mouth.

Kerrick dropped to one knee and placed his hand on the forehead of his enemy. His shoulders slumped.

Her empathy kicked in, one of her softer gifts. She read him in another deep intake of air. She felt his soul-weariness and saw the darkness within. He had carried this burden for a long, long time, longer than a few decades.

A sense of his life passed through her mind. She perceived centuries, only how was that possible? Then again, the man had enormous wings, so apparently he existed outside the bounds of earthly possibility right now. Centuries, then, yet despair pounded from him in hard anguished waves. She wanted to touch him, to settle her hand on his shoulder, to give him just a little relief. But what did she really know of him—and worse, would she hurt him accidentally if she got too close?

With his hand still on the killer's forehead, he closed his eyes then murmured, "May the world be eased by your departure and may you find peace."

Grace in the midst of vengeance?

Who *was* this man? Warrior? Guardian? Vampire?

She took a step away from him.

He rose to his full staggering height. As her gaze slid up his back over his long black hair to his profile, desire once more, and so inappropriate, returned in full measure. She had never seen a face so pleasing, his nose straight and strong, his lips full, his cheekbones high and pronounced. His thick black hair invited exploration. His eyes were an exquisite green, an almost emerald hue.

His height dwarfed her six feet. She actually felt feminine next to him, an unusual sensation. A deep yearning threatened to swallow her whole. She took another step back. She didn't know this man, or angel, warrior, vampire.

So what on earth was he, and what did all of this mean?

He drew a credit card of sorts from the pocket of his kilt then thumbed it. When he brought it to his ear, she realized he held a phone.

He spoke in his low voice. "Hi, Jeannie. Yeah, I got him. One to pick up. Let Thorne know. The other signature?" His gaze snapped to Alison, "*She's* right next to me. I'll disperse the mortals and call back for the second removal."

Disperse the mortals? Second removal?

The unreality of the situation once more worked in her mind. *Psychotic break* seemed more reasonable to her right now than any of what she had just witnessed—still witnessed. She blinked hard. Maybe if she relaxed all this would simply disappear. She closed her eyes and took several deep breaths.

She opened her eyes but her warrior-angel was still there. He smiled crookedly. "Sorry, beautiful. I'm real." He added, "You must think you're going out of your mind."

"Bingo," she whispered softly.

He returned his card-like phone to his kilt pocket and, with his deep resonant voice thrumming over her body like a base viol, he said quietly, "You might want to cover your eyes."

Just as her hand came up to her face, a blinding light filled the courtyard for the space of maybe a second or two.

Sliding her hand away, she saw that the body of the killer had disappeared as well as any remnants of his death. The cement in the area looked pristine.

She recalled the window glass she had shattered, the pocket of time she had frozen, the retrieval of the glass, time withdrawn, a mistake made right. She stared at the warrior next to her. What he did, what he could do, *matched* her abilities. She had such powers, perhaps not exactly the same as his, but earth's basic laws of physics had a different meaning to her than to anyone else. She could pull things from other places on the planet into her hand. She could bake a cake from scratch while sitting in another room.

She thought of the statue. She held her palm out. She brought the absurd unity sculpture into her hand in the way he had retrieved his sword for battle, as if from nowhere. She needed this warrior-angel-guardian to see.

He glanced at it and his jaw grew hard. His brows drew together, forming a furrow. He met her gaze once more and nodded. He held his sword out then released it, not to fall on the cement but to be returned from wherever it had come—*wherever* the hell that was. She thought the thought and sent the statue back to the coffee table in her office.

He narrowed his eyes and shook his head. "I have no idea what to do with you."

That makes two of us, she sent.

Kerrick struggled although he hoped none of it showed. The blond goddess looked confused, frustrated, even despairing though his concern was not fixed on her plight. Instead madness seized him. This woman was still a field of lavender and he wanted to tramp through that field for the next century, maybe forever.

So who are you? The stream was telepathic, which would reach her mind, yet not penetrate. She could choose to answer or not.

Her brows lifted and her lips parted. She sucked in some air, something she seemed to be needing a lot of, then answered from her mind: *Alison Wells, and you are Kerrick? Warrior Kerrick? Is that right?*

He nodded. He squeezed his eyes shut. *Jesus, you smell like lavender.*

"Oh," she said aloud.

When he opened his eyes, her fingers were pressed to her lips. "I'm smelling Moroccan spices," she said aloud. She smiled suddenly. "Not cloves exactly. More like . . . cardamom. Yes, you smell like cardamom. I love that spice."

Oh. God.

She could smell what he was giving, a scent that had only one meaning in his world and could only be detected by someone *meant for him*. Shit. He was in so much trouble. Again, he had the feeling Endelle had set him up. "I find you . . . lovely," he said, gritting his teeth because this was an understatement. "Which explains the scent . . . again."

Her brow puckered. She was so beautiful. Achingly. She looked confused, yet her blue, gold-rimmed eyes glittered. He watched her swallow and another heavy wave of lavender swelled over him. He had to get away from her but he couldn't make his feet move.

Her gaze began a sudden strip search and wandered over his body from head to foot. He wanted her looking and was glad he wore just the leather kilt and simple weapons harness over his chest. The winged battle gear gave her a lot of landscape to cover.

She closed the distance between them, then put her hand on his arm, as though to make certain he was real. She looked up into his eyes. He knew he should stop her from touching him, from being this close, but he couldn't.

"Warrior Kerrick," she whispered, as though trying to understand. Her blue eyes darkened.

"Just . . . Kerrick," he said. His voice sounded like it had fallen down a hole.

He could hear her heart slamming against her ribs. Lavender once more rushed at him and he knew, *he knew*, if he took her somewhere private right now, he'd have her under him in a split second.

Never in his life had he experienced anything so overwhelming as looking into her eyes. He wanted in, not just now. He wanted in forever. Who was she that a mere mortal would have such a profound call on him? How could just being near her make him want to throw to the winds, without a backward glance, the vow he had taken so many decades ago?

A window opened and golden sunshine poured in, teasing long-dead hope to life. Could it be different with this woman who had such power? Could he do what he had been unable to do for his first wife and their son? For his second wife and their two children? Could he keep Alison Wells alive? Could it be different?

Those clear blue eyes beckoned to him like nothing before. Everything about her called to him.

His body tensed. He strained toward her.

His phone buzzed.

"Shit," he muttered. He scowled heavily and drew back. He plucked the phone from his waist and swung it to his ear. "Yeah, Jeannie."

"Just thought you should know, the female is all lit up and right next to you. Any trouble?"

Plenty. "No. Don't worry. She and I are talking right now."

"Aaah. She likee. Smart woman. Does she know you're a vampire?"

"Jeannie," he muttered, a hint of warning in his voice.

"Okee-dokee, then."

"Jeannie, one of these days . . ."

"Promises, promises."

He thumbed the phone and replaced it. He felt disoriented. Everything seemed to be changing beneath his feet and he couldn't find solid ground. And now this woman had met her first vampire. What would she think of spending time with the real thing, of maybe kissing the real thing?

He looked at Alison again, at the rumpled forehead, at the glitter of blue eyes, the swollen lips. He shook his head. "I can't go there. I want to, but I can't."

She nodded in quick jerks, but she still streamed lavender like she'd bathed in it about a minute ago.

He nodded as well. "I realize this must be as confusing as hell and we will talk, but I have to take care of the rest of this first."

She nodded again.

He took two steps.

I'm not going anywhere, she sent, the words hurtling into his brain and freezing his steps again. He turned back to meet her gaze once more.

Cardamom, she sent. Her eyes closed, her lips parted. Unwittingly—he was sure of that—she released yet another wave of lavender, which almost brought him to his knees. Whatever this was between them, it was goddamn mutual.

He trembled inside as he turned away and drew his hands into knotted fists. He couldn't do this. He refused to do this. Whoever she was, *whatever she was,* he couldn't get involved, not with her, not in this way. She wasn't just sex to him. No, she was a helluva lot more. She was mainline heroin, and if he wasn't careful, he'd get sucked into something he had vowed never to do again.

He moved in the direction of the stairs. He laid his hand on shoulder after shoulder though not for comfort. The spectators in turn ambled off to their various offices, no longer remembering the fatality below.

He moved back down the stairs to the crowd gathered around the body and with the same steady, quiet effort sent the rest of the spectators away from the emergency personnel. He approached the EMTs, who in turn no longer remembered that a woman had died. They reentered their vehicles and one by one drove away.

The breh-hedden *occurs so infrequently there is hardly sufficient information to make informed opinions as to its validity. This author believes Warrior of the Blood mate-bonding must be part of ascension mythology. Nothing more.*

—From *Treatise on Ascension,* Philippe Reynard

CHAPTER 4

Alison watched Warrior Kerrick put his hands on person after person. What did they see? Surely not a long-haired warrior the size of an NBA player wearing a black leather kilt and looking like a god. She was amazed as each individual simply turned away from the crime scene and went back into the medical complex.

He worked steadily until even the police and emergency vehicles pulled out of the parking lot. Finally he stood over the covered body. Once more he drew his strange phone from the pocket of his kilt, spoke to a woman he called Jeannie, and made the deceased woman disappear.

He returned to stand before her. He closed his eyes for a moment, his nostrils flaring. When he opened his eyes he scowled. "Why do you have to smell like lavender?" Once more his heavy spice, rich cardamom, flowed around her.

She couldn't believe the way her body responded to his scent, as though it belonged to her and no one else, as though she had to have it or die. Which was absurd, completely irrational.

She drew in another deep breath and gestured to the now clean cement. "What did you just do? Where did the woman and the other winged man go?"

He held her gaze. He reached a hand toward her then let it drop away. "I do interdimensional cleanup work when death vampires hunt on Mortal Earth. We work hard not to leave evidence of our world behind."

Alison nodded as though these words made perfect sense to her. "So, you have a job description, which involves making sure that we, us, this world doesn't learn of your existence."

"In part. Every night I patrol the Borderlands and battle more of these night-feeders. Any of this make sense to you?"

She shook her head. "Does any of this make sense? Death vampires? Borderlands? What do you think?" She hated the hysterical note in her voice. She put a hand to her chest, a sense of deep inexplicable yearning still possessing her. She took yet another deep breath. "Okay. So where are the bodies?"

"In a morgue on Second."

"Second?"

"Second Earth. Same earth, different dimensions. Evolved powers. Shit, you really aren't in your call to ascension, are you?"

"Since I have no idea what any of that means, I guess the answer would have to be no."

"But I watched you fold from the catwalk to ground level right in front of me."

"*Fold?* Oh, you mean the disappearing–reappearing thing? Yeah, I've never done that before in public."

"But you've done it before."

"Sure. Since childhood, although early on it happened mostly by accident."

"Anyone else in your family able to do this?"

She shook her head. "My mother is telepathic but that's about it."

"Yet you can see me," he stated. "You dematerialize, you can fold objects, and you slip into my mind easily."

She nodded, her gaze fixed to his.

He released a heavy sigh and shook his head. "You have a shitload of power, but you don't have the usual hallmarks of a rite of ascension, so right now you're a mystery to solve."

She looked him over. Was he real? Once more, she settled a hand on his bicep, reaching for an anchor. He *felt* real.

His nostrils flared suddenly. He squeezed his eyes shut like he was in pain.

Okay, she had to open the door. She had to know the truth about him, about what she was seeing and touching. "So, you're a . . . vampire."

"Yes. The ascended world is a vampire world but not in the way depicted in the worst of the Bram Stoker traditions."

"Except for the death vampire."

He nodded. "You're seeing the source of that particular aspect of vampire culture since the one I just dispatched used his fangs for some really hard-core shit. However, most ascenders—residents of Second Earth—use their fangs properly, to take blood and to give pleasure without doing harm." He searched her gaze for a long moment. "I can't even read your mind and I should be able to, which means you have powerful shields in place. Who *are* you?"

Once more, she stated her name. "Alison Wells. I have a counseling practice here in this building. Or had one. I've been closing up shop for the last two months. I just saw my last client."

He narrowed his gaze and lowered his voice. "Was your last client Darian Greaves?"

She nodded. "Yes."

"Christ." He shoved a hand through his thick black hair, which gave her sudden cravings. She drew in another breath and shifted back to his green eyes. "Do you know Darian?"

"Shit. It's so weird to hear you call him by his first name. No one does that. Not on Second. He's known as the Commander or Greaves and he's a major player. He has big plans for our world as well as Mortal Earth—*your* earth—and these plans involve war, conquest, and slavery. Right now he's well on his way to succeeding. I take it he didn't discuss his *ambitions* with you or his vampire nature."

She shook her head. "No. But he offered me a job."

"What?" he cried.

His deep rich voice flowed over her, and she forced herself to take a small step backward. Everything he did, everything he was, sent shock waves of desire through her body. "He wanted me to join his ranks. He said he would give me anything I desired and now I see he really wasn't kidding, was he?"

"No."

"I told him I couldn't work for him. I could never work for such a man."

"But you've been treating him." Sort of a question.

She sighed. "I don't think you could ever call what I was doing 'treating him.' He had an ability to manipulate the sessions. I often ended up revealing things about myself I didn't want to, very Hannibal and Clarice. Though he never spoke directly of his wrongdoings, he shared a great many *fantasies* with me, which generally involved an advanced level of brutality. Of course he would insist he would never think of acting out these *fantasies*. If . . . if I truly can believe that *you're* real, and that Darian is from Second Earth as you've said, then it would explain a lot but oh-my-God saying these things out loud makes me think I'm headed for the loony bin."

He smiled suddenly. "I didn't know *loony bin* was a clinical term."

She couldn't hold back a chuckle. "Well, I confess it helps to laugh. But *Second Earth. Mortal Earth.* Really?"

"Where do you suppose *I'm* from?"

Once again, Alison shook her head. "I have no idea but for the past fifteen minutes I've been trying to determine if I'm going insane or not."

He smiled. Even his teeth were beautiful, although it was weird to see the tips of his fangs showing, not nearly as pronounced as when he'd been fighting. In fact, they were hardly noticeable.

"You're not insane," he said.

"What is Second Earth like?"

His gaze softened, something she hadn't expected. "In developed areas, where ascenders congregate, the architecture is amazing and there are gardens everywhere."

"You mean like public gardens?"

"In part. Just imagine a world of gardens, where the most sought-after prizes are given for horticulture and design."

The image, juxtaposed with leather-kilted warrior vampires, jolted her mind. "Gardens?"

"For miles. But at the same time, these gardens are only allowed within the town and city limits. Beyond designated areas, Second Earth is in a raw state. The Colorado River is still without dams and goes through regular tidal bores since it empties, without hindrance, into the Sea of Cortez."

A world still full of primitive wilderness yet thoroughly civilized.

She thought he had just described himself, raw, in a wild state, yet *civilized*. The impression struck a chord. She trembled, and desire once more sent a shock wave through her body. He closed his eyes, flared his nostrils again, and winced as though she had just hurt him.

What returned was his scent, that exotic cardamom smell that once more invaded her body. She restrained a gasp then swallowed hard. She forced herself to the point.

"So why the same place-names, or are they different on Second?"

"Same." He smiled, just a crooked slant to the side of his mouth and absurdly sexy. "Keeps everything simple."

She nodded. Made sense. "I have so many questions. Can you stay for a while? Talk to me?"

He searched her eyes but shook his head. His jaw took on a stubborn line, which didn't bode well for the request. "Unfortunately, Alison Wells, I don't have a legal precedent to allow you to retain any of what's happened here this evening."

"What?" She took yet another step away from him. She shook her head. Her mouth felt suddenly dry. "But what are you saying . . . exactly?"

Before she could react, he closed the distance in one long impossibly fast stride, clamped his right hand to her forehead and his left to the back of her head. Warm waves of power pulsed through her.

"No," she cried. "Don't! Kerrick, please don't."

He released her and spoke softly. "Don't fight me. I have to do this. We have rules. A lot of rules."

Tears stung her eyes. "You don't understand. I'm alone here. I mean, I have family, but they don't really understand me, what my life is like. I want to know more, about you, about this." She waved her hand to encompass the now deserted courtyard.

"You're not ascended, and the presence of a warrior in an environment like this is never a call to ascension. Not even Darian Greaves's presence. As I said, we have careful rules about this. I'm sorry."

"I want to ascend," she cried. She felt panicky, like her future had just arrived on a strong ocean wave but an equally strong tide was dragging it back out to sea.

"I'm sorry, this isn't the way it's done. There are reasons for the steps we take. You have to be *called* to ascension. A warrior in a location like this is not a call."

He caught her head again, a hand before and behind. The strength of these new waves paralyzed her. Tears ran down her cheeks. "No," she whimpered staring into his eyes. "You don't understand."

"I don't have a choice," he muttered between gritted teeth. "But for God's sake relax or this is going to hurt like hell."

"No," she whispered. She couldn't lose this memory, not when for the first time in her life she had actually seen other beings do what she had been able to do since childhood.

"Please stop fighting, Alison. I don't have a choice."

The frequency of the waves increased. Knives sliced through her head.

He leaned close. "Relax, beautiful one," he whispered against her ear. "I don't want to hurt you, but my God you're powerful."

She knew she didn't have a choice. The pain increased and she surrendered abruptly.

She had a sense she had fallen into his arms.

When her brain started functioning again, she heard a very soft, almost chuffing sound. Warm sweet breath flowed over her face and down her neck. More of his incredible leathery spicy scent drifted into her nose all over again. Desire engulfed her as well as tremendous relief.

He hadn't done it.

He hadn't taken the memory.

She drew in a strong breath, opened her eyes, then met his amazing green eyes, shards of emerald glass, sparkling, longing. She drifted the back of her fingers over his cheek. "You're magnificent," she whispered. "Please don't go."

"Shit," he murmured.

She laughed but tears shimmered over her vision.

"Don't fight me again," he said.

She sighed. "I wish you wouldn't go."

"Don't have a choice."

She closed her eyes. Despair forged a wedge in her heart once more. She hurt to her toes.

He put his hand on her forehead. She surrendered. Her mind eased away and the next thing she knew she sat on the third step of the cement stairs, alone. She looked around mystified. Why wasn't she upstairs in her office locking up for the night?

She crossed her arms over her chest and squeezed as though trying to hold something in, but what? She wiped her cheeks. She'd been crying but for the life of her she didn't know why. The feeling was familiar, though. For weeks now her chest had ached, pulling her heart south, which spoke to every longing she had ever had for a full life, a complete life. Maybe she didn't know why she sat where she sat, or the present cause for tears on her cheeks, but alone-and-weeping made complete sense.

She glanced at her feet and noticed a business card sitting between the tips of her shoes. She reached down and picked it up. A red rose, lying prone against a glossy black background, lay beneath words printed in a lovely scarlet script, THE BLOOD AND BITE.

How strange was this? She'd dreamed about this nightclub several times over the past two weeks.

Marcus stood behind his massive desk, phone receiver in hand. He was in shock. Goddamn shock.

He released his strangled grip on the phone then hung the damn thing up. He looked through the glass, which topped his desk, to the sculpted gnarled base below. The base had been assembled from massive pieces of driftwood retrieved from the coast of the Olympic Peninsula and topped by a custom four-inch-thick piece of glass the length and width of a small car. Fabricated by a local artisan, the table had cost him over two hundred thousand dollars, a drop in the bucket compared with his entire fortune.

Yet he felt in danger of losing everything because of this one single fucking phone call.

He glanced at his TV. CNN ran twenty-four/seven. He knew Mortal Earth. He'd made a life here, goddammit. This was his life, the life he wanted, the life he'd chosen.

He turned to face the window, each hand now in a tight fist. He had an office near the top of a high-rise, which allowed for a magnificent view of Puget Sound. Another storm pounded Seattle and rain hit the window in successive waves, like a thousand fingertips tapping the panes all at once, releasing, then tapping again. Usually the sound soothed him. Right now, however, nothing was going to take the edge off.

He hadn't heard that particular voice, an edgy sharp female voice, in two centuries. Endelle had not spoken a word to him since he quit her elite group of warriors, not since he walked out on all the vows he had taken, not since the day he'd flipped off his warrior brothers and left them for good, yeah, two hundred years ago.

And now she'd called him back. She had a job for him, a critical job. The war against the Commander had heated up, her warriors were worked to the max, and she needed him to take Kerrick's place because the bastard had a major ascendiate to guard, or would as soon as the female answered her call to ascension.

Whatever.

For a split second he thought about hunting for the mortal woman himself and warning her away from the shitfest called Second Earth. Then again, who was he to say what was right for anyone else? Even he hadn't left Second because he didn't love his world. He did. He left for other reasons, reasons that still haunted him.

Fuck.

At least he'd only have to return for a handful of days, *a few pebbles from the ass-end of the riverbed of his life,* Endelle had said.

Like hell it would begin and end there.

Nor could he refuse and she knew it.

Goddammit.

His week was jammed. He had meetings with three of his boards over the next few days. Several international construction bids were in the works and one major contract with a Second Earth import firm. Tomorrow night he was scheduled to have dinner with a representative from one of the Middle East royal families and in an hour, he had a fang-date with an exquisite Canadian actress. He had an emerald necklace to give her, and he'd planned on spending most of the evening buried inside her then wiping her memory about midnight. He would leave her with the necklace accompanied by a single memory of beautiful sex and a sweet but necessary good-bye. She wouldn't remember he'd sucked on her neck though she might be a little dizzy over the next two days.

Now he'd have to cancel his evening.

Goddammit.

He turned away from the window. His gaze once more fell to the woody swirls beneath the thick layer of glass, all the twisted limbs, sea-worn, smashed about by the heavy Pacific waves, gnarled and smooth. He thought of Endelle's eyes, the ancient lined appearance of her brown eyes. He thought about her sacrifice of service to Second.

He owed her this.

He pressed the tips of his fingers hard into the block of glass. Too hard. He eased back.

He'd made a life for himself on Mortal Earth, a goddamn beautiful life full of all the money he could want, all the women, all the toys. He'd just ordered a Harley 1200 Nightster and the newest Jaguar. Both would eat up the coastal roads like the blast of a rocket, rain or shine.

But he had to go. He had no choice. When he left the Warriors of the Blood he'd promised Endelle one thing—if she ever needed him, truly needed him, he would come. After all, he wasn't a completely narcissistic bastard.

He thought about what he'd be doing over the next several days, putting his life on the line and all his plans on hold. He thought about his fang-date. To hell with it. Endelle and the warriors would have to wait until goddamn midnight before he left Mortal Earth. He'd get laid first.

Other thoughts intruded, thoughts beyond battling, the reason he'd left the warriors in the first place, the reason he no longer lived on Second. It was simple. At the time, if he'd stayed, he would have killed Kerrick for what he'd done.

He still would.

His fingers ached now from the pressure he once more leveled on the glass. Part of his mind warned him to back off, but the other part had turned a brilliant shade of red. His need for revenge hadn't changed, not even a little. As God was his witness, he'd get Kerrick's neck in his hands and he'd kill that sonofabitch.

The table shattered at the exact same moment a roar left his throat.

Kerrick felt blasted from the inside out. The sheer strain of trying *not* to think about Alison Wells made his eyes feel like he'd rubbed them with sandpaper.

He stood in Endelle's office, leaning an arm on the mantel of a never-used fireplace. Windows formed the north and east walls. A scattering of lights glittered all across the base of Camelback Mountain. Phoenix in any dimension had interesting volcanic hills; this one was named for its shape.

The throne room, as Thorne called the seat of Endelle's administration, was a comfortable space with dark wood floors covered with scattered zebra skins, more a man's room, almost a trophy room, than the place where a bitch-on-wheels administered an entire world government.

He couldn't begin to imagine what she had to cope with as Supreme High Administrator of Second, but right now he had his own problems, a big one with lovely blond hair and blue eyes rimmed with gold, a powerful mortal female, a woman, most likely approaching her call to ascension.

Alison.

Alison.

Christ.

He shoved his hand through his unbound hair. He shouldn't have left that card on the cement step. He was interfering in the process. Bad things tended to follow interference.

The trouble was, he'd held her in his arms, this woman, *Alison,* and the smell of lavender clung to him like honey to skin. Every breath he took brought her scent deeper into his bones. He knew what was happening and he couldn't stop it, yet he had no intention of doing a damn thing to help it along. He would fight to the death on this one.

And still he had left that damn card with her.

"Where the fuck is your *cadroen,* Warrior?"

Kerrick shifted his gaze back to Endelle. He stood up straighter. "On my sink."

She narrowed her eyes. "Why?"

"I'm just a little pissed off."

She rolled her eyes. "Fine. Whatever. Now, you were telling me about the mortal female. She folded and I asked you about place and distance."

He came to attention, slinging his left arm behind his

back. He still wore his kilt and harness, both bloodied, hardly proper attire for offering up a report to the Supreme High Administrator, but she'd insisted on a meeting right after he'd left Paradise Valley. He told her what happened.

"She folded right in front of you. No shit." Endelle's perfectly arched brows rose. Her Supremeness was impressed.

She sat low in a cradle of her enormous wings—yellow feathers this time since she could change the color at will. She wore some kind of spotted hide dress—maybe leopard—which climbed up her thighs. He had no *interest* in Endelle, but she was extraordinarily beautiful, and he was after all a man. She had the exotic features of an Arabian princess, olive skin, thick black hair, but her dark eyes were unusual and had an almost wooded appearance, like rough tree bark. She was also dangerous and possessed powers he couldn't begin to imagine. She wore stilettos, the long narrow heels reminding him of a pair of daggers.

Fitting.

Endelle had a scorpion's temperament.

"I did a quick profile of her powers. She may have all of Second's abilities."

"Goddammit," Endelle muttered. She plucked one of her feathers and ran it between her fingers. He winced. It hurt like hell to have a feather plucked but he supposed she'd been doing it so long the experience was similar to filing her nails. She continued, "The Commander's going to want her and in a few hours this is going to turn into a fucking shitfest. Okay, so where exactly is she in her call to ascension?"

"I couldn't get into her head."

"What?" She actually shifted her legs off her desk and leaned forward to stare at him. "You couldn't get into her head?"

"I could communicate telepathically, but she has shields like you wouldn't believe."

"Wow." She nodded several times. "So, did you ask about her dreams?"

"I'm not a Liaison Officer and you know the rules. Even asking is considered a violation. She had no apparent prior knowledge of anything she saw, either the death vamp or me. Our world, therefore, hasn't commanded her dreams, otherwise she should have known more than she did."

"But her powers . . . ?"

"Off the chart. Only your ascension came with the ability to dematerialize."

"Damn straight. Well, she has to be in the middle of it. I'm playing this as though we have a major ascension in progress. I think it's just a matter of time before she makes her way to one of the Borderlands." She rubbed her forehead. He wondered if she ever slept. But then, none of them did right now, at least not a whole lot of hours strung together.

Sleep. What would that be like?

The feather she had plucked changed colors, from pink to amber to black to green, a kaleidoscope turning along with the flicks of her thumb and forefinger, all the absent workings of her thoughts.

His gaze shifted to the view from the north window. Night had fallen, and Camelback Mountain was in silhouette against a black sky lit with stars. The same location on Mortal Earth would have put her office somewhere near Sky Harbor Airport.

Madame Endelle's administrative building sat in a group of elegant glass high-rises, each building wide at the base, like a pyramid, and staggered inward at each floor, allowing broad patio gardens to make up part of the overall design. By tapping into the underground rivers, the Valley of the Sun on Second Earth, in populated areas, took on a tropical feel. Broadleaf trees and citrus groves kept the temps down and the air clean. Healing greenbelts winding throughout the city were the norm.

She looked back at him. "Central said Greaves was on deck tonight."

He nodded. "The mortal female is a therapist by profession. She served as his counselor, such as it was, for the space of a year."

"No shit," Endelle murmured. "So he's known about her all this time." She shook her head. "Goddammit. I have got to have better information. This is the worst group of Seers I've ever had." She muttered a long string of obscenities then drew in a deep breath.

She nodded slowly, her gaze slicing back to him. "You got pretty chummy with this non-ascending ascendiate, didn't you? She pretty?"

Beautiful. Gorgeous. Tall, so she'd fit me like a glove. I wanted my arms around her, my fangs at her neck, and a helluva lot more. "Very pretty," he said in as flat a voice as he could manage.

"Cut the crap, Kerrick. Do you think I can't read your mind? So you have a thing for her."

What was the use pretending? There was a good chance Endelle knew his thoughts even before he had them. "More than I should. Unreasonably."

"Huh." She narrowed her eyes. "You smell anything *fragrant* on her?"

Lavender, he sent. *Fields of it.* He just couldn't say it out loud.

"Well, this has to be shit for you because it sounds like the *breh-hedden.*"

He stared at her, held her gaze. "I didn't think it existed. We all thought it was a myth."

Endelle shook her head. "It's rare but the damn thing exists. I've seen it in action a few times over the course of my fucked-up life. And it can be a real bitch so good luck with that." She laughed.

He didn't see anything funny in the potent exchange he'd had with Alison. A thought occurred to him and he narrowed his eyes. "Did you know this was going to happen when you sent me over there?"

"I had a hunch."

"Fuck."

"You know if this is the *breh-hedden,* you're not going to have much control over it."

He didn't want to think about it. He didn't want to even

acknowledge the possibility that something so powerful and apparently irresistible was dogging his heels.

He shook his head. "Won't matter if this is the *breh-hedden* or not."

She leaned back in her chair. "Oh, yeah, you took vows. Idiot. *Death happens.* Get used to it, for Christ's sake. And what was it, two hundred years ago? *Hannah* knew the risks. Give her some goddamn credit."

His jaw turned to stone. "Helena," he muttered. "My wife's name was Helena."

She stood up, planted her hands on her desk, then leaned forward. Her wings turned black, unfurled to the fifteen-foot ceiling, and popped into an aggressive drawn-back position. "Don't you dare take that fucking tone with me, Warrior, or I'll have your wings—literally—feather by feather."

She could do it, too. But for just this moment, he wanted to tell her to take them all, right here, right now, and shove them up her ass because he was sick of all this fucking bullshit, the death, the addicted bloodsucking vampires, the mortal children drained and left in goddamn alleys, and of battling a psychopath like the Commander. He leaned toward her. *Yeah, just do it,* he sent.

She stared at him for a long tense moment, her wings extended as high as they could go, each apex rounded, the feathers fluttering at the tips. Suddenly she barked her laughter, brought her wings to half-mount, then sat down in her chair once more. She again settled into the nest of her wings. "Hell, no. Why should you be set free? Suck it up like the rest of us. Besides, I don't get why you're still upset after all this time."

He lowered his chin. "It's simple, Endelle. You've never had children. When you do and you lose them because of *who you are* then you'll have the right to tell me to just *get over it.*"

Endelle grimaced. "Whatever."

Kerrick wanted to leave. If he had been capable of folding he would have lifted an arm and vanished with a sweet *fuck you* on his lips. "So are we through here, or what?"

"Yeah."

He turned to go, but she called out, "Wait. One more thing."

Something in her tone sent a warning chill straight down his wing-locks. He glanced back at her but she didn't speak. Instead she chewed on her lower lip, and Endelle *never* chewed on her lower lip. He got a very sick feeling in the bottom of his gut. All his instincts fired up like the steam engines on the *Titanic*. "Spill," he commanded.

"I've recalled Marcus." She actually looked a little guilty.

Kerrick's nostrils flared. He sucked in air. His shoulders bunched into hard muscles. His biceps twitched and his hands curled into two deadly fists. "You did what?"

"We need him."

He shook his head. "Like hell we do," he bellowed.

She rose again, once more meeting his aggression head-on. "We need him because the Commander is importing death vamps from every territory of Second Earth at the rate of fifty a day—even with all my efforts to the contrary—and even if you and your warrior brothers only take down thirty or forty, *do the goddamn math*!"

He shook his head.

"What? You don't believe me? Then tell me, what language did the squadron from last night speak, the one out at the White Tanks?"

He glared at her, but his face felt burned like he'd been standing in a powerful wind for days.

"They came from the Republic of Chad and spoke Sangho."

Of course she was right, he just hadn't stopped to think about the various nationalities he'd been fighting over the past several months. He'd just figured the Commander was ramping up his effort to keep the brothers working overtime, wearing them out. And fuck, it was working.

"So don't you dare stand there and tell me we don't need

Marcus. We do. He'll show up sometime later tonight and in case you're wondering, he's not happy, either. But the two of you had better find some way to get along. I'm putting you on guardian duty and he's taking your place at the Borderlands. We need this ascendiate. The only thing my fucking Seers were able to tell me was that Alison Wells tips the balance of power and if she ends up dead, our world will suffer for it."

Kerrick stiffened. There were so many things wrong with this situation he didn't know where to start. But the most significant thought rose swiftly into his head and before he could screen the words, he cried out, "If that sonofabitch puts one hand on her, I'll kill him."

"Oh, for fuck's sake. Go home and take a goddamn cold shower."

He was ready to argue but she lifted a hand and the next moment he was on his knees sliding across his basement floor. His hands shook and didn't stop even after he clenched his fingers into tight fights.

Marcus?

Here?

Hell, no.

Hell the fuck no.

Evil forges a tornado.
But goodness battles in a straight line.

—*Collected Proverbs,* Beatrice of Fourth

CHAPTER 5

Why couldn't she remember?

What couldn't she remember?

Alison had the worst feeling she had forgotten something so important that her life depended on it, which was silly of course, yet the nagging sensation remained.

She stood in front of the Venetian mirror in her master bath. She bent over slightly, swung her long blond hair off to the right, and tied the strings of the silk halter at the back of her neck. Was she really going to do this?

She stood upright and flipped her crimped hair back.

She'd actually crimped her hair.

She hadn't gone clubbing in three years, not since . . . well, she wouldn't think about her last boyfriend. She patted a thin rose gloss onto her lips. She pressed her lips together. She glanced down at the card on the sink . . . THE BLOOD AND BITE.

The club had been the subject of one of three recurring

dreams she'd been having for the past month. The second dream had been about a downtown alley and the third about a long, narrow lake on the west side of the White Tanks, a lake that didn't even exist.

As she thought about these dreams, a profound longing swelled within her chest until her heart felt squeezed. She closed her eyes and leaned forward. She knew of panic attacks, but *longing* attacks?

Dreams of the nightclub had sent her to her laptop. She'd Googled the establishment and learned enough to stay away. The location in south Phoenix had ended any desire she might have had to discover exactly why a club, with a wretched name and completely unknown to her, would suddenly appear in a dream.

An image popped into her head of a man bearing large black wings and fangs. A vampire?

Her head thrummed and a chill stirred up the little hairs at the nape of her neck. Vampires with wings. Why was she thinking about something so ridiculous, and yet . . .

The image crystallized. The man had been beautiful and he'd conversed with her. He had a translucent ivory complexion with a faint blue cast to his skin. He bore enormous shiny black wings and twirled in midair.

She winced. A sudden headache bloomed in the middle of her skull, a dedicated throb. She blinked several times and drew in a deep breath. She let it out slowly. The pain diminished then winked out.

Weird.

What had she been thinking about?

Well, nothing.

She glanced down at her man-hunting costume, a red silk halter, short black skirt, and strappy black Jimmy Choos. She loved these shoes but never wore them. She'd never had an occasion until tonight. She'd even put on sparkly eye makeup. Oh, God, was she really going to do this? Did she actually think she would find happily-ever-after at a place called the Blood and Bite?

On the other hand, what if her deep subconscious mind

had been working to redirect her to exactly the man she needed, hence the dreams? She didn't hold to rigid clinical views when it came to her life's calling. She embraced the chaotic nature of existence as well as the mysterious and intricate depths of the human mind.

Besides, all of the psychology in the world couldn't explain her own special powers. So what did she hope to find at this club tonight?

The answer sped to the surface of her mind like a buoy released abruptly from underwater. She hoped that somewhere inside a man existed who could understand her, accept her, perhaps even have the ability to withstand the strange powers she wielded. Did she have a basis for such hope? Only that she'd found a card at her feet and couldn't explain how it had gotten there.

At eight o'clock Eldon Crace, High Administrator of Chicago Two, sat in a pool of his own sweat, which made no fucking sense at all. He was known for his composure.

On the other hand, he was sitting opposite the vampire who had the power to give or to withhold what he desired most in the world. Commander Darian Greaves, with one whisk of his Montblanc pen, could authorize a seat at his Geneva Round Table, the place of all future authority for the Coming Order.

He dabbed at his forehead with a crisp square of white linen. Perspiration leaked from every pore of his body. What was this unbearable pressure inside his head?

The Commander was a complete master in the oldest sense, in his level of personal accomplishment, in power, and in the obeisance he called from those around him. He had the air of European aristocracy and the will of Emporer Qin.

He sat behind a massive ebony desk, the size of a battleship, his being as calm as a lake on a windless day. Behind him was a wall of chipped rock, evidence that the compound existed underground, protected, secure, a vast stronghold.

The Commander wore an expensive black cashmere

suit, probably Italian, at least in design, the yellow silk tie a striking contrast. He had large round black eyes, a bald head that glimmered beneath ceiling lights, a black ring on his right pinkie, and extremely sharp fangs he rarely bothered to conceal. As a finale, he had talons instead of fingers on his left hand.

Crace refused to look at the dagger-like claws, but not looking didn't lessen the amount of moisture his body sloughed in pints.

Jesus.

A faint whirring sound drew his attention to the far wall. A row of immaculately groomed and very phallic Italian cypresses ranged from one end to the other and now swiveled a quarter turn in massive gold pots, shifting to face a bank of grow lights suspended from the ceiling. Even the botanical expression in Greaves's office suggested power and purpose.

A new wave of sweat dribbled down his forehead and he dabbed again.

He held himself together, however. He'd at least learned a great deal of poise in the last few decades.

He'd been summoned to Phoenix Two for a purpose, but he would not hear the Commander's wishes and desires until the Commander wished and desired to speak. Right now silence kept Crace's nerves on the edge of a knife.

Crace had had his lips pressed to Greaves's ass for the last century, doing what he was told and when, stockpiling ordnance, acquiring an army of death vampires, and training, training, training. These activities were no more, no less than the other High Administrators around the globe were doing, all those ambitious men and women who had aligned with the Commander, who hoped for a new order, who hoped *for the spoils* of the Coming Order.

Crace, however, had no illusions. Darian Greaves wanted to rule and rule he would. Two worlds would soon be up for grabs, and Crace meant to be seated *at the right hand of God* when the shitstorm came down.

Right now he sat opposite his deity, dwarfed by his presence in the cleverest way. Crace's chair sat too low and the bottom was angled up at the knees. He couldn't sit forward if he wanted to. He would remember the psychological disadvantage he felt right now, and as soon as he returned to Chicago he'd order a pair just like them. The chairs would sit in front of his desk and with great pleasure he'd watch his inferiors lean back like they were tanning themselves at Lake Michigan. How easily a blade could be thrust through the sternum in such a vulnerable attitude.

"What's Chicago like these days?" Commander Greaves asked. He had a velvet-on-steel voice, soothing with a foundation of malice, a solid promise if things didn't go his way. As one who meant to rule, the Commander spoke as he ought.

Crace flared his nostrils then smiled. "Cold in early March. You know Chicago. We only have two kinds of weather—winter and the Fourth of July. However, the weather's perfect here in Phoenix."

The Commander nodded, his fingers steepled, his expression thoughtful. "And how fares your army?"

"We have followed your lead and work steadily to acquire one new recruit every week." He was very proud of his record. The best time to recruit was during the rite of ascension when mortals were most vulnerable. Later, with a more complete understanding of the nature of dying blood, it was the rare ascender who opted for addiction and military service. Regardless, he made a powerful effort to recruit and had performed past expectation.

"You've done well. Ship fifty to me by the end of the week."

Crace withheld the hiss forming in his throat. He was highly protective of his army for several reasons. First, to send them to Phoenix Two was nothing short of a death sentence for each squad, and second, the Commander always had quotas. What if he wasn't able to fill the required numbers? Punishment would surely follow—or worse, he'd lose his chance at a Round Table appointment. Sweat leaked from the back of his knees and streaked down his calves. If only the pressure in his head would ease up.

"I would of course not hold you to your current quotas although I do recommend you replenish your forces as quickly as possible. I suggest you go farther afield. Head down to Texas. Who will know, except you and me, should a little meaningless rule get broken?"

"Thank you, Commander." He'd just received permission to venture into a Territory aligned with Endelle. Truth? He enjoyed breaking the rules. He smiled.

"My, my, we are eager."

Hell yes, *we* were eager. *We* should have had a promotion to the Round Table fifty years ago, but the Commander never did anything in haste. He should take a lesson from his superior; instead his gums flapped. "I've earned the post."

The Commander's eyes narrowed.

Shit.

The words came out in his quietest voice, and the talons flexed ever so slightly. "You've earned the post when I decide you've earned it. You must learn patience, Crace. Your *eagerness* has always been your downfall. Now, now, don't despair. You will be happy to know that I have a job for you."

At last. The reason for the summons. Crace released a deep breath, oh-so-quietly. He pressed his right hand over his heart and bowed, a less-than-elegant action in the sloped chair.

"I offer myself willingly."

The Commander lifted a single sheet of crisp white paper, held between the long sharp claws. Crace's gaze shifted to the talons. Sweat blossomed all over again. Greaves had so much power. No one else on Second had the ability to alter DNA and sprout a claw. He could retract the damn thing as well, although not for this interview apparently.

Sweet Jesus.

"Do this," the Commander said, a smile easing over his fangs, "and you will sit *at the right hand of God.*"

He shoved the paper forward. It moved just a few inches, which forced Crace to haul his ass out of the low chair by pushing up on the arms with both hands. He took the sheet and slid back into place once more, the pooling sweat soaking his Gucci briefs.

As he glanced over the first few lines of the assignment, he shook his head. He didn't understand. Was this all the Commander required?

He lifted his gaze and met the large round eyes of his deity. "You want me to kill a mortal woman?" He almost laughed. Could anything be simpler?

"Put your plans together. However, do not take even the smallest action until I have permission from the Committee. Even then, we can only begin the moment the ascendiate has answered the call. Are we clear?"

Crace stared at him, his lips parted. Of course he knew the rules, he just couldn't believe the simplicity of the assignment. He even wondered why a man of lesser talents wasn't brought in to get the job done.

The Commander smiled, just a little. "Is there a problem, High Administrator Crace?"

"Not at all."

Crace knew joy. The sensation was a flock of butterflies flitting through his veins. He got a hard-on the size of a sledgehammer. Victory sang in his ears. He grinned though he knew he shouldn't. Maybe this was a simple form of justice for all the labor he had performed, karma coming home to roost.

A fever now worked in him. "I will not disappoint you," he cried. His hands shook. The paper rattled between his fingers. He had many things he wanted to discuss with the Commander. He had a thousand ideas about how to administer the Coming Order, the vast spectacle he would help create worthy of the Commander's vision and power.

Kill a mere mortal woman and he had a seat at Commander Greaves's Geneva Round Table.

Sweet, sweet Jesus.

And he had so many ideas for the Coming Order.

He was dizzy with excitement, a bride on her wedding day. He was ready to speak, to share the enormous plans he had. Instead the Commander rose to his feet. "You must forgive me for ending the interview. I have other matters to attend to."

"Yes, yes, of course," Crace said, once more pushing himself out of the chair, his damn pants clinging to his thighs. The interview was over.

He bowed and remained in the subservient position as the master passed by. A scent of lemons arose along with a faint resinous smell, something like paint thinner.

A moment more and Greaves vanished. At the same time, the pressure within Crace's head eased.

Of course Greaves had been in his head. Of course. Yet he had somehow cloaked his presence.

So much power.

Crace glanced at the paper. One final task to complete, and not nearly as difficult as a dozen others he'd performed over the decades. He smiled once more, baring his fangs. He laughed and threw in a throaty growl. He wished his wife were with him. She was the great love of his life, the partner in his ambitions, the finest hostess of the North American continent. Most certainly his darling wife would understand the monumental nature of this opportunity.

He'd take her, right now, here in the office of his deity, on the Commander's big fat ebony desk. They would drink champagne and commune. Oh, God, would they commune.

Maybe he should bring her to Phoenix Two while he took care of business. He would have need of her, great desire for her body and for her blood.

He glanced once more at the paper.

Now where, oh where, to find the mortal Alison Wells?

After showering . . . *again* . . . Kerrick dressed in black cargoes, a snug black tee, and steel-toed boots. This time he pulled his hair back and secured the leather *cadroen*. The ritual bound him to the warriors, to Second Earth, to his avowal of service to all immortal ascenders. He took his vows seriously.

Most nights he wore flight gear to meet up with the warriors at the Blood and Bite, because for whatever reason the ladies always made a beeline for the kilt. Right now, however, he wasn't in the mood.

As Central folded him to the Mortal Earth club, he stood on the threshold and took a long look around, the music a loud wild frenzy, strobes flashing over the dance floor. He flared his nostrils and breathed in. He was only concerned about one scent right now, although he feared the smell of lavender more than a hundred of the Commander's death vampires.

However, when nothing returned to him, not even a hint of lavender, instead of feeling relieved, he cursed. Where the hell was she?

He ordered his mind. He should be grateful she hadn't made her way here. Alison Wells would do well to remain unknown, hidden in the safety of her life. Any association with him would put her in harm's way.

What had he been telling Thorne just a few hours ago: *You ever had an itch you couldn't scratch?*

Fuck.

He headed to the bar where Thorne, Medichi, Jean-Pierre, and Zacharius bellied up and drank, four of his warrior brothers. Well, they all drank except Jean-Pierre. He had his tongue in the ear of a brunette.

Thorne sat in his usual spot, at the top of the bar where he had the best view of every corner of the room. The club was full of Phoenix Two Militia Warriors who also had permanent passes to the Mortal Earth club. Thorne made sure all the vampires treated the mortal women with respect. Right now his right heel thumped to the music.

Kerrick went down the row and slapped shoulders. Medichi shoved an elbow at him as he jerked his head up and down once. He held a glass of red wine in his hand. Kerrick didn't know how his brother could stand the shit.

Zach presented his hand, and Kerrick grabbed five. Zach drew him close. "Heard Greaves was with the ascendiate," he shouted. The music roared by this time of night and the strobes bounced light and dark around like a pinball machine.

"You got that right."

Kerrick acknowledged Jean-Pierre with a nod. The brother was a little too busy to do more than cast an eye in Kerrick's direction as he tended to the female. Jean-Pierre was one helluva player, just as he'd been during his mortal life. Ladies were his game, no restrictions. The woman leaned close, her lips parted, her body molded to the warrior.

Kerrick turned around and headed back in Thorne's direction. The lighting over the bar cast spotlights over each stool, and the last thing he needed from Jean-Pierre was a visual reminder of what he wanted to do to Alison.

As he drew close he saw that Thorne's hazel eyes were not only red-rimmed but also bloodshot, and still he had his fingers around a sweating tumbler of Ketel One. He gestured for Kerrick to take the stool next to him then swiveled in his direction. "Good job," he shouted, his gravel-pit voice raking the words hard. "Jeannie said the death vamp drained a mortal."

Kerrick nodded. He spoke in a strong, clear voice. "Had to spend a few minutes wiping memories."

"No doubt." Thorne picked up his tumbler and took a deep swallow.

"So . . . Marcus." Even saying his name caused Kerrick to twitch and his shoulders to bunch. "Endelle said she'd recalled him."

Thorne scowled. "Yeah. You gonna be okay?"

"Fuck, no."

"Exactly what I thought."

Kerrick turned to Sam, ready to call for his Maker's only to find a glass filled with liquid gold already sitting in front of him. He smiled. Sam was the best. He mouthed a *thank-you* to the barkeep. Sam merely nodded in response and kept moving up and down the line, tending to the warriors.

Thorne cut into his thoughts. "So how'd the cleanup go? We good?" He spoke in a loud voice but he still sounded like the low rumble of an idling Corvette.

Kerrick nodded, took a long swig, then leaned in close, aiming his words at Thorne's ear. "With one exception."

Thorne shifted toward Sam, lifted his left arm, and with his hand made the cut sign across his neck. Sam nodded, picked up a phone, and a few seconds later the music came to a halt. Sam always obliged Thorne.

"Tell me everything."

Kerrick related the battle at the medical complex, then his experience with Alison.

"So what is this ascendiate like?"

She's . . ." *Perfect.* "Like most women. Curved, soft-looking." *Hot as hell.* Okay, he had to stop thinking about her. Now. He added, "Assuming this really is an ascension, it's already without precedent. She has a boatload of power. Telepathy, empathy, and she folded. A profile indicated at least twenty others. I think she has all of Second's abilities."

Thorne dipped his chin. "Are you shitting me? And she folded, just like that? I couldn't dematerialize when I ascended, not for another decade or so. And you still can't."

"Don't rub it in."

Thorne laughed. He threw back his Ketel, popped the glass on the bar, and Sam was ready to pour. "If you weren't in all other respects the most powerful of our band of misfits, yours truly included, I might just feel sorry for you. Your speed makes up for everything since you prove it every night. Bastard."

Kerrick laughed then shook his head. "I watched her fold. I had my wings at full-mount and would have risen to the second-story catwalk where I thought the death vamp had her trapped, but the next moment she appeared a couple of yards in front of me on ground level." He then told Thorne about the difficulty he'd had doing the memory slice.

Thorne's face knotted up. "Jesus. I've never heard of a mortal with so much resistance."

"I've never had to go that far before." He had his tumbler to his lips, but he just kept shaking his head at the memory. He'd practically punched her head with an ice pick to get inside—and even then, that she'd withstood the pressure without stroking out meant only one thing. Power. A lot of it. "Greaves was there."

"Holy hell. When?"

"Just when I arrived. He acknowledged my presence then walked away. After that, Jeannie couldn't read him on the grid so we presume he folded. The mortal's been his therapist for a year. Can you believe it? She said he offered her a job. She refused."

"Goddamn. So essentially she's already declared her intention of aligning with Endelle."

"Again without precedent, since she still hasn't answered her call." He shook his head. "None of this makes sense, does it?"

"No." Thorne frowned. "A complete anomaly."

Kerrick felt compelled to make his confession. "I left a card for her."

Thorne snorted then backhanded his arm. "What the hell were you thinking? We are *never* supposed to interfere."

"I thought between the Commander's presence and the death vamp's knowledge of her power she was already in the middle of a call to ascension. Couldn't be a coincidence that the vamp went to the complex hunting for her, and apparently with a purpose to drain her, nor that I showed up shortly after." He dropped his voice, turned slightly, and met Thorne's gaze dead-on. "Something else happened. I really got into her."

Thorne shook his head. "So exactly what are we talking here? How much?"

He dropped his voice one more notch. "Like I was the fucking German army and she was Poland."

Thorne frowned, caught Sam's eye, then popped his glass

on the bar again. Sam moved in smoothly and filled. Thorne took a swig and met Kerrick's gaze. "Is she here?"

"Nope, and believe me I'd know."

"She's *fragrant*, then?"

"Yep."

"Damn. You know what this means, although, hell, I thought it was a myth."

"We all did. I'm trying not to think about it. Besides, even if she shows, I have no intention of going after her."

Thorne clapped him on the shoulder. "Think about it, though. If she's so powerful, she'll be right for you. This could be a good thing."

Kerrick really didn't want to hear any encouragement, not from Thorne, not from any of the brothers. "I took vows after Helena died." EOS. He finished off the Maker's.

Medichi leaned in from the side. "I've got a question."

Kerrick turned in his direction and waited.

He swirled the Cabernet in his wineglass. He was the tallest of the brothers, topping out at six-seven with lean, powerful muscles. "What the hell are you ladies talking about?"

Before Kerrick could answer him, Zacharius rounded Medichi and butted in as well. "Yeah. You exchanging recipes or what?" Kerrick flipped him off.

Zacharius was *the man*, a vampire full of shit and swagger. His thick curly black hair, when he chose to release it from the *cadroen*, drove the ladies wild.

Thorne's gravel-pit voice broke over Kerrick's shoulder. "Well, assholes, though it's none of your business, we were just discussing warrior *mate-bonding*. Any thoughts?"

Zacharius turned white and headed back to his stool. Medichi crossed himself. Both warriors hunched over their drinks and disappeared for a while. Kerrick waggled his empty glass at Sam. Sam nodded and refilled.

A feminine moan shifted his attention down the bar, just past Zach. Jean-Pierre whispered a string of tender French words into the ear of his now panting female. He traced a long index finger along her collarbone. The other hand slid deep into her skimpy blue silk top.

Sam called to him, "Jean-Pierre, you know the rules. Mist and a booth or I'll have to throw you out."

Jean-Pierre met his gaze and lifted an arrogant brow. He bared his fangs and a lovely Gallic growl eased out of his throat.

Kerrick had to smile. The barkeep was half Jean-Pierre's size, a small vampire, born on Second Earth, who'd find himself broken in half if he pushed the warrior. One of his privileges, however, since he served Endelle by keeping the club specifically to serve her warriors, was to order even the Warriors of the Blood around, at least on his premises.

Sam tipped his head to his bouncers, and a couple of giants stepped forward. Kerrick's smile broadened. Regardless of their size, if they intended to engage Jean-Pierre, they'd both end up in the hospital in less than a minute.

When the warrior didn't back down, Thorne lifted his head from his drink. "Goddammit, Jean-Pierre, get a booth. Now. Though why you have to *forget* the rules every other night . . ."

Jean-Pierre shrugged, laughed, then wrapped a ripped arm around the female's shoulders and drew her away. The only order he would ever take was from Thorne.

He had a different take on the *cadroen* as well. He tied up his wild-looking brown waves with varying strips of brocade, a leftover affectation from his years at the court of Louis XVI.

"Fifteen minutes," Thorne called after him.

"*Quinze,* bah." He made use of his tongue again and the female sagged against him.

Zacharius hooted after Jean-Pierre, who in turn flipped him off. Jean-Pierre disappeared behind a layer of mist as he hauled his mortal female into one of many red velvet booths.

Fifteen minutes.

As usual, the warriors would be working the Borderlands throughout the night, on both Mortal Earth and Second, hunting the Commander's death vampires. Kerrick's muscles twitched. Fifteen minutes? He couldn't wait.

Movement at the entrance caught his attention. Alison? Adrenaline punched through his veins once more, but it was only Luken and Santiago, the two remaining warriors. They strolled in, tall powerful vampires, each six-five plus.

Damn but if a petite redhead didn't run at Santiago, leap on him, and throw her legs around his hips. He caught her easily and sucked on her neck. Her giggles rose above the noise of the club. Alcohol tended to elevate any voice, so even with the music off until Thorne wanted it back on, the place was alive with whistles, catcalls, and loud conversation. There were other sounds as well. Those, however, Kerrick ignored.

He picked up his glass, slid off the stool, and once more leaned his hips against the bar. He hooked Luken's arm and palmed his hand.

Luken nodded then spoke in a low voice. "Heard about the mess in downtown earlier. Kids. Shit."

Kerrick was taken right back there to finding the mortal woman and her children, broken and drained. He nodded then sucked back the rest of the Maker's.

Luken clapped his shoulder, afterward moving down the row to greet his brothers. Kerrick followed with his gaze. Luken kept the peace and eased suffering. He was a massive warrior, with more muscle than even Kerrick, yet lean as hell. He had the heart of a saint and it meant something to have Luken acknowledge when shit went bad.

Kerrick shifted his gaze to the dance floor. Several couples remained, chatting, waiting until the music came back on, exchanging a few erotic kisses. Even Santiago waited with his redhead, his lips still fixed to her neck. He had the whole Latin thing going on and knew how to work it.

One Militia Warrior already had his fangs deep, his body arched over the female, who, hell, looked like she was ready to come.

Damn. Kerrick's thoughts flew back to Alison, and desire pumped through him so fast he had to turn back into the bar. Holy shit. He only had to *think* about the blond goddess and he was hard as a rock. He eased back onto his stool and spent the next minute memorizing the labels on the bottles opposite.

Normally he'd be out there taking care of business as well, easing his tension, letting the ache of his solitary life leak out of him for a minute or two, yet ever since he'd held Alison in his arms, he'd lost interest in smelling anything but lavender.

Kerrick brought his tumbler to his lips once more. As he took another hefty swig, his gaze hit the mirror opposite and landed on a space between a bottle of Absolut and another of Bacardi Superior. In that small, mirrored spot he caught Thorne's tight expression as he stared into his tumbler.

Shit. Boss looked fazed, his expression fixed and staring. He clasped his hands on the bar, caging his tumbler of vodka. His right thumb dug into the well of a long deep scar, a sword wound that had nearly severed his left thumb from his hand many centuries ago. Thorne bore his responsibilities seriously yet he'd never appeared quite so blasted, and it wasn't just because of the drink. Something was eating at him.

Thorne had seen over two thousand years of mortal and immortal life, and he'd borne the weight of the Warriors of the Blood for the last millennium. He was even responsible for handing out the Militia Warrior training assignments, although lately none of the brothers had been to the camps. Greaves had kept the Borderlands lit up for months so that improving Militia Warrior skills had fallen by the wayside.

Worse for Thorne, however, was his duty to Endelle. As her numero uno, he was linked to her telepathically, and that had to be one helluvan assfuck.

As Supreme High Administrator Endelle was in charge, but damn she gave *bitch* a bad name. She had reason, of course, since for God only knew how many centuries she'd shouldered the burden of keeping Greaves from nuking two worlds.

And Thorne served as her second-in-command.

Tonight he looked it as he sat rubbing his thumb into the scar, his eyes glazed, the lower half of his face hanging low like gravity had him by the jaw and was pulling hard.

"Hey," Kerrick said quietly. "Why don't you head out there and get busy?" He jerked his head to the dance floor where couples waited for the music to resume.

Thorne's face moved through half a dozen expressions, ending in horror. "What the hell are you talking about? You know I'm celibate."

Kerrick looked at him hard.

Thorne flipped him off but not in a friendly way.

"I meant no disrespect."

Thorne turned and faced him. His eyes grew wet and he pinched his lips together. He shook his head several times. He clearly wanted to say something. He ground his molars then muttered a couple of obscenities. Finally, he said, "Aw, fuck. Just forget it."

"Done."

Thorne caught Sam's gaze then swirled two fingers in the air. Once more Sam picked up his phone and ordered the music on full blast.

As the Black Eyed Peas's "Pump It" started up, Kerrick returned to his glass and took a strong pull. Was this his future in a few more centuries? Staring mindlessly into a mirrored wall and lying to his friends, drinking like a fish, walking around like a dead man? Now, there was a vision to get excited about.

Once more he thought of the ascendiate, of Alison, but he clamped down hard on the images racing through his brain. *Lust* was too small a word for what he felt when he thought about her.

He ordered another Maker's and decided he'd spend the next few minutes sinking into his own tumbler. Just as he raised his glass to his lips, the door to the club opened. A number of scents plowed into his brain and he sorted through them one after the other. The last faint bouquet reached him like the rumble of a tank just beyond the hill.

Lavender.

However, as he rose and stared at the doorway, only two Militia Warriors crossed the threshold. He waited, but no one else followed.

He turned back to drop onto his stool then sipped his Maker's. Great. Now he was imagining Alison's scent.

The rite of ascension only creates difficulty for those with highly evolved powers, but the contributions of service, which follow, astonish even the gods.

—From *Treatise on Ascension,* Philippe Reynard

CHAPTER 6

At eight o'clock Alison stared up at the sign hanging from a scrolled wrought-iron standard. The words THE BLOOD AND BITE gleamed in a beautiful red script against a black background just like the card she'd found at her feet earlier.

Beneath the words, like the card, a red rose lay prone.

Why was she here? She pressed a hand to her stomach then took a deep ragged achy breath. She could lie to herself and say she'd come solely to figure out why she had found a business card, bearing the club's logo, lying at her feet. But the truth went deeper—so deep she trembled.

Oh, God. Was her future inside this club?

Looking up at the sign, however, she shuddered. The name of the club, the Blood and Bite, harked back to vampire lore. What kind of person would name a club something so obvious and so absurd? She could only imagine that those who frequented the establishment sported artificially sharpened incisors, tattoos, a whole lot of piercings.

Though the quite beautiful sign alone offered sufficient warning to make her skitter back into her log, right now she had to at least have a look inside.

Taking another cavernous breath, she put her feet in motion.

When she entered the club, the darkness of the environment as well as the flashing strobes shut her vision down for a few long seconds. As she waited near the entrance, her heart pounding, her fingers touched something soft.

Glancing to her right then squinting, she discovered she was looking at a long length of scarlet velvet. Her fingers glided down the soft fabric. How strange.

As her vision adjusted and she glanced once more around the club, she caught sight of a lot more red velvet covering a host of booths to her right. The choice struck her as bizarre, out of place, yet very sensual, which all added up to *purpose*. A woman might let down her guard in a place lined with such a sensual fabric. She had an odd impression she'd walked into a velvet trap.

The music pumped through the building. Gwen Stefani's "The Sweet Escape."

Her heart rate kicked up another notch.

The club was jammed, a real hot spot. She shifted her gaze in the direction of the dance floor. She could only see the bouncing heads and arms of a whole lot of people. She could barely make out a bar off to the left. To the right were rows of the velvet-clad booths, which, given their tall backs, provided a great deal of privacy. Did she just hear a moan?

Two quite handsome men, at least as tall as she was, even in her heels, moved toward her. They appeared to be dressed in expensive clothes that shouted *Armani*. Another surprise.

What kind of place was this?

Both men were loaded with confidence. She really hadn't expected *GQ and* swagger in a place called the Blood and Bite. Once again she was struck with the sense of everything being not-quite-right.

Their voices jabbed at her in quick alternating blows.

"Are you new here?"

"You'll like the club."

"It's a little loud."

"But you'll get used to it."

Again warning bells sounded because something didn't feel right about the exchange. Underneath their spoken words, she felt a very specific and heavy mental pressure. When she released her shields, different words, their words, flooded her mind.

You're so beautiful—and what a body . . .

You've come to the right place.

We're going to take good care of you.

Yeah, the best kind of care.

She was stunned. They were communicating telepathically. Worse, they were *seducing* telepathically. Had she been without all her special abilities, she wouldn't have been able to *hear* their enthralling words.

Despite the fact that she disapproved of what these men were doing, she couldn't believe she had actually found two other human beings who could do what she could. Yet somehow the exchange seemed familiar, as though she had recently conversed with another *man* in just this way—telepathically.

Images started flying through her mind, of a huge gorgeous warrior, a vampire, with white wings, and another vampire with pale translucent skin and black wings. They had been fighting, with swords, in the air.

She gasped at the memory. But the headache that followed these thoughts took her into the stratosphere and she winced until she couldn't remember what had brought it on. As suddenly as it had come, the pain just floated away.

The Armani duo each took hold of one of her elbows and the nightmare officially started as the one on the left pressed hard with his mind, *You'll enjoy every moment with us. You'll give your neck freely, your blood, your body. You'll experience pleasure like you've never known before.*

The companion added, *Open for us, lovely flower.*

Her muscles tensed. They wanted to drink her blood? Okay, this was getting way too weird.

She considered dematerializing back to her home. However, given the telepathic abilities of both men, she suspected she'd walked into a den of vipers and needed to pick her way very carefully out of the situation.

She closed her mind as she allowed them to usher her down a crowded row of booths, maneuvering her through a maze of clubbers. She glanced around, looking for an avenue of escape.

Oh, Lord, she shouldn't have done that. She wished she hadn't seen the erotic events taking place in some of the velvet-encased booths.

Wait a minute. Some kind of disguise overlaid the couples, like cobwebs, something an average human probably couldn't detect or even see through, some sort of shield.

Oh, great. Rack up one more supernatural power for Alison Wells—the ability to see through unusual shields. Yet what sort of people could create something so intricate? Once more her heart went into overdrive. Whatever was going on here mirrored her own abilities.

She looked away, ignoring the squeals and moans, the writhing limbs.

Instead she turned her attention to the dance floor, which she could see just above the backs of the booths, but oh-my-God the action out there equaled anything she'd already seen. She drew in a sharp breath. Several fanged men sucked on the necks of the women they danced with. The other half were working up to the same thing and the women . . . were *loving* it.

The purpose of the club as well as the nature of those who frequented the establishment became clear.

Her heart pounded all over again and she felt dizzy. One of her admirers flashed a smile and showed off—of course—his fangs.

Vampires?

Vampires.

A deep cold sensation invaded her stomach. She could hardly breathe. Vampires . . . who made use of telepathy to seduce their victims. Creatures, looking *very* human, who had fangs and drank blood.

How was this possible?

Since she could read minds, and take herself from one place to another with a mere thought, she supposed she could allow other unusual creatures to exist as well. Why not vampires? Earth had a lot of room, certainly enough for all kinds of freaks—for instance, those who read minds and teleported and served as psychotherapists—why not those who attended hot nightspots and dressed in Armani and drank blood from veins?

When the man, the vampire, on her right once more started in with his mind pressure, she'd had enough.

Reaching the end of the row of booths, she turned to face her way-too-confident squires. She lifted her hands to each and without either knowing, she kept them from assaulting her with steady, quiet blasts from the palms of her hands. Then she went to work on each of *their* minds.

Turnabout . . . fair play!

She sent subtle messages about respecting women more and about avoiding this absurd club in the future. She gave each a longing to date intelligent women who would make good wives, then she littered their heads with all the delights of fatherhood. That should keep these two vampires busy for the next several decades.

She only had one problem remaining: how to get the hell out of the club without anyone noticing . . . or possibly following.

Kerrick tossed back his third Maker's and set the empty glass on the bar in front of him. He sniffed the air. He could still smell the lavender scent. Wait a minute. The scent was stronger.

He flared his nostrils and drew in a deep breath.

Yep . . . stronger.

He rose upright and took a step away from the bar. He

breathed in again. His heart set up a sudden furious hammer-like beat inside his chest. His eyesight dimmed while his olfactory system flared into high gear.

The heady lush scent assaulted his nose again, sped into his brain, and this time triggered a host of reactions, each of which splintered one after the other and shot a cascade of fireworks through his central nervous system.

He smelled her. Alison. *Alison.*

Goddammit. She was in the club right now.

Urgency crowded him.

In a brilliant flash he transformed into a heat-seeking missile. He glanced at the entrance but saw only an array of Militia Warriors ready to pounce on new arrivals. Somehow Alison had come into the club and had already gotten lost in the play.

Holy shit.

He had to find her *now.*

He penetrated the various mists cloaking the Militia Warriors on the dance floor. She didn't seem to be there. However, the club was deep and there were many hidden alcoves and way too many booths.

His mind touched female after female. He picked up each woman's scent and cast it aside again and again, his search specific, his hunger rising, his fangs lengthening. Where was she?

Thorne's commanding voice thumped the bar. "Leaving in four."

When Kerrick turned around to face him, Thorne shifted to look up and met his gaze. Kerrick pulled his lips back over distended fangs and growled deep in his throat. His consciousness shuffled off to a distant part of his brain and watched this unheard-of behavior in astonishment.

"What the fuck?" Thorne muttered, leaning back. He grinned. "No fucking way. Medichi, Zach, you tracking this?"

Kerrick turned away.

He had to find the woman.

He stepped past the bar. He smelled the trail coming from the direction of the booths straight across from him.

His blood boiled. His shoulders hunched. His muscles flexed and twitched, ready to engage in battle over what he knew in the depths of his being belonged only to him. His wing-locks itched, ready to release full-mount, to catch her if he needed to.

"I've got your back."

Kerrick whirled and glared at Thorne. "Do whatever the fuck you want. Just keep away from the woman."

Thorne nodded. "Understood."

Kerrick wanted to knock him flat . . . for no reason. He shifted back around, his hands closing into heavy fists. He flexed his wing-locks.

The row of booths was jammed with people, coming and going. The wet sounds of sex slugged at his ears and ratcheted his temper up a notch, and then another. He didn't know what he would do if he found *her* engaged in any of these acts.

He sharpened and lengthened his vision.

Halfway down the crowded row, the path cleared and he had a perfect view of a tall woman who faced two Militia Warriors.

Alison.

Alison.

Time froze; his feet as well. He couldn't move. He could only look, wonder, crave, stunned like a beast caught in the headlights.

She was sexy as hell with soft crimped curls dangling past her shoulders and down her back, so different from the tight, controlled twist at the medical center. She wore a short black skirt, which revealed long legs that kept on going. Her scarlet halter was cut low enough to expose a swell of high firm breasts. God, her beauty lit up his head. His body followed. *He craved her.*

The trail of her scent reached him and struck hard. Woman and heady lavender formed a cocktail and set off grenades throughout his suddenly starved body.

Breh-hedden ripped through his head.

Bonded-mate.

In a fraction of a second he slid his mind over hers, pressed hard, broke through her shield—damn, what power—and finally read her. She stumbled because of it but at least now he knew what was going on.

She had come to the club because of a series of dreams and because of the card he'd left her. So he was right. She had been in the middle of a call to ascension. She'd also come in hopes of a slow dance against a hard male body. He could give her a slow dance and anything else she wanted.

He also read the lustful state of the warriors who had tried and failed to sink her into a seductive thrall. He had to get her away from them. The muscles in his arms tightened and a maroon haze clouded his vision. His mind shouted to her, *Come to me now.*

She shifted her gaze to him and looked him up and down. The lights flashed erratically in the dark club, and his vision adjusted for every discrepancy. The sun might as well have illuminated her every feature. Her cheeks turned a dusky rose, her lips parted, and her breathing grew shallow.

Oh, yeah, she liked what she saw.

His mind reached for her again, *Come to me, Alison.*

Much to his shock, she shot back, *And who the hell are you to command me?*

Damn, she didn't remember him. He wished now he hadn't sliced her memories. Still, he had no intention of arguing with her.

He lowered his chin and moved with preternatural speed. He intended to rescue her from the unwanted attentions of the two males and to claim her for his own. But by the time he reached her she had disappeared. She had folded from the club.

He clenched his fists again, drawing his forearms up at the same time. Sonofabitch. Though he had the capacity to mentally trace her path, he couldn't give pursuit because he couldn't fold from location to location. Goddammit. He stood within an arm's reach of *his woman* yet because of his folding weakness, she might as well have been in Paris or Beijing rather than fucking Phoenix One.

Unfulfilled need raged through his body. He lifted his head and roared at the ceiling, the full-throated cry of a male caught in the hard-core grip of *breh-hedden* and unable to complete the act.

The maroon sheen darkened his eyes further. His neurons scrambled. His thoughts lost all remaining sequence. The two Militia Warriors, smaller in stature than any of the Warriors of the Blood, backed away. Thorne shot in front of them and shouted, "Fold! Now!"

Kerrick slammed into Thorne as he reached for the warriors, but grabbed air. He turned to Thorne and lifted his fists ready to do battle. Thorne caught one of his bunched hands in a powerful grip, held on, then folded them both out of the Blood and Bite.

Kerrick blinked. A new location. He vaguely recognized the Cave, the place where the Warriors of the Blood went just to chill, usually after a night of battling.

There was no lavender here, and in quick stages his consciousness returned.

More figures entered the space. A wall of hard male bodies appeared, some in flight gear, others dressed in cargoes and tees like he was. Some smiled. Others watched, stunned. His mind opened suddenly. He recognized the men, warriors all—Thorne, Medichi, Luken, Santiago, Zacharius, and Jean-Pierre. *His* Brothers of the Blood. What the hell was he doing here?

"Get him a drink," Luken called out.

"I'm on it," Medichi said, heading to the bar opposite the pool table.

Liaison Officer Havily Morgan knew she could make a difference in the war, if given half a chance. She was sure of it. She felt it to the tips of her fingers, to the ends of her toes.

Central had just called. The Supreme High Administrator had finally summoned her, and though the hour was late, nearly nine o'clock, she didn't care. At long last her chance had come to begin her campaign.

She stood in the center of her living room, a hand pressed to her chest, her heart ramming out a fast cadence. She was dizzy, excited . . . and, yes, relieved.

Fifteen years ago her fiancé, a dedicated Militia Warrior, had been taken from her, his body brutalized by a death vamp and drained of his precious blood. Since that time Havily had lived with a fire in her belly, driven to make sure that his death had not been in vain.

She had met him shortly after his transfer from Los Angeles to Phoenix. She had fallen for him so fast, a brilliant tumbling that had led to a betrothal a mere six months into his tour of duty in the Valley of the Sun.

She had waited a long time for love, nearly one full century from the time of her ascension. Losing Eric, after having waited for decades for exactly the right man to come along, had destroyed her heart, her belief that she would ever know love in this ascended world.

Her life had been altered irrevocably when he had failed to come home after his shift, when she'd received the dreaded call, when she'd learned of his horrible fate.

Yet out of her suffering her passion had been born, passion for finding a way to change the course of the war. Above all, she had promised herself that Eric's death would not be in vain.

Unable to serve on the front lines, since she was in no way suited to wield a sword, she applied herself to figuring out what she could do. The more she researched the difficulties facing Madame Endelle as Supreme High Administrator of Second Earth, especially from the time the first High Administrator defected to the Commander's side, the more she saw what needed to be done. Call it a vision, but she knew, *she knew*, that a completely redesigned military-administration complex would go a long way to preventing more defections from the ranks of the High Administrators.

And tonight she would begin the process of making a difference in her world.

She smiled. She looked through the window at the night skyline visible from her Camelback Mountain home. Her town house was situated at the foothills, and the location gave her a stellar view of South Mountain as well as Endelle's administrative headquarters farther to the east. She had bought this house in order to be close to Madame Endelle's place of rule.

Still buzzing with excitement, she hurried to her office. Madame Endelle had demanded her immediate presence, so she had only a handful of minutes to make her preparations. Her primary concern was which of her presentations to take with her. She immediately dismissed the idea of PowerPoint since it would involve setting up a screen, running cables, and interfacing with a computer and digital projector. She sighed. Endelle would not have the patience for setup time.

She wished she had the preternatural ability of presenting her vision directly from her mind to the screen. However, to her knowledge no one could stream mental images, at least not on Second Earth. Maybe Third or Fourth, but not Second. There were a great many limitations to personal power on Second.

Okay. No PowerPoint.

Still, she smiled. She could not believe this was happening. Madame Endelle had summoned her. All her e-mails had finally gotten through. Or perhaps her beautifully crafted professional correspondence, for which she used the best letterhead with a watermark depicting a pair of full-mount wings, her own design. In the end, she had only one real choice, a project that had taken a full three years of off-hours to create. On a table tucked into a corner to the right of the door sat a large portable display case, in black leather, which bore a sturdy handle.

The size of the case was deceptive. Once she set the case on the table and unlatched the sides, the cleverly designed multi-layered complex, coupled with her telekinetic powers, rose to a height of five feet, spreading some eight feet in length and another three feet in width. She had worked with an architect for months to get every detail exactly right.

Beyond the excellence of the architectural display, she was ready for this moment. She had practiced her presentation over and over. Fifteen years of hard work and she now had her meeting.

She waved a hand and changed into her best Ralph Lauren jacket, black of course, including a black pleat-front blouse. She wore four-inch heels, putting her at six-two and hopefully somewhere near Madame Endelle's six-five height depending on the size of heels the Supreme High Administrator wore. Havily intended to leave nothing to chance.

She stepped in front of a full-length mirror. Appearances were important, especially to Her Supremeness. She chided herself for using the slang appellation. Madame Endelle. *Madame Endelle.* She repeated the words and kept her voice clipped and formal.

She scrutinized her reflection. She didn't have time to affect a formal chignon so she left her hair loose, a flow of soft peachy-red over her black suit. She nodded. Her makeup was still flawless from the morning's effort. Thank God for improved cosmetics on Second Earth. She nodded again.

Her eyes, however, were a little bloodshot, not unexpected given the lateness of the hour.

No more stalling. Havily Morgan, get your beautiful self over there . . . now.

She went back to her office then took the display case in hand. With her briefcase in the other, she thought the thought then folded into the building that housed the administrative offices. She moved quickly to the wide glass entrance of Endelle's suite. The interior was dark, of course, because the admins had already long since gone home for the night.

She stepped in front of the sliding doors. Nothing happened.

She tried several times.

She drew her phone into her hand and thumbed.

"Central." She recognized Jeannie's voice. Something about her tone eased Havily. She had no idea why, although she'd always heard that the women chosen to work at Central—and they were always women—had a calming effect on the warriors.

"Good evening again, Jeannie. I'm outside the offices, but the doors are locked and everything's dark. Are you sure Madame Endelle is here?"

"Oh, yeah," Jeannie drawled. "Her Supremeness has been holding court and wrecking everyone's night for the past six hours. She's there. I'll give her a holler."

"Thanks," she said.

She thumbed her phone and as she waited, her heart once more took to hammering inside her chest. Yes, indeed, there were many changes that needed to be made.

And they began tonight.

After ten minutes of being back in her home, Alison finally stopped trembling. Yet her mind still spun like a top and couldn't seem to land.

Her head wagged back and forth. This couldn't be happening.

Vampires?

She stood bewildered in her family room staring at a wall of books, her favorite books, collected from the time she was a child. She stretched her hand out toward them, toward that which was familiar, trying to find purchase for her spinning thoughts and fears.

Vampires.

My God, they really did have fangs and suck down blood. They enthralled and used women.

She should never have gone to the Blood and Bite but the dreams had called to her and then the club's business card had appeared at her feet.

And the longings, oh the longings, which never stopped. She took deep breaths, one after the next.

A new, horrific thought intruded. She crouched then turned 360, looking around for an intruder, examining every shadowy pocket of the rooms she could see—the front entry, the living room, the open kitchen, the hall leading to the master bedroom suite. What if one of those creatures had followed her here? Could they even do that? Did they know how to dematerialize like she did? What if they now knew where she lived?

She held her breath and waited, listening hard for the smallest movement, the smallest sign she had been followed.

Finally, after several minutes, she took her first deep breath, concluding she was safe, at least for now.

The club had been too much, a radio on full blast in a confined space—the fanged men at the necks of women, the red velvet booths, the Armani twins.

She put a hand to her head and rubbed her temple. The headache had returned, this time deep inside her brain, a throb that made her think of migraines and going to bed for days.

She sank to the green sculpted carpet in front of her coffee table. She slid off her Jimmy Choos and sat with her legs crossed in front of her. She leaned forward and put her head in her hands.

Events at the club once more played over her mind. Despite the actions of the Armani duo, it was the other vampire who claimed her attention right now, the powerful creature who'd gone gorilla, his chin low to his chest, his fangs distended and pressed against his lips, his wild gaze fixed to hers, his powerful body tensed for action, his mind breaking through her shields.

She had been overcome by his presence and even then she had thought, *God, he's gorgeous,* thick wavy black hair drawn back from his face, angled stubborn jaw, light-colored eyes, the shade hard to determine in the flashing strobes of the club. He had tried to command her with his mind. So what exactly had his intention been? Had he meant to hurt her? She lifted her head and stared at all the rows of books. No, he wouldn't have hurt her. He would have done something else. He would have *taken* her.

She put her fingers to her mouth. A powerful wave of

pure desire flowed through her body until her back arched and her mouth opened.

A single thought shook her—*she would have let him.*

Oh. God.

Once more, as had happened for weeks now, a wave of painful longing swamped her chest. She struggled to breathe, unable to comprehend what she was feeling. Was she merely longing *for him,* for this oversized vampire, or was this something more?

As she searched her heart, she knew she felt something greater than just a primitive mating urge. Her desire for this man, this vampire, was part of the need she felt, but not the whole.

So what was this yearning that once more possessed her? For what exactly did she long?

Tears burned her eyes. She was frustrated on so many levels. She just didn't understand what was happening to her.

After a few more minutes she realized her thoughts had begun to travel in an endless loop; nothing would be settled tonight. Suddenly she wanted a shower. She wanted her short skirt and sexy halter off her body.

She rose from the carpet and headed to the master bedroom.

She sighed. She lived alone in a house she had bought two years ago, a lovely piece of property in the north metro Phoenix area, in a community called Carefree.

Carefree. Well, not tonight exactly.

She crossed the living room and entered the hall, which led to the master suite. Once in the bathroom, she met her reflection in the mirror, the beautiful Venetian mirror her mother had bought for her as a housewarming present several years ago, when her practice was thriving and she had officially thought of herself as an adult.

Right now, as she looked at her crimped curls and once more thought about what had happened at the club, she felt bad. Really bad. Why had she been born so different? Why couldn't she have had even a single day of *normal*? Why did the one club she had checked out in over three years have to be full of . . . vampires?

She swallowed the sudden knot in her throat. All right, so her life had just gotten a lot weirder, something she had not thought possible.

Once more she recalled the gorgeous vampire who had moved like lightning in her direction. She had a profound feeling she had met him before.

The moment the thought struck, the headache bloomed, only this time she dove deep within her mind, closing her eyes and focusing on the area in her brain that seemed to be causing her so much trouble.

She explored the affected area and suddenly she could smell an intriguing spice, a very familiar spice . . . like *cardamom*. As though attempting to pull a sticky portion of adhesive tape from very tender skin, she started mentally plucking at the strange area. She winced. She prodded, poked, and peeled until at last the seal gave way.

The memory beneath exploded and she grabbed the sink in front of her to steady herself.

She saw it all, just as it had happened earlier in the evening while she stood on the catwalk outside her office, Darian beside her—the dead woman on the sidewalk, the police, the EMTs, the pale-skinned death vampire who had decided her blood needed to be down his throat.

And . . . Kerrick. The warrior vampire with massive white wings. The vampire from the club, one-and-the-same. Warrior Kerrick who had protected her. Her knees buckled yet not in fear. She had been so into him. Desire once more ripped through her, pressing into the well of her abdomen.

She had spoken with him, touched him, looked into his very green eyes. Yes, his eyes were green. She had wanted answers about—what was it he had said? Yes, about ascension. She had begged him not to take her memories. He had held her in his arms. He had nuzzled her neck. She had not wanted him to go.

No wonder she had thought she would have given herself to him. She had met him before and he had saved her life. At that time, however, he'd been sporting wings, the angel-vampire, or whatever Kerrick was, the being that had fought the death vampire at the medical complex.

As she clung to the sink, a familiar desperate sensation returned to her, an intense awareness that she had at long last met a man, a warrior, yes, even a vampire, who could match her in ability, who would not be afraid of knowing she could move from one room to the next with a mere thought, or move objects in a room around in the same way, or communicate telepathically. Kerrick would have no such fear or concern because he could do the same things and *he wanted her.*

But . . . he was a vampire, for God's sake.

A vampire living in a different dimension.

Yes. *Same earth, different dimensions.*

Vampire.

As the word settled in her mind, another wave of yearning swept over her so powerfully that she gripped the sink once more and hung on. The sensation intensified, gripping her lower back and riding up her spine. She felt her back muscles shift about. She felt strange tingles all along her back in a wide V-pattern. *Wings.*

What was happening to her? Was she feeling the presence of wings? *Wings?*

The sensations eased, drifted away, disappeared.

Still she held on to the sink. She forced herself to breathe as tears dropped onto the white porcelain.

Oh, God. Could her night get any stranger?

After a few minutes, when she had absorbed the reality of the renewed memory, when her tears had ceased, when her heart beat in normal thuds within her chest, fatigue hit and she wanted her bed. Now.

She stripped, got in the shower, then washed the crimp from her curls and all her makeup down the drain. As the hot water beat down on her shoulders, exhaustion took a toll.

She had to get some sleep.

Ready for bed at last, she climbed between the covers. She tried at first to force herself to sleep, but for a long time all she could think about was the warrior called Kerrick. How strange to want a man so much, a man she barely knew. Yet he wasn't a man at all, was he? He was that *other thing*. She slung her arms over her face and refused to think one more thought on such a hopeless subject.

Somewhere among all her worries, frustrations, and desires, she began drifting off to sleep. She just hoped she didn't have another dream.

God help her.

After Kerrick had swallowed at least three tumblers of Maker's, he sat on one of the leather couches, leaning forward, his forearms on his knees, the cool glass cradled in his hands.

His warrior brothers were close by, waiting, he supposed, until he finally regained his senses and told them why he had just done what he'd done.

The Cave was a men-only club, not because they didn't allow women but because most women were revolted by the place—beat-up leather sofas, a few stricken end tables, a pool table that took the brunt religiously of all the warriors' tempers. A huge flat-screen TV hung at an angle off the wall awaiting repair . . . yeah, for three months now.

Chasing after Alison like a madman, his vampire body raging to protect her, the experience had left him wired, like he'd been up for three nights driving across a couple thousand miles of open land.

"I must have been out of my mind," he mumbled. He took another swig of Maker's.

Thorne sat down beside him then grasped the back of his neck. "You lucky sonofabitch! This has to be the *brehhedden*. I mean, we all thought it was a myth but this has to be it!"

The other warriors drew close then offered up their congratulations as well, thumping him on the back, calling out the appropriate jibes.

He sat holding the tumbler, unable to respond, his chest in agony.

So the *breh-hedden* had come to him and the woman meant for him was here. Unfortunately, he couldn't act on it, couldn't go to her, couldn't bring her close. Any degree of proximity to her was a death sentence.

The litany of his failures wasn't particularly long but it was *complete*. He'd majored in failure. He'd gotten an A+ in all the big fuckups of his life. The hell he'd add one more to the list, and this had *failure* written all over it. If he ever claimed her physically, her death would essentially be guaranteed. "I won't see it through."

All the hearty backslaps, the jokes, the good-natured taunts ceased.

"What?" Thorne cried. "You can't turn it down. *She's* here. The woman meant for you, who can engage your mind, an ascendiate who matches you in power and can I just say, holy shit but she's beautiful."

Kerrick felt his biceps flinch possessively. His fangs thrummed and started to emerge. He dipped his chin, sucked in a gulp of air, then threw back the last of the Maker's. He turned to face Thorne, his boss, his best friend, his brother. He shook his head. He tried to swallow but couldn't dislodge the lump in his throat. After a few more breaths he said, "I won't marry again, not so long as I'm a warrior, no way in hell. And I sure as shit won't complete the *breh-hedden* with that woman."

"How can you even think about turning this down?" Luken asked. "The recorded documents say that completing the *breh-hedden* is about as close to heaven as you can get."

Kerrick met his gaze knowing the golden warrior couldn't possibly understand. "Well, take a wife and lose her because you're a Warrior of the Blood. Hell, take two. See how that feels. Birth a couple of Twolings and have the Commander blast them into a fine spray of blood and bone just because he wants to hurt you. Believe me, you'd rather cut your own heart out than try again. I shouldn't have married the second time. I knew it going in and I will always blame myself for Helena's death and the deaths of our children. Eternity alone? Not such a bad fucking idea."

"Aw, hell," Thorne muttered.

The room writhed with the singular reality of the warrior's life. They were all goddamn targets, every day and every night, and anyone connected to them.

Curses rent the air, issued from one warrior to the next, passed around like a peace pipe. The air cooled, and his determination shored up.

"Your call," Thorne said quietly, his gaze shifting to the bar then back to Kerrick. "Whatever you want to do, we'll all support you. There's just one thing—I'm not so sure you can refuse the *breh-hedden*."

"Well, fuck that," Kerrick said, rising to his feet. "I'll just have to be the first."

Thorne nodded then turned away. He punched at the air several times. Kerrick watched him cross the room, heading in the direction of the pool table. Once there, he slid his hands beneath the top then lifted. Thorne had heavy broad shoulders and muscles to match. Grunting, he gave one hard jerk, which flipped the damn thing onto its side, breaking two of the four legs supporting the heavy table. One more dip of his knees and Thorne, in his rage, flipped the pool table all the way over. Christ.

Kerrick stared at the massive legs, two leaning and broken, two standing straight up. He started to laugh and couldn't stop. Others joined him. Somehow this was just perfect. If Thorne lost it, none of them would be far behind.

They were all on edge, riding their nerves like horses whipped to a frenzy.

The war had shifted, ramped up. They all knew it but couldn't talk about it. What was the point? They were fighters, they had to fight, and they would do what they had to do.

Still, an undercurrent ran through the Warriors of the Blood, a goddamn streak of lightning that never let up, kept them juiced, warning them something big and bad was on the horizon. Thorne's behavior alone told them what they needed to know.

The simple question rose to his mind: *How are we—*

seven men—supposed to keep on fighting death vamps *imported nightly from all over the fucking globe, one after the other, squad after squad?*

His laughter blew out, a candle snuffed in the wind. He crossed to the bar, set his tumbler down, then made his way to the upside-down pool table. He clapped Thorne on the shoulder. Thorne met his gaze, bleary hazel eyes in pain, lots of pain. They all felt it, every damn one of them.

Medichi came forward next and shoved at the back of Thorne's head then put his hand on his other shoulder. Luken followed, another hand on Thorne. Jean-Pierre's hand slid around his waist. Santiago let go of a long string in Spanish, but it sounded soft like a prayer. His hand found a place next to Kerrick's. Zacharius, however, stepped between Thorne and the upside-down table. He smiled a crooked smile, held out his hand, and folded his sword into his palm. "With you to the end, boss," he said, nodding.

"To the end" slipped from one voice to the next, another kind of prayer, a shared promise among warriors, one that had been spoken from the beginning of time.

"Well, shit," finally erupted from Thorne's mouth. Like a signal flare, the warriors moved away from him, except Luken who once more slapped Thorne on the shoulder as he stared at the pool table. Despite Thorne's mass, the power of Luken's friendly shove rocked Thorne forward.

"Thanks, boss, you just won me a hundred bucks. I bet Santiago we wouldn't go another month without having to replace the damn thing."

Thorne shook his head from side to side, a weary gesture. He turned to face Kerrick looking like ten kinds of ruined.

Kerrick had his own problems, however, and he needed to address them now. "I want out tonight."

Once more Thorne's head wagged. "Endelle has already assigned you to guardian duty." His voice was rough, low, desperate.

"Thorne, you gotta back me on this one."

Thorne planted his hands on his hips. "Fuck," he muttered. "You sure you can handle another warrior being so close to her, day and night, for at least three days?"

Kerrick's jaw hardened. "I'll have to."

Thorne held his gaze steadily for a long moment then finally said, "You sure about this?"

"Yeah. I'm sure."

"Okay. Head home but keep your phone at the ready."

Kerrick nodded. "You'll call if things go south?"

"You know I will."

Thorne cleared his voice. The gravel deepened as he addressed the warriors. "Endelle will no doubt be on our asses all night. So just be prepared."

A string of softly muttered obscenities rumbled through the room, every mouth grinding molars. The air smelled burnt.

Shit. This really can't be good.

Whatever.

He'd be going back to his house. No, not to his house, to his basement, the hole in which he lived, his shrunk-down but oh-so-necessary existence.

At least he wouldn't be seeing Alison again. Hopefully not for a long, long time.

Dreams create the gateway,
But the feet must cross the threshold.

—*Collected Proverbs,* Beatrice of Fourth

CHAPTER 7

As High Administrator Cracc reviewed yet another report about the mortal female Alison Wells, he had a new sweat issue developing. Even his breathing had taken on a gurgling sound.

He sat in his recently commandeered office, his brow low as he held one of several reports in hand. How was this possible? He'd never heard of a human of Mortal Earth capable of dematerializing. Shit.

He looked around. At least he had an office now.

At ten he had removed one very pissed-off general from his massive seat of authority. Though not as large as the Commander's office, the general's workplace proved the axiom "Size matters." Cracc might have taken the smaller space offered to him, but the general had made the mistake of curling his lip at Cracc upon introduction so of course he'd had no choice but to dispossess the bastard.

The space was pristine, as it ought to be, a reflection of

the disciplined military mind. The desk was clean, large, and rectangular, the chair, ergonomic. One wall of the office held a bank of four-drawer black steel, locked-down filing cabinets. On top of the cabinets sat a long planter that extended the entire distance of the file drawers. Maidenhair ferns filled the space spreading all the way to the ceiling.

He approved. The plants cleaned and humidified the desert air. The oxygen kept the mind sharp.

In his office in Chicago, he had a full-time Japanese gardener who kept both his indoor and outdoor gardens in immaculate condition. He had won successive awards for his specialized azaleas. He missed the calming effects of walking the gravel paths, and with his Guccis sliding over his damp ass right now he sure as hell could use a little calming green.

On his desk was the latest PC, the CPU built into the large screen. The keyboard was also ergonomic. Though the hardware appealed to his aesthetic sensibility, he was old-school and liked the feel of the reports in hand, the slick outer binder, the individual sheets between thumb and forefinger as he turned the pages

All well and good.

But the contents.

Holy hell.

He had spent the last hour reviewing the stack of reports, a foot deep, which Commander Greaves had provided for him concerning the mortal ascendiate Alison Wells. Suffice it to say his chest now felt strapped with steel bands and his briefs were, yeah, damp.

So much for an easy kill.

What he had believed would be a simple task—offing a female mortal—had taken on the quality of a nightmare, the one where you tried to run but your legs wouldn't move.

He read, *The mortal is the most powerful ascendiate since Endelle's arrival nine thousand years ago. She has all of Second's abilities.*

Jesus.

The Commander had sent his spies after the ascendiate

every day for the past year, assessing her, reading her powers, watching her activities. There was even an absurd notation about the level she had achieved at sudoku.

Of course his mind tripped over this information and fell flat with the next bit. *The ascendiate will no doubt have a Warrior of the Blood in full guardian mode protecting her during her rite of ascension.*

Sweet Jesus.

So, yeah. He was in the middle of a nightmare. As he continued to flip pages, a new thought emerged, one that kept tightening his groin with possibilities. If he were to drink the woman to death himself and seize her powers, would he then be as strong as Commander Greaves? Stronger?

He flexed his buttocks and shifted in his seat to make room for a sudden erection.

The Commander materialized in front of his desk. "Lay that thought aside, Crace. Make no mistake. Once you got near enough to ascendiate Wells with such a proposition in mind, she would incinerate your gray matter."

Crace looked up from the reports then shot to his feet.

Shit.

The Commander had read his thoughts before he'd appeared in the room. Crace had to be smarter than this.

"Commander," he murmured. He bowed low, remaining in the same position in hopes his obvious *excitement* would diminish quickly.

"The Committee has been informed of the ascendiate's refusal to join my ranks. You hereby have permission to proceed in preparation for an imminent rite of ascension. Lay in your plans. Keep me informed. I'll be in Geneva for the next few hours. After that I have several High Administrators to tend to. I'm not sure when I'll be back in Phoenix Two. In the meantime, please move from your hotel into the suite next to my chambers here in the compound. Are we clear?"

"Yes, Commander. Thank you, Commander."

Permission to proceed.

Move to the suite next to the right hand of God.

He rose from his bow, his vocal cords humming, his parted lips ready to engage the Commander. Unfortunately, his deity had vanished.

Crace released a sigh. He sat back down, aware again of his clinging pants. He really needed to change them again, but he didn't want to leave his desk. He could not believe all this good fortune was happening to him. A chance at the Round Table and now *the suite next to the Commander*. His star was rising, ascending.

He laughed at his joke.

Okay.

This was good.

Holy shit . . . *the suite next to the Commander*.

His arousal throbbed. He needed his wife. He had already summoned her from Chicago. She would take up his rooms at the Bredstone Hotel, and later he would get the relief he needed: her body, her blood, her mind.

As he glanced at the reports once more, a plan began to form. He believed in keeping things simple. The ascendiate would be answering her call to ascension soon, at one of the Borderlands, near a dimensional Trough, and when she did, he would have three squads of death vampires in place to finish her off. Simple, to the point, the task accomplished.

Since her warrior guardian would probably be at the Trough as well, he would need to send along at least one of the Commander's generals, a powerful warrior, to make certain the guardian died along with her. Fortunately, Commander Greaves had turned a Warrior of the Blood over a century ago. Yes, the warrior General Leto would do, a most appropriate assignment for him.

What could be simpler?

Oh, God, a seat at the Round Table.

Havily tapped her foot and glanced at her phone.

For the twentieth time she stepped in front of the sliding doors.

Nothing.

She called Central. Again. She heard Jeannie's voice then suddenly the doors flashed apart, a soft whoosh of air over her face.

Finally. She glanced at the time. Just after ten o'clock. She had been kept waiting an hour.

She slid her phone back into her pants pocket, picked up her carry-case and her briefcase, then marched through. A path of lights lit the way to the office.

Her steps slowed when her peripheral vision caught sight of the chaos of the administrative pool. She stopped and turned in horror. There were rows and rows of desks going on forever, each one piled high with papers. She shook her head back and forth, back and forth.

This is ridiculous.

Had no one heard of a paperless office?

She dipped her chin and resumed her course, picking up her pace. She turned down the wide corridor to the left. At the far end, a wedge of light angled into the hallway. Madame Endelle's office.

After passing a dozen glass-walled executive offices, also piled with papers, she reached the doorway. She drew in a deep purposeful breath and at the same time crossed the threshold.

Endelle glanced up at her. Barely a glance, a brief batting of thick black lashes, nothing more as she resumed reading a report on her desk. "I need you on liaison duty, Havily." Liaison duty? Endelle never spoke to her directly about liaison assignments. "This is important." She tossed a clear lavender folder in Havily's direction across the desk. The folder slid just to the edge. "Everything you need to know is in there. Things will get messy, but I have Kerrick on guardian duty so you probably won't need a flak jacket. Nice to see you again, blah-blah-blah. Thorne will contact you when you're needed. Good night."

Havily stared at the bent head. Madame Endelle shuffled papers and started reading another report. She felt a quick flush to her cheeks, a familiar tingling, which meant she ought to retreat right now and gather the reins of her vampire temper. "I beg your pardon?" The words came out clipped, even brittle, certainly a challenge.

Endelle froze, lifted an icy gaze, then eased back in her chair, back against a mountain of light blue feathers. How did she do that? How did she sit in a nest of her wings? Havily's back ached just looking at the bent and contorted feathers.

Endelle's chin rose and her gaze came at Havily full-throttle, two hostile brown eyes, lined like ancient oak bark. She wore some kind of animal print, cheetah perhaps, which added to the sense of menace in her eyes. "And apparently *I beg yours.* What the fuck do you mean by talking to me like that? You have your assignment. Thorne will call you when he needs you. Now get the hell out of my office."

Again Havily felt her cheeks tingle, another warning to start moving backward, to put her feet on the bicycle pedals and start wheeling out of the office, at light speed, preferably. Instead she actually stepped forward. She had waited for years to speak to Madame Endelle face-to-face. She dropped the briefcase from her left hand and heard the soft thunk on the carpet. Her right arm came up, then the rest of what she accomplished, to her horror, occurred in preternatural time.

Before Endelle could blink again, the proposed military-admin complex lay before her, on top of the report she was reading, the portfolio as the base, the entire thing an architectural pop-up. It was a work of great beauty, and took up a good portion of Endelle's oversized desk.

Far more important than the physical structure was the complete reorganization of duties and responsibilities, which would create an efficiency currently lacking in Endelle's operations. Havily moved to the side of the desk so that she could see the Supreme High Administrator as she began her prepared speech. She started to explain the freedom that would accrue to Madame Endelle by adopting her plan. She didn't get more than four sentences in when Endelle's wings shifted color from the present light blue to a dark midnight black. She rose to her feet. Her nostrils flared.

Despite the displeased nature of these signs, Havily pressed on, giving statistics about hours and efficiency, when suddenly the architectural mock-up burst into flames, a monstrous sudden conflagration. As the flames reached to the ceiling, Havily backed up several feet, almost to the fireplace.

The next moment the flames disappeared abruptly, as well as even the smallest dust mote of her project. Vanished. Gone. Kaput.

Havily had the mildly hysterical thought that her work of three years had just gone up in smoke.

Her lips parted. Of all the things she had expected to happen during the interview, she had not expected this, a complete unwillingness on Madame Endelle's part to hear even a word she had hoped to say, the speech she had practiced before her mirror dozens of times.

The Supreme High Administrator held Havily's gaze for a long, tense moment, then said, "I'm trying to keep a mortal alive, not to mention attempting to prevent all of Second Earth from falling into the hands of a monster, and you brought me a goddamn dollhouse? Just do your fucking job, Morgan, and get the hell out of my office."

Havily glanced at the lavender folder, which had fallen to the floor in the chaos. She held out her hand and brought it in a long glide through the air into her palm. She turned on her professional black heels and left her briefcase sitting there. What was the point? She hoped Endelle tripped over it.

She moved swiftly down the wide corridor with all the glass walls and ignored the tears tracking down her cheeks.

When she was within ten feet of the sliding doors, something large whizzed past her head—oh, her briefcase, in the form of a rocket—which then struck and demolished one of the glass panes leading into the hall. She paused for a moment, staring at the shattered glass.

Perfect.

She lifted her arm and dematerialized back to her office. She walked the length of the room back and forth, forcing her heart and mind to settle. Her disappointment was severe, painfully so. The tears wouldn't stop. What was wrong with the Supreme High Administrator that she would not even listen to an idea?

She breathed in as she took brisk steps. She swiped at her cheeks, folded a tissue into her hand, and blew her nose. She had so much to contribute. She could make a difference in the war. Why couldn't she get Madame Endelle to hear her?

After a few minutes, she began to calm down. A few minutes more and she brought the lavender folder once more into her hands then popped it open.

"Alison Wells," she murmured. "Blah-blah-blah . . . preternatural empathy, dematerialization of objects, mental shields, blah-blah-blah." With so much power, the Commander was probably planning her demise. Even with all seven warriors guarding her ass, Alison Wells would not likely survive her first two hours on Second. Hah!

These truly ungenerous thoughts had an effect. Havily's rage fled as her conscience kicked in. To say she was severely disappointed was to say the least. She knew she had it in her power to make an enormous change for the better in Endelle's administration. However, this ascendiate, the mortal Alison Wells, should not have to pay for her temper.

As she read the document, her eyes widened and she sucked air between pursed lips. The mortal could even dematerialize! Good God, she was powerful. She'd probably been in hiding on earth, maybe not literally but in a dozen other ways. She would need information, and lots of it, just to keep her sanity.

Very well.

She turned her organized mind to the task at hand and moved to her desk. She began making notes, all sorts of notes, starting with, *Attempt to explain a difficult, callous, and quite ancient Supreme High Administrator to a hopeful ascendiate.*

At midnight, as promised, Marcus folded to the steps outside Endelle's administrative headquarters. He hadn't been on Second in a very long time, not even to see what changes had occurred. As he looked up at the massive building then turned around in a circle, the architecture stunned him, as did the extensive intricate landscaping. Hanging gardens cascaded from dozens of floors.

Since he'd built half his massive fortune on the highly lucrative trade between Mortal and Second Earth, he'd seen many pictures, of course. However, the photos failed to capture the beauty of the modern world Second ascenders had created. Phoenix One had many strong buildings, but nothing like this.

The air smelled different than on Mortal Earth as well, cleaner, of course. There were fewer inhabitants to wreck the environment and there was also a deep commitment to plant life, which went a long way toward keeping the planet healthy, clean, oxygenated.

He took a deep breath. His chest felt strangely tight, absurdly emotional. Second had been his home for thirty-eight hundred years before he'd had his fill and returned in self-exile to Mortal Earth

Now he was . . . *home*.

Goddammit. His ascended vampire nature knew the difference between Mortal Earth and Second. He hadn't expected to feel this way, to have such a profound sense of belonging.

He ground his teeth. Whatever the global society had been able to achieve in terms of the environment, however, the power struggles had been a disaster and his sister's death had been the last straw. He'd blamed Kerrick for having married her, for having made her a target, and yet he'd also blamed so many other things. The Commander, for instance, should have been offed centuries ago, and Endelle's administration was a sinkhole.

He moved into the building. Not knowing the layout, he took the elevator to the top.

Once in the hall, he saw the broken glass and paused. Turning around, he noticed that a black briefcase lay against the far wall where the glittering debris trailed to an end point.

Instinctively, he dropped into a crouch. His wing-locks set up a steady vibration. He took deep breaths. He extended his senses, reaching for the enemy target. Nothing returned to him.

Huh.

As he rose, he assessed the situation then snorted. Someone had lost *her* temper, no doubt. Typical.

He didn't bother with the sliding doors. He stepped over the low metal casement of the broken window. The lights were off over the entire southern stretch of workstations. His gaze made a quick pass, hunting for anything out of place, a wink of light, a piece of furniture, anything.

But the only thing he detected as unusual was an odd scent in the air, a kind of perfume that made his neck muscles jump . . . and, shit, his groin muscles tighten.

What the hell?

He looked up and down the wide hallway. All he saw were a few ill-tended palms in enormous bronze pots and a row of sickly-looking pink plants fronting the glass office wall—nothing that could account for the fresh and rather sweet floral scent that assailed him. He flared his nostrils, parted his lips, and took in the scent, breathed it in, all the way into his lungs and into his brain. He exhaled and breathed again.

The fragrance made him dizzy and his heart sped up, like he needed to be prepared to give chase. Once more his wing-locks responded, thrumming, preparing for flight.

Fucking weird.

What was Her Supremeness pumping through the air-conditioning system and why did it give him the strangest sense of well-being? It even affected his libido. He had a sudden hard-on.

Holy shit.

He ignored the odd smell and his body's reaction to the scent. His gaze drifted over the sea of desks. A mountain of disgust followed. With all the modern technology available to Second Earth, why were there mile-high mounds of paper everywhere? Had Endelle not heard of a paperless office?

He shrugged.

Whatever.

He would only be here for three days, four at the most.

He followed the path of lights into a corridor off to his left. He moved past glass-fronted offices. Again all the rooms were weighed down with stacks of paper. He shook his head then stopped in his tracks outside the door to Endelle's office. The scent was stronger now and very familiar. What was he smelling? He closed his eyes and ran through a litany of flowers, starting with the ones he sent to women he intended to bed—not roses, not carnations, not lilies. What the hell was that?

An old memory struck.

Of course. His sister, Helena, had planted this shrub in Scottsdale Two—on the mansion grounds of the home she'd built with Kerrick. She had trained a dozen or so shrubs against a long stone wall at the back of the property. The plants had thrived, growing into huge mounds. Green-throated hummingbirds came around to enjoy the fluted red flowers, and sparrows built nests deep inside. Yeah. He was smelling goddamn honeysuckle, a fragrance he loved. He always had and right now he even weaved a little on his feet. He was hard again as well. So, where the hell was all this sensation coming from?

He planted his hands on his hips and shook his head. Second Earth bullshit.

Again . . . *whatever.*

He dipped his chin and forced his senses to clear. When he was ready, he gave the door a shove, caught sight of a woman he hadn't seen in two hundred years, and barked his laughter. "Sleeping on the job, Madame Supremeness?"

Endelle jerked her head up, a trail of saliva draining from her mouth. She swiped the drool with a quick backhand. "Marcus, you dumbfuck! You nearly scared me half to death." She glanced at the clock on her desk. "Well. I slept for half an hour. Just set a new record."

Marcus might have had a comeback if these simple

words hadn't slapped him hard across the face. Endelle never slept?

"Oh, shit. I drooled all over the Buenos Aires report." She finally met his gaze. "The Commander had my ambassador killed about an hour ago."

Holy shit. "So he's killing ambassadors now?"

"Sure. Why not? He's an ambitious man." She looked him up and down. "And you are still one hot vampire. Goddamn, Marcus. Two centuries on Mortal Earth has not changed you at all except you look bigger." Her gaze skated from shoulder to shoulder.

"I work out," he said.

She arched a brow. "So I see." A smile curved her lips. "Thanks for coming."

"I told you I would. I just hope to hell this is important."

"It is. I've had Seer reports from around the globe that this ascendiate has the ability to shift the tide of war. No specifics, though."

Marcus nodded. "So how far along is she on her rite of ascension?"

"She hasn't answered her call yet."

Marcus scowled. "Then why the hell am I here?"

"Relax, gorgeous. Should be any time now. The ascension is imminent."

"That's it? *Imminent*." This did not make sense, not in any dimension. He narrowed his eyes. "And by the way, what the hell do you mean *no specifics*? You used to have an incomparable Seer network. The information you got always kept you one step ahead of Greaves."

Endelle lowered her chin, and her striated brown eyes darkened. "Intel from my Seers Fortress has shrunk to the size of a frog's nut and no, I don't know why since the administrator of the facility, *by law,* doesn't have to let anyone on Second pass through his front door. Yeah, you should look shocked. We have a lot of new rules on Second because we've got this fucking committee, COPASS, which now tells me where, when and how to wipe my ass.

As for global Seer information, it's much less reliable. Most Seers, as you know, are beholden to their local High Administrators."

He frowned. "COPASS?"

"The Committee to Oversee the Process of Ascension to Second Society."

Marcus laughed. "Who the hell made up that name? It's a joke, right?"

Endelle rolled her eyes. "Nobody thought to check the acronym before the vote went through."

"Another bunch of fucking bureaucratic idiots."

"Pretty much, but it has simplified the war, brought it in close, and for that I should be grateful."

"In what way is the war *simple*? Kind of an oxymoron, don't you think?"

Endelle shrugged, and for just a moment she wore every one of her nine thousand years like a weight on her shoulders. "One of the first rules put in play was a proximity rule. Attacks involving the Warriors of the Blood only occur at the Borderlands now—legal attacks, that is. Homes, estates, *whatever,* of both Greaves's generals and my Guardians of Ascension are off-limits. No bodily harm is allowed, either."

"What happens if the rules are violated?"

"Complaints are filed, court dates set, judges preside, and death vamps executed, usually fall guys, but the bottom line is that the war is more contained now than it was."

He frowned. "But this doesn't stop death vampire depredations on regular citizens in either dimension, does it?"

Endelle shook her head slowly. "Death vampires need dying blood, so no, but our Militia Force is strong now. Although the inherent problem has not changed—"

"Four Militia Warriors to bring down one death vamp."

"Yep."

"And Greaves agreed to this *proximity* rule? Really."

"Shit, yes. Do you know how many of his generals we offed before the proximity rule?"

"A lot. So why the hell did *you* agree to it?"

Endelle was silent, her mouth grim. He waited but she
didn't speak. She just looked at him from her ancient brown
eyes.

Then he realized the why of it, and his temper flared.
"Goddammit," he cried. He punched the air and paced in a
circle. "This was because of my sister and her kids. You did
this because of them. A buck short and a day late, Endelle."

She caught his gaze and held fast so that he stopped
moving. "You think I didn't feel guilty as hell about what
happened to them?"

He looked away. Jesus, the pain of the whole damn thing
started at his feet, flowed up his legs, hit his abdomen, and
twisted his stomach into a knot. Shit. "It wasn't your fault."
Not even a little since he knew exactly where the blame lay.

She released a sigh. "I know this isn't what you wanted,
to come back, even once, but it's fucking great to have you
here."

Marcus resisted the pull, the deep tug on his soul whispering to him that he was home. He had known Endelle all
of his ascended life, four millennia. They had a long history together, twice as long as even Thorne. But the hell he
was staying. He just couldn't.

"Three days, Endelle, from the time the female answers
her call to ascension until she ascends, and not a second
more. So why did you recall me? Why now?"

Endelle shrugged. She drummed her fingers on her desk.
"I have a spasm in my back telling me the Commander's
ready to give us a good assfucking."

"Your language has gotten even more flowery since I
was here last and speaking of flowery, what the hell have
you been doing? Have you got a PlugIn bouncing a perfume around? It's even stronger in here. Sort of like honeysuckle."

Her brows rose to perfect black arches over her brown
eyes. She actually leaned back in her chair, and a smile
formed off to the left side of her mouth. "Something flowery, huh? Sorry. No perfume, no PlugIns. Maybe one of the
admins brought in a spray-bottle of Febreze. Of course,

there was a woman in here a couple of hours ago. Maybe you're smelling *her* perfume."

He felt uneasy, like his nerves were being scraped raw one at a time. He glanced around. "Whatever it is, it's bugging the shit out of me."

"Affecting your Johnson?"

He just stared at her. Like hell he would cop to that.

For some fucked-up reason, Endelle started to laugh. "Well, well. Isn't this a kick in the pants. Two in one night. Can't be a coincidence. Jesus. I'm starting to feel . . . *hopeful*."

"What the hell are you rambling on about? Two what?" He kept glancing around trying to place the scent, which right now tickled his balls. Jesus H. Christ.

"So," Endelle drawled. "You still know how to use a sword?"

Within the dream, the downtown Phoenix alley pulsed with energy. Alison walked along the fractured asphalt, her heart light, her mind aglow. She had been waiting for this her entire life, for an event so extraordinary that her life would be changed forever, transformed, that all would at last make sense to her, the strangeness of her abilities and powers, her sense of not fitting in, the deep longings she experienced that had for the past few weeks formed a powerful ache in her chest.

The dream shifted. Suddenly Darian appeared, the man now known to her as Commander Greaves. He materialized in front of her, beckoning her to come to him, to be with him, to serve him. Fear rained down on her head in heavy waves. Her heart pounded in her chest. Her legs trembled. The alley had become a place of danger.

Darian smiled in his gentle manner at first, then his large round eyes narrowed. A feral light entered his eye. His left hand transformed into a frightening claw.

Her heart thundered against her ribs. She had to leave the alley now. She tried to move, to turn away from him, to go the other direction, but her feet wouldn't move. He advanced, closer, closer. *There is still time. Come to me.* The claw reached for her.

Alison woke up. Sat up. She was soaked and trembling. She covered her face with her hands. What was happening to her? Why the dreams? Why Darian? Why the alley? Why this longing so fierce that her heart felt ready to burst?

Why vampires and a vampire club?

She slid her legs over the side of the bed. She wore a camisole and soft cotton pajama bottoms, but the damp fabric irritated her suddenly too hot, too sensitive skin.

Sleep would not find her again anytime soon. The dream had wrecked her in every possible way. She even fought a heavy bout of tears.

Her thoughts turned back to the club, to seeing the warrior called Kerrick. Some of the tension inside her eased as she brought forward her memories of him.

At the medical complex, he had called himself her guardian. What had he meant by it, and what exactly was this dimensional world in which he lived? And why was she so ridiculously attracted to him?

She stood up, crossed her arms over her chest, then paced her bedroom, back and forth. She just didn't understand her present reality. She felt compelled to action, to do something, but what?

She glanced at the clock. The minute hand ticked just past two in the morning. She made a quick decision. She would go to the alley right now. There had to be a reason why this particular Phoenix backstreet kept calling to her, kept appearing in her dreams.

As she dressed in a T-shirt, jeans, and a light sweater, doubts assailed her once more. Two in the morning didn't exactly bring out the best in a city, especially in some of the impoverished areas adjacent to downtown Phoenix.

On the other hand . . . *the dreams!* She was sick of them, of waking up to them, of waking up *sweat-slick* because of them.

The night's events had tossed her life up into the air, and she needed to find out exactly where all the pieces were meant to land. After all, there had to be a very specific reason why she kept dreaming about this godforsaken alley.

At a quarter past two in the morning, Kerrick awoke to a stiff neck. He'd fallen asleep in a chair in his library and apparently crunched his neck in the process. He rubbed out the muscles, finding some relief though not much.

He looked down. He'd dropped off to sleep with a book about ascension history on his lap written by a rather pretentious Frenchman by the name of Philippe Reynard. Reynard taught at the university in Scottsdale Two and had risen as the acknowledged expert in his field. However, the information Kerrick sought, as in how to overcome the *breh-hedden,* or even any useful information on the subject, just hadn't surfaced in this really pompous tome, *Treatise on Ascension: A Cultural Perspective and Analysis.* Jesus.

Reynard had called the Warriors of the Blood "the righteous backbone of modern society, the hope of the future, the wellspring of all good things." He liked a compliment as well as the next guy, but this bullshit rankled. The warriors were anything but righteous, and as for a *wellspring of all good things,* "a death squad for pale blue things" would have been a lot more accurate.

Well, thank God he had the night off. Things seemed to be pretty quiet. Thorne hadn't called once. Good. He could rest, set his resolve, and put some strategies in place for avoiding all contact with Alison should she choose to ascend.

He glanced around the spacious, two-story room. Shelves, ladders, books, and a spiral wrought-iron staircase. An upper landing and walkway traveled in a semicircle at a distance two-thirds of the way above the floor, where more shelves and books rose the remaining nine feet to the domed ceiling. A pair of crimson velvet drapes, which flanked a north-facing multipaned window, protected the museum-like contents of the library from direct light.

The whole mansion had been a combined effort, his sturdy masculine influence, and Helena's ability to overcome his absurd rigidity and give real grace to every line. This had truly been *their* house and Helena had made it a home, especially once the children had come, his son and his daughter. Of course they were going to have a big family. Ten years later, Helena, Kerr and Christine were gone. They had left behind an enormous hole in his heart, one never to be filled, one covered with his vows.

His cell buzzed.

He slid the slim phone from the pocket of his pants and thumbed the strip. "Give."

"Sorry, Kerrick. Time to rumble." Thorne's gravel voice had split into three resonances, a sure sign his stress level had cranked up another notch. Of all of Thorne's abilities, and they were numerous, he could split his resonance better than anyone Kerrick knew.

He closed his eyes and gritted his teeth. "No problem. Where do you want me?"

"Central detected a large deployment at the Trough over downtown Phoenix. I've got Medichi in Awatukee, Zacharius and Jean-Pierre are working the White Tanks in Buckeye, Santiago is at New River, and I'm with Luken covering the Superstitions. I waited as long as I could, but I've never seen so many death vamps out in one night. We need you, buddy, and be prepared the moment Central folds you. There could be as many as twelve downtown."

"Twelve? Three squads? Shit."

"We've been up to our asses tonight."

"You should have called me sooner."

"Wanted to respect your sitch."

He took a deep breath and asked the question. "Any sign of . . . the ascendiate?" He refused to say her name.

"Nope. Oh, shit. Five more just showed up."

The line went dead. Kerrick stared at it and cursed. He waited. The phone buzzed again. Thank God. "Give."

Thorne spoke fast. "Sorry. Luken's got everything under control. Jeannie just patched in. She said she's identified Leto at the Trough over Metro Phoenix as well."

"Holy shit." Leto never joined in the usual fray, since he served as one of the Commander's most powerful generals.

Then again, he ought to be since he was a former Warrior of the Blood, the Commander's biggest prize in the last two hundred years. "Well, isn't this a night for surprises. I guess this has to be about the ascendiate."

"Looks like it. Sorry, brother. Oh, shit, *motherfucker,* four more pretty-boys just showed up, of an Asian variety this time. You know the drill with the ascendiate—seize and protect. The coordinates are laid in. Call Central when you're ready." Thorne hung up.

Kerrick stood up, folded off his jeans and tee, then folded on winged battle gear. He adjusted the weapons harness and with a thought brought the dagger into his hand from his weapons locker, securing it into the slot. He drew in a deep breath then adjusted his thick, heavy sandals. The kilt felt so very right and his wing-locks had already started to thrum.

With a thought, he folded his sword into his hand. He called Central and cursed silently, yet again, that he still couldn't just dematerialize wherever the hell he needed to go.

"Hi, Jeannie. You still on?"

"Sure am. I'm taking Carla's shift. She had a date. You ready, *duhuro*?"

He couldn't believe she'd used that expression. *Duhuro* was an ancient form of address that annoyed the hell out of him. "You haven't called me *duhuro* in at least a decade. You'd better cut that shit out, Jeannie, or I may have to come over and rough you up a bit."

"Who's stopping you," she said, giggling. "My husband and I have an agreement. He gets Angelina Jolie and I get any of you warrior brothers, any time, any place."

"Yeah, yeah." Something inside him relaxed a little. He even smiled. The Twolings at Central were chosen for their calm under pressure, for their ability to handle tragedy, and mostly for their general all-around good humor. They were also a gum-popping bunch and they had his number.

"Fold me when you're ready."

"You got it. And Kerrick?"

"Yeah?"

"We're all grateful for what you and the brothers do."

Before he could respond, the vibration whispered through him.

A moment later he crouched right next to the Trough, sword in both hands. An extensive park covered the Borderland on Second Earth.

The Trough was the distance between the dimensions made of nether-space, which extended who knew how far below him. On Mortal Earth the downtown Phoenix Borderland made up the rest of the sandwich; two Borderlands and a Trough in between.

He shifted his gaze slowly, past Arizona sycamores and the occasional overgrown oleander. How many times had he battled death vampires in just this place? Tens of thousands of times. Yeah, he'd been fighting that long.

But tonight everything would be different. He could feel it. So, shit.

And no sign of Leto.

He felt his presence, though, the goddamn traitor.

The call to ascension burns in the heart,
But the rite of ascension begins with the mind.

—*Collected Proverbs,* Beatrice of Fourth

CHAPTER 8

At two forty in the morning, Alison rolled to a stop beneath a lone security light in the middle of the downtown Phoenix alley. She sat in her beat-up Nova, letting the engine idle for a few seconds before turning it off. Her heart slammed in her chest.

Why was she here?

So many reasons—a warrior who smelled of cardamom and had enormous white wings, death vampires, pale skin with a faintly blue hue, beautiful creatures, persistent dreams, dimensional worlds, a yearning.

Yes, a deep persistent yearning that never seemed to leave her.

Ascension.

A call to ascension.

She peeled her fingers off the steering wheel, settled her hands on her lap, then closed her eyes. She took deep breaths.

After a moment, the thumping of her heart settled . . . a

little. Kerrick had said he wasn't certain she had received a call to ascension. She wished now she'd thought to ask him some details about the process. Yet her instincts told her this was her call, all of it, the alley, meeting vampires at a club in downtown Phoenix, the dreams, the powerful yearnings.

She yearned for this world. Even the vein in her throat throbbed. Her eyes flashed open. She felt the pulse at her neck and she thought of Kerrick. She thought about his fangs piercing her neck and taking her blood.

She leaned back against the seat as desire bloomed between her legs, specific, real, sexual. How was this possible? To feel so much for someone she hardly knew, someone who was a vampire, and without understanding why, to want to give him her blood.

Reality tugged on her mind. If ascenders were vampires—some good, some very bad—then . . . logically . . . wouldn't she become . . . a vampire?

She tried on the word, but how could it possibly fit? Vampires were supposed to be creatures of the dark, *the undead,* that which had no heart and lived on blood to survive.

She took another deep breath. Once more her hands gripped the steering wheel. The explanation that came to mind made sense: that somehow the darker element of the world of ascension, the habits of death vampires, had made its way into the culture of her world, enough to create the vampire mythos, creatures that moved in the shadows, enthralling humans, draining their blood.

But Kerrick, *Warrior Kerrick,* fought these addicted beings, killed them, worked as his conduct suggested, to protect both Mortal and Second Earth against their depredations. And he was a vampire, the best of vampires.

It all made sense . . . and yet . . . the reality of her present situation kept her fingers fused to the steering wheel.

She swallowed hard, once more forcing herself to relax. Tonight, this night, she would open a door to a different world, the world of the vampire, of winged beings with power matching her own, a world that included a man-warrior-vampire who was her equal.

Tonight, she would change her life forever. A tremor raced through her, of excitement, of fear, of hope.

She opened the car door, slid out, then drew in a deep breath. Even with her sweater on she was cold. She rubbed her arms and shivered. The desert temps dropped at night in early March.

As she looked up into the night sky, she recalled Kerrick mentioning the Borderlands. Without being told she knew this alley was a Borderland to the Second Dimension, a gateway to the world of the vampire. Her heart beat faster.

Her instincts shouted at her to run and hide, to leave this place, this moment of responding to a world she knew so little about. She looked down at the crumbling asphalt and thought again about just climbing back into her ragged car and running away.

But where would she go? Back to Carefree, to her su-doku puzzles and slavish addiction to old movies, to reading every night yet not really living, to working out in a gym and getting strong but for no particular purpose, no boyfriend, no possibility of children and a family, to be of only partial use to her future clients?

No. That was her old life and tonight that life *passed away*.

Once again she looked up. On opposite sides of the alley, two rows of buildings, also two stories in height, boxed in the backstreet. Beyond, only a handful of stars broke through the wedge of dark night sky.

Still looking up, she held out her right hand, palm up, the same hand that had recently held a pocket of time. The pressure in her chest grew, of longing for a new world, of needing to answer her call to ascension. The need swelled then spread to her limbs until she trembled. She felt tingling in a V down her back, the promise of wings.

All paths had led her here, to this moment, from the first time she had moved a toy as a toddler with just the wave of her finger.

Ascension was her destiny.

She seized energy from all around her, gathering power into her hand, as she never had before. Her heart thudded, swift and loud. She took a deep breath and without questioning what she was doing, she flipped her wrist backward then whipped it forward, sending at the same moment a concentrated blast upward into the night air.

The quick release flung her down hard onto the asphalt, bruising her backside, as electric shocks drove through her veins, muscles, and bones.

She pulled herself up and into a crouch, then hunched as close to the Nova as she could. If so much power had gone up into the air, something else might come falling down.

Kerrick remained in his crouch, near the Trough, waiting, listening, every sense on alert. He didn't immediately mount his wings. He needed to see what the enemy intended first. He gripped his sword hard, his vision in constant motion, his hearing sharp. He heard laughter and extended his vision. Half a mile away Leto stood with twelve death vampires, just as Thorne had said.

There was only one reason such a large contingent would be present right now, and the truth hit him square in the face—Alison was below the Trough at the downtown Phoenix alley right in the middle of her call to ascension.

Shit.

As he watched the death vamps in the distance, he tried to understand what had brought him to exactly this point, above the Trough with the woman meant to be his *breh* waiting below. He'd been trying to escape this moment from the time he'd first caught her lavender scent.

Yet here he was, apparently destined to serve as her guardian.

Suddenly Leto's unit dematerialized.

He kept very still.

All twelve materialized a hundred feet away, at the edge of the wash, all facing away from him and staring down into the Trough, waiting.

Kerrick's heart beat a strong cadence in his ears, a heavy thump preparing him for what was going to happen in the next few minutes. No matter what, he had to get to Alison first. If even one of these death vamps preceded him, she'd be dead within the next ten minutes.

What he needed was for Endelle to dump him into the Trough, since she was the only one who had that kind of power. He also hoped like hell the opposition didn't do the same. Provided that neither Leto nor any of the death vamps got dumped, a fall through a dimension would give him a lead time of four minutes, enough to get Alison to safety. Nothing less would do, even though it would hurt like hell.

Greaves could do a dump, and he'd heard rumors that at least one of his minions also had sufficient power. One more disadvantage for Endelle's side.

He just had to trust the situation to work out. What he could do was keep all the death vamps in front of him so busy they'd have to stay put.

Endelle, he sent, hoping against hope she was tuned in to him.

Hang tough, Warrior, she responded instantly, straight into his head. *Your lavender sweetheart's call hasn't made it to Second yet. That's what all these morons are waiting for.*

He took a breath. Thank God for Endelle.

I should give you a little warning, though. Leto's packing a bomb, a little shredder package he won't hesitate to use, so keep your nuts tight.

Don't I always, he sent.

Endelle laughed then fell silent. After a moment, her voice pummeled the inside of his head. *Holy shit! Can you hear that? Damn, this ascendiate has power.*

Kerrick turned his attention to the Trough. He could feel it now, a deep vibration within the dimension. Beneath his sandals, the earth rattled back and forth, earthquake-fashion, and a sound like a freight train grew louder and louder.

The next moment an explosion ripped the air. The sand

rose like a geyser straight up out of the Trough, a quarter of a mile high and a full ten feet across. He'd never seen anything like it in his life.

Holy shit. A hand-blast through a dimension.

He had never known an ascendiate with such a highly developed level of power. She would be one helluvan asset to Endelle and one huge threat to Greaves. No wonder he'd sent Leto and three squads of death vamps to head her off. He needed her dead. Period. And despite the big rule of *no death vamps* on Mortal Earth, this was war and the bastards would follow him into the Trough anyway. When Leto and his crew showed up on Mortal Earth, COPASS would treat it as part of the ascendiate's rite of ascension and not the usual violation of Second Earth Law.

He sighed. Same old shit.

He thought of Alison, of having held her in his arms and how difficult it had been to penetrate her mind, the same woman who had folded out of the Blood and Bite.

He moved back several yards as the sand began cascading back on itself, falling into the wash as well as the surrounding lawn. Leto and his men dropped into crouches and took the brunt of the sand on their backs. One of the vamps writhed under the onslaught. The others held steady. Leto, as expected, didn't flinch.

Kerrick focused on securing the ascendiate for Endelle. Nothing else mattered.

Leto rose and reached for his phone.

Kerrick called to him sharply, not wanting him to contact anyone who could start sending death vamps into the Trough. "Hey, dickheads. Looking for me?"

Twelve. Thirteen, counting Leto. Well . . . this would be a challenge. He dipped his chin. Bring it on.

Leto turned around, dispensed with his phone, folding his sword into his hand at the same time. "Well, if it isn't Thorne's lapdog. Look, boys. Cocksucker just arrived."

"Fuck you, Leto."

"You first, asshole."

Kerrick would have preferred to mount his wings but

since he'd be heading into the Trough, he couldn't. You never got dumped in full-mount. The wings would never survive the fall. Besides, he could manage this bunch on solid ground.

Endelle? he sent.

Just get me some blue skin first then prepare to get dumped. Whatever you do, don't mount your wings.

Got it.

He lowered his head, lifted his sword, and with preternatural speed launched at all thirteen vampires at once.

"Will you look at that," Endelle cried. Her chest felt on fire as she watched Kerrick fight. She had Marcus's wrist in a stranglehold to keep him from folding into the fray. "Three down and the rest of those motherfuckers are scratching ass, wondering what the hell happened."

Marcus shouted, "Endelle, let go of me. Now!"

"No can do, gorgeous." Of course he was anxious to do battle. He was a goddamn warrior and she was streaming Kerrick's moves straight into his head, a blow-by-blow event, which caused Marcus's face to darken and his lips to curl into a fierce snarl.

She stood with him in front of her desk, restraining him. She wished she could have sent him immediately to back Kerrick up, but as much as she valued his readiness to wield the sword, she couldn't risk the two of them being together right now, not with so much bad blood between them.

"Let me go!" he cried. "Ten to one. If Leto engages . . ."

She smiled. Marcus was a warrior at heart, in every cell of his body, no matter what he'd been doing for the last two hundred years.

"Relax. Be patient. Leto's too busy texting, which tells me things have gone awry at the fucking compound. Besides, Kerrick is doing just fine."

He outmatched all the death vamps in preternatural speed, which meant nearly every thrust or slice of his sword counted. She let out a loud whoop. "Two more bastards down and he's barely started." There was nothing so fine as watching one of her Warriors of the Blood, all virile, muscled, highly sexed vampires, doing what he did best with a sword in hand. She drew deep breaths, all the while keeping Marcus in check.

"Turn me loose," he shouted. "He can't defeat them all."

Endelle met Marcus's gaze straight-on. "I thought you hated him, wanted to kill him."

"Fuck you."

Endelle smiled. She knew her men well. "You sure you're ready to go back to work? You sure you're strong enough after so much soft living on Mortal Earth?"

She watched a red haze slide over his eyes as his chin dipped. "Don't I look ready to you?" He split his resonance three times.

Nice.

Again she smiled. He was almost as tall as Kerrick and as muscled. Of course he wouldn't have let his training lapse. "I have to send Kerrick into the Trough and the moment I do, I need you ready to take on the rest of these motherfuckers. Keep as many of them from entering the Trough as you can. Have you got that?"

"Yes," he growled.

From the vision in her mind, Leto continued to function separately from the battle. He shouted into his phone, once, twice. He made call after call, which all told her that something had gone wrong.

Thank you, Creator!

"On my mark, half a minute from now and not a second before. Do you understand? Will you obey because I'll have your nuts if you don't? Nod if you agree."

She watched him draw a shallow breath. That was good enough for her.

She released his wrist and focused on Alison as well. She wished she could just fold Kerrick directly to her, but she'd be breaking a big rule. No resident of Second Earth could await an ascendiate on Mortal Earth while the mortal answered a call to ascension. If that rule wasn't upheld, no powerful ascendiate would ever survive even the first three seconds after demonstrating preternatural power.

No. This was the way it was done.

She gave Kerrick a single mental warning then a damn solid shove with the powers the Creator had given her. Down he went through the dimension, flying, his kilt flapping like a black leather wing. At least he wouldn't be conscious for the trip.

She shifted to the downtown alley, mentally charted his course, and had to laugh. Would you look at where he was going to land? How about that for fucking *destiny*. But boy, it was gonna hurt.

With the dump well under way, she nodded to Marcus and told him to do his worst.

Alison now stood beside the Nova, completely still, her hand on the car as an anchor.

Her heart pounded in her ears, the toms still beating out a painful rhythm. She'd heard the voices of several men and she knew for certain one of those voices belonged to the winged vampire warrior she'd come to know as Kerrick.

She had also heard the clanging of metal like swords being struck hard together, which made sense since she'd already witnessed a sword fight. Then suddenly, as quickly as it had begun, the fighting ceased and silence followed.

A third man with a nasally voice gasped, "Where the hell did he go? Fuck. We've lost him."

"He got dumped into the Trough." She recognized the voice of the man called Leto, the one Kerrick had taunted. "Shit, where the hell is Crace? Goddammit."

"He's not answering?" another voice asked.

"No." A string of obscenities followed, then, "What the hell?"

"Hello, Leto. Wanna stop playing with your phone long enough to show these numbnuts how a real fight is conducted?"

"Well, fuck me," Leto said, "look what just crawled out

of the swamp—Marcus the fucking Coward. You done hiding on Mortal Earth?"

"So you went traitor, you goddamn sonofabitch."

More steel clanged . . . then silence, like someone had punched a mute button.

Alison stared hard up at the dark sky. So, Kerrick had gotten dumped. What exactly did that mean?

From out of nowhere, a blast of arctic air descended on her. The temperature had been a little chilly a moment earlier and yet a powerful stream of icy cold air suddenly flowed from nowhere. She started to shake. What on earth was happening?

The airwaves above began to pulse. Her heart thumped all over again. She sensed that something—no, *someone*—was coming.

Kerrick, her winged vampire warrior?

Her heart beat heavily in her chest all over again. She shouldn't want to see him so much, but she did.

The air now pounded on her as though the sky expanded and contracted in slow heavy waves. The pressure increased and her head started to hurt. An intake of air rushed from both ends of the alley, sweeping up in a funnel around her then taking her off the ground. She cleared a whole foot of space. Loose papers whirled everywhere.

She thought, *Tornado, maybe?* However, not even the faintest wisp of a cloud marred the black sky.

Her chest constricted and she couldn't breathe. She trembled all over. Maybe she shouldn't have sent a hand-blast into the air after all. Maybe ascension was something she didn't really want to take on.

A little too late for that.

Suddenly the air collapsed. She fell to her knees and cried out as rough asphalt bit into her skin. She rose up and plucked grit out of the palms of her hands.

What the hell had just happened?

Again she looked up.

Silence followed.

An awful, deafening silence.

She dropped into a protective crouch again, hunching as near to her Nova as she could get. Something bad, really bad, was about to happen.

She heard a fluttering, which got louder in incremental bursts as an object came into view heading straight for her. Not an object, a man in a kilt. Oh, God! He was going to fall hard.

She turned away from the sudden crunch of metal as Kerrick landed on the hood of her car. At nearly the same instant an odd metallic clattering sounded onto the asphalt in front of the vehicle.

The airwaves stopped pulsing.

Silence followed. No breeze, no voices, nothing. Even the chill had disappeared.

She rose up to look at him, her legs locked in place.

Surely he was dead.

Tears stung her eyes.

She blinked several times.

Okay, Alison, get a grip. At least see if he's still alive.

She rounded the front of the car and looked down at him. He wore his black leather kilt with a harness belted around his waist and covering his chest, shoulders, and back. His arms were muscled and corded just as she remembered. He'd held her in his arms like she'd been a feather.

He lay in a depression in the metal, his legs hanging off the side of the car at an awkward angle. Part of his long thick wavy black hair fanned over his face; the other part was held back by some kind of leather clasp. She wanted to push the strands off his cheek to look at him again but he couldn't still be alive, not after falling so far. Her heart constricted. She really didn't like the idea at all that Kerrick might be dead.

Oh, God. Please don't let it be true.

Something rattled on the asphalt behind her. She turned around. His sword vibrated against the asphalt.

She bent down to pick it up.

"Don't touch the sword."

She gasped as she rose, turning to stare at Kerrick.

Through the thick strands she caught sight of a glistening eye then he blinked at her.

"Don't touch it," he said, more quietly this time. His deep voice drove into her chest, wrapped a couple of times around her heart, then pulled tight. "You'll die."

"Kerrick?" she asked, wanting to make certain she had not mistaken his identity.

"So you remember me."

"Yes."

"Do you remember what happened?"

"Yes."

The eye closed. *Come to me* whispered through her head, then his body went limp.

She stared at him for a long moment. This really was Kerrick, her warrior-vampire from the medical complex and from the club.

So what had just happened? Had he given her a warning about the sword, spoken tender words over her mind, then dropped dead on the hood of her car?

She settled two fingers on his neck.

Thank God. His pulse beat steady and strong. She pushed the hair away from his face. How had he survived such a terrible fall? She placed her hand on his cheek.

"You are so beautiful," she whispered. A new ache settled deep in her chest.

Come to me.

Could he really speak to her while unconscious?

I'm here, she sent.

His chest rose and fell as if on a sigh.

She felt dizzy, her legs weak beneath her. How had they both ended up in the same alley right now, here, tonight? She had never been big on *destiny,* but given the evidence in front of her she could almost believe.

She stepped forward and couldn't resist pushing his upper lip back. And there they were, lengthened incisors. She touched the left one at the tip but apparently pressed too hard. Blood pooled instantly and dripped against her lips.

He moaned and sucked at her finger yet didn't awaken.

The feel of his mouth doused her in sharp arousal. As she withdrew her finger, desire sank low. My God, even unconscious this man-vampire-warrior had the power to undo her.

He was as she remembered him, unutterably handsome, even more so up close like this, the planes of his face strong, his lips full and sensual. She felt drawn to him like sun to the desert. The smell of him struck her nostrils and buckled her knees.

She leaned close and drew in a deep breath. His familiar scent assailed her, of cardamom and his tough leathery musk. The combination caused her internal muscles to clench and shivers to fly down her neck and back. She wanted to touch him . . . everywhere.

Her conscience assaulted her. The warrior was clearly out cold, severely wounded, and all she could think about was putting her hands on him? Where had her professionalism gone? Her humanity? Had she no sense of decency?

Apparently not since she settled her hand on his arm, the swell of his muscles warm and thick beneath her fingers.

Come to me.

She heard his voice again within her head.

Once more she sent, *I'm here.*

He groaned.

Alison closed her eyes. Winter drifted out of her life and spring emerged, little shoots of bright green rising everywhere. Her lungs opened. For how many years had she been holding her breath, longing to breathe, hoping to have a man in her life who wanted her in this way? *How long?* Tears bled from her eyes.

The answer was simple.

All her life.

She took in a mainsail full of air. She opened her eyes and looked down at the vampire. She fell into the addiction of him, hard, complete, secure.

She worked her hands down his body. Nothing seemed to be broken, but her fingertips hummed strangely and her attraction to him increased tenfold. Shivers stole up her arms and down her neck. His warrior world had hardened every muscle of his body. The scent of cardamom rose again. She leaned close and inhaled once more.

She wanted him painfully but she worked to get hold of herself. She continued down his legs. All his bones remained intact. She couldn't find even an abrasion, let alone a deep gash or wound—nothing to indicate serious trauma.

Unfortunately he was still unconscious, so he must at least have a concussion.

It dawned on her that she should call 911.

Could emergency services treat a vampire?

Well, no time like the present to find out.

Maybe the circumstances surrounding his accident were a little bizarre but he obviously required medical attention.

Still, she found it almost impossible to leave his side. It was as though an intangible force bound her to him.

Seriously, she should tear herself away from him long enough to make sure he stayed alive.

She drew in a deep breath and ignored the humming of her fingers as well as the profound need she felt to keep touching him. She took two steps away, took another frayed breath, then hurried around to the driver's side of the car.

She got in and reached for her purse then withdrew her cell. She had just poised a finger over the number nine when Kerrick started to move. He flexed his right arm like he was simply enjoying the feel of his muscles.

CHAPTER 9

Crace bid good-bye to his heavenly wife, his body sated, sex hormones drifting lazily through his veins. He thought the thought and returned to the bathroom in his new suite next door to the Commander. He washed his hands and smiled.

The planets were most definitely lining up.

His dear Julianna had arrived in Phoenix Two half an hour ago and he'd installed her at the Bredstone at White Lake, the finest hotel in the Western Hemisphere. The Bredstone had every amenity, suitable for visiting dignitaries and especially for his wife, who deserved the best that immortal life had to offer. Tracing to her, thank God, had been but a single thought.

His wife was the most perfect partner a vampire could ever wish for, beautiful and rich, extremely well connected, powerful, and she loved his body.

He checked his Rolex. He'd been gone a bare nine minutes. Excellent.

Now a little cleanup, then back to the war room to see how things were progressing. Leto had been as good as his word. He had been checking in every ten minutes, each time with a text of three zeros to indicate there was still no sign of the ascendiate.

There could be no question—the ascension was happening. He felt it now, in his bones, in his mind, a vibration, which had the entire compound jittery.

He felt wired yet exhausted at the same time. It was after three in the morning, which meant five in his beautiful Chicago. No wonder he felt strung out. He'd been awake for about twenty hard hours.

He had just splashed water on his face when he heard a thumping noise. He toweled off then headed into the living room. For Christ's sake, who was pounding on the door?

His face flushed red hot. If there was one thing he would not tolerate, it was this sort of disrespect. He reached for his phone, which he had turned off, *for nine minutes.*

Then he saw the messages.

All of them.

Oh, shit.

No. No. No.

Leto had called. And called then texted. *Need a dump to Mortal Earth. Now.*

His heart seized.

The window had opened then closed and he'd been gone the exact nine minutes he'd been needed.

How was that for fucking *destiny*?

He pulled the door open. An administrative assistant stared at him wild-eyed. "General Leto needs a dump through the Trough. You're the only one with enough power. The Commander can't be reached."

If he'd been a woman, he would have fainted.

Nine fucking minutes may have just cost him a seat at the Round Table. There still might be enough time. He folded to the war room.

But when he got there, all six of the Commander's Phoenix Two generals stared at him with unmitigated hostility and a bounty of rage.

"Where are we?" he shouted.

"Well, you finally made it," the general sneered, the vampire whose office he had taken. "Let me fill you in. The female ascendiate finally answered her call to ascension, one helluva hand-blast up the Trough, so we were good to go in pursuit." His sarcasm fired Crace's temper but the bastard continued, "Naturally, Madame Supreme High Administrator dumped Kerrick into the Trough on the three-minute cycle, you know, because of all the power she has, and if you remember you were supposed to be here to do the same thing for Leto as needed. However, because you weren't here, I had to glide Leto down on the seven-minute cycle, along with two of his death vamps, since no one here but you has enough power to effect the fucking dump. We won't know anything for a few more minutes but he'll be too fucking late since the ascendiate has a car in the alley.

"If Warrior Kerrick recovers fast enough, and why the fuck wouldn't he, they'll leave in her car before Leto touches down. And you know what that means." He got close into Crace's face. "Once they're on the move, we won't be able to get to them. Remember? No wings on Mortal Earth and no Second ascender I know of has the ability to fold to a moving object. Even if they stop, the grid won't be able to find either of their signatures for hours. So unless Leto touches down fast enough with the bomb he took, it looks like we're at square fucking one!"

Crace ignored the general. He took a step back and turned to stare at the grid where not only the ascendiate's powerful signature pulsed, but Warrior Kerrick's as well.

Shit.

For the space of about five seconds he thought about cutting his dick off.

Marcus flew straight up into the cold, dry desert night air, chasing the last of the death vamps. Goddamn he'd forgotten what this was like, the sheer blaze of adrenaline, his wings plowing the air, his sword pressed against his thigh.

Power. That's what this was. The incomparable sensation of sheer physical and preternatural power combined. What a rush.

The pretty-boy had thought to outfly him, the last of the death vamps left alive after Leto took two others and headed into the Trough.

But this one was flat-out scared. As he ought to be.

Marcus lowered his chin. He focused on the death vamp's mind and sent, *You started drinking people into the grave and now you think to run from me?*

In response, he heard a kind of mental shrieking. He laughed and worked his wings in long hard thrusts. With each one, he drew closer to his prey until he reached forward and grabbed the asshole's ankle. He gave a solid jerk and a twist, which sent the bastard into a wicked spiral, his wings locked in place, his body spinning out of control.

Marcus halted midair and watched. After a few seconds, he drew his wings into close-mount, tight against his body, then headed like a rocket after the bastard. He kept his sword close, caught the pretty-boy's arm, and unfurled his own wings at the same time. He floated both of them back to earth. At the last moment he flipped his enemy onto hard solid ground.

The death vamp's spirit was broken as he looked up at Marcus. There was no more fight left in him.

How familiar all this felt, like hopping on a Harley after not riding for a few months. He knew just how to hold the clutch and rev the gas. He lifted his sword and at the last split second, as the blade swept in a load-bearing arc through the air, he saw the relief in his enemy's eyes.

He severed the head. Nothing less would do.

But the finality of the act caught the back of his knees and brought him hard next to his enemy, onto the grass of the Second Earth park. His body shook, adrenaline slamming through his veins. He leaned over, breathing hard. He barely kept the nausea at bay.

He looked around. There were bodies everywhere. And body parts. And broken feathers. God, there were feathers everywhere.

He had expected a real high, a warrior's high. He had looked forward to it. Instead a terrible emptiness followed, something he had forgotten.

He thumbed Central and spoke to Jeannie. Two seconds later a bright flash and all the gore disappeared.

Maybe there had been more than one reason why he'd exiled himself to Mortal Earth.

Kerrick opened his eyes as he flexed his right arm. He had a clear view of an alley and everything looked quiet, but his mind fuzzed in and out like a computer screen hit with a virus. He couldn't place his current location. Damn.

It was still dark, though. Somehow, that was a good thing. His back, his left hip, and his left knee hurt like hell. He looked at his arm again then wondered why he wasn't covered in blood from all the fighting.

What fighting?

Sudden images flashed over his brain. Oh, yeah. He'd been battling Leto and a host of death vamps, twelve if he remembered right. He had worked hard to shift the battle away from the Trough and then the ground had dropped out from under him anyway.

He'd fallen . . . a long way.

Oh, yeah. He'd been dumped. Hence, the absence of blood and sweat. Traveling through a dimension like that, instead of just folding, had a cleansing effect on the clothes and the body, like he'd showered up and put on fresh gear.

Now he was on Mortal Earth.

He just couldn't exactly remember why he was here. He had a mission, but what?

More images crowded his mind.

A woman and his sword rattling on the ground.

He sniffed the air. He smelled something *very* familiar. He lifted his arm and dragged his nostrils over his skin. A rich scent hit him like he'd walked into a perfume shop.

Lavender. A woman, not any woman, *his woman,* Alison—yes, her name was Alison. She had touched him recently, within the past few minutes.

In exactly how many dimensions was that even possible?

The scent of lavender took him on a rocket ride and he hardened painfully. A moan drifted out of his mouth. He ran his tongue over his lips. He tasted blood not his own.

His breath stopped. This was *her* blood. Oh, God, how had he gotten her blood on his tongue? He knew it as though he'd read her DNA signature a thousand times.

Oh. My. God.

He remembered now. She had pressed his lips back and touched one of his fangs a little too hard and pierced her skin. He had sucked her finger.

The blood on his tongue sent him spiraling into a cursed need to commune with her. His fangs thickened in his gums. He swallowed potent saliva. He throbbed everywhere.

But what the hell was she doing in this alley below the Trough? He was at the downtown Phoenix Borderland. Still night. A Borderland. The Trough. Alison.

Shit. Of course. Her call to ascension. The sand of the wash shooting up into the air.

He took deep breaths and calmed his body.

He had to think straight. He wouldn't be mate-bonding with this woman. He'd taken vows. Never again would he put a woman's life in jeopardy because of a mating. Never.

Yet by some wretched twist of fate she'd been plummeted into the danger of his world, *on his watch,* and now it was up to him to keep her alive.

He sat up and rubbed his neck. He could feel his bruised bones knitting together rapidly and his muscles and skin repairing at lightning speed. Christ, his head still felt thick. He shoved a hand through the loose strands of his hair, pushing it away from his face. He drew the pick from the *cadroen* then rebound his hair.

He was in Phoenix One, all right, below the Trough to

Second Earth, one of several favorite descent points of the
pretty-boy bloodsuckers. Oh, shit, he could feel the air
above him start to pulse.

Yep. Leto and his playmates were on the way, only this
time they'd be armed to the teeth. Swords were the only
battle weapons allowed on Two. On Mortal Earth, however,
there were no limits, with the exception of atomics and full
regiments.

If he didn't take action, he and Alison would be toast in
little less than a minute.

So where was she?

He could feel her presence now as well as smell her.
Even her heartbeats sounded in his ears.

He gave his head a shake and cleared away the last remaining aftereffects of the fall.

He drew in a sharp breath. His nostrils flared. Her scent
stroked him again. In twelve hundred years he had never
been so affected by a woman, but Alison was a perfect
mate, designed to torture him even at inconvenient times.
Her pheromones charged the air and dragged over his skin
like sharp, erotic fingernails. So this was what the *breh-
hedden* did to a man? And just how easy was this going to
be to disengage? Holy hell.

He paused. He reached out with his mind, located her,
then turned around on the hood of the car, crouching low.
He looked through the windshield.

Time once again slowed to a standstill.

There she was staring at him, her large blue eyes opened
in surprise. Sweet merciful God. *He wanted her.* He
wanted her like he had never wanted a woman before, like
he had just figured out what *woman* was.

Heat and desire cascaded off her body in brilliant red
waves. His lips curved. The not-so-subtle mating experience was apparently mutual.

As cold air spilled over the car, he drew his mind out of
his present need. He had to get Alison to safety . . . now.

He rolled off the hood then picked up his sword. He

caught her gaze again as he rounded the driver's side. She tracked his moves and stared at him unblinking. Her lips were parted in a soft expression of shock.

He strode to the door then jerked it open. "Move over . . . now . . . or we'll both be dead in about twenty seconds."

She compressed her lips and searched his face. He could see her mind spinning, processing. A moment later she slid her backside over the lump of her purse, which she tossed into the backseat, then latched her seat belt like her fingers were on fire.

He folded his sword back to the locked case in his basement before he climbed into the driver's seat. As he slid in, his knees hit the steering wheel. He moved the seat back with a swift jerk but even then he barely fit into the confined space.

He looked at her as he started the ignition with a touch of his finger. "Let me say this again: whatever you do, don't handle another warrior's sword. They're forged to individual recognition and if you touch one, other than your own, you'll die. Got it?"

He hoped the woman had good instincts. If she was able to blast a hole in another dimension, she ought to. On the other hand, instincts often went to character and right now he knew nothing about this woman except of course that he wanted to be inside her, *like now*.

"Got it," she said. She finally blinked.

He met her gaze. He hoped like hell she had a sense of humor because damn, she was going to need it over the next few days. Okay, hours. Whether she understood it or not, her life had just been blown all to hell.

He put the gearshift in reverse, stepped hard on the gas, and began backing up.

Slowly.

He gripped the steering wheel and withheld a lengthy string of expletives.

The car chugged along like it had all night and all day to get out of the alley.

Dammit.

He hit the steering wheel. "What the hell is this?" he cried.

"Well, it's a 1993 Nova," she said. "Top speed sixty if you don't mind the shaking."

"We're screwed."

He kept backing up anyway. He ground his teeth. If he'd been able to fold, as any proper resident of Second was able to do, then he could have just put a hand on her and taken her to his house in Queen Creek. Now his safety and hers depended on a junk pile gaining speed like a tortoise headed for a siesta.

Goddammit.

Alison stared at her warrior-vampire-guardian as he drove the Nova backward down the alley. The desert couldn't have been drier than her mouth and her chest fired off heartbeats like rounds of ammunition. "So what is it? Are the death vamps on their way?"

He shot his gaze to hers. "So you do remember?"

"I found the memories you took, so yeah, I remember the battle at the medical complex."

"Christ," he muttered. He slung his arm across the back of her seat as he looked through the rear window and guided the car at an increasing speed toward the street. "And yes, the death vamps are on the way."

"Exactly how many?"

"At least three, maybe more."

"But they'll fall like you so we'll have more time. Right? They'll be hurt? They'll need time to recover?"

He shook his head. "Nope. They'll float down and they'll most likely have a bomb with them."

"A bomb." Her breath came out in one long slow drag. "You know, you're kind of scaring me."

"Good."

He backed into the street, the wheels squealing as he made a turn. He shifted to drive and once again the car lurched forward at a snail's pace. He hit the steering wheel a couple more times and appeared to work his mouth over another obscenity or two. He moved into the sparse three AM traffic.

"Watch behind," he said, "and tell me what happens."

Just as Alison turned around to look out the rear window, a loud explosion ripped the air. Her whole body jerked in response.

"There's smoke and fire, stuff flying everywhere," she cried. "What was that?"

"A nifty little bomb called a shredder. It's full of shrapnel and, when tossed in grenade fashion, explodes in a pre-set direction. One of the Commander's little creations."

The Commander again. Darian. *Her* Darian. The psychopath who talked about his fantasy kills the way most people described a family dinner. She shuddered all over again.

"We wouldn't have survived if we'd been back there."

"Blown to bits."

She glanced at him. Her heart seized. What did this mean? "So Darian, *the Commander,* wants me dead?"

He nodded. "Yes, but keep watching. Tell me what else you see."

She arched around again and sucked in a quick breath. "There are three men, one as big as you and the other two are like the death vampire at the medical complex. No wings, though."

She turned to face him again. "Will they come after us? The men on the street?"

The Nova reached top speed and started rattling, but the warrior kept his foot to the pedal.

He shook his head. His arms and shoulders both relaxed. "No. High-speed chases aren't allowed on Mortal Earth."

"They won't be sprouting wings?"

"Nope. No wings, which was why I'd been sent to the medical complex earlier. Our Second Earth technology picks up wings-in-flight pretty fast. The death vampire had been flapping his black pair for quite some time before I got there."

Alison strove to calm her heart down. "So what are you

doing here? I mean, you were at my office complex this evening, then at the club, now here you are."

He glanced at her. "I'm here to protect you, Alison, as best I can while you go through the ascension process. I'm here to serve as your guardian." He glanced in the rearview. "Have we left them behind?"

Alison turned around and scanned the street. The car had covered at least a mile and a half. Maybe more. He had the Nova at full throttle now and the car shook almost as badly as her legs. She could barely see remnants of the explosion at that distance.

"All clear."

"Good." He breathed a heavy sigh and eased off the gas a little. The shimmy evened out and the engine no longer sounded like it was being strangled. "Thank God."

She felt numb and her mind had stopped working. She placed her palms on her legs and rubbed back and forth trying to ease the shaking. Could her life get any more bizarre?

"So let me understand," she said, her throat in a knot. "We're talking same earth, different dimensions, right?"

"Yes, Mortal Earth and Second Earth, but there are four more dimensions . . . that we know of."

Okaaaay. "Just so I've got this straight, were you fighting several death vamps just a few minutes ago? And was one of them called 'Leto'?"

"Yes." He glanced at her again, his eyes wide. "How the hell do you know that?"

Her gaze skated back to the street. Only a handful of cars were out and about at this hour, cops and bad guys, and apparently vampire warriors and novice ascenders. Her brain felt fuzzy, disordered. "I think I heard the battle or at least part of it."

"I guess you did."

"I wish my legs would stop shaking."

"Breathe," he said.

For the next minute she focused on breathing, one in, one out. One in. One out. When her legs had settled down, she asked, "So why aren't you dead? I mean, I watched you fall out of the sky and you landed on my car." She waved in the direction of the battered hood. "There's the proof."

"The ascended heal quickly in most situations."

She put a hand to her chest, knowing she had to make her confession. "I think I should tell you . . . I sent a blast from my hand up into the sky, back at the alley, I mean."

"I know. I saw the results."

She turned toward him. "So, I have to know . . . did I hurt you?"

"What do you mean?"

"You were unconscious after you crashed down on my hood." She had just voiced her deepest fear, and her heart hammered out a few more loud beats.

"You think you caused my fall?"

"Yes."

He chuckled. "The two events aren't connected. The truth is, I got dumped. The woman in charge, Endelle, sent me into the Trough—the space between dimensions—so that I could get to you before anyone else. It makes for a quick trip but it hurts like hell."

She nodded. She even managed to breathe a small sigh of relief. "So exactly how did Endelle send you into the Trough?"

"The same way you brought the statue into your hand earlier tonight. She just thought the thought."

"She must be powerful."

"You have no idea. Endelle is very old and should have ascended to an Upper Dimension long before this. She's the Supreme High Administrator for all of Second Earth."

"I have so many questions and you can answer them now, right? Unlike at the medical complex?"

He nodded. "Yes, because you answered your call to ascension."

Call to ascension. The words spun around in her head. So, she had done it. She had answered her "call to ascension." "So exactly what does this mean?"

He looked straight ahead and his voice dropped a notch

or two. "Once a mortal answers a call to ascension, he or she begins the rite of ascension, a period of time that lasts three days, no more, no less, during which the ascendiate, if powerful, is vulnerable to attack, just like what happened in the alley."

"So for the next three days I'll be attacked?"

He nodded slowly. "Probably, but that's why I'm here, to see you through."

She felt queasy but ignored the sensation. "What happens at the end of the three days?"

"There will be an ascension ceremony, probably conducted by Endelle—again because you are so powerful—during which time you will profess your loyalty to her and to Second Society. She will then give you the power of Second Earth, through her hands, by which you will be permanently ascended."

"And once I'm ascended, I won't be attacked."

"No. At least those are the rules. So far the Commander abides by the rules, although I'll apologize up front about this despicable 'trial period.' Once you're ascended, however, you won't be hunted like this. You'll take up your place in society in whatever way Endelle wants you to begin your service, and you'll be left alone."

Alison pondered what he'd said. "I guess what I don't understand is why Darian wants me dead. It makes no sense. It's not as though I'm a warrior or any kind of real threat to him."

When he didn't answer right away, she glanced at him. His jaw flexed several times like he was grinding his teeth.

"Tell me, Kerrick. I have a right to know."

He eased back on the gas, signaled then turned left onto a residential street. He parked beneath a spindly palo verde tree. He shut off the engine. "All right, here it is. We're at war, Alison, not a declared war like World War Two or anything like that but war nonetheless." He raked his fingers through his hair in the direction of the leather clasp. He rubbed his neck then sighed. "Darian Greaves, *your Darian*, has ambitions to rule two worlds. He's been developing an army for centuries made up of death vamps and ascenders alike. My warrior brothers and I battle death vamps every night as part of this ongoing war. We also serve as guardians to powerful ascendiates, which is what you are, a powerful ascendiate."

"So not all ascendiates are powerful—" She paused.

"Not at all, and the bottom line is that when an ascendiate has your level of power, he or she can by the nature of that power become useful to either Madame Endelle or Commander Greaves. It's kind of a tug-of-war for assets, albeit a deadly tug-of-war. And right now, you're considered an asset."

Alison held her hands together so tightly her fingers ached. She forced herself to relax and let her hands ease apart. "So then what exactly is a death vampire, the ones you battle?"

Kerrick's shoulders bunched. "An ascender who by any means partakes of *dying blood* is a death vampire. The drinking of dying blood creates all the features you saw at the medical complex: the blackening of the wings, the paling of the skin, the faint bluing of the skin, the beautifying of the face, as well as increased and quite superior physical strength."

Death vampires. Ascension.

Alison resumed breathing. One in. One out. "But once I've passed this trial period—"

"These three days," he said.

"Then I'm home-safe?"

"Yeah. That's the way it's set up."

She glanced out the side window, frowning. Why exactly had she answered her call to ascension? "I didn't know I was choosing war."

"You weren't choosing war," he stated emphatically. "Look at me."

She shifted her gaze to him.

"You were choosing a better life for yourself, a better fit. I know how powerful you are and I also know it must have

been hell for you trying to always hold back, always restrain yourself. When you ascend, you can be everything
you were meant to be. Try to remember that."

Alison stared into passionate green eyes glittering in the
dim light of the Nova. "I wanted to ascend." She put a hand
to the dip between her breasts. "I have felt such a yearning
here, in my heart, every day for weeks now. I know this is
the right path for me, but I didn't expect . . ." Her voice
broke. "And Darian was my . . . client. I cared for him. I
worried about him. All in vain, I guess."

"Well, shit," he muttered.

"That about sums it up."

Alison swiped at her cheeks, straightened her shoulders,
and took in a big solid breath. She unlatched her seat belt
then turned toward him.

As she met his gaze, the familiar and very crazy attraction she felt for him flowed through her once more. She
became painfully aware that he was only inches away from
her. He was huge and more than filled his side of her way-
too-small car. He shifted his gaze away from her, cleared
his throat, and this time he stared out his side window.

He looked uncomfortable, though she wasn't quite certain why.

"Okay," she said. "So tell me everything."

He nodded and, after drawing a deep breath, turned back
to her. He spoke for a long time about the structure of immortal earth, of ascending dimensions, to which individuals received a call. In her case the dreams she'd been having
as well as the sense of longing she had experienced were
her calls. He gestured a lot with his hands and more than
once dragged his fingers through his hair in the direction
of the leather clasp, until he undid the piece, refit all his
thick wavy hair, then secured the prong through the leather.
She didn't know long hair on a man could be so damn
sexy.

When he fell silent, she asked, "So what's with the vampire thing? I thought vampires were the undead."

He smiled, a slight crooked curve of his lips. "There's a huge difference between fictional vampirism and what exists in real-life, real-time ascending worlds."

Apparently.

"So you weren't always a vampire, before you ascended?"

He shook his head. He even smiled again. "No. Vampires aren't born to Mortal Earth. Vampiric traits are given during the ascension ceremony, traits such as increased physical power, sharpened vision and hearing, sometimes new unexpected powers, as well as fangs, in order to both take blood and to release chemicals into the blood and surrounding tissues. I know this must sound barbaric to you, but the experience of taking and receiving blood is revered on Second Earth."

She snorted. "Yeah, there was a lot of *reverence* going down at the Blood and Bite."

At that, he chuckled, a deep low rumble. The vampire had an amazing voice, a soft elegant bass, warm, rich. "You've got me there," he said. "I suppose it's like sex. It can give tremendous relief in stressful situations, like before a battle. Shared between husband and wife, yeah, *reverence* is the right word."

She stared at him. "Husband and wife?"

He seemed to fall inside himself as he said quietly, "My second wife and I shared blood. It was . . . a very fine experience." His expression dimmed, like the memories had pulled the shades down on all the windows. He also spoke in the past, and given his drive toward her, she thought it a fairly good guess that his wife was no longer living.

He drew out of himself in slow stages. She knew better than to hurry the process.

He flicked his thumb over the steering wheel and finally said, "As you already know, given events at your office complex, the blood ritual can be profoundly abused. Mortals and immortals alike can be drunk to death and often are. The most significant sign of this act you've seen already, the paling out and faint bluing of the skin."

She nodded. "He was beautiful."

"Yes." He shook his head. "A cruel irony."

"Why are these kinds of monsters allowed on Earth? I mean Mortal Earth?"

"It's not allowed. It's illegal and we work to contain them."

"So you, as a warrior, battle death vampires, as in, that's your job."

He nodded, staring straight ahead. "Yes. Myself and six other warriors. Warriors of the Blood. The problem is, the Commander—Darian Greaves, *your* Darian Greaves—has gone global in the last fifty years, and with the increase in Mortal Earth's population, the number of death vampires he and his allies can create has increased exponentially." He shook his head back and forth. "You don't really need to know this shit." He scowled and once more tapped the steering wheel.

Alison sat quietly, her thoughts tumbling inward. Ascension. Ascending dimensions. An entire world adjacent to Earth. Mortal Earth. *Mortal Earth.* Mortal. Earth.

All the vampire lore she had ever heard sped through her mind. She had read Bram Stoker's version. She watched *True Blood*. But this was real and apparently something she would become if she kept going down this road.

Alison Wells. Vampire. She shivered suddenly.

"You okay?" he asked, not looking at her. His thumb again tapped the steering wheel, slower now, a dull thud in the confined space.

"Sure," she said. "I'm sitting next to a vampire and if I follow this path to a logical conclusion, I'll grow a pair of fangs myself."

He glanced at her, his features solemn. "You're doing fine."

"You know, you have the most beautiful voice."

His smile emerged once more.

He looked incredible in the weapons harness and black kilt. Her fingers itched to slide her hands under all that leather. She glanced at his legs and noticed the twitching of his thighs.

"You're jumpy, too."

"Kind of," he said, his voice rough. "In a different way." Once more, he looked out his side window and drew in a series of long, deep breaths.

"And if you don't mind my saying, you have the most wonderful . . . *scent* . . . like cardamom."

He nodded, yet he still wouldn't look at her.

She laid a hand on his arm. "Thank you for getting me out of the alley."

He jerked, stiffened, then relaxed. When she withdrew her hand, thinking she might have offended him, he caught it and pressed it back in place.

"You're very welcome." He took another deep breath. "But I need you to know a couple of things."

"Okay."

"First, I want to explain about earlier at the club. I was caught up in what is a rare experience called the *breh-hedden*. I was crazed when I went after you, but I wouldn't have hurt you."

"I know that."

"You do?" He glanced at her, relief in his eyes.

She nodded.

"Good. And I'm going to do my best not to let it happen again."

"Okay." She became acutely aware of his hand covering hers and his thick muscled arm beneath her palm.

"So it's the 'bray' something?"

"The *breh-hedden*." He spelled it for her. "An old expression from a language no longer much in use, just the occasional term or phrase."

"What is it exactly?"

"First, it's rare, very rare, but presents itself as an almost impossible drive where the man feels a need to possess a woman sexually, to protect her as well as to exchange blood and to engage the mind in a very deep way, to be in the other's mind."

"You're not talking about telepathy."

"No. Something much deeper. Mind-engagement, sometimes called mind-diving."

"Does it have to be all three?" She didn't want to say them aloud. It all seemed so personal, so intimate: blood, sex, and the mind.

"To complete the *breh-hedden,* yes, all three, all at once, both parties, at the same time."

Alison released a long breath. The thought of being so fully joined to another person, to a man, possibly the man sitting next to her, made it difficult to draw the next breath. She swallowed . . . hard. "So, the attraction I feel for you is part of the *breh-hedden.*"

"Yes, but I hope you can just forget about it."

"Kerrick," she whispered, her face tingling, her breaths shallow, desire flowing. "I don't think I can."

He turned toward her and met her gaze. "Oh, God, you smell like lavender."

"I do?"

He nodded. "Alison, listen. I'm hanging on by a thread here. This *experience* is powerful, like almost everything that occurs on Second." He gently slid her hand off his arm. "So you would be really wise not to touch me again, to do what you can to resist this *attraction.*"

Alison felt completely and utterly trapped between a desire to move forward and an urgent need to restrain herself as she always had, to make certain she didn't hurt the man beside her. For a split second she wanted to run home, pull the covers over her head, and stay there, like forever. On the other hand, ever since she'd thrown the hand-blast into the air, something deep inside her had shifted and changed. She would never again return to the safety of her simple, *lonely,* cloistered life. For the first time in a long time, perhaps *ever,* she felt like she was coming alive.

Her breaths sat high on her chest. She needed to know something important—whether she could be with this man, this vampire, and not hurt him. The level of his powers gave her hope, but could he handle who she was?

She put her hand back on his arm and watched his lips part and his chest rise. He turned to meet her gaze. She overlaid his mind with a question. *Would you do me a favor?*

He didn't hesitate, not for a second, as he sent, *Anything, beautiful one.*

What a perfect response.

Aloud, she asked, "Would you kiss me, Kerrick?"

A dream brought to life is more precious than gold,
But beware the price.

—*Collected Proverbs*, Beatrice of Fourth

CHAPTER 10

Thorne whipped his phone from the pocket of his kilt, ran his thumb over the strip, then wiped his forehead with his arm. The sweat ran. As it should. He'd been battling on and off for hours. His muscles twitched, a couple of them screaming for relief.

"Central."

"Hey, Jeannie. We've got a mess for you to clean up at the Superstitions." He stood with his back to a wall of cliffs. The land in front of him was lit by starlight and strewn with unfriendly cacti and the bodies and feathered debris of slain enemy . . . the usual.

Luken sat nearby, his hands planted in the dirt behind him, which enabled him to lean back. Horace tended a deep sword cut on his thigh. The warrior didn't flinch as the healer held the wound closed and murmured soft prayer-like intonations. Jesus, that had to hurt.

"How many, *duhuro*?" Jeannie asked.

"Hey, what's with you and the *duhuro* shit?" His hands shook and he felt like his entire chest cavity was on fire.

Jeannie chuckled. "Just showin' the love, boss."

"Yeah, but you haven't used that expression in, what, the last how many years? What gives?"

"Thought it needed a comeback."

"You know what Medichi says, don't you?"

"About *duhuro*? Yeah. He says it means 'slave' but we know different."

"Whatever." But he laughed.

Jeannie's throaty chuckle rippled through the line as well. What would they do without the women at Central?

"By the way, why are you still working?" He glanced down and kicked at a small rock.

"Carla had a date."

"That Militia Warrior again?" His gaze scanned the horizon, ever-seeking. Dawn, unfortunately, was still a couple of hours away, and since death vamps preferred to hunt at night he'd be stuck out here for a while.

"Yeah. She's really into him. He's six-four, two sixty, all muscle, just like you warriors."

"Well, you just make sure he treats her right. If he doesn't, you know where to find me."

He heard a very deep sigh. "Aye-aye, *duhuro*. So, what kind of numbers are we talkin' about at the Superstitions right now?"

"Twenty-three."

"Holy shit. At least you got 'em all."

"Amen to that." Sweat once more rolled down his face, dribbled off his nose. He folded a washcloth from his house in Sedona Two and scrubbed his face. "Luken got sliced across his left quad. I had to bring Horace in to do his healing magic."

"Ouch. Tell him to feel better."

Thorne just grunted. He heard a series of taps on the screen, then Jeannie came back on line. "Cover your peepers."

Thorne called out to Luken and Horace, who both closed

their eyes. A flash of light and this time a faint rumbling. Twenty-three was a big number.

When the light disappeared, Thorne looked around. All the carnage had vanished. Thank God for technology. It wasn't so long ago he and Luken would have spent part of each night doing the large folding work themselves, which wasn't too bad. But on-the-ground debris work was one helluva job: dropped weapons, body parts, feathers, you name it.

For some reason his knees went watery and he sat down on the ground. "Thanks, Jeannie."

"You headed over to the Convent later?"

"What do you mean?" *How does she know?*

"You always do about dawn."

"I do?" Jesus. Had he been so obvious? He needed to break up his routine, although the thought of anything preventing him from going where he needed to go tied his stomach into a double knot. A visit to the Convent had become part of his survival strategy.

"Hey. Everyone knows you're worried about your sister. How's she doin'?"

Oh, yeah. His sister. "She's the same. Excessively devoted."

"Convent," Jeannie murmured. He could feel her shudder.

"I hear ya. Horace is just about finished. Holler if you need me."

"Always do."

Thorne thumbed his phone and remained sitting on the ground, his forearms resting on bent knees, his leather kilt hanging low. He reached out with his senses, but didn't detect any shift in the airwaves or cooling of temps. He sniffed the air. Only the sharp smell of the desert returned.

He glanced at the tall, thin healer, his head bent over Luken's thigh, his hand on the wound, his brow furrowed. A faint glow emanated from the area he worked. Luken leaned back on his palms, his expression disinterested. After a few centuries, what was one deep cut? After all, the artery hadn't been hit.

"How you doin', Luken?"

"What? Oh, fine. I was just thinking how beautiful the desert is at night. Just listen to the quiet, and shit, those stars are something else. You don't see them like that near the city. And I love the smell. Like sage, I guess."

Leave it Luken to marvel at the work of the Creator after having been flayed like a fish.

A few seconds more and Horace drew upright. Luken rose to his feet as well, shook out both legs, then stomped around. "Horace, you are a fucking genius." He faced the healer then clamped his hands on both shoulders. "As always, thank you, my man."

Horace looked up at him and smiled. "My pleasure." When Luken's arms returned to his sides, Horace bowed, an absurd sign of respect, which the warriors couldn't seem to train him out of. He bowed to Thorne as well, lifted an arm, then vanished.

Luken moved to stand in front of Thorne. *"Jefe?"*

"Yeah?" Thorne looked up. Luken's legs and shin guards were spattered with blood. He rubbed his hand along the scar by his thumb, savoring the feel of the ridges, thankful he still had all five digits intact.

Luken shook his head. "Twenty-three of those bastards and I almost bought it."

Thorne's throat tightened. "I know."

"Thanks for having my back."

Thorne just shook his head. The interior of his chest still burned like a sonofabitch. He wanted his Ketel. Now.

Kerrick looked into blue eyes, which were little more than a soft glitter in the darkened car. The smell of lavender rushed at him, bathed him, worked his senses into a frenzy.

So she wanted him to kiss her. She wanted to open that door.

Goddamn *breh-hedden.*

His vows rushed at him and his heart pitched south. Memories ripped through him, of a lost village twelve hundred years ago, of Marta, his first wife, and her torn-up, drained body. Fast-forward several centuries—Helena and their two children vaporized in an explosion. And during all those twelve hundred years, he had battled with a sword every day and every day he took life again and again. Christ. Before the sun had even set this evening he'd battled four death vamps and sent them to perdition.

"I kill, Alison. That's what I do."

He heard her heart rate increase. She couldn't disguise such a reaction, and still she said, "You are a warrior."

He nodded. "I am a warrior. I've also taken vows. I will not marry again."

He heard a slight intake of breath then a slow release of air. "I never thought to marry in the course of my life." Her voice was little more than a whisper.

He turned toward her, shifting in the too small seat. "Why not?"

"I hurt a man once. I . . ." She lifted her chin. "I almost killed him."

He checked the growl forming in his throat. "Did he hurt you? Was that why?"

She shook her head then winced. "He got hurt because of who I am. When I asked you to kiss me, I wanted to know if—" She looked away.

"You're worried you'll hurt me."

She nodded and her gaze fell to her lap. "I know what it is to take a vow. It's just that it would be really nice . . . once . . . to know I could kiss a man, be with a man without hurting him."

"You wouldn't hurt me," he stated.

"So you say."

He really shouldn't open this door. His vows spun around in his head, slamming against the inside of his skull, but she was next to him and she had said words he said to himself. *They get hurt because of who I am.*

Jesus. He knew exactly how she felt.

He struggled to remember all the reasons to refuse her. He knew the right reasons were there, he just couldn't find his rational thoughts, not one of them. Besides, he wanted to do this for her. He wanted her to know that although many things had been impossible for her here on Mortal Earth, it was only because she needed to ascend, to be with a man on Second Earth, someone like him, a powerful vampire who could take all she had to give.

The thought of all her power did him in, what it would be like to have her under him, to be connected to her, his cock buried deep, his fangs in her neck, his mind drifting through hers. He wanted it all.

He sent the question softly into her mind, *You sure about this?*

Uh-huh, she responded, her telepathic abilities just about perfect. "We could start with one kiss," she suggested, "and if it doesn't work out . . ."

Like hell it won't work out.

She sighed. *That's what I'm hoping.*

He turned toward her. His rib cage hit the steering wheel. He could hardly move his knees, the car was so damn small.

He tried to relax but his body was a cauldron. He gripped her arms and hauled her against his chest. He kissed her fiercely, claiming at least her lips, imprinting that much of his body onto her memory.

Oh, God, she parted her lips.

He drove his tongue hard, taking possession of her mouth, maybe too hard because she pulled back then twisted sideways out of his arms. He was about ready to apologize, but she shifted a little then tucked herself against him so that her head now rested in the well of his shoulder. *Oh, she was just getting more comfortable.* She even slung an arm around his neck. Yeah, the car was small and they both had to adjust.

He slid his palm over the back of her head, caressing. The silky strands drifted over his fingers.

"Kiss me again," she murmured.

He bent over her and kissed her as though he'd never had his tongue in a woman's mouth before. He searched every crevice, rimmed her teeth, her lips, and battled her tongue. He couldn't get enough.

Desire roared through him.

God help him.

Little moans escaped her as she trembled in his arms.

Was he hurting her? "Are you okay?" he asked, his voice trimmed with rough bark.

She moaned softly. "Yes, yes. God, yes. I'm not hurting *you,* am I?"

"Not even a little. I promise you, I can take whatever you've got."

She whimpered then lowered her head back to his shoulder and once more he took her mouth. Her hand slid over his shoulder and down his arm, squeezing, gripping, savoring his muscles. He loved it but man . . .

He pulled back in utter agony.

"Do more of that," she whispered. She slid her fingers lightly over the back of his hand. Damn, he was pawing her breast through the soft cotton T-shirt. He glanced around at the neighborhood. The hour was late, the night dark, but just in case, he created a complex mist around the car. Any mortal looking in their direction would experience confusion and it would be as though the car didn't even exist.

Was he really going to do this? He should stop now, so help him. However, his willpower had vanished. It had been too long. Too fucking long.

He pushed her sweater aside, pulled her top up then her bra down. Her soft warm flesh felt like heaven against his hand. She had an idea of her own as she rose up then arched over him, her breast pressed to his cheek.

Oh, yeah.

He turned, settled his mouth on her lavender-drenched breast, and suckled until her body undulated against his. He wanted to use his fangs. Oh, God, how he wanted to use his fangs. He wanted to sink them deep and make her come. He growled heavily, which caused her to throw a leg in his direction. Unfortunately, she hit her knee on the dashboard and cried out.

He drew back and looked at her. "This car is too damn small," he said. "Are you okay?"

She nodded until her gaze fell to his lips. She gasped. His fangs had emerged. Dammit.

She drew back. "Maybe this wasn't such a good idea," she whispered, leaning back into her seat, her gaze fixed to his mouth. The waves of lavender receded.

He winced and closed his eyes. He had no choice. Had to rein himself in but the dam had broken. He ached in his groin like he'd just gotten kicked.

He took deep breaths, a lot of them, until his fangs retreated. "You're right. This wasn't such a good idea. Let's get you home. Where to?"

"I live in Carefree."

He nodded several more times. "On the way you can ask me more questions." He met her gaze.

She finally looked into his eyes. "This is real, isn't it?"

"Yes."

"Vampire."

"Yes."

She shifted her gaze to the windshield. "Oh. What am I looking at? I saw it earlier at the club."

He touched the ignition and started the engine. He growled his frustration. He was a starving vampire sitting next to a nine-course meal and forbidden to eat. He waved a hand and dispelled his creation. "We call it mist."

"How does it work?"

He glanced at her. "Well, for ordinary mortals and most Second ascenders, mist is designed to confuse the mind. For instance, if a mortal walked by right now, his mind would simply glance past the car as though the vehicle wasn't even there. But I take it you can see it."

She nodded.

"What do you see?"

"Like cobwebs sort of, but more like a really beautiful intricate yet loose mesh. And white. It's white."

He shook his head and chuckled. "That's amazing. That's what I see as well, and my warrior brothers see the same. But up until this moment, I've never had an ascendiate capable of detecting the physical composition of mist."

She put her seat belt back on. She fell silent. No doubt she was feeling overwhelmed—and why wouldn't she? This was a lot of information to take in.

He turned the car around and headed in the direction of I-10.

Silence reigned for a good long while. He gave her time. Finally, she asked, "So what prompted you to leave the little black-and-red invitation at my feet?"

He shook his head. "I hated leaving you in such despair. I thought, maybe, if you were in the middle of your call, it would help."

"I guess it did because here I am."

"Here you are."

"So why the Blood and Bite? Couldn't you have just invited me to a Starbucks or something?"

He chuckled. Oh, God help him if she made him laugh. He tended to fall hard for a woman who had a sense of humor.

"You know that club is really sexist."

He glanced at her and smiled. "Tell me honestly, down the road, if you and I had never met, do you think you might have gone back?"

He sensed her sudden discomfort, but when a rush of lavender wafted beneath his nose he had his answer.

She shrugged. "Well, okay, maybe. Once. Just to see what it was like."

"The women who go there enjoy themselves."

"And those *warriors* enthrall the women."

"In part. Try to think of it as a shortcut to the usual seduction. It's really not much different."

"We're talking levels of power. It *is* different."

"Except for one small thing. A woman has to be *willing* to be enthralled. Period."

"Oh." She was silent for a moment then asked, "And have you found most women *willing*?"

He glanced at her. He saw the challenge in her eye. Honesty might serve him in more ways than one, and he saw no reason to yield to a lie. "Yes."

She looked away from him. He could guess her thoughts, especially since he couldn't detect even the smallest trace of lavender shedding from her body right now. Good. If she found him disgusting, like maybe she thought of him as a sexist pig, then she'd leave him alone.

"Are any of the warriors married?"

"None of the Warriors of the Blood but a high percentage of Militia Warriors take wives . . . or husbands. We do have women who serve as Militia Warriors."

"So there's a difference between the two groups?"

"Unfortunately there's a big difference. There are only seven Warriors of the Blood, but across the world there are hundreds of thousands of Militia Warriors. The militia serves as a peacekeeping force, sort of like your National Guard, but with many of the same duties as regular police officers, you know, handling disturbances, theft, home invasion, domestic disputes, homicides, the usual."

"And the Warriors of the Blood?"

"We mostly serve Endelle fighting death vampires as a unit here in this part of the world."

"I'm not sure I understand. Death vampires only reside in the Phoenix area? No other place in the world?"

He shook his head. "Not at all. There are death vampires in every territory, every country on Second Earth. Militia Warriors all around the world battle death vampires but only in large units, since it takes at least *four* Militia Warriors to bring down *one* death vamp. As for the Warriors of the Blood, we're here as a layer of protection for Endelle, which tells you why the Commander keeps rounding up death vamps from other continents and shipping them to battle us. If he can break our ranks, put us in our graves, then he can break Endelle and her administration."

"Seven men against one man who appears to command an army of death vampires? How does that work?"

"It didn't used to be so bad but with the explosion of the population of Mortal Earth and the increased number of ascensions that occur on all seven continents of the world, the number of conscienceless ascendiates, ready and willing to drink dying blood, has increased as well. We're a little overworked at present, and the number of Militia Warriors who die each year is heartbreaking."

She shook her head. "Which leads me back to my original question—the Warriors of the Blood don't marry?"

"I guess we got off topic but the answer is, rarely."

"Why?"

The question pierced him straight through the heart. His memories of Helena and his children surfaced yet again. "It's just too damn dangerous. Not for the warrior, but for those he loves."

Alison held her arms around her sides like a vise. Her fingers plucked at her sweater. Chills kept running through her even though she wasn't cold.

She fixed her gaze out the window and watched a blur of streetlights and old worn-out houses go by. How long since she had spoken? She glanced around. They were approaching I-10. That long, then.

Her thoughts had become a stormy sea, the waves high, a lot of crashing surf. She couldn't seem to make sense of what was happening to her, the mind being a limited thing and only able to absorb so much.

Then there was the continued onslaught of Kerrick's massive presence in her car, the lingering erotic male scent of him, his nearness, and the temptation of touching him at will . . .

She drew in a long shaky breath.

"You've grown quiet." His deep voice filled the car and once more battered her senses.

"A lot to think about." She shifted toward him. "What was your rite of ascension like?"

Did he just shudder? Great.

"Every ascension is different. You can't compare the two."

"Try me."

"You don't want to know."

"Yeah. I do. I need answers, Warrior."

His gaze snapped to hers then back to the on-ramp.

When he'd merged into the light early-morning traffic, he said, "Well, I was a wild beast, full of rage. I still am when I think about what happened. The death vamps raped and drained my wife, Marta, my mortal wife, my first wife. She was dead before I found her. My son Evan, not a month old, was fussing in his cradle but alive.

"My ascension involved abandoning my son that same day. Once I completed the ceremony, I went on a rampage, killing and then more killing until I'd found every last one of those bastards who had essentially destroyed my family."

Alison felt the depth of his pain. He remembered those days or weeks as though they were yesterday. A wife raped, a son abandoned. Jesus. "You ever wish it undone? Your ascension?"

He nodded. "I would undo it for Evan's sake. I hate that I left him. I still think about him, hurt for him, wish I'd thought of him instead of my need for vengeance. I think abandonment is one of the worst things you can do to a child. You don't have children, do you?"

Alison shook her head, even laughed. "Not possible."

"You mean you can't have children?"

She glanced at him. "As far as I know I can. I was referring to the *power* thing I was talking about earlier. Every year, my power kept getting stronger, and by the time I was in my late twenties, well, I couldn't be with a man anymore, not without . . . causing damage."

"I'm not surprised," he murmured.

Alison needed to change the subject . . . fast. "If I ascend, do I have to leave my family behind? Is that one of the rules?"

"Every ascender's situation is different. Some are happy to leave Mortal Earth and never look back. Those who want to sustain the connection to loved ones face a variety of dilemmas. For one thing, every visit requires a pass, as well as counseling.

"The greater dilemma becomes the nature of immortality. Once ascended, you have the potential of living *forever*. Each day that passes in which you do not age creates a problem for your family, your friends on Mortal Earth. As the decades wear on eventually a separation becomes not just necessary but sensible. And of course, there's always the matter that we keep our world hidden from mortals, hence the counseling."

Alison couldn't imagine saying good-bye forever to her parents, to her brother, to Joy, to little T. J., even to Joy's husband, Ryan. Her heart ached just thinking about it.

"Hey," he said quietly. "The best thing to do is to take this one step at a time. Let's get you ascended first."

She nodded, staring straight ahead. "Good idea."

After a few minutes, as he merged onto the 51 now heading north, the more pressing aspects of her current predicament shook the foundations of her mind all over again. A shiver rolled through her. "So," she ventured into the stillness, "what are the odds I'm even going to make it through the night?"

"I'm right here," Kerrick said. "It's my job to see you through this. The warriors will help. And Endelle."

She thought of Darian, of having counseled him for the past year. What had he meant by it, by being in such close proximity to her all that time but not lifting a finger against her? It didn't make sense.

"Why didn't Darian—the Commander—take my life when he had the chance? I saw him every week for a year."

His thumbs once more drummed the steering wheel. "Again, we have certain rules we have to abide by. An ascender isn't fair game until he or she has answered the call to ascension. Endelle would have had the right to demand a trial to prosecute Greaves if he'd harmed you. But that law works both ways. Endelle, all of us, have to be careful how we do our jobs."

He scowled. "But I'll tell you what *I* really don't get. Do you see that car in front of us? That's a BMW M3 with a four-liter, V-8 engine, some of the best handling in the world, and the driver is going fifty-two fucking miles an hour!"

The warrior next to her was irritated at how a mortal drove a car?

Alison jerked forward and laughed, which helped a lot. In this moment, the vampire next to her seemed so, well, normal.

Warrior Kerrick, however, was not amused. "You think that's funny?" He changed lanes, sped by the BMW as fast as he could in a car that started to shake. He eased back to fifty-five so that her Nova could relax.

"I take it you're not the patient type, are you?"

"I have no patience for someone driving a car that could easily fly at a hundred miles an hour."

Alison shrugged. "Think about it, Warrior. At this hour of the morning, the driver could easily be drugged out or drunk off his ass. Slower would be better."

He grunted but still wore his scowl.

"Okay. You've told me a lot of bad stuff about Second Earth. So now tell me what's so great about ascension? I'm not exactly *feeling the love.*"

When he didn't speak right away, she shifted to look at him. "Having a hard time answering the question?"

Once more his head wagged and his thumb tapped the steering wheel. "It's just been so long since I've stopped to think about it. Well, you'll never have to worry about gum disease."

"What?" She barked her laughter.

"Hey. It can be a real issue." But a smile played at the edges of his mouth. "We don't have diseases on Second. It's awesome. No tooth decay or hangnails or goddamn cancer. You can smoke 'til you puke and you'll never get sick. We don't age. When we get a cut or a bruise, we heal fast. We're not completely immortal, though. Decapitations will end a life, strangulation, explosions."

"Terrific."

He shrugged, as in, *Get used to it.* But he continued, "And you'll never see more beautiful gardens than on Second. Horticulture is the highest form of art."

"Huh. Sort of like the Garden of Eden."

"Pretty close, but with paled-out, blue-tinged death vampires just to keep things interesting."

Her turn to shrug. "There's always a stinger on one of the insects."

He glanced at her then looked away. "What else? Oh . . . God . . . *spectacle*. If you like a good fireworks display, or flags, or squadrons of DNA-altered geese or swans, you'll think you've died and gone to heaven. If there's a chance to celebrate in an open-air arena or outdoor amphitheater, Second will proclaim a goddamn holiday. Think Cirque du Soleil meets Beijing."

She narrowed her eyes. "So when was the last time you attended a *spectacle*?"

Once more his eyes stared out unblinking.

"That's what I thought. You need to have more fun, Warrior."

Apparently this was not the right thing to say. His jaw worked back and forth like he intended to pulverize his molars. "I'm usually a little busy at night . . ." The air in the car cooled about twenty degrees. "And I sleep during the day."

She couldn't help herself. "In a coffin?"

"Oh, you're hilarious, ascendiate."

But Alison laughed.

Okay. So that was something she could work on—Kerrick needed to loosen up.

But even as the thought sped through her brain she stopped herself. What was she thinking? Oh, she knew what she was thinking. The vampire next to her was some really awesome boyfriend material. Given the nature of his life right now, how great would it be to lighten him up a little, give him some ease?

Okay, so she was way ahead of herself.

She decided to switch the subject. "Tell me more about Madame Endelle—a name, by the way, that makes me think of a psychic you'd find working her trade in downtown Phoenix, or Sedona, maybe."

He chuckled. "I think you're right." But then he frowned. "Endelle is complicated. The thing is, she's a real piece of work but I'd give my life for her. She's the Supreme High

Administrator of Second Earth and she's basically sacrificed everything to keep this world in order. She's been around a very long time, more than nine millennia."

She whipped back to stare at him. "Nine thousand years?" Her breath caught in her throat and once more she felt dizzy.

"Why not?" he asked. "If I exist, if you exist with all your unbelievable powers, why not immortality?"

"You're right. Of course." But she felt like she'd taken a serious blow to the head.

"Her name is interesting. Endelle. She's also known as She Who Would Live. Both names reflect her birth name. The only person who can pronounce the original version is Thorne. It involves three clicks or something. Every once in a while I'll hear him let loose with it and think a cricket climbed into his mouth."

She just looked at him. She knew he meant to distract her with his innocuous explanation of Endelle's name, but for some reason *nine thousand years* had sunk her. Her chest folded up a little more.

"You said a decision is involved. So this means I can still choose *not* to ascend."

He kept glancing at her, probably debating just how much he should say. Finally, he said in a quiet voice, "Theoretically, you can decline. With your level of power, however, the Commander won't let you go very easily, if at all."

"Oh."

She felt a sudden pressure on her mind. She glanced at Kerrick and knew he wanted inside her head, not just mere telepathic conversation, but that deep kind of mind-engagement he'd talked about earlier.

She didn't debate long. After all, he ought to know the level of her confusion. *Nine thousand years.* Vampires. She suddenly felt like she was swimming underwater. Even her hearing seemed distorted, so she let him in.

When he dipped inside her mind, however, it was the strangest sensation, a powerful connection that made her gasp.

He drew out almost as quickly. "Shit," he murmured. "I know this has been too much but this isn't exactly my best skill set, so how about we change the subject. Why don't you tell me something about yourself?"

She looked at him then blinked.

"Are you okay?"

She blinked again. Finally, she said, "What would you like to know?"

He released a small sigh. "Have you lived in Phoenix long?"

"I was born here."

"Do you have family?"

"Yes, I have a brother and a sister. My sister is married. She recently had a baby and I just found out she's pregnant again." She thought back to her conversation with Joy. Only a few hours had passed, not even twelve, yet she felt as though she had just lived an entire lifetime.

"Parents?"

"They're both doing well. Dad's a cop and Mom has worked part-time at the Fry's deli ever since I can remember."

"What do you like to do for fun?"

"I love books of all kinds. I can't get enough. I'm hopeless in a bookstore."

The fatigue of the night seemed to settle into her bones and right now she wished herself out of the whole situation. Unfortunately, if Kerrick was right, it was way too late for regrets.

He glanced at her again. "Hey, I have an idea. Why don't you rest for a bit while I drive you home? You must be exhausted."

"I couldn't. Not after all this."

"I can help. First, tell me where we're going."

She gave straightforward instructions in a flat voice.

They were well along the 51 now, still heading north, almost to the 101. He mentally sent her a powerful sleep suggestion and she grasped it tightly, like she was drowning and he'd just thrown her a life preserver.

She yawned. *I like you in my head.*

I like being there.

And he was there as he had been a few minutes ago, more than just telepathy, more like a shared presence, at least for a moment. Then he withdrew, leaving a great deal of peace behind. She closed her eyes.

Crace was living a nightmare. Still, like any good High Administrator, he had gone on the offensive the moment Leto folded back to the war room. Chaos had reigned for the past forty-five minutes. All the generals shouted, and Crace shouted back. Chairs had been knocked around, phones rang, monitors flickered. If someone had folded a gun into the room, shots would have been fired.

The argument had waged for some time now. Fortunately Crace knew how to do verbal battle, how to spin the spin. "You stand there and blame me, General Leto? I gave you a simple assignment. Wait at the Borderland, take out Kerrick then the ascendiate. How hard could that have been? You had twelve death vampires with you. I only left the command center for nine minutes and"—here he used his most powerful voice with seven-split resonance and added telepathy for the entire room—*"you fucked it up."*

Several of the officers fell on their knees, holding their heads in their hands. Telepathy coupled with the spoken word was a powerful weapon against lesser minds. Throw in a little preternatural resonance and just about everyone caved. A few moans went around the room. Hands shook. Not Leto's, though. Jesus, the vampire had power yet he had still failed to take out Warrior Kerrick and the ascendiate.

Leto narrowed his eyes. "I will say it again: Madame Endelle dumped Warrior Kerrick into the Trough right in the middle of the battle. We lost four fucking minutes since we had to float down in the usual way. By the time we reached the alley, Warrior Kerrick had ascendiate Wells in a car, a goddamn car, and into the street, and you know damn well none of us could have dematerialized to a moving vehicle.

And mounting wings is illegal. We couldn't give pursuit and you know it."

"You should have anyway!" Crace shouted. "And the fuck if I will listen to any more of your excuses." Leto was right, of course. Once Kerrick took off in the car, the opportunity vanished. No one he knew could fold to a moving vehicle, and vampires in full-mount and in flight on Mortal Earth were easily detected by Central's fucking grid. Warrior Thorne would have been called, and the bastard would have been within his fucking rights to send a regiment of Militia Warriors after the offender.

Militia Warriors weren't anywhere near as powerful as the weakest death vampire, but enough of them could get the job done. On top of that, COPASS would have been required to prosecute the Commander despite how much control Greaves had over the Committee. Given time, he would have more control, but for now, what a shitfest.

Still, Leto pressed his point. "All we needed was the same boost to Mortal Earth and we would have had her." His face darkened and his voice altered as he employed the same dangerous shouting-combined-with-telepathy Crace had. *"And I'll ask again, where the hell were you?"*

Crace's knees buckled—so, yeah, Leto had power—but he didn't fall. More groans erupted throughout the war room. The only problem Crace had now was his inability to hear out of his right ear. His head throbbed.

However, this situation, and his nine minutes with his wife, would not sit well with the Commander. He was merely fronting in a room loaded with testosterone, something he had to do to save his ass. Greaves was a different story. His bowels turned to water at the thought of facing him.

"General Leto," a familiar velvet-on-steel voice intruded. The Commander was back from wherever the hell he'd been in his ongoing efforts to turn High Administrators. "You are too hard on our visitor. He did his best, I am sure. I beg you will apologize to High Administrator Crace. At once."

Leto bowed quickly from the waist. "I apologize, Mr. High Administrator."

"Good. We must all be friends for the Coming Order. Leto, continue if you will to monitor the dispatches from my *discretionary network*. I will confer with you later."

"Yes, Commander."

"Crace, come with me."

Crace squared his shoulders then moved quickly to follow the Commander from the War Room. Thank God his deity didn't speak because he still wasn't hearing properly out of his right ear, which was the ear facing the Commander. He reached out with his senses, probing Greaves's *feelings* ever so lightly. Nothing returned to him. Usually he could read any individual's state of being with a mere whisper of a thought, but the man beside him was a walking piece of steel . . . emotionally.

Once inside the Commander's office, Crace stood before the desk while Greaves once more took up his seat behind the ebony battleship. He smiled at Crace, his eyes cold. "You have always enjoyed your wife, have you not?"

Crace nodded. So the Commander knew. Jesus, how did he know?

"I do not suffer fools lightly."

"Of course not."

"You celebrated a little too early."

He nodded. "Yes, Commander."

"I will need you to sign a breach-of-promise form as well as a disclaimer against your life should anything befall you in the next few days. You will remain in Phoenix Two, of course."

"Of course, Commander." He wanted to fall on his knees and beg for a second chance. He'd been so foolish, yet his wife had called and said such things to him. She had shared his euphoria over the coming offer of a seat at the Round Table. Perhaps he could explain how his wife had seduced him. He dismissed the idea as ridiculous. He knew the Commander's temper extremely well. Any passing-of-the-buck would result in his nuts being held in a very tight grasp.

So . . . he waited.

"You have disappointed me, Crace."

"Yes, Commander." The fewer the words spoken, the better.

Greaves nodded. "I want you to contact COPASS. Set up a meeting with Harding. We will have need of the Committee's support in the coming hours. Harding will be desirous of a mortal female at this time. Provide one for him. Help him to understand our needs."

"Yes, Commander." The Committee. Of course. The word among the High Administrators who had joined Greaves's coalition was that the Commander had taken pains to work his magic with the various Committee members. To his knowledge, almost a third of them were now addicted to dying blood and making use of the antidote, that little concoction of Greaves's that prevented the acquiring of death vampire traits, especially the faint bluing of the skin. With more and more of the Committee under Greaves's thumb— including the chair, Daniel Harding—the Commander frequently had Endelle's legal complaints delayed and at times her court verdicts overturned. Harding's conversion had been a profound triumph for the Commander and in Crace's opinion the signal that the war had turned permanently in Greaves's direction. It wouldn't be much longer before the balance on all fronts would force Endelle's administration to collapse.

"As for our little project," the Commander said, "I want you to send a regiment to Carefree. You are familiar with what is there?"

A test. At least this one he could pass. "The ascendiate's private residence." He rattled off all the details he had memorized from the satellite photos until the Commander lifted a hand. Crace shut his vocal cords down with a quick snap of his jaws.

"Good. I have had word from my Seers Fortress in Singapore that the ascendiate will be in Carefree sometime within the next twenty-four hours. Have General Leto monitor the grid in the war room for the ascendiate's signature.

See to the destruction of both Warrior Kerrick and the ascendiate. And remember, we have one significant advantage— Warrior Kerrick cannot dematerialize. Do not hesitate to use the big guns. Get them both this time. Take the house down to rubble if you have to. I need this done. Do you understand?"

"Yes, master."

Crace admired his deity very much. An entire regiment was forbidden on Mortal Earth, which meant the Commander was relying on present influence with the Committee to get around these details.

His shoulders eased and he no longer felt like puking. A regiment would get the job done, which then explained the need to consult with Harding. The chair ought to be warned about what was going down.

Of course it occurred to him that the Commander, by using Crace, removed himself from any culpability in the matter. He didn't mind being cast as the fall guy because in this case, he knew he could get out of any situation he desired.

"You may go."

Crace did not wait. He bowed, turned on his heel, then strode as confidently from the room as he could. Once outside, with the door shut, the shaking started. Yes, the plan was excellent but the other matter! The disclaimer! Shit.

How quietly, how calmly the Commander made his threats. A *disclaimer* was essentially a suicide note. If anything went wrong, and Crace got offed, the Commander would simply offer the signed disclaimer to the Committee and the matter would be dropped.

Struggling to even breathe, he folded to his suite. The honor of being situated so close to Greaves's quarters now took on an entirely different meaning.

Okay. Get a grip. All is not lost.

He would set his strategy then return to the war room to deliver his next set of orders to the generals. Afterward, he would tend to the chairman of COPASS.

He and Harding had always gotten along, quite well.

Although he confessed he'd been shocked when he'd learned that Harding had for at least a year been in the habit of drinking dying blood. But he was also intrigued. As a hedonist, Crace had always wondered what the experience would *feel* like.

As he considered the Commander's new plan, hope resurfaced. Even a Warrior of the Blood was no match for a regiment and a rocket launcher. This he could do and no screwups. He no longer worried about a seat at the Round Table. How inconsequential that seemed compared with the preservation of his own sweet neck.

The odd thought rippled through his head, *How many times has a man fucked up his life because of a need to ejaculate?*

CHAPTER 11

Kerrick gripped the steering wheel hard and focused on the freeway. He drew a deep breath and tried to calm the hell down. The sloth inherent in Alison's Nova wasn't helping at all.

He had effected a very superficial pathway to sleep. He would need to use his hand in order to take Alison the rest of the way, but so help him if he made skin-to-skin contact one more time he didn't think he could be responsible for the outcome.

Despite the fact he'd controlled himself, his body roared with need for her, to make her his own, to stake his claim so thoroughly that every other immortal on Second would know she was off limits. Thank God it was dark. He was hard as a rock and had been since she'd parted her lips and he'd pushed his tongue into her mouth.

He cursed the *breh-hedden* then shifted his focus back to what she needed. He breathed again.

With one eye on the freeway, he overlaid her forehead with his hand. He sent the image of sleep past the first layer of her mind. Once again the power of her shields stunned him, but he kept working her mind until all resistance faltered. He pressed deeper and deeper until she released a heavy sigh and her head rolled to one side.

This was surely one of the most difficult experiences he'd ever known, wanting to touch this woman yet holding back, sort of like trying not to sneeze while inhaling black pepper. She was so beautiful and he could still taste the kiss and feel her body pressed up against his, the pleasure of suckling her breast. His veins hummed with the memory.

And her scent. The car smelled as if the lavender she shed had become locked onto every surface of the vehicle.

Of course, it wasn't helping to relive what had just happened, so he focused on just breathing, air in, air out.

Once in Carefree and parked on her crushed-granite driveway, he carried her into her house, past the living room and kitchen, all the way to the back of the house to what he supposed was the family room. He stretched her out on the couch then flipped on the lamp near the bookshelves. He stared at hundreds of books and yet again time stopped. Hemingway, Kingsolver, García Márquez. She had said she loved books. So she did and he had a library most mortals could only dream about, so many first editions because, well, he'd been collecting over a long period of time.

Great. Something in common. A shared passion.

He looked down at her. The *breh* pressured him, spikes in his chest. This woman was meant for him, designed for him, and he for her. She wouldn't hurt him with the power she released when she became aroused. He knew it in his bones.

The thought of her power coming at him while fully engaged . . . he weaved on his feet.

Shit.

He so didn't need this.

He turned his attention to the rest of the house. He

walked through each room, created a mist around the outside of the house.

Christ. If the Commander wanted her, what could stop him?

He doubled the mist.

He continued patrolling. He wasn't sure he'd done the wisest thing bringing her to Carefree. But then where exactly would she be safe given that her signature was strong enough to appear on the grid? Greaves could easily assign one of his minions to search localities until either of their signatures was located.

He felt confident, however, that he could handle any number of death vamp squads that showed up and he could always call his brothers for backup.

Beyond those considerations, the Carefree property was nicely located. The house sat on a good quarter acre and backed up to a wilderness of cacti, native desert shrubs, gullies and washes. He could do battle here, under a cloak of mist, without disturbing the neighbors.

An hour passed. Dawn wasn't far away now. If only vampires had the fictional quality of being *allergic* to the sun, then he could be at ease, because all ascenders would go to bed for the day. Death vampires did have a mild sensitivity to sunlight, but nothing serious. They could battle at high noon if necessary. A pair of Ray-Bans would keep them in business; a thick layer of sunscreen helped, too. Bastards.

He returned to the family room to look down at Alison again. His lips parted as he struggled to draw a decent breath. She was so damn beautiful.

His desire for her rose sharply . . . again. Fucking *breh-hedden*. He wanted to stretch out on top of her and, as she awakened, gently grind his hips into hers and bring her to a state of arousal to match his own.

Hell, maybe it wouldn't hurt to be with her, say, *just once*. After all, the completion of the *breh-hedden* involved a lot more than just sex. Minds had to merge—not just in telepathic conversation, but much deeper. At the exact same time, blood had to be shared, his and hers. Just one person making use of fangs wouldn't do it; both had to be engaged at the same time. So, yeah, an exchange of blood, deep mind sharing, and penetrating sex; all three activities had to occur *at exactly the same time* to complete the *breh-hedden*.

His body melted down as the image of engaging Alison in all three ways took hold of him.

Her blood . . . his mouth.

Her mind . . . his thoughts tunneling deep.

His cock buried inside her.

Her throat . . . his blood.

His mind . . . her thoughts taking possession.

Her body clenching around his shaft.

A soft chuff and a low growl broke from his chest. His abs tightened. His eyes burned. *Desire* seemed like such a small word.

Guilt followed as it always did, a rabid dog racing behind him and finding purchase on his neck. He shook his head from side to side. How could he move forward with his thoughts, with his *desire,* when he sucked at keeping those he loved alive? He was responsible for Alison now, to keep her safe during these treacherous three days of ascension.

And yet, he had to have at least part of her, a taste of her. He couldn't deny himself that much, even as paltry as it would be compared with completing the *breh*.

He didn't understand all the forces that had brought him to this place, here and now, staring down at a woman built for him in every possible way.

He thought of Thorne and his despair. Of all his brothers-in-arms and the lack of women in their lives.

They all needed this, some kind of connection, an anchor in stormy seas, which a woman could provide.

Okay, he knew he was rationalizing, but he'd come to a decision. He would have this woman, at least in part. Here. Now.

His heart once more slammed against his ribs.

He knelt beside the couch, moved in close, and dipped

his face into her neck. He breathed in her fragrant skin, her intoxicating lavender. She had asked *why* vampirism? As he thought about driving his thoughts deep, sinking his fangs, and plunging into her, *he* knew why. He knew what it would be like with her, to take her fully, his body, mind, and blood engaged, the oneness, the connection.

Hunger swamped him, a tidal wave, relentless, powerful, demanding. He craved her.

Alison, he sent, drawing her out of sleep. He drew back, unbuckled his weapons harness, and slid it off his shoulders. He laid it carefully on the adjacent love seat. He removed his *cadroen* and set his long warrior hair free.

Alison opened her eyes, her mind loose, her vision unfocused. Her head felt stuffed with cotton. She looked up at some kind of ceiling. The room was dark except for the dim light from one nearby lamp. Something heavy, though not unpleasant, rested on her stomach. Warm puffs of air teased her neck and raked shivers down the right side of her body.

Weird. Maybe she was still dreaming.

After a long moment, the ceiling took better shape and she recognized the texture pattern of her home in Carefree. Oh, she was home . . . in Carefree.

So, how did she get here?

Where had she been? Why was her mind so unfocused? Oh, yeah. The alley, falling men, a bomb, and her Nova. Oh, God. Kerrick.

He had kissed her like he needed to explain to her in precise detail just what kinds of things made up a real kiss. Then she had seen his fangs, and her mind had started unraveling.

On the way home, he'd put his hand on her forehead and she had drifted into the most beautiful, peaceful sleep.

She blinked a couple more times and came fully awake. Kerrick's arm rested on her stomach and he was suckling the right side of her neck. A wicked streak of desire flowed from the point of his lips all the way down her body. She slid her hands into his thick black hair, now loose around his bare shoulders. Without thinking, she slipped into his mind, bypassing his shields, and going beyond the level of mere telepathic communication. *She was inside his head.*

She retreated, shocked. Her vampire warrior was in a state of full arousal, his mind a tornado of need and desire. He had told her something had hold of him, *breh-hedden.* Evidently. He gave off heat in waves.

I need you, he sent, his deep voice saturating her mind, like water soaking into thirsty ground. *I want you, to be inside you, to have your blood in me.*

She rasped a heavy breath. *My blood in you?*

I won't hurt you.

He wanted to take her vein. *I know you won't. I can see into your soul,* vampire. *You have a golden heart.*

The words once conveyed to his mind seemed so inadequate to express what she had seen in him: his dedication to Second Earth, his perfect submission to Endelle, his love for his warrior brothers, his desire to do the right thing, always, his desperate guilt.

How could she resist a man she could admire like this?

He sighed and kissed her neck. "I love that you were inside my head, but I can't believe you pushed past my shields and I didn't even know it! Damn, what power."

"You couldn't tell I was there?"

"No, which means you must have abilities like Endelle. She can do that, too."

"And you don't mind?"

"Truth? I loved it."

She drew in another deep breath, and his cardamom male scent flooded her nostrils. Desire, pure and simple, drifted over her body like a warm breeze. Beautiful, exquisite pheromones. She would have fallen backward if she hadn't already been stretched out on the couch.

Are you feeling better? he asked.

Much.

He rested on his knees beside the sofa and must have been bent at an awkward angle over her, but he wasn't complaining.

He dragged his fangs over her neck. The sensation caused her heart to skip a beat and her body to clench . . . hard.

Alison?

She heard the question beneath her whispered name. Was she really going to do this? To allow such an invasion? Such a release of herself into him?

He lifted up and looked at her. *Lavender,* he whispered over her mind.

The sight of him did her in, beautiful, fully masculine, incredible green eyes, thick black hair now framing his god-like face.

Desire flowed through her like a river. She wanted to throw herself into the current and swim.

He nodded as though understanding.

He bent down to again nuzzle her neck.

She moaned at the new set of chills whipping over her body. She touched his hair and pulled the coarse strands through her fingers.

He growled against her neck. More shivers. Her fingers wound through his hair.

Be strong for me, he whispered in vaporous trails that condensed in her mind. He shifted slightly and kissed her neck. She rolled her head to allow more room. He groaned heavily and moved in closer. He pulled her hips toward him then slid her head away from the back of the sofa to give him even more access.

His tongue flattened and rasped up the side of her neck as though drawing forward what he wanted. Again and again he licked. Her pulse throbbed. The duller sides of his fangs scraped the skin above her vein. She had touched one of them when he'd been unconscious on the hood of her car. The sharp tip had drawn blood. How little it would take to puncture her throat.

Was she *really* going to do this thing? Allow this penetration?

He nuzzled, kissed, licked.

An ache formed deep within. Desire gripped her and

again she clenched internally. She moaned. What had he said about the sharing of blood? An act of reverence.

Reverence? she sent.

Yes. God, yes.

He slid his hand over her stomach, pushed aside her sweater, then lifted her T-shirt. The callused pads of his warrior fingers drifted over her ribs, creating sliding jolts of pleasure. He found the waistband of her jeans, unhooked the button, and unzipped. He slid his palm lower beneath the fabric and rubbed in circles, moving deeper with each pass, digging his fingers into her flesh. Her hips rose and fell in response.

He scraped her neck again. *I tasted the blood on your finger. I want more. I need more. More of you. Will you give me what I desire?*

She wanted to. Was this what he meant when he said the woman had to be willing? She was so absurdly willing.

Do you have me in thrall?

No, but I can put you there if you want.

No, she whispered through the rugged contours of his mind. *I want everything just like this, awake and aware.*

She arched her neck.

He growled heavily. As he rose up, he slid his hand the rest of the way down her pants and cupped her. He pivoted his shoulders and overlaid his fangs above her vein. *You must give me permission.*

Alison had a thousand reasons to say no. She didn't even know this man—vampire—*whatever.* He admitted he was caught in something even he didn't think was such a good idea, bonding of some kind. And hey, it was her blood, *her blood* she'd be giving up. Truth? She ached with need from her head to her toes. She was in a process of ascension, which still confused her and freaked her out and he was asking for blood and oh, damn, she was so going to give it up for him.

Take me now, her mind whispered.

He emitted the most erotic sound, something between a

gasp and a growl. He sank the razor-sharp tips, a quick sting then just the presence of his fangs. The next moment he sucked long and hard from her vein.

At the same time, his fingers worked her delicate folds. Desire rushed over her in lightning flashes. She gasped and moaned. It would take so little. The pulls on her neck were connected to the well of her body and each time his mouth suckled, she clenched internally, over and over. The lightning strikes continued, pulsing down her sensitive flesh, streaking into her core. The clenching became exquisitely unbearable. She should warn him how close she was, that she might . . . oh, God . . . she came so suddenly she cried out. Pleasure climaxed like nothing ever before. At the same time, power rolled from her, a burst of energy that struck him before she could give the warning. She felt his body react as if he'd taken a hit, although the only sound he made as he continued pulling at her neck was a deep satisfied groan.

Are you okay? she sent.

More than okay. That was amazing. Do it again.

I didn't hurt you?

Not even a little bit, he sent, his fangs still deep, the pulls on her neck gentler now as he conversed telepathically. *The blast felt like an erotic punch to my chest. More. I want more.*

You don't know how relieved I am. Her eyes burned suddenly and unexpected tears slid down the sides of her face.

She hadn't hurt him and he wanted more of what she could give.

Relief merged with pleasure, heightening every sensation. More growls rumbled in his throat. He pushed his large hand deeper, taking her jeans to their limit as he pressed two fingers inside.

She whimpered as he rhythmically worked her core and at the same time took from her vein.

I have so much more to give you, Alison. I want you to have everything, my mouth sucking your beautiful breasts, my cock inside you pumping hard, working your body, driving your passion. I want to feast on your sex, taste your honey.

His words forged a new fire. His driving fingers stoked the flames. Her cries rose to the ceiling. *That's it,* his voice murmured inside her head. She was breathing hard. Her core clenched around his driving fingers. Lightning slid over her flesh again and she screamed yet another orgasm. And another. Each time her power pummeled him, but he merely growled as though deeply satisfied.

Tears once more trailed from her eyes as her body quieted.

After a few minutes, he withdrew his fangs. He remained settled against her neck, his lips kissing in tender swipes, his fingers still possessing her core.

Will my neck bleed? she sent.

Not at all. When I withdrew, chemicals left the tips of each fang and gave you a quick seal-and-heal.

She took deep breaths, settling into the reality of what had just happened as well as how happy she was. She could get used to this, to being with him.

Even so, her heart tensed. After all, what did she really know of him? She had an overwhelming desire to stay with him forever, but how sensible or even possible or likely would that be? By his own admission, he said he could never really be with her, not in any permanent sense.

Oh, God, what did she risk by drawing this close, by allowing her blood into his body, by giving herself to him?

She was in so much trouble.

Her hands were still buried in his thick hair, a couple of her fingers knotted up completely. She started untangling them. When she was free, Kerrick slowly withdrew his fingers from the well of her body then looked at her. She dropped her gaze to his lips. "You have blood on your mouth and you look really pumped, stronger."

He nodded. He appeared sated as he carefully wiped his mouth with the fingers that had been inside her. Green eyes bored into hers as he sucked his fingers clean of every last bit of her. *Lavender,* he sent.

Her entire body became a pool that just kept sinking deeper and deeper into the couch. She didn't want to get up . . . ever. She wanted to stay here and watch this man, this vampire, lick his fingers, his green eyes dark with passion and need, his strength enhanced by her blood.

He leaned over her and planted a hand between the sofa back and her side. His dark hair fell forward onto her face, her neck, her chest. Even his hair smelled of exotic cardamom. His fangs lengthened. Arousal, maybe? Probably.

A new wave of heat rolled from his body and blasted her. She lifted a finger and touched his left fang. So smooth. Her finger strayed to his lower lip and as he had done while unconscious he drew her finger into his mouth. He closed his eyes and moaned. She had the most profound sensation that she could never tire of this man, this vampire, not in a hundred million years.

He released her finger, leaned down and kissed her, the weight of his fangs pressed against her lips, his tongue dipping inside. She suckled and he groaned. She was so into this. If this was ascension, give her more, a lot more.

He started pushing down her pants around her hips. He had just managed to free one cheek when a really bad sensation stole up her spine like a spider with claws. She planted a hand on his thick shoulder. "Kerrick," she called sharply. "Something's not right."

"No," he said, his voice husky. "This is right. This is *very* right."

She sat up and pushed at him. "I'm serious, Kerrick. Something's wrong. I can feel it. I *sense it*. We're in trouble."

He drew back and scowled. "What kind of trouble?"

"I think death vampires are on the way." She shook her head. "A lot of death vampires."

Kerrick shook his head. "Shit." He started to pace.

Alison leaped from the couch, pulled up her jeans, zipped, then buttoned. She glanced out the family room slider, which faced east. The mountains opposite were trimmed in a faint light. Dawn would not be far behind.

He looked at her. "So you're sure about this." He crossed

to the other couch, grabbed his weapons harness then slid it on. In a blur of motion he drew his hair back and secured it in the leather clasp.

She nodded. "We need to get out of here. Now. But Kerrick, this isn't fair to you."

"What?" He looked like she'd slapped him.

"Why should you be put in danger because of *my* ascension?"

He actually laughed. "Oh, please. This is my job. Shit, I can't believe you said that." He drew his phone from his pocket. "Now I need to ask again, are you absolutely sure? Because what I'm about to do is illegal."

Alison nodded. "I keep seeing the word *regiment,* and I feel the pressure of an army coming—not just one man or even two or three."

He dipped his chin. "That's good enough for me." He thumbed his phone then a moment later said, "Central, I'm calling an emergency lift . . . repeat, an emergency lift. Have Thorne retrieve two at this signal and make it fast. We will be on the move." He thumbed his phone again and slid it into the pocket of his kilt. He cursed. He was so fucking limited in the action he could take. Even if he'd had the capacity to fold Alison to another location, chances were good Greaves could track their movements and send death vampires right on their tail. When Thorne performed the fold, he had the power to block a trace.

But what he really didn't understand was how Greaves had found them in the first place. The complexity of the mist Kerrick had created this time in order to disguise Alison's house should have prevented detection, even from Greaves, which of course meant the Commander had increased his technological capability. So . . . shit.

"Kerrick. The regiment is here. Right now. Outside."

He blurred to her side and took her hands in his. "We have no time. You said you had a Hummer. You must fold us there now—only please tell me your Hummer is good to go."

She nodded.

Kerrick squeezed her fingers. "Just relax."

Relax? Really? She smiled but she took his words to heart, drew in a long deep breath, and concentrated. She felt the vibration.

Just as she appeared by the vehicle with Kerrick in front of her and his hands still holding hers, an enormous blast sounded on the other side of the house. The walls shook. The garage sat on the opposite side of the house, separated by a courtyard and a wing of bedrooms, which she suspected was exactly what had just saved them.

"So Darian's army just blew up the rest of my house."

Kerrick nodded then thrust a hand toward the vehicle. "Get in."

She mentally hit the lights, both for the garage and the headlights for the Hummer.

"Maybe I should fold us somewhere else?"

"Too late. Greaves's army has a fix on you, with death vamps ready to trace no matter where we go, and believe me, if they've sent a regiment to your home, they'd be happy to send another regiment in pursuit. They'd engage me in such a way that I'd be forced to leave you unguarded. Then you'd be dead. Right now only the call to Thorne will get us out of this."

"Lead on," she cried. She vaulted around to the passenger's side then hopped in. She started to tell him she had forgotten the keys but there was nothing holding her back. She pointed to the ignition and started the vehicle. She could use any of her powers right now, in the presence of this warrior, and it wouldn't matter. He wouldn't be freaked and he wouldn't judge her. Maybe he wouldn't even get hurt.

She turned toward the garage door and began forming the thought to open it. Instead his words zipped through her mind: *No time, duck down.* He aimed his hand at the door, fired away, shattered the back window of the Hummer, and sent the garage door flying off its hinges.

The Second Earth vampire had power!

A heartbeat later he backed out of the garage at the devil's own pace.

He turned, skidded, and shifted into drive.

He hit the accelerator.

The tires squealed.

He didn't bother with the driveway. He drove straight through the wire fence and the hilly open desert away from the front of the house. The Hummer's lights bounced over the terrain like a lantern swinging wildly.

As her eyes adjusted, she looked around. Greaves's army attacked, heading toward her house on the ground and in black combat gear or flying down out of the sky. Some of the soldiers looked normal, but the rest were death vampires bearing the hallmark beauty of their kind as well as the pale, almost bluish tint to the skin. Those soldiers in flight wore the same gear Kerrick did right now: kilts, gladiator sandals, and weapons harnesses. However, the weapon of choice involved bullets rather than blades.

"Oh, God."

One good spray from an assault rifle and game over.

"Get down," Kerrick's deep voice thumped inside the Hummer.

She dropped low in her seat though she felt compelled to keep an eye on what was happening.

A death vamp flew close then lifted his rifle.

Without thinking she raised her hand, blew out the front windshield, and knocked the warrior down. The resulting bounce of tires caused her stomach to lurch. Oh, God, they'd run him over.

Kerrick cried out, "Keep doing what you're doing. Right now you're our best weapon. Goddammit." He jerked the heavy vehicle to the right, bounced down into a wash, then climbed up the other side all in the space of seconds. The maneuver left behind a platoon of foot soldiers.

More death vamps, in flight, headed toward the Hummer.

With one hand on the steering wheel, Kerrick held out his right hand and a pistol appeared. A death vamp landed on the hood. Kerrick fired, chest center, and blew the vamp backward. Another crunch under the wheels. Alison's stomach heaved north.

Her peripheral vision caught movement. A death vamp

flew at window level. He slowly raised a pistol. Her eyes widened. Once more she sent a blast, which in turn sent the death vamp spiraling out of control and piled up at the base of a saguaro.

"Goddammit, Central. Where's Thorne?"

He fired his pistol until the trigger clicked on empty. He folded another weapon into his hand and pulled the trigger, the sound deafening inside the Hummer. Death vamps fell right and left and still more came. He fired as he drove through the desert, up and down gullies, busting apart creosote, sideswiping tall spindly ocotillo, and crunching fat barrel cacti.

Alison kept aiming her palm at anything that drew close. Her heart had ramped up, doubled its beats. She had never been so frightened in her life.

A thumping sounded on the roof. Alison sent a blast up. The top of the Hummer lifted, separated, then fell off the back of the vehicle. From her side mirror she saw a winged death vamp slide down the side of the wash then struggle to gain his feet.

"Shit," Kerrick cried out. "Thorne, where are you?"

Alison turned around and cried out. In front of her at least twenty death vamps rained down from the sky directly in the Hummer's path.

Do your best, Alison, or God help us, he sent.

She blasted away with her hand in a wide arc in front of her, but she knew her power had weakened. She'd never thrown so many hand-blasts in her life. Not all the warriors fell. Her left shoulder jerked backward.

She felt a strange curdling in the pit of her stomach. Another winged death vamp landed on the hood of the Hummer. Kerrick pulled the trigger, but only a series of clicks followed.

The pretty-boy aimed his pistol directly at her, a feral look in his eyes, a smile pulled back over thick, heavy fangs. Alison lifted her hand, but the blast that followed had little effect. She was finished.

Time slowed.

So this was how she was going to die?

She laughed. So much for ascending to Second Earth. She hadn't even survived a handful of hours.

She closed her eyes and waited.

A brilliant light flashed in front of her eyelids.

The next thing she knew, she stood before a tall handsome man with long light brown hair. He was almost as tall as Kerrick and just as muscled. His hazel eyes were badly red-rimmed like he hadn't slept in a year.

He scowled at her. "You're hit."

She didn't know what he meant exactly. No one had *hit* her, but her mind felt as if it was moving in circles at the bottom of a drain. She couldn't see very well. She glanced around. She had landed in some sort of very dark rec room that housed a bunch of really ugly couches. A pool table was on its back, all four legs up in the air, two of them bent at a weird angle. On the other side of the room was a long bar fronted by several tall stools. An assortment of gleaming hard-liquor bottles in a variety of shapes and sizes decorated a row of cabinets.

She weaved on her feet. Pain pierced her shoulder suddenly, like someone had just taken a chain saw to the joint. She glanced down. Blood soaked her shirt and sweater. She pulled the neck of the T-shirt away and sure enough, blood pumped sluggishly from a bullet wound.

Well, what do you know? She'd gotten *hit*.

Oh. That's what the guy with the red-rimmed eyes had meant.

At least she wasn't dead.

At least, she didn't think she was dead.

Her knees gave way. She had a vague impression of someone catching her as everything went black.

Let the healer come,
For when the wounds are well-tended
A land is saved.

—*Collected Proverbs*, Beatrice of Fourth

CHAPTER 12

Kerrick stood near the pool table, Alison in his arms. Christ, they'd barely made it out alive.

Guilt powered down on his head, tensing his neck and tightening his chest. This was what happened to the women in his life. Proximity meant danger. Danger meant injury and death.

Goddammittohell.

Blood still seeped from her shoulder. She needed help. Now. "I think you'd better call one of the healers. My powers don't encompass torn arteries."

"We don't need to," Thorne said. He grimaced, his brows drawn into a deep furrow as he stared at Alison. "Endelle is on her way."

"Thank God. In the meantime, pressure on the wound would help."

Thorne stepped close and with the heel of his palm stanched the flow. "She's very beautiful," he murmured.

"Yeah," Kerrick muttered. Dammit, he shouldn't have taken her at the neck earlier. What the hell had he been thinking and just how much blood did she have left? The level of Alison's powers demanded she battle her way into Second and she needed every resource, including a decent amount of red cells. *What the hell had he been thinking?*

He hadn't.

Ever since the *breh-hedden* had taken hold of him his brain had been functioning on fumes. If he hadn't been working her out on the couch, this wouldn't have happened. He needed to get a grip. Now.

"So why the *emergency lift*?" Thorne asked, shifting his gaze to Kerrick. "How many death vamps were there? I've seen you battle eight by yourself and barely break a sweat."

"There were dozens. A regiment."

"What the fuck?"

"Greaves sent *his army*." Which was another part of the truth. He'd been prepared to take on two or three squads of death vamps but not a regiment.

Thorne hissed. "That goddamn motherfucker. So there weren't only death vamps present."

"That's right. Good old working soldiers." He told his story ending with, "Things would have been different if he hadn't sent his army. That much I know. It just never occurred to me that he'd send a regiment, that he'd break such a big fucking rule. Shit."

"Don't beat yourself up. We knew from the medical complex that her signature showed up on the grid. Any way you look at it, you were screwed."

Right. Whatever. "Someone else should have charge of her."

"Doesn't sound like it would make one lizard's turd of a difference."

Kerrick huffed a laugh. "No. I guess not."

"No question we're in for it, though. And you know what the Commander will do when he hears we used an emergency lift."

"You got that right." He ground his teeth. There weren't

enough obscenities to cover the scope of his thoughts. "But we'd both be dead otherwise and isn't it kind of illegal to be dropping an army down on Mortal Earth?"

Thorne snorted his disgust. "The Committee will overlook that *little indiscretion*."

COPASS. The Committee to Oversee the Process of Ascension to Second Society. "Bullshit committee."

Kerrick had a sick-gut feeling all over again, the one laced with despair. He had been a warrior one century too long. He couldn't seem to find his feet anymore, and by the looks of it Thorne wasn't in much better shape.

Thorne glanced at Alison. "So, what do we have here? Endelle said she sent a hand-blast up the Trough."

"Yep. Saw it myself at the receiving end. Straight up. A sand geyser about a quarter of a mile high."

"Damn."

"Where the hell is Endelle? Alison can't lose much more blood."

Thorne scowled, his gaze shifting back and forth as he scanned the room. "She'll be here."

"I need to get Alison back to Mortal Earth. I have no idea how long she can tolerate being on Second." An unascended mortal couldn't handle being in the second dimension for more than a couple of hours at a time. In a wounded state, the draining effects would rob the mortal of the much-needed energy to recover. An extended stay of longer than twenty-four hours, wounded or not, always ended in death. Only when Alison received from Endelle's hand the ascended vampire nature at her ascension ceremony would she be able to tolerate living on Second Earth.

The air shimmered suddenly. Endelle. She caught Kerrick's gaze and without a single nicety cried, "What the hell have you done? An emergency lift? Do you know what this means?" Kerrick's ears rang. "Did you just lose half your IQ points, Warrior? *Shit!*" The decibels she employed in that one word, spoken as it was both aloud and with telepathy, pounded the hell out of his eardrums and shattered all the bottles on the bar. The sudden reek of alcohol drenched the air. "You might as well have handed Alison's head on a platter to that motherfucker. Calling an emergency lift just gave Greaves one more piece of ammunition against us. He'll take this to COPASS and demand retribution and they'll give it to him. So, again, what the hell were you thinking?"

"Didn't have a choice, ma'am," Kerrick began. He told her what he'd told Thorne.

She scowled as she glanced at Alison. "You know, you're really letting me down here, Warrior."

Kerrick drew in a long deep breath through his nose. "Yes, ma'am. But there wasn't much else I could do. The Commander didn't just send a war party to Carefree, he sent a regiment."

"Whatever."

Her wings, a ruddy scarlet this time, extended to their fullest height and breadth, a reflection of her temper. She had changed her clothes from earlier in the evening and wore tight black leather pants and some kind of dark hide halter with long bristled fur. He thought buffalo, maybe.

"You'd better take her back to Mortal Earth," she barked.

"But where?" Thorne asked. "And how do we sustain secrecy?"

She huffed a sigh. "All right, let's take care of our little troublemaker." She drew her feathers abruptly into her wing-locks, a movement that jostled the halter but didn't dislodge it.

She laid a hand on Alison's forehead. The air pulsed slowly, then rapidly all around them.

When the pulsing stopped, Endelle straightened up. "You can take her now. I've given her a shield, which will last about thirty-six hours. No one will be able to locate her."

"It may not be that simple," Kerrick said. "Both Alison and I have signatures that show up on Central's grid. If Greaves or his generals located us because of our signatures, that means they've improved their technology. Your shield might block Alison's signature but not mine."

"Shit," Endelle muttered. "All right. Let me think. Okay. I can put my mist around the Queen Creek house and as far as I know even Greaves won't be able to find you."

Kerrick nodded. "Yeah, I'd like to see him bust through your mist."

"Damn straight about that. Okay. So, we're done here, right?" She didn't wait for an answer but turned to leave.

"*She'when'endel'livelle!*" Thorne called after her. At least three very pronounced clicks broke up the proper name.

Yep, crickets in his mouth.

Kerrick lifted a brow. How could Thorne even remember her birth name, not to mention pronounce it?

Endelle turned around and scowled at her second-in-command. "What?" she snapped.

"Could you take care of the wound, please? Neither Kerrick nor I have the ability to heal a mortal whose shoulder has been shredded."

She clenched her jaw. "I hate details." She blurred back and touched the wound. The flesh re-formed flawlessly, and a vibrant pink color returned to Alison's face. So much power. She replaced the bloodied sweater, T-shirt, and jeans with a soft white, but very short, tunic.

"Thank you," Thorne said, averting his gaze from Alison's now bare legs. Endelle rolled her eyes, tossed an arm, then folded. She left behind a blast of wind full of stinging grit to remind her warriors just how much she disliked being taken from her usual routine.

Kerrick whirled away in order to shield Alison. When the wind stopped, he turned back to Thorne, who in turn just shook his head. Endelle was one fine piece of work. "What the hell was she wearing?"

Thorne shrugged. "I don't know. Bear hide?"

Kerrick snorted.

Just as he was going to ask Thorne to give him a fold to Queen Creek, a double shimmer appeared near the bar some twenty feet away.

Medichi . . . and *Marcus*.

Kerrick's jaw hardened and a hideous growl erupted out of his throat.

Thorne automatically threw an arm in front of Kerrick. "How'd it go?" he called to Medichi. "And what the hell happened to Marcus? Hey, asshole, your pansy-ass life catch up with you?"

Marcus had a huge bump over his left eye and a deep cut on his right arm that dripped blood onto the floor. He met Kerrick's gaze and his shoulders hunched.

"Motherfucker," he called out, his teeth gritted. At the same moment, in a move lightning-quick, Medichi grabbed Marcus, slammed him to the floor, then put a foot on his neck. Medichi held him in place as Marcus started cursing the dust Kerrick walked on and everything else he could think of.

"Goddammit," Thorne muttered. "Just what we need."

"Take the ascendiate," Kerrick cried, trying to shove Alison at Thorne. "Let me at the bastard! I'll break his fucking neck!"

Thorne turned back to Kerrick and over Alison's body he caught Kerrick's face with both hands, getting up close. "You just get her to Queen Creek and keep her safe," he cried, splitting his resonance.

Despite the fact that Alison was caught between them, Kerrick shifted his knees as well as his shoulders in a primal effort to bust out of Thorne's hold on him. He breathed hard through his nose. He wanted at Marcus like nobody's business.

"Calm the fuck down!" Thorne shouted. "You have guardian duty right now. You can beat the shit out of Marcus later. Right now, *take care of your woman.*"

These last words, spoken as they were aloud and in Kerrick's head, brought his focus straight at Thorne's red-rimmed hazel eyes. The pain of the combined mind-voice speak nearly brought Kerrick to his knees.

He started nodding without quite knowing what he was agreeing to. However, in deliberate measures, his breathing slowed and he didn't see quite so much red as before.

"Ready to go?" Thorne asked.

Kerrick nodded.

The vibration began.

Kerrick stood in the middle of his Queen Creek living room on Mortal Earth.

He concentrated on steadying his heart. When Marcus had folded to the Cave, if Alison hadn't been in his arms, he would have gone apeshit on that bastard's ass. It sure as hell wasn't helping his blood pressure to think about what he would have done, what he still wanted to do to his former brother-in-law. *Hatred* didn't begin to describe what he felt for Marcus.

Jesus. After two centuries he still wanted to kill the man for all the things he'd said after Helena had died, all the blame he'd laid at Kerrick's feet, even if it was the same blame he heaped on his own damn head.

With *his woman* still in his arms, he started walking around in one large circle, yeah, calming the hell down. He looked down at Alison and let her presence work on him, even in her unconscious state. He took massive breaths and focused on her beautiful face.

The living room smelled of leather couches and chairs, though not sufficiently enough to block the powerful scent of lavender that clung to Alison's skin. As he savored her peaches-and-cream complexion, the *breh* started to replace all the stinging rage. Damn, but she was beautiful, lovely straight nose, high cheekbones, and her lips . . . so fucking kissable. He wanted to kiss her . . . right now.

Take care of your woman.

His woman.

The words fit. They felt so fucking right. He didn't want to let her go. He wanted to hold her for hours, years . . . okay, centuries.

He needed to keep her safe, to protect her, to keep her alive, dammit. So far he'd been barely one step ahead of the adversary, to the point that she'd almost bought it in Care-

free. He had to do better. At least Endelle's mind-shield
would give them a reprieve.

Her face held him entranced. She had a small freckle
just off to the side of her left eye, barely a mark at all. He
couldn't help it. He drew her close, leaned down, and covered the freckle with his lips. She sighed in her sleep. He
drifted his lips over her cheek. He breathed in lavender and
hardened—yet something else happened as well. Great
chunks of metal, several feet thick, began dropping away
from the sides of his heart. The crashing sound chipped at
his resolve.

His gaze drifted over the soft arch of her eyebrows, down
the straight pretty line of her nose, to the sensual fullness
of her lips. Her beauty worked him like a boxer in a ring,
punching at him until she dropped him for the count. The
breh-hedden couldn't possibly answer for everything he felt.
Maybe the ritual merely heightened what was essentially a
godawful attraction.

Yet the vow he'd taken after Helena's death hadn't been
done in haste or on impulse. He straightened his shoulders
then carried Alison into the guest room. He rounded the
bed then with a thought drew the covers back. As he lowered her, she awoke slightly, blinking up at him. "Kerrick?"

"I've got you. Just sleep for now."

"Okay. I'm so tired." She rolled onto her side. He drew
the comforter over her.

"Of course you are." He patted her shoulder. She caught
his hand, turned into it, and, oh, damn, she kissed the back
of his fingers. Desire flowed through him like gasoline on
fire.

"Thank you for getting us out of there," she murmured,
her eyes still closed. Then she turned her head into the pillow, released his hand, and sighed.

He made himself back away from the bed. He took one
step then another although it was like moving through
quicksand.

This is for the best. Let her sleep.

One more step.

One more.

He finally reached the doorway and could breathe again, but he kept the door wide in case she called for him.

He turned into the hall then moved to the front door and opened it. What he saw mesmerized him. A well-constructed mist confused even the strongest mind, ascended or otherwise, but oh . . . my . . . God. Endelle had created one incredible superstructure of mist around not just his house but his property as well. This was helluva lot more complex than the one he'd composed in Carefree.

He moved onto the porch then well out into the yard. He looked back at the house. He had to work hard to see the house at all since Endelle's mist confused even his powerful mind. Only by focusing could he see that, yep, a dome of mist covered his home, a constantly moving swirl of white gossamer threads. Yet, beyond the threads, he could see the blue sky. Amazing. Just amazing.

He shook his head back and forth. Holy shit. Sometimes he forgot just how powerful Endelle was. He couldn't imagine Greaves, or any of his generals, getting within a hundred yards of his home.

Only then did he relax.

He crossed to the guest room to check on Alison. Hell, he just wanted to look at her once more. If he ever communed with her fully—entered her body, exchanged blood with her simultaneously, and engaged her mind at the deepest level— she would be bound to him in a way that would haunt her if he died. The *breh-hedden* wouldn't be like a simple Second Earth marriage, not between them, not with so much power on each side. They would be linked, joined, bonded, an inseparable pair. Death would never be a straightforward matter because grief, for the one left behind, would be magnified to the tenth.

For these reasons, he would never engage in full communion with Alison. He had a high-profile warrior job and the chances of his buying it one day were way too high to let her bear the burden of having to cope afterward.

So, yeah. He wouldn't complete the *breh-hedden* with Alison. It was too much to put on the shoulders of a fellow vampire ascender. As much as his groin strained toward her, as painfully as his chest tightened while he watched her roll onto her back, even as much as death seemed a welcome alternative to this denial, he wouldn't bond with her.

He forced himself to move on. He went into a utility room off the garage and folded his sword and dagger onto the long table he'd had installed just for this purpose. With Choji oil and clean rags, he cared for his weapons.

After he was satisfied with the sharpness of both the sword and the dagger, he returned them to his weapons locker on Second. He located his guns, still in the Hummer, and mentally folded them back to the same location. He went to his master bath, stripped, then hopped in the shower. As he soaped up, the warm water eased his aching body.

So much power on Second.

So much responsibility.

And the temptations were a hundred times harder to resist.

When the heat had worked some of the tightness out of his neck and shoulders, he rinsed, shut the water off, then wiped down with a towel. He sat on the side of the bed, a second towel draped over his ritual long hair. He felt better. He had a plan of action now. Maybe things would happen with Alison, involving blood and sex, perhaps even a sharing of minds, but he could make sure the ball game didn't play to the end. Yes, he could do that.

Screw the *breh-hedden*.

As he finally climbed between the sheets, and as sleep overtook his mind, he wondered what anvil would drop on his head in the next twenty-four hours.

Marcus wiped the blood off his lip as Horace tended to him. The healer, who looked like all those retro pictures of Christ, had his hands over the deep cut on his arm, taking care of biz.

His heart finally beat like it was supposed to. Yet from

the moment he'd folded to the Cave with Medichi and caught sight of the bastard-from-hell, he'd been in a state. Even now, as he sat forward on the ratty brown leather couch nearest the bar—that bar with all the broken bottles— his left knee bounced. He'd tried to make it stop several times but he was so damn juiced, too much damn adrenaline and nowhere to put it.

Luken and Santiago worked to clear up the mess, which had to be done manually. Only Central, or maybe Endelle, had the power to clean up debris without a mop or a broom. However, a lake of combined alcohol and broken glass hardly qualified as a crisis demanding Central's intervention. The boys were almost done anyway, although they might want to throw away the reeking mop afterward.

Whatever.

If only his foot would stop thumping on the cement.

"Are you in pain, Warrior?" Even the healer's voice had a soothing quality.

"I'm fine." His words came out clipped. He blew the air from his cheeks, leaned forward, and planted his forearms on his thighs. Horace moved with him, his hands still hovering above the wound.

"Almost done," Horace said.

"Oh. Sorry," Marcus muttered.

Marcus had spent the entire night at the downtown Borderland above the Trough, battling wave after wave of death vamps. Medichi had joined him just before dawn, thank God.

Marcus found himself grateful, beholden to the warrior. He wasn't used to fighting and as much as he'd savored the first twelve or so engagements, after that his muscles ached in places he'd forgotten he had. So yeah, Medichi had saved his ass, something he hated to admit.

Who gave a fuck?

The rest of the warriors stood in a group not far from the upside-down pool table, shooting the breeze. Luken and Santiago, having finished their chore, joined them. His gaze skated beyond the group to a smashed-up TV hanging at a weird angle off its wall mount. If the TV had worked, he would have fired up the dimensional hookup to Mortal Earth and started running CNN. He kept the network on in his office, day in, day out, just to keep up.

Horace's hands shifted to his face. He felt the soothing warmth travel through the fat lump over his eye. He glanced at him. The healer's brown eyes had a gentle appearance, a kind expression. He tried to imagine being a tender sort of man. Impossible. He'd always have his hard abrasive edges. He was who he was. Though he had lived on Mortal Earth for two centuries, he was still a warrior.

Speaking of which, he sure as shit could use a little jugular time. He'd love a woman right now. He felt his iPhone vibrate, slid it from the deep pocket of his kilt, then scanned the text. He let a couple of obscenities fly. One of his corporations, the one that exported to Second, had just lost a major contract. He really needed to get the hell back to Mortal Earth before his empire turned to dust. His nerves shot off skyrockets and his muscles jumped and twitched.

He hated being hamstrung like this. After all these decades, he'd learned a goddamn thing or two about running massive businesses. Bottom line, they all depended on one thing—his fucking leadership.

Horace asked him to tilt his head back a little. Marcus complied, his gaze landing on the ceiling. There was one fine collection of spit wads up there, glued to the texture. He chuckled. Now, this was something he missed—the outer limits of male bonding.

The small bit of laughter eased something inside his chest. As the bump above his eye lessened, he said, "You're the man, Horace."

"Thank you, *duhuro*."

"Hey. Don't use that address with me. Any of these warriors hear you say that to me, they'll crucify you."

Horace chuckled. "I think not, *duhuro*. And no matter what any of them say, you were battling death vamps when the rest of them were made up of trees, frogs, and daisies."

Marcus met his eye. "That's one helluva generous thing to say."

Horace smiled as he kept the healing warmth flowing.

His gaze shifted back to the warriors. He still didn't know the story about the pool table but he could imagine a dozen scenarios that would have provided the same result.

Every once in a while, the group of six hardened vampires burst out laughing. A drift of tobacco swirled to the ceiling. Zacharius had a cigar in hand. Yeah, he had forgotten the best part of being a Warrior of the Blood, sharing stories at dawn, having a last drink, a last smoke before heading home to bed.

At the sound of a feminine voice, he leaned his head sideways. When had the woman arrived? He couldn't really see her. Just her legs and feet. Medichi and his massive shoulders and height blocked her from view. Luken ranged close, though, like he had some claim on her. She had on really conservative brown pumps, the kind a lot of his admins wore. *Boring.*

He closed his eyes. He drew in a deep breath. His nose was clear, finally. So clear that for just a moment, he caught a familiar scent, the one he had smelled at Endelle's. Had all of Second started using Glade PlugIns laced with honeysuckle? Jesus.

The trouble was, his body really liked this particular smell. The small of his back developed a knot and his groin warmed up. He ground his teeth and worked at keeping himself under control or Horace here would get ideas that he was into men. What the hell was going on with him?

He breathed again. This time the scent was stronger and his eyes rolled back in his head. Oh. My. God.

He heard Thorne's shredded-bark voice. "Havily, I don't know why the hell Endelle hauled you out of bed and sent you over here at this hour. The ascendiate has gone to Queen Creek with Kerrick and is recovering from a serious wound. She probably won't wake up until later this afternoon. I can call you when you're needed. By the way, have you met the ascendiate yet?"

"No, not yet. You know, I think this is really odd. When I spoke with Endelle, she was adamant I come over here, right now, to get the details from you."

The musical lilt to the woman's voice affected Marcus, like he needed to hear more. A lot more.

"She sent you here . . . at dawn . . . to get details? I don't get it. I don't have any details. I met Alison for the first time about an hour ago and she was unconscious."

"Well, I guess there's been some mistake but I'm not sorry I came. I always like seeing you boys. Please tell me you're done for the night."

A general flow of affirmatives went around the group.

So the woman's name was Havily. Didn't sound familiar. None of the warriors had mentioned her. He supposed she was the ascendiate's Liaison Officer. He still couldn't see her, just her legs. Her ivory linen pants looked tailored from where he sat. They had a firm crease like his suits did.

"Your healing is complete, Warrior Marcus," Horace said.

Marcus sat up a little straighter. "Thanks." He touched his face and couldn't believe how thoroughly he was healed. "You've got one helluva gift."

At that moment the honeysuckle scent struck him all over again, like taking a hard swing of a baseball bat to his stomach. He leaned over and groaned. Dammit, now he was hard as a rock.

"Warrior Marcus?" Horace cried, his voice ringing through the rec room. "What is the matter? Have you suffered an injury, perhaps to one of your internal organs?" He squatted beside Marcus and searched his face. "Tell me where you hurt."

Marcus stared at him. Like hell he'd try to explain. He could feel the heat on his face, though he wasn't embarrassed. He was overcome. Dammit, what the hell was wrong with him. "Just a cramp. It'll pass. Trust me, I'll be fine." *As soon as I leave the building and get away from that erotic smell.*

Horace's concern, however, spoken in a sharp tone, had

disrupted the conversation across the room, and all talk in the Cave had ceased.

Medichi turned in his direction, scowling, and unblocked the view . . . *holy shit* . . . of the most beautiful woman Marcus had ever seen in his entire existence, including all the actresses he had known, Canadian or otherwise. She was an angel, a denizen of the heavens with thick auburn hair cascading in soft waves past her shoulders, a beautiful peachy-red against the ivory linen of her suit jacket. The desire he felt doubled, then doubled again.

Goddammit. One stroke and he'd come.

He sat well forward, his hands slung between his knees. He hurt now because his throbbing erection was twisted and he couldn't do a thing about it. If he stood up, he'd make a fucking tent out of his kilt. She met his gaze and frowned. He had an overwhelming sense of needing to get to her, to stand at her back, preferably with his sword drawn.

What the hell?

Havily stared at the warrior she had heard so much about, particularly from Luken who worried that this vampire could cause a war in the Brotherhood.

Warrior Marcus.

The renegade, *the deserter.*

He sat forward on one of the absurd worn leather couches against the far back wall. He looked like he was in pain but as Medichi had just told her, Warrior Marcus had come in pretty beat up from his first night of battling after two centuries. Hence, Horace's presence.

Horace's cry of concern had sent everyone turning in the deserter's direction. She didn't know him at all, of course, since he had been residing on Mortal Earth for two centuries. She did know he was despised among the warriors, as he ought to be. She could think of nothing worse than an ascender abandoning Madame Endelle and his brothers-in-arms.

His leather kilt hung in a deep loop between his legs, his shins covered with leather. He watched her with the oddest expression on his face, as though he were seeing a ghost. She didn't know what to make of him yet somehow, for reasons she could not explain, she was surprisingly drawn to him. His hair was dark, perhaps not black like Kerrick's, but a very dark brown, yet quite straight. His skin was a beautiful olive in tone, and he had an intensely fierce expression with dark brows slashed over light brown eyes. God, he was gorgeous.

She drew a breath, ready to turn her attention back to Thorne and ask if he knew when she should visit ascendiate Wells, but the strangest scent assailed her, an earthy musky scent that reminded her of—and this was quite ridiculous—fennel. She closed her eyes and took a deep breath in. She could picture an entire bouquet of black licorice vines, which was just . . . well . . . heaven to her. She'd always had a great fondness for licorice. Had the warriors started keeping some kind of strange air freshener in the Cave? If so, she needed to find out what brand it was because she would buy it, maybe a dozen cans. She might even wear it as a perfume.

The strange thing was, the scent appeared to be emanating from where Warrior Marcus sat, his hands clasped so tightly together she could see the whites of his knuckles. He was still staring at her, that same odd, almost pained expression on his face.

Without warning, her skin bloomed, tingled, even her nipples drew up into hard beads. She struggled to catch her breath and she was so dizzy. What on earth was happening to her?

Thorne's deep rough voice broke into her thoughts. "Endelle gave the ascendiate a thirty-six-hour mind-shield, so I suspect you'll have plenty of time to officially welcome her to our world."

She glanced at him. What was he saying? Something about the ascendiate. She should pay attention since this was her job as a Liaison Officer. She hadn't been happy about the assignment, but the fact that she got to visit with the Warriors of the Blood always made her day. They had taken her under their collective wing from the time of her ascension a hundred years ago when Luken had served as her guardian. She seemed to have a natural understanding of the men and certainly she appreciated the level of their sacrifice in keeping Second Earth safe.

In rank, the Warriors were above her, but then they were above everyone, with the exception of Endelle, since they also served in the position of Guardians of Ascension and kept powerful ascendiates safe during their rites of ascension. Only Endelle had a higher rank. Even the High Administrators around the globe were lower in rank than the Warriors of the Blood.

For no particular reason her gaze drifted back to Warrior Marcus, who had given up the prestige of guardian status to take up a useless life on Mortal Earth. He still watched her. But as her gaze met his and held, her lips parted and deep, so very deep inside her body, desire spun an erotic slow dance almost as though the warrior held her in thrall.

How else could she explain her inability to look away, except to shift her gaze from one heavily muscled shoulder to the next, visible because of the traditional flight gear, solid ribbons of muscle that made the very tips of her fingers tremble and her tongue ride the back of her teeth.

An image took hold of her mind, of her hands on his back, her fingernails sunk into his flesh, her body beneath his as she held him tight . . . and he moved over her.

The fennel scent sharpened, broadened, laced with a pure male musk. She drew in a long deep breath, dragging air through her nose and into her mouth at the same time. She was intoxicated as another wave of desire traveled over her skin, into muscle and bone, then descended lower until she felt gripped from within. The very core of her wept as her internal muscles clenched, not just once, but over and over and over. She was . . . oh, God . . . she was perilously close to orgasm and all she was doing was staring at a warrior.

The vein in her neck started to pound. She put her hand there and stroked up and down. The slash over light brown eyes sank lower, a predator's stare, and she watched his fangs descend onto his lower lips. Oh, how she wanted this vampire who could put his fangs into her neck and take right now what she wanted to give.

When he started to rise from the couch, a gasp rose out of her throat. With every ounce of strength she possessed, she tore her gaze from his and looked at Thorne.

He grabbed her arm. "What is it, Havily? What's frightened you?"

"I must go." And before he could argue with her, she lifted her free arm and folded. Unfortunately, her mind was so confused, she ended up not in her home but standing in the middle of the fountain outside her town house complex.

She felt the water on her heated skin and started to laugh. To say she needed a cold shower was to say the very least.

As she stepped out of the fountain, however, she just couldn't figure out the *why* of what had just happened. In what dimension did it make the smallest sense that she could ever desire a vampire, warrior or not, whom she despised for the deserter he was?

The future speaks in a dream,
But morning unveils all truths.

—*Collected Proverbs,* Beatrice of Fourth

CHAPTER 13

Crace sat on a stone bench in the very center of the Commander's extensive peach orchard. Waiting. At least he wasn't sweating this time, although what he felt was far worse—like he'd been stabbed in the chest.

From the time of his ascension he had known hunger, his basic personal drive not just to get ahead, but to rule. With the single exception of his lovely wife, his beloved Julianna, he had only one great love—his ambition.

From the moment he first saw the Commander during his rather mundane rite of ascension he knew he would one day align with him, belong to him. He understood the Commander, because he shared the same naked, unrefined, crippling need to have power and more power and more power.

Two dimensions? Oh, come on. Greaves had more vision than that.

The opportunity to work beside Commander Greaves

had meant, literally, *the world* to Crace. Yes, Geneva was part of it, a huge part, but his sensibilities went deeper. He thought of the Commander as a true comrade, a brother-in-arms in spirit, in motivation, and in a complete lack of scruples.

He tapped his left foot on the intricate pattern of the patio made up of terra-cotta pavers. He had arrived early just to think. His wife would join him when she had put the last touches to her coiffure, the subtlety to her makeup, her ensemble. She was fastidious in such things.

The orchard, near the base of Estrella Mountain, was a thing of beauty. The trees were laid out as though radiating from a large hub, the circle ever widening as it traveled in what seemed like miles in every direction. The entire orchard was covered with a variety of shields, which allowed for a gradation of microclimates. Some trees were heavy with ripe fruit, others just budding, others in a state of wintry rest. Beneath the trees, a natural collection of grasses and weeds grew. The Commander had won awards for his organic methods.

More than any other aspect of the Commander's life, this orchard and what lay below typified his essential character. Beneath the rows of peach trees, buried in the earth, was the Command Center for his entire global operation. Below the Command Center ran miles of bunkers and a variety of training facilities for his army. Below the bunkers was a vast cavern dedicated exclusively to research and development. The Commander had a passion for armaments. He was creative with weaponry of all kinds, always working on improved killing methods.

An hour earlier, despite the failure in Carefree, Greaves had requested that Crace and his wife join him for breakfast. He would serve mimosas, fresh peaches, egg-white omelets, and all because he knew such a breakfast would delight Julianna. In the center of a table covered in beautiful Irish linen sat an elegant arrangement of orchids growing from a bed of some sort of small-leafed green ground cover. Yes, Julianna would be enthralled by the attention to detail.

There was so much to admire about his deity.

How heavily he sighed.

He had showered and shaved. He wore a formal white tuxedo, black trousers, the finest black shoes. He had tried to scrub the stench of his failure off his tanned arms, legs, and face but couldn't. He bled remorse from every pore of his body.

He sat on the hard stone awaiting his wife's arrival. She had told him to quit being so nonsensical, that the Commander, being a practical, sensible man, would not, *would not* in any way blame Crace for the failure of an entire regiment to slay the ascendiate. In her opinion such an elegant private breakfast meant he held Crace no ill will.

Usually, Crace's wife knew best. She had great abilities. She could sense things before they happened. He therefore shouldn't feel as though he would soon be ground to dust by his deity's displeasure.

Yet how could it be any different? The Commander would hold him responsible for what had happened in Carefree.

Crace rarely despaired. An optimist by nature, his present sensations were foreign. He didn't like the way his body felt, heavy in every muscle, tight around his heart, tense in his lungs. He even had to force himself to breathe.

Was it his fault the ascendiate had so much power? She had disabled his men over and over from a series of hand-blasts. *Hand-blasts.* He could not even conceive how she'd done it. He shuddered at the memory. Beyond the hand-blasts, however, who could have foreseen that so noble a warrior as Kerrick would have called an illegal emergency lift? It was unheard of.

And just how had the pair known to take off in the ascendiate's fucking Hummer? How had they been warned? He shuddered all over again.

He felt the air stir and he rose to his feet.

He melted at the sight of his incomparable wife. She had the beauty of Aphrodite, and looked particularly splendid in a peach-colored soft linen gown—an excellent choice given the occasion—her dark tresses arranged in several loose elegant knots down the back of her head. She wore soft pearls, which the early-morning light and the shields over the orchard set in a gentle glow. She was perfection, her taste unequaled. Gems of any sort would have been wholly unsuitable. She had taught him this, and many other things. She knew how to present herself in such a way to add to his worth and to his power.

She had sharp blue eyes, angled slightly at the corners along with her brows. Her cheekbones were high and pronounced, her lips full. Her breasts were large, round, very supple, and moved completely unfettered beneath the fabric. The sight of her breasts so well displayed, yet still covered modestly, brought a sharp arousal. She approached him, kissed his cheek, and took his hand in hers. She whispered in his ear, "You will take me to bed after this, you will drink from me, and I will soothe your fears."

She always did. He drew in a deep breath and relaxed . . . a little. She was the best of wives. He was the most fortunate of men.

The air stirred once more. She stepped away from him slightly. Given his rank, she did not believe in public displays of affection. When the Commander appeared, she offered a courteous inclination of her head coupled with a slight curtsy, a tradition she had begun and which had caught on throughout Second Earth. "Julianna, how lovely to see you."

"And you, Commander."

"Please. Call me Darian."

His wife, his darling wife, merely smiled, offered another bow, then said, "As you wish, *Commander*."

Crace marveled at her adroitness. She always passed the Commander's little tests, which seemed to please him immensely, for he smiled and even chuckled. She lifted her hand to him.

He approached her and took her proffered hand, offering a polite kiss on the arch of her fingers, a sign of great respect. Crace felt a wave of heat roll from his wife. A surprise. The Commander's gaze dropped oh so briefly to her breasts. Crace followed suit and found his wife's nipples peaked, stretching the lovely peach linen. He understood in this moment all over again how clever his wife was. He blinked and more of his fears dissipated.

The Commander lifted his hand and snapped his fingers. A moment later three wait staff materialized as well as a large serving cart.

Julianna clapped her hands in an innocent expression of pleasure at the meal the Commander had provided for her. Naturally, Greaves seated her himself. And naturally, Julianna smiled up at him, just over her shoulder, and whispered her thank-you.

Crace sat down to eat with his fears settled to a dull roar, so much so that by the time the meal had been consumed and the champagne had eased through his veins, he leaned back in his chair.

"I was sorry to hear of Warrior Kerrick's illegal maneuver," Greaves said. "Wholly unexpected."

"Yes, it was, Commander."

"Very well. We shall simply move forward."

Crace withheld the gasp rattling in his throat. There would be no recriminations. Thank the Creator for small mercies.

"I want you to see Harding and make arrangements for the next leg of this journey. We will have every legal right to pursue any course we wish. I rely on you, my dear Crace, to make the finish *remarkable*."

Crace stared into the eyes of his deity. *Make the finish remarkable. Every legal right.* The emergency lift may have saved the ascendiate's life, but it had also given the Commander a profound, irreversible advantage.

On Second Earth, there was always one way to make anything *remarkable*.

Spectacle.

Yes, *spectacle.*

Within his mind, he began to weave a glorious exhibition. He would use swans, of course, and fireworks. He would call in a favor or two from Beijing. The local theaters would have all the actors he required for a full-mount display . . . yes, he knew exactly what needed to be done. And of course the event would be televised worldwide. Yes, that would work . . . *remarkably*.

As for the ascendiate, well, her demise would be the highlight of the entire evening, of course.

"I believe I have the answer," he said.

Crace felt a now familiar pressure in his head. Greaves's serious expression softened then lightened. He nodded several times and afterward smiled.

"My dear Crace, you have outdone yourself. You are to be congratulated."

"You may congratulate me, master, when the ascendiate breathes her last."

The lake.

Alison floated inside a familiar dream high in the air. She looked down at a very long, somewhat narrow lake, perhaps only half a mile across in the widest place. However, the body of water extended several miles in a north–south direction, making up in length what it lacked in width.

The floating was pleasurable.

Wait. She wasn't floating at all. She was flying and she had wings, beautiful pearlescent light blue wings edged with gold at every tip, a shimmering gold. She felt euphoric and deeply content. She flapped her wings, which had mounted from within her back, like Warrior Kerrick's wings.

What a strange sensation to feel the presence of wing-locks as well as the thickened muscles of her back and the heavy dose of hormones gliding through her veins. She had a sudden and tremendous sensation of power. She stretched out her arms and felt within her mind the key to movement— the wing-locks combined with thought.

Her wings were an amazing part of her, both mind and body. When she envisioned a downward thrust, her wings responded almost magically. Flight was therefore a learned skill, the way an infant would learn to bring his fists together and feel the clasp of his hands for the first time. Wings were another set of muscles to learn to manipulate.

Exhilaration. She envisioned a spin and her wing-locks responded until she was twirling oh so high in the air. On instinct, she spread her wings wide and the spiral stopped. She laughed.

Looking down, she spun in another circle, much slower this time, and discovered that the lake was at the foot of the range of mountains she knew well—the White Tanks. She also, for some reason, knew the name of the lake—White Lake. Yet how strange to see a body of water here. On Mortal Earth nothing much existed on the west side of the White Tanks except a small development of homes and the occasional lone house or trailer. Certainly not a lake.

As she glided over the water, she experienced a sense of destiny, of the future, that her future was here, with this lake. A strong yearning took hold of her chest, the same profound longing that had prompted her to answer her call to ascension. She felt *protective* of the lake, almost painfully so, as though the fate of the world depended on her ability to keep White Lake secure.

The word *guardian* slid through her head, the same word Warrior Kerrick had used to describe his relationship to her, that he was her guardian. And she was the guardian of this lake. Only what could it possibly mean?

As she drifted toward consciousness, the dream formed the backdrop of her mind. She awoke on her back in an unfamiliar bed staring up at a tall vaulted ceiling painted a beautiful burnt orange and overlaid with dark stripped branches. She had never seen a ceiling like this, a real work of art. So where was she?

The last ceiling she'd awakened to had been her own and . . . Kerrick's arm had been slung over her chest. He had burrowed into her neck, teasing her awake with erotic movements of the duller parts of his fangs nudging her throat just above the vein.

Potent desire whipped through her at the remembered sensations, and she arched on the bed. Recalling the powerful orgasm brought her legs pressing together, trying to find some relief. Oh, what Kerrick had done to her. She slid her hand over her neck. She groaned at the memory of coming apart while he took her blood and tormented her with his fingers. She couldn't begin to imagine what full-on sex would be like with him.

Once more her back arched off the bed.

Okay. She had to stop thinking about him, or at least about having sex with him. She had to dwell instead on exactly where she was and how she'd gotten here and why on earth she had been dreaming about a lake.

She sat up and looked around. Near an open doorway, leading to a bathroom, stood a rack hanging with clothes, women's clothes. She looked down at the very soft, white nightie she wore, more like a tunic, she supposed. Where had this come from? She frowned as she thought about the blast, which had no doubt destroyed her home. Did she even have any clothes left? She mentally reached out to her house, but found her mind blocked very strangely. She couldn't reach farther than twenty or thirty yards from her present position.

Some kind of shield was in place, a very powerful shield, one she knew instinctively had been put there to keep her safe.

She flopped back down on the bed. She was right back to the very bizarre world she'd entered, from death vampires and warriors with rasping tongues and erotic fangs, to inexplicable mind-shields and dreams about a lake and being a guardian.

Ascension. Her ascension.

She closed her eyes and for a long moment took deep breaths. She let the reality of her present circumstances drift through her head. Last night, twice, she'd barely escaped with her life, once from the alley, once from the attack of death vamps at her home in Carefree.

And then there was Kerrick, her guardian, the one assigned to protect her, the one she felt drawn to like cactus to the desert. Her heart raced when she thought of him and of the wonderful musky cardamom smell of him, the one that made her think of exotic marketplaces in Morocco.

She had come to a new world, engaged a new life full of danger yet also of possibility.

An odd question surfaced. Just how was she going to explain to Joy, or to the rest of her family, her new life?

Kerrick sat in his kitchen at a stool drawn up to the large square granite island. He sipped his coffee.

Coffee was good.

God, he loved this era—plug it in, turn it on, cook, fry, bake, and boil. Centuries ago he would have spent a part of every summer day chopping wood in order to keep the home fires burning through the cold season.

He'd made a pot of coffee and set out a cup for Alison. He wondered if she drank coffee. He wondered about a lot of things where she was concerned—which authors got her going, why she owned a Hummer, and whether or not he could keep her alive, goddammit.

He exhaled on a heavy sigh.

Whatever.

The Queen Creek house had no close neighbors and plenty of windows. Afternoon light brightened all the west-facing rooms. As homes went, this one was . . . comfortable.

He sipped again. He liked his coffee like mud. Did Alison prefer hers weak?

He shook his head. His thoughts had been full of her from the time he'd awakened, of wanting to hold her in his arms, take her to bed, bury himself in her body for maybe a year. Two. Three. A thousand.

In Carefree the power she had released when she orgasmed had been as erotic as hell. Shivers slid down his back just thinking about it. He shifted to make room for an erection that never seemed very far away.

He was driven to distraction by his need to commune with this woman, to be inside her mind, to take more of her blood—rich heady wine laced with erotic lavender—to be physically joined with her. He throbbed for her, at his neck and in his groin. He had to set his coffee cup down since his hands started to shake.

Christ.

And he was only *thinking* about her. What would happen if . . . *when* . . . he made love to her? He shook his head and picked up his cup once more. He drank this time then breathed. So how the hell was he supposed to keep his vows when the *breh-hedden* had fucked up his head so completely?

Damn *breh-hedden*.

A roll of lavender reached him and he leaned forward on the stool sucking in his breath. He'd already been hard as a rock. Now? He could have pounded nails. Okay, time to work up his resolve, to shape it into a mountain and hold steady.

Breathe, dammit—suck one in, shove one out.

So his woman was awake and thinking about him. Great. How was he supposed to keep away from her if she got worked up as badly as he did? He muttered a string of curses as he stared at the green-black granite. What was it going to take to get rid of this absurd drive?

He sat back up as Alison appeared in the kitchen doorway straight across from him. The mere sight of her, however, fresh as she was from a deep sleep and so beautiful, brought an entire brigade of heavy equipment scooping away at the mountainside of his resolve. Diesel engines chugged along, tires the size of SUVs rolled everywhere, and trucks the length of football stadiums hauled away rock and dirt in droves.

She looked beautiful in a pair of simple black pants and a light green tank top—thank God Endelle's assistant had provided something more than just that short white tunic. And yeah, thank God she'd changed. One sight of her long legs and he was sure he would have lost it.

Unfortunately, the top fit her really well and had a small glittery firework in the center just below her cleavage and yeah, she had some awesome cleavage showing. He'd like his tongue running up and down . . .

He drew in a rough breath.

He took a sip of coffee then let his thoughts drift toward her. He gave shape to one potent idea and sent it straight to her mind, the one he just couldn't contain any longer: *Naked and on your back* . . .

She smiled. "Anything particular on your mind, Warrior?"

Warrior. Oh, shit. Calling him by his vocation made her more real in his life. He sent her a string of powerful images, all of which involved him doing things to various parts of her anatomy.

Her lips parted and a fresh wave of lavender returned, which nearly knocked him off his stool.

The air grew charged though she remained where she was. She rubbed her arms and drew in a long raspy breath. *How much do you want me?* she sent. The voice in his head floated and writhed. She could seduce him even with her thoughts.

Like dry earth begging for rain, he responded.

He was so screwed.

Alison couldn't move. She wanted to. She wanted to run to Kerrick, throw her arms around him, and hold him tight.

Dry earth begging for rain, she sent.

He nodded.

She wanted to be the rain, to cover him with moisture, to bring life to his seed.

As she met his gaze, looked at his long wavy black hair hanging loose past his shoulders, at the size of those shoulders, her body thrummed, wept, cried out for him. This was what she had longed for ever since she was a goofy teen getting crushes on boys. This was what Joy had. Could this truly be hers?

She reached out with her mind. She touched gently not to enter, but to be close for just this moment. He closed his eyes in understanding. She let her mind rest next to his and at least a dozen tender fantasies rolled through her.

She could really be with this man. Yes, this vampire.

She gazed deep into the future and saw an eternity of him. She took his hand and smiled into his face. She laughed with him and cried with him. She bore his children and nagged him about putting up Christmas lights and helping the kids with homework. She admonished him to keep his sword-hand wicked and his tongue in her mouth or anywhere else he wanted it.

She wanted these things painfully.

Yet she still couldn't move. She felt pinned to the spot where she'd landed, her bare feet stuck like chewing gum to cement. Fear of this new world held her fast. She still didn't know the rules. Besides, wasn't it possible she could still end up hurting Kerrick because of her powers in ways she couldn't yet conceive? She hadn't hurt him earlier on the couch in Carefree, but he'd been beside her, not in her. Oh, God. Okay.

He opened his eyes, smiled faintly at her reticence and nodded. He slid off his stool then moved to the coffeemaker. Her gaze followed hungrily. The muscles of his arms bunched and twitched. His knuckles paled as he grabbed the coffeepot. He topped off and returned to his stool.

He struggled, just as she struggled.

He set his mug down then gripped the counter. He stared into the flecked green granite. He released a heavy sigh, picked up his mug, then sipped again.

Her heart strained toward him. She suppressed the sensation. "You have a lovely home," she said.

He met her gaze. Did she see relief in his eyes because she'd mentioned something so ordinary? "Thank you," he responded.

"I really like the twigged ceilings."

He nodded. Sipped.

She glanced to her right and had a clear view through a second doorway into the living room. Her gaze skipped up to the ceiling where more branches, stripped bare, were laid side by side. "Beautiful texture, unique, especially with the terra-cotta color behind. You must love this home."

"I do . . . today," he said.

She shot her gaze to his. A wave of cardamom nearly knocked her flat. She braced a hand against the nearest kitchen cabinet and took a deep breath. Okay. She really shouldn't go there.

She tried another subject. "Did you know there's a rack of clothes in my room?"

"I'm not surprised. Endelle's staff would want to take good care of you. So tell me, what do you remember from last night, after the attack in Carefree?"

The gum disappeared from the soles of her feet. She moved, albeit slowly in his direction, crossing the kitchen to the massive granite island. She moved to stand at the side of the island off to his right, the coffeemaker behind her. Her palm slid over the mirror-smooth stone. "I recall a flash of light then standing in front of a man with long sandy-colored hair, though not much else."

"You passed out from your injury. Do you remember the shoulder wound?"

"That's right, I got hit." She rotated her left arm. "What happened? I mean, I hardly feel anything. Only a little muscle ache remains."

"Endelle healed you."

"She was there? The ruler of Second Earth? And she healed me?"

"Of course," he said. "She also gave you a mind-shield that will protect you until about seven tomorrow evening."

"Oh. Now I understand. I tried to reach out to my home, to see if anything was left, but couldn't get far. I suppose I should thank her."

"I'm sure you'll have plenty of opportunity to return the favor."

"She's the demanding type?"

"You have no idea."

"Who was the man I saw? He was almost as tall as you and quite good-looking. Very muscular." His gaze hardened and his fangs made an appearance, a sudden reminder she'd entered not just a world of dimensions but a vampire-warrior world as well.

She blinked as her gaze rested on the sharp tips of his incisors. Assuming she survived this journey, one day she would sport a pair of fangs and . . . she'd make use of them. Her lungs seized at the thought of putting her fangs at Kerrick's neck. The breath she drew sounded like she was dragging air through a fine-mesh screen.

She thought she heard a faint growl. She listened harder. The warrior with all the gorgeous black hair *was* growling. Because she'd said the other man was good-looking and muscular? Uh-huh. A clear case of caveman possessiveness . . . and it kind of got to her.

He didn't meet her gaze as he sipped his coffee. "Thorne. He's Endelle's right-hand man, the leader of the Warriors of the Blood."

He drank again, though shifting his gaze this time to watch her from just above the rim of his mug. A new growl formed, deepened, then got louder, a sound that rumbled right through her chest, weakened all her stomach muscles and the tendons supporting her knees. The smell of cardamom grew stronger.

Wow. If she hadn't been working out she would have dropped to the tile by now.

Still, some devil worked in her and she couldn't resist teasing him. In a strong voice she said, "You know, Thorne has a real aura of command, doesn't he?"

The growls escalated but he chugged his coffee once more then did some more granite-staring.

Okay, so maybe she was being a little mean, teasing him as she was. She'd stop now. She looked him up and down and all her desire for him once more made an appearance, whipping through her like a wildfire. He wore jeans that did little to disguise his powerful thighs, and a snug tee molded to massive pecs. She stifled a groan. Her gaze skated lower, all the way to the floor. The man was also barefoot. Damn. Even his feet were sexy as hell. More wire-screen breathing.

Her gaze took a turn and shifted to her own shoeless feet. A strange dizziness passed through her mind. *They were alike.* Oh, no.

She swallowed and spoke quickly, "My head feels fuzzy. Is that the shield?"

"Yes."

"And no one can find me?"

"No one. A shield like this causes confusion but it's also illegal to use on ascendiates so we're awaiting the repercussions."

Alison nodded. "As with the emergency lift you called?"

"Yep."

"So we're in trouble."

"Yep."

She looked away from him. "Well, what's the deal with my house and my Hummer? By now I'm thinking the police will be all over the rubble, probably looking for terrorists or something."

He shook his head. "Thorne sent Zacharius out to take care of things after the Commander's war party went home. The Hummer's fine—well, except for the blasted-out windows, fender damage, and oh, yeah, you need a new roof. As for the house, mostly rubble. Endelle has already arranged for a crew to rebuild."

"Is she doing that for me?" she asked, surprised.

"Sorry. This is about appearances and secrecy. There's a very complex mist around the property until the renovation is complete."

Alison shook her head. "Okaaay, then."

"So why a Hummer? You have a sad little Nova and then a powerful, environmentally unfriendly vehicle."

"I've had it several years and I admit I love it. It's so big and roomy. My height is an advantage in many ways but not in small cars. The Nova I've had with me since my teens."

"The Hummer's more of a man's car, though."

"Yes, I suppose so."

She nodded and rubbed a hand once more over the smooth granite. She glanced up then shifted her gaze anywhere except in his direction. He was staring at her and she so hoped he wouldn't guess her thoughts because a quite humiliating epiphany had just swamped her brain. She had bought the Hummer as a promise of the future. She wanted a man in her life big enough to fill a vehicle that size and . . . there he was sipping coffee and looking incredibly *hot* in a snug, pec-shaping T-shirt, blue jeans, and, oh, yeah, sexy bare feet.

She turned around and crossed to the coffeemaker. A second mug sat beside a bowl of sugar along with a small pitcher of milk. "Did you put this here for me?" she asked, over her shoulder.

"Of course."

There was no such thing as *of course*. Dammit, the man was thoughtful about small things. Great. Just great. One more reason to like him way too much.

She poured herself a cup, added just a dollop of milk, half a teaspoon of sugar, stirred then took a sip. She almost choked. "You kind of like your coffee strong." She turned back to him and cleared her throat. Twice. Her eyes watered.

He smirked and crossed his arms over his broad chest. "I would have warned you if you hadn't gone on and on about Thorne and his *aura of command*."

She laughed. "Yeah, the whole Thorne thing was a bitchy thing to do."

"Yes, it was."

Unfortunately, he was really close, and when she took her next breath she smelled his wicked cardamom scent all over again. She felt the strongest impulse to launch herself at him and end this ridiculous misery.

Havily stood on the front porch of Warrior Kerrick's Queen Creek house. She had her attaché in her right hand and she held her left fist poised at the solid wood door, ready to strike, to let her presence be known, but her mind traveled in circles around the recent events at the Cave.

Fennel had become fixed in her sinuses and leached into her brain every now and then to remind her she had seen the recently recalled Warrior Marcus for the first time and had experienced several inexplicable reactions to him.

She flared her nostrils and tilted her head back. She lowered her fist back to her side. She closed her eyes and let the remembered smell tease her senses. And every time she did, her breasts swelled and tightened, her abdomen rolled down and down, then the most delicious sensation tugged at her deep internal muscles. Even her fangs tingled, anxious to emerge.

She had known all the warriors for decades now, having met them during her ascension nearly a hundred years ago, when she had needed their protection. While Luken had served as her guardian at the time, the process had given her the opportunity to get to know each one.

Since then she had remained close to the warriors. Even though she served as a lowly Liaison Officer, similar in rank to the girls at Central, the Warriors of the Blood had come to treat her as one of their own, in part, no doubt, because Luken had a serious crush on her. She loved the men as brothers. However, this was the first time a warrior had ever affected her so powerfully, like a designer drug created just for her.

The more she stood there, the remembered fennel working inside her, the stronger the drug acted on her body. She should stop the roll of sensations—she had her liaison work to do—but the pleasure she experienced had become *addictive*. Now her fangs throbbed, seeking a point of entrance. She imagined the tips sinking into his throat. His blood would taste of fennel, very sweet, very earthy, and she wanted his elixir down her throat. Desire drove deep and she clenched, hard, almost to the point of orgasm . . . again.

Her face grew flushed, first in desire then in acute embarrassment. She had seen how female ascenders, wings mounted and on display, often threw themselves at the Warriors of the Blood, out-of-their-senses women who were normally intelligent and, well, moral. Of course the warriors were superb specimens of maleness and tales of their sexual prowess were legion. Still, until now she had never once engaged in a fantasy of being with one of them.

Until now.

She clenched once more, her body weeping and out of control. Again her face flamed.

This was completely absurd.

And beyond humiliating.

She was not this kind of woman. She had never been a warrior-chaser. She was sensible, governed by rational thought and careful about her conduct on every level. She had enjoyed the act of love, especially with her fiancé, the powerful Militia Warrior nearly equal in size to the Warriors of the Blood. But that had been fifteen years ago.

Since then she had dedicated herself to finding ways to shift the course of the war. Havily Morgan had a mission and she would stick to it.

She forced herself to calm down. She took deep breaths and regained control of her senses. She would not be this sort of woman.

When her cheeks no longer felt torched, she knocked on the door then called out in a loud voice to announce her presence. A warrior on serious guardian duty ought to be warned. "Warrior Kerrick. 'Tis I, Havily."

After a long moment, the door opened. A frown split Warrior Kerrick's brow as he stepped onto the porch. He shoved her backward toward the doorway, an arm thrown in front of her protectively. His head panned ever so slowly from all the way left to all the way right. The muscles of his shoulders flexed beneath a very tight T-shirt. He wore his hair loose in long black waves. He had beautiful warrior hair, so long and touchable. Again, she had seen women touch and stroke his thick hair.

Warrior Marcus, on the other hand, had a modern corporate cut, though not unattractive. She remembered his expression as he sat forward on the couch and stared at her, her gaze locked onto his. He had seemed so *intent* on her.

More desire descended and she gasped. Why on earth had her thoughts again become fixed on *him*?

"What is it?" Warrior Kerrick snapped, turning to stare at her.

She met his gaze. Oh, God, she could hardly share with

Kerrick her unholy thoughts about a fellow warrior, especially a warrior whom Kerrick despised. So she looked past him and prevaricated. "Your mist is so beautiful," she said. "I . . . I just noticed it from this side.

"You see, I arrived over there on the edge of the wash and could see nothing of your house. I had to have Central fold me directly to your front door."

He turned back to her, his green eyes serious and in full warrior mode. He nodded once. "I can't take credit for the mist. This is Endelle's work."

"Oh. Well, it is amazing but it wouldn't have surprised me if you'd been the author or any of the Warriors of the Blood. You're all so powerful."

He shook his head. "None of us can make mist like this. Trust me. But let's get you inside."

He hustled her into the foyer and closed the door so hard the frame shook. He stood facing the door and listened for a long, tense moment.

At last, satisfied, he turned to her. "What the hell are you doing here?"

She took a step back and lifted her attaché a few inches. "Liaison work. There are forms to fill out, to sign. Questions to ask."

At that his shoulders relaxed. "Shit, yes, of course. Come in, Havily. I'm sorry. I should have expected you. Let me introduce you to ascendiate Wells."

The tongue is a blessing.
The tongue is a sword.
Beloved, my beloved,
Pray know the difference.

—*Collected Poems*, Beatrice of Fourth

CHAPTER 14

Alison stood by the granite island. She had heard the exchange between the woman and Kerrick, the woman he had called Havily, an unusual name, a very pretty name.

When the rapping on the door had sounded, Kerrick had gone into full warrior mode. As her adrenaline spiked, forgotten in a heartbeat was all the crushing need to throw herself at him. He'd ordered her to stay in the kitchen then contacted Central. Yes, the woman named Havily had been sent to them. He had said, *She's a Liaison Officer.* Alison had waited.

Hearing their voices fall to normal levels, she moved into the doorway leading to the living room.

Havily. As the woman turned around, Alison had an instant impression of beauty and tremendous determination. She had a fount of glorious red hair flowing in waves past her shoulders and was an absolute angel, a visual work of art. Her features were delicate, her skin clear and smooth as though molded by a master's hand, her eyes an exquisite light green. She wore professional clothes, a cream linen suit, nicely tailored. *You're lovely* slid from her mind before she could stop the words.

And you are powerful, Havily returned, her eyes brightening. *I've been told my shields have no equal, yet here you are, in my thoughts?*

"I shouldn't have gone inside your head. I apologize."

The young woman looked up at Kerrick and blinked again. "She laid her thoughts over my mind."

Kerrick nodded. "And your shields are like granite." He smiled his crooked smile. "Welcome to my world. Liaison Officer Havily Morgan, may I present ascendiate Alison Wells."

The next few minutes involved a general exchange of greetings, explanation of duties, then a sit-down at the adjacent round table, which began with an enormous sheaf of forms. "Is all this really necessary?" Alison asked. "I thought ascension meant everything was improved."

Havily sighed. "Unfortunately, the same difficulties of entrenched bureaucracies are alive and well on Second Earth. I'm hoping to make a difference. After all, what is the purpose of one form that says ASCENDIATE APPLICATION and another, ASCENDIATE DATA, each presenting a list of identical questions with the exception of one or two? And what's worse, it's all done on paper as though the computer had never been invented."

Alison heard the increase in both pitch and speed of the Liaison Officer's speech. She glanced at both forms then at Havily. She saw the wrinkled brow and heard the quiet clucking of her tongue. Alison reached out once more and felt the young woman's passion, her dedication. "You'd like to see many changes."

"You have no idea." Her cheeks grew pink and her eyes widened.

"What kind of changes?"

Havily turned toward her, shifted her knees, and met her gaze straight-on. She gestured with a sweep of her left hand. "At the very least, each entity should be led by a person of vision, of passion, who understands the concept of a *mission-oriented* plan. At the very least."

Alison smiled as her own heart rate kicked up a notch to match Havily's. She encouraged her to speak, to elaborate on her ideas, and the Liaison Officer opened up to the point that after a few minutes Havily rose to her feet and paced the room. She gesticulated with an ever-widening throw of her arms and covered subjects like *competitive performance* and *empowering staff*. Even Kerrick moved to sit on a stool, coffee cup in hand, his gaze fixed on the vibrant movements and gestures.

When at last Havily drew breath, Kerrick said, "I didn't know you cared about these things. I mean, I know you've been working with an architect on a new military-admin complex. Jesus, Havily."

She glanced at him then back at Alison. Her fine peachy-red brows rose over her delicate features. She pierced Alison with her vibrant stare. "You're an empath."

"I . . . suppose."

Havily returned to her seat in her brisk movements. "You are. Of course you are." She opened up a lavender folder. "Yes, of course, since you have all of Second's abilities. That's how you got me to talking." Once more her passionate nature asserted itself and she laid a hand on Alison's arm, her light green eyes blazing. "You must get to know Madame Endelle. You must find some way to help her, to get through to her about all the ways she's misdirected. You see, she's grossly overworked trying to hold our world together, and her administration is sunk in all the reports she receives from all over the world. We none of us really know her, or what makes up her day, since who among us comes near to having her powers? But you could. With all of Second's abilities, you could."

Alison hardly knew what to say. As it was, the little she knew of Endelle made her feel sorry for *anyone* who might have to work so closely with her.

Kerrick moved from the island to stand next to Havily. He

settled a hand on her shoulder. "Hey, O Passionate One, our ascendiate barely knows anything about our world. She's just getting used to the fangs and having to battle for her life. Asking her to be of use to Endelle—it might be a little early in the process."

Havily shifted her gaze to stare at the papers once more. "You're right." She nodded. "Yes, of course." She then pulled forward the first sheet and began gathering Alison's basic information, date of birth, height, weight, medical history, schooling. Alison found the interview soothing in an odd way. To be talking of such mundane things made her feel there was some normalcy to the process.

She sat back in her chair and sipped her coffee as Havily checked boxes and filled in spaces. When Havily jotted down Joy's name, Alison asked, "So how does this work? Kerrick told me I will still be able to see my family. I can still visit them, be with them."

Havily glanced at her and smiled but there was a hint of sadness in her eyes. "Of course you can. However, we require counseling for ascenders who wish to continue to visit Mortal Earth. In the beginning everything will seem strange, awkward. You might even want to repress memories at some point or create new ones to explain your absences, that sort of thing."

Alison sucked in a breath. "You mean tamper with the minds of family members."

Havily nodded, frowning. "I know it seems invasive, even unkind. However, one of the goals must always be to keep Second Earth a secret from Mortal Earth. We even have departments worldwide that monitor eruptions about dimensional worlds, or the world of the vampire. Again, lots of memories are suppressed."

Alison nodded, but she couldn't imagine being anything but forthright with her family. "I'm very close to my sister. She'll wonder where I am. As it is, I'll be missing a family dinner."

"Actually," Havily said, "I've often found it helpful, just until this process works itself out, to pretend you decided to take a spontaneous holiday, like to Hawaii, or better yet, Mexico, for oh, say, three weeks."

"Fake a vacation? A three-week vacation?"

Havily consulted her notes. "Well, you're in between gigs at the moment, having given up your practice, and your grad program wouldn't have started for another month."

"I just don't know if my family will buy it." She shifted in her seat.

"I'm not fond of fabricating my way through life, either. In this situation, however, the truth won't serve. Think of it as giving yourself a period of time to adjust to your new life here, to receive some counseling, to know what you can tell your family, to figure out how to move forward." Alison didn't know what to say. Havily pressed on. "Once you complete your rite of ascension, the first few weeks of ascended life will be rigorous. We are an industrious world and everyone plays a part. Pretending a three-week stay in Mexico or Hawaii will give you time to settle in before having to tackle the more delicate job of incorporating visits to Mortal Earth with your new life on Second."

Alison held out both hands, palms up. "What do I do?"

Havily whipped out her iPhone. "Call your sister and start learning to *elaborate* on the truth."

Alison blinked. She didn't know which shocked her more, that she'd be lying to her family or that Havily held a Mortal Earth iPhone in her hand.

Havily laughed, a musical trill very much like Joy's. "The import business on Second is enormous. We take advantage of all Mortal Earth technology."

Alison once more had that strange underwater sensation, the one she had experienced earlier when Kerrick drove her to her home in Carefree. All the information he had blurred in her direction had made her feel like she'd dropped below the surface of a large body of water. She felt that way all over again.

Despite the sense of being overwhelmed, Alison took the phone and made her call—but when she heard her sister's voice, tears started to her eyes. The reality of what would become in time a huge gulf between herself and her family threatened to overtake her.

"Where have you been?" Joy cried. "I've left you three messages and you're just now calling?"

Joy's peeved tone allowed air to rush into Alison's lungs. She smiled. "Where have I been?" Alison suppressed a laugh thinking of her blown-up house in Carefree. She glanced at Kerrick. He shook his head back and forth, not as a negation but as a hell-if-I-know-what-to-say.

"Well, you're never going to believe this," she began. Havily gasped and opened her mouth wide. She wagged her head briskly back and forth, clearly afraid Alison meant to spill the beans. But Alison said, "I'm in Mexico . . . Cancún, actually."

"What?"

Alison pulled the phone away from her ear then back. "Hey, I have *acute* hearing, remember?"

Joy laughed then expressed a mountain of *I can't believe it,* but the more Alison assured her she'd hopped on a plane, checked into a hotel, and was now by a pool sipping a margarita, the easier the lie became.

Silence. Alison closed her eyes. Would Joy buy it?

"I can't believe you actually took a vacation."

"I needed time to think. I've really started to question whether grad school is the answer for me. And do you realize that the last time I zoned out on a beach was over four years ago?"

"Lissy, I'm so glad. You've earned a break, but why didn't you tell me?"

"Well, I'm not sure. But after you and I talked on the phone, I just got to thinking about what you told me. The next thing I knew . . . well, the plans came together really fast." She let the words hang.

Joy gasped. "Tell me you're taking my advice . . . about . . . you know."

Alison shifted her gaze to Kerrick, to his wonderful height, to the massive plane of his chest, the ripped shoulders and pecs, his sexy jeans and bare feet. "Actually, I think you might have given me the best advice ever and I'm going to do something about it."

Joy squealed. "Go get 'em," she cried. "But you'd better call me . . . a lot. I want updates."

"Hey," Alison cried, "if my plans work out I may be a little busy."

"That would be so awesome, sister mine. Okay. You do whatever you have to do right now. If you need time to, well, *relax*"—she pretended to growl—"then you *relax* as long as you want."

"I love you, Joy."

"Love you more."

Alison touched the screen to end the connection. She handed the phone back to Havily, who had already stuffed her papers back into her briefcase, preparing to leave.

For some reason Alison recalled her dream of flying over a lake. On impulse she said, "Before you go, there's something I'd like to ask you."

"Yes, of course, anything."

"Can you tell me about White Lake?"

"White Lake? You mean White Lake near the White Tank Mountains?"

"On the west side of the White Tanks?"

"Yes."

"So it does exist," Alison murmured.

"Why do you ask? What is it you want to know?"

"I've dreamed about the lake. I just wasn't sure if it was real. There isn't a lake here by that name."

Havily's lips parted and a frown furrowed her brow.

Kerrick returned to the table. He stared down at her, his emerald eyes flashing. "What kind of dream was it?"

"Earlier, when I woke up, I had been dreaming that I had wings—and it was so awesome to be flying. I was over a lake, and in the dream I knew the lake was called White Lake. I just wondered if it had any particular significance."

Kerrick whistled.

Havily put a hand to her chest, her expressive fingers

plucking at her ivory silk blouse. "What was the nature of the dream?" she asked. "I mean, what were you feeling in the dream?" Her voice had a hushed quality.

"Well, I guess I just felt very *protective* of the lake, like somehow this was my job, to protect White Lake. Also, I kept hearing the word *guardian* in my head."

"Holy shit," Kerrick murmured.

Havily glanced at Kerrick, but he just shrugged as though unable to give her direction on this one.

"The lake," Havily said, "forms a Borderland between Second and Third Earth."

"A dimensional Borderland?" Alison was shocked.

"Precisely. However, the Trough to Third is closed to us."

"Like Second is closed to Mortals."

"With the important difference that we know Third Earth exists."

"Yet you have no contact with Third Earth or any of the Upper Dimensions. So how do you know any of them exist?"

"Because Third Earth wasn't always closed," Havily said. "Several millennia ago there was constant movement among all the dimensions. Then it was just shut down. No one here knows why. But that was a long time ago."

"And you don't have any idea what the significance of this dream might be? Why I might have experienced such protective feelings about the lake, the Borderland?"

Havily tilted her head. "Dreams are an important element of ascended life, and we never take them lightly. It sounds like you have a very real connection to the White Lake Borderland. The interpretation, however, shouldn't be forced, and I'm absolutely certain you'll discover the meaning in time."

Havily stood up, taking her briefcase in hand. "Be at peace, ascendiate," she said.

Alison rose as well. Havily extended her hand and with a smile, Alison took it in hers and gave a firm shake. However, the moment she did, Havily froze in place, her brows high in the air. Her lips formed a silent *O*.

Then Alison felt it as well, a strange vibration flowing up her arm from the hand clasping Havily's. She experienced a connection with this woman, an inexplicable bond. Alison closed her eyes and a heavy sensation flowed through her mind, a prescience, then a specific image of Havily flying next to her over White Lake, her expression hard, determined, focused.

Alison gasped then released her hand. "Did you see that as well?"

"A vision?" Havily's brows rose higher.

"I guess that's what it was."

Havily shook her head, smiled, chuckled. "You *are* powerful. As for myself, no vision, though I did feel a tingling in my hand and all up my arm." Once more she tilted her head. "Ascendiate, I wish you the very best in the coming days and weeks. If you need anything, do not hesitate to summon me. Should you require a place to stay until you get settled, my home is open to you. I've left my cell number with you." She gestured, again with her elegant lively hands, toward the lavender folder on the table.

She offered one last smile, lifted her arm, then vanished.

Alison turned to Kerrick. "I've noticed ascenders often lift a hand or an arm before folding. What is that?"

Kerrick shrugged. "Just a warning, I guess, like hitting the turn signal in a car."

Alison laughed. "That makes sense. I suppose it's nice to have notice before someone disappears."

Kerrick refilled his mug and tried to quiet the hammering of his heart. This was getting worse and worse. During the time Havily had conversed with Alison and performed her job, his gaze had been all for Alison. He'd been struck by her kindness toward Havily.

This was Alison's true gift, and it had nothing to do with preternatural power. She listened and she cared. Goddamn that got to him, worked in his heart like a miner after a vein of gold. And for whatever biological reason, the same sensation drove straight into his groin demanding possession.

Why the fuck couldn't she have been selfish and small-minded? Instead, while she was in the middle of an experience that essentially meant she was battling for her life, she had culled from Havily a single stunning fact—Havily was passionate about making significant changes in hopes of altering the course of the war.

We need Alison, he thought. *Hell, I need her.*

Then there was the whole business about White Lake. He had lived too long on Second not to comprehend that the dream was significant, which meant her role on Second Earth would become increasingly important, another reason she shouldn't be anywhere near a Warrior of the Blood. Christ, this whole thing kept getting more and more complicated. Fucking *breh-hedden.*

"You're very quiet and you've been stirring a mug of coffee I happen to know has no sugar or milk in it."

Even her voice worked over his body as though every part of her was designed to torment him. "Yeah," he responded. "Just cooling it off." A lie. He just didn't know how to turn back to her without picking her up in his arms and carting her off to his bed. Like now.

"I'm smelling spice, lots of spice, sweet exotic Moroccan spice."

He still didn't turn around. He nodded and kept stirring.

"Did I do something wrong? I mean, I know I have a lot to learn. Do you think I offended Havily? Do you think talking about White Lake upset her?"

He let go of the spoon and the mug and turned to face her. "No, not at all. Havily looks delicate but she's tough as nails, and no, you didn't offend her." He returned to the stool he'd inhabited earlier.

"So I didn't do anything wrong?"

He refused to meet her gaze as he said, "Actually, you've done everything wrong. You've been kind and generous, tender, concerned. Shit, this has become a fucking nightmare. I don't want to do this, you know. From the first moment I saw you, I knew I was in trouble, and the longer I'm with you the worse it gets. I took vows, Alison. I won't go back on them."

Alison saw the set of his jaw and the way his green eyes darkened and shifted over the granite, his gaze hunting for a place to land. His fangs would emerge next because the room was so rich with his scent, she was sure if she took a deep enough breath she could taste it on her tongue.

She saw his struggle, and she appreciated he'd taken some kind of vow, which was now directed against her, yet in this moment everything shifted for her.

The past caught up: how he'd protected her from the death vamp at the medical complex, the kiss in her Nova, how she'd awakened to his fangs on her neck and let him drink, how he'd used his hand to give her such wonderful release, how she had only to look at him and desire tightened her internal muscles and sent shivers over her skin.

She touched her fingers to her neck. From his peripheral vision he must have seen the movement because he turned and his gaze followed. He growled softly and his eyelids fell to half-mast. She couldn't feel the puncture marks, but she remembered the sublime sensation.

She didn't fully understand what was happening between them. Part of it made no sense. He had lived for centuries, he had fought as a warrior for over a millennia. He had transformed into a vampire when he ascended. She, on the other hand, had grown up in her cloistered world, protecting everyone else from her powers. Though she'd gotten a master's degree and had set up a practice, she had lived a bare thirty-plus years of an isolated life, of tight self-command and no relationships to speak of except with her family. How did being with an ancient winged vampire warrior therefore make any kind of sense?

She moved to stand next to him. The height of the stool allowed her to meet his gaze straight-on. His lips parted and his nostrils flared. His scent tormented her. She could barely draw breath.

She put her hand on his bicep, savoring the feel, as she had before, of the sculpted muscle. When she shifted to look at him, her gaze fell to his mouth. He had the most sensual lips she had ever seen, and she already knew exactly what they felt like. The tips of his fangs showed again. This time, instead of being afraid or overwhelmed as she had been in the car, and because he'd already taken her blood, desire flowed. The same growl, throaty and possessive, rumbled in his throat.

You're throwing lavender, he sent.

That sound you're making is getting to me.

Good.

He growled a little more, only louder this time. The vibration hit her chest and shivers slid down her abdomen.

I want in, she sent.

Funny how she knew he meant her mind. While he remained seated, she drew a little closer to him. He moved his right leg wider. He slid his arm around the small of her back and pulled her deeper between his legs. She put her hands on his shoulders then opened wide, letting down all her mental shields.

He held her gaze and dipped heavily into her mind, an experience well beyond simple telepathy. He was inside her head, deep inside her head. She gasped. It was like being surrounded, comforted, and taken all at once by an enormous wave of warm tropical waters. Pleasure cascaded through her body all over again. He growled as he swam through her thoughts and memories.

To be possessed in this way, his mind penetrating hers, moving over her, was a sensation she had never imagined before, yet it made sense. If telepathic communication was possible, why not this kind of deep penetration, even possession, of the mind?

She opened her mouth to breathe better and he took the opportunity to pull her against him fully and kiss her, his sensual lips warm and soft against her mouth. He drove his tongue deep, all the while remaining inside her mind. She moaned as his tongue pleasured and teased the sensitive recesses of her mouth.

Yes, she could really be with this man. It scared her yet it explained so much, the how and why of everything. Now she understood. What she needed was a powerful warrior, even a vampire, who could command her mouth while he moved an ocean around in her mind, who apparently didn't get blasted against a wall when she orgasmed.

A little more of her tightly held self gave way.

Kerrick, I want you inside me. We have some time, don't we?

He shifted, slid off the stool, and gathered her into his arms, his lips still molded to her mouth, his tongue thrusting hard.

His presence in her mind worked her body into a sudden outrageous frenzy. Her muscles ached everywhere. She drove her hands into his hair, her fingers tingling from the sensation.

Your thoughts are so beautiful, Alison. I love being in here. I want to stay forever but I can't. Tell me you understand.

I do. You've lost too much, haven't you?

Yes.

Kerrick, please take me.

Are you sure? Even if this is temporary?

Yes.

He caught her buttocks with one hand and pressed her against him. She writhed against the hard ridge of his sex. A long string of moans left her throat, the sound trumped by a powerful growl that passed from his chest to hers and reverberated like a steadily blowing breeze.

This wouldn't take long. This would be quick, hard, and fast. She wanted nothing more. She began tugging his shirt out of his jeans. His hands slid under her top and all her movement stilled as he found her breasts, then with one large hand fondled them both at the same time.

Kerrick . . . so good.

Yes.

His kiss deepened and the pressure on her nipples reached a place of pleasurable pain, which buckled her knees. He caught her waist with his free arm and held her close.

He lifted her up and planted her on the granite. He spread her legs and moved between them, reestablishing the connection. "Pants off," she whispered as she dragged a breath into her lungs.

"So impatient," he murmured. He pushed her onto the granite until she lay flat against the cool stone, one hand still kneading her breasts. She closed her eyes and let go of the burning need to having him inside her. Clearly he had other plans and as he stripped her pants off her, then her thong, she let go of a long lusty cry.

I'm here, he whispered deep in her mind, a sensation that sent ripples of desire . . . everywhere.

I love you in my head.

He growled then kissed her breasts, the fabric shoved up high, the bra as well. He suckled. Oh, how he suckled. She writhed against the granite, her body on fire, the cool stone below, his calloused warrior hands working over her thighs, her abdomen, her ribs, her shoulders. One finger found her mouth and she took him inside and sucked hard.

He nipped at her breast then pulled hard.

She arched off the granite and because he was present in her mind she almost came. *Kerrick . . .* No words followed, just a series of whimpers as he released her breast and started a burning trail of kisses down her body. Her skin and muscles jumped, her hips rocked. He kept moving down and down. He drew his finger from her mouth and grabbed her waist with both hands. He pushed her farther up the granite until her feet found purchase and almost at the same moment, his lips met the soft curls then the flesh of her labia. He nuzzled and kissed, nipped and sucked, all in tender little flurries. Yet he avoided reaching the sweet spot.

She moaned and her fingers found his hair, digging deep and guiding.

So impatient, he sent.

*Kerrick. Such torture. Oh, your mind inside me . . .
your lips . . . oh, God, your tongue.* He pressed her apart
and blew a stream of air over her until tears tracked down
her cheeks.

Please.

Please, what?

Lick me.

He obeyed the command and raked his tongue in one
long sweep up her aching flesh. She cried out. He licked
again. Her hands became reckless over his long hair, diving, tugging, as her hips rocked hard into his face. He settled in and licked in quick purposeful swipes.

Her cries echoed around the kitchen.

Come for me, Alison. Let it all go.

Power gathered. She could feel it. *It's coming.* She tried
to warn him, but her thoughts were scrambled, her mind
fixed on the intense pleasure, building, building.

Let it come. I'm ready.

His deep voice, so present inside her head, his mind still
connected to hers, made her come apart, pleasure streaking
over her sensitive flesh as her internal muscles pulsed over
and over. She cried out again and again. Power gathered
and released from her abdomen, pushing him away, but he
only laughed and returned to tending to her with his tongue.
He kept the sensations rolling again and again, spinning
out another orgasm then another, until she lay slack against
the granite.

Her hands fell away from his head. He didn't rise. Instead his tongue stroked the insides of her thighs. He kissed
his way to her opening. "Lavender," he breathed against
her core. "I must taste it." With his hands on her waist, he
dragged her to the edge of the island this time so he could
reach her in just the way he wanted. Her legs lay over his
back. He was so powerful. Her mind felt heavy and de-
cadent with the weight of his mind in her. His thoughts expressed his intense pleasure, which fired her own.

His tongue stroked over her opening in heavy laps, taking the nectar into his mouth. She cried out as new pleasure

began to build, the walls of her core pulling at him as he licked into her.

You're so beautiful, he laid over her mind.

Kerrick was all she could manage.

The strokes went deeper each time until his tongue worked her in a strong steady purposeful rhythm. He grunted, his hands on her buttocks now, his thumbs pressed into her hips. He pulled her toward him with each thrust of his tongue. She'd never been taken like this before. She'd never dared let a man get so close. She felt her power gathering again, as well as the grip of another orgasm.

This one barreled down, the power releasing. When she came and the power hit, he held her firmly in order to sustain the fast driving rhythm of his tongue. She came over and over as he possessed her with his mouth. He was pushing hard into her, determined. She felt blissfully used as another wave of power and another orgasm hit her. She screamed and gripped his head, holding him against her.

She panted.

Slowly, he decreased the speed.

Her own pulses faded in strength and intensity until once more she released his head and fell against the granite.

She was breathing hard, struggling to catch her breath. "That was amazing."

You're amazing. His deep voice flowed within her head, still joined heavily in her mind, possessively. She lifted up on her elbows to look at him. He cradled her, his arms beneath her knees. He placed kisses over her blond triangle of hair, her thighs, her abdomen.

"Take me," she whispered. "I need you inside me." Tears threatened. She was overcome by a strange combination of intense satisfaction and burning need to be joined to him, a great paradox.

He shook his head, the expression in his eyes pained. In a slow movement within her mind, he began to withdraw. She held him fast with a thought, *Stop. Don't go. Don't leave yet. I want you . . . now. And I love that you're here in my mind with me.*

He withdrew anyway, leaving her dizzy and strangely bereft, close to tears as, with a final jerk, his mind separated from hers.

He smiled crookedly. "I'm so sorry. I didn't have a choice. My fucking phone has been buzzing for the last ten minutes. Given our circumstances, I have to take this call, and I already know it's Thorne and it won't be good."

She folded her hands over her stomach and stared up at the ceiling. Her breath hitched a couple of times. She felt fabric fall onto her hips. Oh. He had bent down to retrieve her pants. However, she didn't move to put anything on. She hoped maybe he was mistaken and with just a little effort, he could still complete what they'd started.

"Give," he barked.

After a good long minute, he thumbed his phone, then a long curse, impossibly joined together, left his mouth. "Goddamsonofabitchmother . . ."

He slipped his phone into the pocket of his jeans. He turned to face her.

She had seen that look before, when he'd told her to fold them both to her Hummer.

She sat up, pulling her bra and shirt down. "We're in danger, aren't we? Is the house surrounded again?"

She started to unravel her rolled-up thong, but he caught her hands.

He shook his head. "We're not in any immediate danger. I'm sorry, Alison. I've just had word from Thorne. I've been ordered to train you for battle. Tonight. And it's going to hurt like hell."

Marcus woke up slowly. He was curled up on one of the ratty leather barges, facing the back cushions. As sleep went, not bad. He'd been asleep for hours and had an erection that he was just about to shift around and make more comfortable when he realized he wasn't alone. He reached out with his senses and felt the presence of six large pissed-off warriors, not a difficult deduction when there was a taint to the air, like someone had lit a box of matches.

"Looks like Sleeping Beauty is never going to wake up. Aw. He must have had a hard night of fighting. He's not used to the sword and dagger. *Pobrecito* . . . we should just let him sleep." Santiago, the bastard. Marcus lifted a hand and expressed his feelings with his middle finger.

"You were so wrong," Zach said. "Looks like Sleeping Beauty is up after all."

Marcus felt his wing-locks thrum and his biceps flex. As his cock settled down, his aggression wound up. He smiled, rolled over, then sat up. "So what the fuck do you assholes want?"

When Zacharius went for him, Marcus jumped to his feet, but Thorne moved like lightning and slid between them.

"Settle down, boys. Don't waste all this precious juice on each other." He turned to Marcus and shoved him back. "You can go to my digs, shave and shower. Don't even think about folding back to Mortal Earth. Endelle would have me by the short hairs if you left Second, even to freshen up. She wants everyone tight.

"Kerrick has ascendiate duty until tomorrow night, at which time we expect all hell to break loose when Her Supremeness releases her mind-shield. And if you think Greaves won't have something spectacular planned while we wait, you're wrong." He then delivered the assignments. "Luken to New River. Santiago, White Tanks. Zach take Awatukee. Jean-Pierre, you'll be with me in the Superstitions, and Medichi, I want you with Sleeping Beauty downtown."

"Fuck that," Medichi said. "Can't someone else babysit?"

Thorne got in his face, tight, hard. "You'll do as I say."

Marcus felt the heat off Thorne's back. After a long tense moment, Medichi murmured, "Whatever you say, boss."

Marcus scoffed, just a little snort off his left nostril. He only realized he'd fucked up when Thorne's fist landed on his face and broke his nose. Goddamn, he didn't even see Thorne move.

"Shit," he cried. Fortunately, the couch was behind him so he had a soft landing.

Blood poured down his face. Thorne bent over him and grabbed the hair at the top of his head. "That's for taking off for two fucking centuries, you worthless piece of shit."

Thorne pulled back, cradling his hand in the crook of his arm. Bending over at the waist, with his free hand he dipped into the deep pocket of his kilt then palmed his phone. After a moment, he said, "Yeah, Horace. I need you at the Cave. One of the warriors walked into a door." He grimaced as he put his phone back in his pocket.

"Fuck you," Marcus cried. Rage pounded through him now, a series of heavy waves pulsing against the inside of his skull. "I never asked to come back. I never would have come back." He pulled up his tee and caught the blood flowing over his mouth.

Thorne stood over him, his hazel eyes red-rimmed, his mouth grim. "You're not welcome here. Unfortunately, I have my orders just like you. I serve Endelle and will do whatever she asks of me, but I don't have to fucking like it. And while you're here, you'll respect the warriors who have fought on while you were playing with your balls on Mortal Earth." He put his hand on Marcus's forehead then relayed the location of his home. "Go there now, before I really lose my temper. I'll send Horace to you after he repairs the bones I just broke in my hand."

Marcus didn't wait. He felt like twelve kinds of shit. Thorne was right. He shouldn't have left all those decades ago, yet if he'd stayed, he would have killed Kerrick. Those weren't just words he'd said. The fury he had experienced when his sister and her kids died had demanded only one outlet—Kerrick's blood—so he had left, without a word, without a good-bye to any of his brothers, only a message via Jeannie that he had exiled himself to Mortal Earth. The only conversation he'd had was with Endelle, a promise that if she ever truly needed him he'd come back—though only once, as a favor. So here the fuck he was and he hated every goddamn minute of it.

He dematerialized into the foyer of Thorne's house, his shirt still pressed to his nose. He felt cool Mexican tile under his bare feet. The house had a warm feel and one helluva view of the Sedona cliffs, the massive two-thousand-foot Mogollon Rim.

So this was where Thorne had chosen to build his home. The colors were desert shades—sand, terra-cotta, a deep turquoise, purple, representative of the land, of the dusty sunsets, of a sun-drenched world, a dry world, the opposite of Marcus's wet, cold Pacific Northwest environment. The change was oddly . . . soothing.

He waited where he was. His nose still bled freely and hurt like a bitch. His shirt wouldn't do the job much longer. He needed Horace's healing power before he took one more step into the house. So he'd stay put.

The rooms radiated off the entry in several directions, a sprawling maze ending in glass walls, which let in all that Arizona light. Doorways were arched from room to room and the texture had a hand-troweled look. Still, the place had a *weird* feel, an empty feel, even though the pillows on the various sofas and chairs were crushed like they'd been well used.

"Huh."

He recognized the *weird* feel. It was just like his primary residence on Bainbridge Island. Well designed, architecturally pleasing, and goddamn solitary.

Shit. Didn't that define them all? A bunch of lonely fighting bastards. He may not have brandished sword and dagger for the last twenty decades, but he'd run his corporations with same single-minded zeal, never leaving a single minute open for living a normal life.

Learning occurs,
When the body remembers.

—*Collected Proverbs,* Beatrice of Fourth

CHAPTER 15

"I think this is ridiculous," Alison cried. "I'm not a warrior. I don't know the first thing about fighting and why would I need to be trained to battle?" She felt stuck inside a nightmare, unable to get out. Wasn't it bad enough she'd already been hunted by a regiment in Carefree, then wounded? "Talk to me, Kerrick."

The man in front of her, *the warrior,* now a stranger, merely dropped into a crouch position and stared at her abdomen. She felt the airwaves shift and knew he meant to attack. A jolt of adrenaline sent her flying into the air. She levitated swiftly as far as she could then held the position, spread-eagled, her back pressed into the long branches that covered the vaulted ceiling.

"Good," he stated. "Anticipation is everything."

"Did you hear what I said? I'm not a warrior! Stop this!"

He shook his head, lowered his chin, then launched toward her. She folded to the family room beside the sliding glass doors. She had never felt so out of control. Her mind raced, trying to find purchase, and her legs trembled.

Oh, God, what if she hurt him?

Her heart started pounding as he attacked again. His six-six powerhouse of a body blurred toward her and just as he would have struck her in the chest, she shot away from him.

"Good" was all he said, the word brusque, clipped, cruel.

Alison's throat ached from holding back a flood of tears. Her ears pounded with each quick powerful beat of her heart.

She didn't even have time to think as he charged again.

And again.

And again until each breath she took wheezed in and out of her lungs like an air compressor heading south.

He finally stopped in front of her. Sweat poured from his body, his green eyes pinched, determined. His fangs had emerged. "Good," again, was all he said.

He put both his hands on her arms. She had thought he meant to comfort her. Instead she felt healing warmth invade her muscles. *So I can continue learning how to fight.*

"I'm not a warrior," she whispered. Tears tracked down her cheeks. He ignored her pleas. He gave her Gatorade, fed her carb bars. He still would not speak to her.

When she reached out to his mind, wanting to help him feel what she was going through, red streams of rage flowed back at her.

She drew in a quick breath and pulled back, shocked. He seemed so in control. Instead his emotions were off the charts, his anger condensed into hard filaments that pulsed crimson. He was simply too angry to speak, certainly not in a frame of mind to either console or explain. It eased her to know how much he despised what he had to do.

He repeated the process of attack until she simply dropped to her knees gasping for air. Sweat now trailed off her face and splashed onto the tile. Her T-shirt stuck to her ribs. She couldn't remember sweating this much, not even in the gym.

Of all the ways she had imagined the evening progressing, playing attack-the-ascendiate was not one of them. If anything, she had hoped . . . against hope, it would seem . . . he would have taken her to bed. Instead he started Warrior Training 101. *Great.*

"Can you tell me now why you were ordered to do this?" she cried between deep inhales and exhales.

"Doesn't matter," he responded.

"The hell it doesn't. This is my life. Talk to me." She struggled to her feet and moved to the island. He wouldn't make eye contact.

"Maybe so you can protect yourself. I don't know. Drink. Eat." He thrust Gatorade into her hand again, his voice as hard as flint. "We're done with the first part." He folded a box into his hands. "I've got your sword. You'll need to create the identification. Just take the handle and hold on. Whatever you do, don't let go." He thrust the box toward her, the polished steel glinting in the light.

"Fuck you," she cried.

Only then did he meet her gaze. His green eyes calmed down, but a deep sorrow shuttered over his irises, so deep Alison gasped. Oh, shit. She saw her death in his eyes. He believed she would die, that she would not make it through. So basically, she got one day of ascended life? One day?

She didn't take the box. She turned away from him and chewed on what now tasted like sawdust instead of a bar of sticky-sweet granola. She swallowed, but it was hard pushing food past the lump in her throat. "I'm not doing very well, am I?"

Silence returned.

She put her hand on her forehead and let the tears fall again. She heard the box drop onto the island. She felt his hands on her arms. "You're doing just fine. The problem is time, not your skills. You've got some of the finest instincts and reactions I've seen in decades. Endelle didn't tell Thorne the why of it, but it can't be good and I have only hours to train you, not months. I don't mean to be a bastard. However, this is my job, and I feel way too much for you to do anything but keep my distance. And . . . I'm just a little pissed off about it."

"Yes, I know." She wiped at her face. "And there's nothing I can do to change the order?"

"No. Not a damn thing."

When she looked up at him, a deep frown furrowed his brow. "What is it?" she asked.

"Training this way just isn't going to cut it and you have one huge advantage over other ascendiates. You match me in power, which means I want to try something with you, something that might just work."

"What are you thinking?"

"I can train you with my mind."

He moved to stand directly in front of her and took her face in his hands. His green eyes beckoned, an intense expression as he stared at her.

How strong is your mind? he asked, his words a powerful question within her head. He narrowed his eyes. She felt pressure now, deep within her mind, a familiar frightening sensation.

She tried to pull away but he wouldn't let her.

Answer me.

I'm afraid to, she responded, blinking. Her heart constricted. What he was doing reminded her of the experience at the medical complex when he'd taken her memories. She wanted to tear herself away from him, to fight him, or better yet, to run away.

Listen to me, he sent firmly. *I have one goal here, to get you through this. You have no idea what you're up against. I do. And there's only one way to get this job done. It will hurt at first, this kind of mental joining, but if you let go, flow with it, you'll be okay.*

I'm scared. Understatement.

He searched her eyes. *You fear losing control. I get that. You've lived as I've lived, independent, taking care of business all by yourself, isolated. You had control. Right now, however, you're going to have to let go and frankly, I don't give a damn what you want. This is the only way.* His expression softened and he smiled, a small crooked curve off to the side of his mouth. *Do you trust me?*

Dammit, he was so not playing fair because there was only one answer. "Yes," she muttered aloud, her jaw bobbing in his hands.

His smile broadened. He leaned forward and kissed her firmly on the lips. He nodded. *Then trust me now and try to relax.*

Once more, she nodded in his hands.

Good. Ready?

She took a deep breath. *Yes.*

Suddenly his thoughts penetrated her swiftly and it hurt, like the hard bite of a wasp sting. He sent sensory images, one after the other rapid-fire, of several of his most recent battles.

Alison wanted to scream. The images afflicted her as though a series of knives whipped through her head.

Let go came as a sharp command between frames.

But she held on tight and the knives sliced her up worse than ever, worse than when he'd tried to strip her memories.

Dammit, Alison, don't be stubborn. Let go!

Alison had no choice or she would pass out. She relaxed her mind and in a split second the pain slid away like water in a dam released in a rush. *Thank you, God!*

A new sensation took over. She felt as though she had *become* Kerrick as he fought death vampires one after another. She was *in his skin,* wielding his sword, throwing his dagger. She could feel his wings move at his command, propelling him through the air in pursuit of the enemy.

Deep within the fibers of her muscles, she experienced exactly what he felt when he fought, the flex of his biceps, of his calf muscles, the way his knees bent and moved, the shift of rib cage, thrust of arm, the absolute ballet quality of his movements. She saw through his eyes. A battle edge skipped through her blood. Excitement pounded in her heart.

She began to know when his movements would quicken and when his legs would retreat, when he would raise his sword-arm, when he would strike, and when he would shield a powerful blow. When he would mount his wings and fly into the air. When he would stay the thrumming of his wing-locks to remain close to the earth. She felt the leather of his kilt slap at his legs, the pull of his T-shirt when he fought in cargoes and steel-toed boots. Every strike of an enemy's sword against his sword now sent vibrations up her arm.

A few minutes more and he began to pull out of her mind, not in a rush but in a long, slow glide that reminded her of stretching pizza dough. One last tug, and he freed himself. Again, how bereft she felt, just like before, on the granite island when he left her mind. She put a hand first to her chest, then to her head.

Her body felt rubbery, disoriented as though some of her muscles pulled two ways at once. Of course. Since she now possessed his muscle memory alongside her own.

She set her feet apart and slung her left arm behind her back.

He looked her up and down, nodded his approval. "A warrior's stance."

Some of the images flickered up to her conscious mind. There he was standing before a woman with black hair and a dress made up of some kind of spotted animal skin, a beautiful woman who looked Arabic and exotic.

She knew the woman was Endelle, the leader of Second, even though her name wasn't spoken. She knew because he knew. Endelle appeared angry, her enormous wings all the way to the ceiling but drawn back aggressively. The words came from her mouth, *"Don't you dare take that fucking tone with me, Warrior, or I'll have your wings—literally— feather by feather."*

"Okaaay," she murmured, shutting the memory down. She was so out of her depth.

"You'll need your weapon now." He held the box bearing what would become her personal sword, her identified sword.

She took the box from him and looked down at a really beautiful weapon resting on a bed of dark green velvet. The steel glimmered beneath the recessed lights high in the vaulted twigged ceiling overhead.

"Carbon steel, extremely sharp. You'll need some instruction on the care of it."

She looked up at him. "How exactly does this work? You said the sword accepts an identity and then that's it, the sword is mine, only mine."

He nodded. "Once properly identified, no one on Second or Mortal Earth can touch any part of the sword without dying."

She nodded. "So how do I do this?"

"Take the handle in a tight grip and the identification process will complete itself. Just maintain contact steadily for a few seconds. You'll know."

She shifted the weight of the box to one hand, holding it firmly beneath. She reached for the handle but hesitated. She was taking another step on her path to a new life, a new world, literally a new dimension.

Oh, God.

"I'm still pissed at you," Medichi said.

Marcus sat on the curb near the downtown Borderland, his kilt slung between his legs, sweat dripping with blood from different parts of his body. He looked up at his fellow warrior. "Who the fuck cares?"

Medichi stood on the sidewalk as cars on Mortal Earth whizzed by. He looked like a god from the Roman pantheon, all six-seven of him, lit by the overhead streetlight. His hair was long, black, and straight, and he wore it pulled back slick and bound up tight in his *cadroen*. He had pronounced cheekbones and a strong jaw. He was powerful, lean, a warrior with dark secrets. No one messed with Medichi.

He wiped down his bloodied sword with a clean, soft white cloth. He didn't seem to notice the traffic and of course no one could see either of them. Marcus had misted the area, a gossamer cloud that none of the mortals would be able to see. The presence of the mist would simply create a confusion of mind.

"So, Medichi, you still keeping your wings a secret?"

"Fuck off." Nobody knew the why of Medichi's refusal to mount his wings. No one. In fact, no one, to Marcus's knowledge, had ever even seen his wings.

Medichi asked, "You still planning on running back to Mortal Earth with your tail between your legs?"

Marcus took the jibe in stride. You did that when the other vampire had saved your ass about a dozen times over the last two nights.

He wiped a hand across his forehead, which caused a cut above his left eyebrow to sting like hell. Their most recent engagement, which involved snapping an enemy's wing, had sent quills scraping him raw. Central had just done a cleanup on eleven death vamps. "You know why I had to leave. It wasn't exactly a secret."

Medichi peered at his sword and rubbed back and forth in a quick motion. Blood trickled from a slice on the back of his thigh and ran down the back of his knee, into the calf straps of his shin guards. He didn't seem to notice. His scowl sat heavy on his brow. "I never believed you'd actually hurt Kerrick."

"Everyone thinks they were just words," he said quietly. "But I would have killed him and my sentiments on the subject haven't changed. Endelle's been smart to keep us separated like this."

"Your beef with him is two centuries old. You need to get over yourself." He didn't add the usual *asshole* tag. A few hours of fighting a common enemy would also do that to a couple of warriors. They weren't exactly buddies, though some of the I-want-to-cut-your-liver-out had left Medichi's dark brown gaze.

Marcus scanned the area, from the burned-out smears of old gum on the sidewalk, to the litter in the gutter, the car across the street with a smashed-in fender. "Helena was the last of my family and I begged Kerrick not to marry her. I begged him for months. I begged her as well, much good it did."

"She loved him," Medichi said, his tone deep, resonant, dark. "What else mattered?"

Marcus gathered a wad of saliva in his mouth then spit. "Well, aren't you the fucking romantic."

"Time to move on."

Marcus gained his feet. "I did move on. I said to hell with this world and returned to Mortal Earth. I like it there . . . I mean here." He swept an arm to encompass the downtown cross street and alley. "I'm only fighting because I promised Endelle one favor. After this gig is up, you won't see me again . . . ever."

Medichi nodded. "I know." His eyes had gotten old in the past two hundred years even if his body had remained exactly as Marcus remembered.

Medichi's gaze scanned the area. "You make fucking great mist and you fight like hell." His jaw tensed, relaxed. "I would have died here tonight if it weren't for you." He nodded several more times.

"You gonna get soft on me and offer up a *thank-you*?"

Medichi turned his head slowly. His lips curved. "I'll offer a *fuck you*."

"Accepted." Marcus looked away. "How soon before we have company again?"

"Any time now. For the past few months they've been coming in waves, not like before when you were here and we sometimes had hours until another squad showed up." His head wagged. "I remember when we had time to take care of some business at the Blood and Bite. Not anymore. We'll be busy just like last night . . . all night."

Marcus drew in deep breaths. He could feel the air start to ice up. His wing-locks responded with a dedicated thrum. He stepped away from Medichi, not wanting to injure him. During a wing-mount, anyone too close could get knocked flat.

Medichi's chest swelled. "They're coming."

Marcus looked up at the night sky. "Floating down on the Commander's breath."

"Three of his generals can perform the trick as well."

"Shit."

"You got it."

The air turned icy cold. Marcus folded his sword into his hand. Medichi dropped the now bloody cloth, letting it fall to the asphalt. He whipped the dagger from the slot in his front harness.

Eleven so far.

Jesus H. Christ.

And now another squad . . . or more.

Marcus felt his wing-locks twitch all down his back. He took two more deep breaths and mounted his wings. Three times now, in one night. Goddamn, that felt good. His wings, light brown with bands of light green, expanded in a vast sweep over his head. His abs tightened as the death vamps dropped out of the sky.

"We need you, Marcus. Thorne will never say it but I will. We need you to come back."

"Never gonna happen." The air had dipped to arctic levels, and he shivered.

"Huh," Medichi muttered.

"What?"

"That green banding on your wings. Same color as Havily's eyes."

Shit. Marcus really didn't want an excuse to think of Havily . . . and now every time he popped his wings, dammit, he'd think of her.

Great. Just great.

He focused his attention on the pretty-boys. This group had a Latin look, brown skin, dark eyes, black hair, and so good-looking that for just a moment Marcus forgot why he had a sword in hand. "So goddamn beautiful," he muttered.

"They all look alike to me," Medichi said, laughing. "Hey, Marcus . . . you sure have one helluva pair on you. Wings, I mean."

Marcus didn't want to laugh, but he did. "Bastard," he muttered. He held his sword straight up, both hands on the leather-wrapped handle, his gaze glued to the, yeah, two squads, eight death vamps, all winged up and flying in their direction. "Come on, motherfuckers. Don't be shy."

One second more and he launched into the air.

Alison couldn't stop smiling. She had been working the sword in large, now familiar arcs and she was still surprised by how it felt. She paused, holding the sword upright in both hands. Even after several minutes small jolts of lightning still swept over her fingers and rippled up her hands and arms. How magical it felt. A rush of pleasure kept swirling through her head.

The sword was hers, 100 percent. She could feel it. She had the weirdest sensation of both ownership and belonging and she *loved* it. *Home.* The sword felt like *home,* which hardly made any sense at all.

She glanced at Kerrick. For the entire duration of her sword love-fest, he'd been pushing furniture to the edges of every room in the house. Right now he was corralling one of the warrior-sized leather chairs in the direction of the far wall near a massive fireplace built of stone.

This is so strange, she sent.

He gave the chair a final shove and it banged against the wall. He turned to look at her. "Third technology. One of the few gifts we've received from our next highest earth. More like a bond than ownership, right?"

"Yes, exactly."

She started swinging her sword again, slashing, moving, twirling. She felt Kerrick's learned experience in the muscles of her legs and arms, shoulders and back. Even her wrist moved differently and the sword made sense in her hand, an old friend.

"Jesus," she murmured. She turned once more to meet his gaze. "This is like some kind of miracle."

He was done moving furniture and stood in front of her. "You've got the right grip on your weapon and your stance is perfect."

She nodded. Her mind still felt a little loose, like it had been stretched to great lengths and was finding its way back into itself. However, when he folded his sword into his hand, she felt a thrill roll through her, a *warrior's* thrill. Holy hell. A smile pulled at her lips and cheeks. A smile? Goddamn, she wanted to fight and now she had a new vocabulary.

All down both sides of her back, angling in a wide V-formation, she felt a tingling sensation. Wing-locks?

What a rush.

She didn't have them yet, of course. Kerrick said given her level of power she might develop wings before the first year was out. Right now, she did feel their presence, their beginning, and it was a rush. If she ascended, she would grow fangs and wings. Of course, that was one thought too many, and she weaved on her feet.

Better to focus right now on just the sword, just learning to fight for who-knows-what-reason.

When he narrowed his eyes and dropped his shoulders, her biceps flexed as though understanding exactly what he meant by those simple physical signs. She brought the sword in front of her and held it with both hands, fully upright. She felt a need to growl, which was ridiculous but then in this moment she was more warrior than therapist, more Kerrick in muscle memory than Alison.

He nodded in approval but his chin dipped and his eyes took on that fierce cut-emerald appearance, entirely without compassion.

He came at her, a blur of preternatural speed. She folded behind him, he whirled, she engaged. *Engaged.* Her arm rang with deadly vibrations as the steel of his sword met hers. Her muscles bunched and jerked with a wild thrill.

She no longer *thought,* she *anticipated.* Every technique Kerrick possessed now flowed into her mind, became part of her. The sword was a mere extension of response and reaction, which translated rhythmically into attack.

The Queen Creek house filled with shared grunts, a deafening sound of clashing heavy steel, and the smell of two bodies full of sweat and aggression.

The Matrix came to mind.

What a tremendous gift he had given her. Something eased inside and she sent him a mental message. *Kerrick, cease!*

He drew back, his sword at the ready, which he quickly lowered as soon as he saw her blade drop at an unprotected angle toward the floor. "I have a chance now, don't I? Say it. I need to hear you say it."

His sword disappeared. He closed the distance between them, shoved her sword-arm away from him, and drew her into a tight embrace. She felt the shudder flow through him, a rippling that began in his arms and shoulders, then passed through the heavy muscles of his pecs, his abdomen, even his massive thighs. "Thank God," he murmured against her ear.

She folded her sword to the far corner of the guest room and held him tight. Only then did she understand how completely hopeless he had felt about her plight. Tears burned her eyes as she nestled her drenched face against his cardamom wet shoulder.

After barely a minute, however, Alison stepped away from him, her mind caught up in her new reality. She folded her sword back into her hand then swiped the blade twice through the air. "The Commander has plans for me, then Endelle ordered you to train me, but for what kind of engagement is unclear?"

"Exactly."

"So this isn't just about being able to defend myself if, say, another regiment of death vampires would happen to show up at your front door?"

He shook his head. "I doubt it," he responded.

Okay. She really didn't want to consider just what Darian had in mind for her. If she did, she'd go crazy.

For the next quarter hour, he worked her hard until she was once more gasping for breath and her muscles were screaming. She folded her sword to safety.

He brought her another Gatorade. She took it, unseeing. She drank. He massaged her arms and shoulders and healed her muscles to the extent he could. She ached, though not nearly so badly as she would have without his help. She consumed another carb bar.

The next session involved even greater speed. In the beginning, she struggled. A few minutes later, she got the hang of countering his speed, moving swiftly, folding swiftly, and anticipating the swings and thrusts of his sword until she met him blow for blow.

She wasn't, however, used to the physical demands of battle. She grew weary as he forced her backward down the hall in the direction of the guest room.

She decided to try something. She threw a blast at him with a flick of her wrist. He returned the blast in even greater force and she barely got out of the way as she rolled into the guest room. Unfortunately she tripped, stumbled, and fell on her arm. She barely missed cutting her leg with her sword.

"Ow," she shrieked.

Of all the ways she might have been hurt while training with a sword in her hand, spraining her wrist seemed the most ridiculous. At the same time, she knew Kerrick wouldn't stop, especially not when she was at her weakest.

She felt his attacking airwaves and used all her power to set up a field. She didn't even know what that was, but she saw it in her mind and erected it. When she looked up, all six feet six of him, all tough muscled dips and swells of her warrior teacher, lay suspended in the air above her.

Suddenly he smiled. The room was dark so all she saw was the glittering of his teeth and the flash of his eyes, but he was smiling.

She felt his sweat as it dripped through the field onto her chest.

I fell on my wrist, she sent, laughing. *Can you believe it?* She folded her sword back to the corner of the room out of harm's way.

She gently released him. He dropped off to the side of her and rolled onto his back.

"This is so awesome," he cried. He folded his sword away as well and crossed his wrists over his forehead.

She sat up. Her T-shirt and pants were completely soaked and every muscle in her body hurt. She twisted at the waist to look down at him. She took a deep breath before asking, "Why did you say that?" She rubbed her wrist.

"In all the decades I've trained warriors I've never had one capable of creating a field." He glanced at her. "You can use that. If you have to battle death vamps, you can use a fucking field."

The act of love,
Swallows all pain.

—*Collected Proverbs,* Beatrice of Fourth

CHAPTER 16

Still on his back, Kerrick said, "Now lie down and give me your wrist."

Alison stretched out beside him and held her left arm out. Where her damp skin touched the carpet, she itched.

Still on his back, he massaged the muscles and ligaments, working his thumbs over her skin. Warm healing flowed through her wrist. She sighed as the pain subsided.

When he was done she rolled to face him, reclining her head on her arm. The room was dark. Somewhere in all the training, night had fallen. With just a thought, she turned on the bedside lamps.

Kerrick shifted onto his side toward her as well but leaned up on his elbow. His long black hair hung in damp strands, but he looked hot as hell. He brought a dry cloth into his hand then wiped her cheeks and her forehead.

How normal this all felt—*I turned on the lights with a*

*thought and he folded objects into his hand from other
parts of the house.*

"What am I doing here?"

"You're staying alive. Same thing you've been doing on
Mortal Earth. It's just a little harder now, at least for a time."
He mopped his own face. "That was pretty great, you
know." He lowered his chin as he met her gaze. A smile
eased over his lips. "I launched myself at you and then I was
just lying in midair. I think you're amazing. Just amazing."

Alison looked into intense green eyes. Heat climbed her
cheeks. She smiled.

So, he thought she was amazing. No one had ever said
anything like that to her before. Her parents had always
been kind and supportive. But they had never said she was
amazing—how could they when they were so busy being
worried about her all the time?

Solitude, even loneliness, had made up her life until this
moment. She didn't want to overlay this time with Kerrick
with too much meaning, but she fit in this world, in his
world. For the first time in her life, her strange abilities made
sense to her.

He even taught her to battle with a sword by streaming
his memories because she was powerful enough to receive
the information from him.

"Amazing, huh?" she responded. She extended her hand
toward him and with the backs of her fingers touched his
cheek.

He drew in a quick breath. "With a capital *A*." As his
cardamom scent once more rolled in a powerful wave over
her, he frowned and shook his head. "We should get back
to work." His deep voice sounded rough, even hoarse.

He started to get up. Alison quickly slid an arm around
his neck. "Stay just a second." She leaned up on her elbow
now, and her arm tingled where it lay over the thick muscles of his shoulder. "I just want you to know that I'm really
grateful you're here with me, that you're training me and
taking care of me. Thank you." She rose up a little more

and planted a kiss on his lips then drew back, but only an inch or so. She kept breathing in his wonderful scent.

His gaze dropped to her lips. "We should keep working," he muttered, more quietly this time. "We really should."

She leaned in again and drifted her lips over his cheek. She licked his salty sweat. He growled softly. More cardamom broke over her senses. She closed her eyes and moved back to his lips. She kissed him again, her tongue rimming his lips. Her hand drifted over his powerful pecs. Her fingertips tingled this time even through his soft, damp T-shirt. His chest rose and fell rapidly. As she worked his lips, she sent, *You took care of me. Now how about we take good care of you.*

A heavy growl left his throat. Even so, he drew back and looked down at her. "This isn't a good idea for so many reasons."

"Then stop with the spice."

He closed his eyes and drew in a ragged breath. "Lavender," he murmured.

Kerrick tried to shut down his olfactory system but all the hard training of the past several hours had every part of his body humming. His nostrils flared and he drank in Alison's heady scent like he was dying of thirst. His groin ached. No, it burned.

Her hand climbed his chest, drifted up his throat, then slid over his cheek.

He turned and caught a finger in his mouth. He suckled the lavender flavor off her skin. The moans, which drifted toward him, carried on her equally lavender-scented breath, brought him shifting toward her. She drew the finger out of his mouth, and the sensual slide made him hard as a rock.

He slid his hand up her arm. "You work out," he said. He arched his body over her. He could feel a possessive need building in him. He should stop this right now. He should take every second possible just to train her.

Still, he didn't move except to rub his hand up and down her arm.

"Yes. Every day because when I don't, I go crazy."

"I know what you mean."

He thought of his basement, of the tight isolated nature of his life on Second, of how he punished his muscles every afternoon just for a little relief. He pushed her thick, damp blond hair away from her face.

The battle training had pinked up her complexion and turned her lips a dark rose. Or maybe it was because she'd just been kissing him. Her blue eyes gazed at him as though she didn't believe he was real.

She slid her fingers into his damp hair. She didn't seem to mind he was slick with sweat. She rolled ever so slightly onto her back and tugged at the back of his neck, drawing him in her direction.

The invitation did him in.

He followed as though connected to her by a short heavy leading rope. He slung a leg over her hips. He planted a hand on the floor beside her head. God, she was beneath him, just where he'd wanted her from the moment he first caught her scent, the moment at the medical complex when she had folded in front of him.

Her lips parted.

Now would be the time to pull back, to remember the futility of what he was doing, but what harm could there be if he got inside her? Sex alone wouldn't complete the *breh-hedden*.

She leaned up and caught his lips, her tongue dipping inside. The kiss settled everything.

He crashed down on her hard, kissing her fiercely, letting the roar of the *breh-hedden* flood his veins.

He lost track of his actions. He stripped her shirt and pants off her then kissed her, or maybe it was the other way around. He got rid of her bra, somehow, although it involved a lot of giggling on her part. He palmed her breasts yet managed to work himself out of his jeans. He groaned as she stroked the length of his cock.

Things evened out when she was perfectly naked and his clothes were piled . . . somewhere. The full wet length of her body, her fingers intertwined with both his hands, her legs spread and wrapped around his hips, his cock poised at her core came into sharp erotic focus.

He kissed her again and began to push inside. She let out one long deep moan and stroked him with tight internal muscles. He groaned and dammit, almost came. He'd been so ready for this from the second her trail of lavender had assaulted him, all those painful hours ago at the medical complex. Too ready. He suckled her neck and rubbed the thick base of his fangs over her skin, avoiding puncture at the tips.

"Hey," she murmured hoarsely, panting. "If you snack on me while we're doing this and you've already been in my head, won't that cause a big problem—you know the *breh* thing you talked about?"

"We're good," he said, struggling to breathe. "It all has to happen at the same time. Separate events don't count. But don't worry." He pushed at her neck with the sides of his fangs. "I won't be drinking your blood."

"I don't understand."

"You will in a minute." He thrust into her hard.

She arched against him. She threw her head back, moaned, and cried out, "You're so perfect. Oh, God. And you're sure I won't hurt you if we're joined like this?"

He laughed. "Not a chance."

He was deep inside now, his cock surging and pulling back, driving in and out, teasing all the sensitive nerves. He was where he belonged. She made delicate mewling sounds and panted in between. Her muscles clenched around him. He was so damn hard and she was a fist pulling at him.

He shuddered with the effort it took to keep from spilling inside her. He wanted to wait. He wanted to wring every drop of pleasure from this time with her. He wanted to watch her come at least half a dozen times before he spent himself.

He drifted his lips down her chest and kissed the swell of her breasts, his fangs thick in his mouth. He knew what he wanted to do but he didn't want to lose contact.

She seemed to understand because as he angled over her chest, she tightened her legs around his buttocks and kept his hips seated against her. He thrust slowly as he licked her breast then set the sharp tips of his fangs over the swell of her skin.

He overlaid her mind. *May I taste you?*

So polite for a vampire.

He cupped her breast and felt it swell in his hand. She groaned and whimpered.

May I? he asked again, avoiding puncture. He ground his hips into her.

"Please," she whispered aloud, her voice hoarse.

He lowered his mouth to her nipple and ran his tongue in a circle several times until her hips bucked beneath him. He slowed his thrusting, holding back, spinning the moment out as long as he could.

He positioned his fangs just above the pink areola. In a swift jab he sank the razor-sharp tips deep, exuding a chemical to keep the blood from flowing. With her blood held at bay, he slowly started releasing a potion designed to heighten sensation.

Alison cried out. Pain and pleasure merged in a driving duet of incredible sensation. She looked up into the twig ceiling and slid her fingers once more into his hair. She panted and gasped, unable to believe that this wonderful thing had happened. Her warrior-vampire was inside her, at last. And she wasn't hurting him. Not at all. At least not yet. Never, she hoped. Oh, God, please *never*.

Her breast tingled where his fangs had penetrated her skin. His tongue lapped low, stroking the tight bud. Her internal muscles clenched rhythmically around his driving cock. Her hips shoved back into him while her legs locked him in place.

She gasped and clutched at the nape of his neck, encouraging him.

A strange sensation began spreading at the place of puncture. She felt a hot sting, then a steady rise of pleasure, which diffused like lightning through her breast as though he touched her from within and without in quick pulses. Her nipple drew up further into a taut hard bead. She moaned loudly. Her back arched.

Oh, God, Kerrick, what have you done to me?

This is only the beginning.

I may pass out.

He chuckled against her skin as he laved the aching nipple, his fangs still deep within her, his hips a slow steady rhythm.

Do you want me to suckle you?

Hard. Now. Please.

He removed his fangs and drew his hand firmly around her breast, forcing the nipple to rise up into his mouth. He took a generous portion and pulled with a deep sucking motion. At the same moment, he slid an arm under her waist and drove into her hard.

Alison knew the moment had come. She wanted to warn him but couldn't. She was locked inside the orgasm as it carried her on a heavy wave. At the same time, she felt power gathering deep inside. He left her breast and rose up over her, pumping hard now as if he understood her need. She moaned, trying to form the words to warn him but failing. As the intense ecstasy caught her, the power released and the climax took her in a sharp beautiful agonizing grip of pleasure that went on and on. She heard Kerrick grunt then chuckle then groan loudly.

He leaned down to her. "Oh, my God," he whispered against her ear as he continued stroking her, wringing the last bit of sensation. "That was incredible. My God."

"You're not hurt?" she asked, still breathing hard. She planted a hand on his chest. She had to know.

"I'm beyond aroused. I didn't know it would feel like that when I was inside you. Alison, do it again."

Relief flooded her. Tears poured from her eyes. She was so happy. And still he was hard as a rock and continued to pump into her. If he kept going, she'd come again.

Now, however, she became aware of a different sensation, a kind of pleasurable burning. Her breast, where he had driven his fangs, now felt on fire in the best way. *You put something in my breast.*

He smiled down at her. "A potion. One of the best gifts of ascended life."

She rolled her head back and forth as another orgasm began to build. The potion wasn't remaining at her breast, either, but had spread and now seeped low into her abdomen.

She moaned and rocked her hips into him.

That's it, Alison. Did I tell you I love it when you're in my head? So damn sexy.

She wrapped her arms around him and squeezed. He thrust heavily into her once more.

The vampire had staying power.

Desire bolted through her all over again as the potion continued to descend. She didn't know how much more she could take.

She whimpered as she slid her hands down to caress his buttocks. He was so thick-muscled, so physically powerful, a man, a vampire, a warrior. Her hands moved over him, riding the dips and swells of his beautifully contoured flesh. He was flat-out gorgeous in every possible way, not less so in the honed muscles of his warrior's body.

She worked her hands up to his waist then over the ripples of his back. She fingered the ridges from which his wings would emerge.

His hips jerked and he moaned. "Better stop that now," he whispered, his body twisting. "Wing-locks are very sensitive."

Her fingers couldn't stop. She loved the way his body moved when she touched him there.

"No, really," he gasped, rising up to look at her. "Stop or I'll come and I don't want to. Not yet. I want to feel you come again. I want to watch you come."

She slid her hands down to his waist.

More, she whispered in his head.

He rose up over her and growled. His fangs emerged, his

green eyes dark, fierce, as he met her gaze. She reached up and stroked his fangs, avoiding the tips. He moaned then rolled his hips into her. She arched and whimpered. She touched his lips, his chin, and stroked his neck with her hand. He was beautiful everywhere. Her chest hurt looking at him.

"I feel your potion inside me still, very deep. Oh, God. It's almost all the way down." Once more, unexpected tears tracked down her face and into her hair.

He caught her lips with his, his fangs heavy on her mouth. His tongue pierced her.

He drove hard now, his hips flexing, his cock driving. When the potion finally penetrated her core, the sensation was like nothing she had ever experienced before, a fire burning in the well of her body. She panted in heavy gasps, weeping, writhing beneath him.

"Oh, God! Kerrick!" The next climax hit her like a hard punch. She screamed at the breadth of the sensation as the orgasm rolled through her, pleasure spiking, flowing, flooding her. At the same time, power gathered, then, in an enormous wave, released.

Once more he grunted hard, taking what she could give. "Oh, shit," he whispered. "That was—" He groaned and growled over her now, more beast than man, more erotic, wild, hot as he pumped into her hard, faster and faster. "I'm going to come."

Another wave caught her. She cried out and on instinct as the climax gathered, as power once more bunched within, she drove her fingers on either side of his back between the ridges of the wing-locks, teasing the sensitive ridges. Her orgasm peaked, the power released against him, into him, and she screamed with the pleasure that took her on a long, exquisite ride.

"Can't wait any longer," he grunted. His back writhed beneath her fingers as she continued to work his wing-locks. He lifted his head. His throat opened as he roared his climax. She came with him again, unable to believe the sensations pummeling her entire body, especially since his orgasm went on and on, his hips bucking into her, his torso punching the air, his lips parted, his eyes squeezed shut.

At last, he rode her the rest of the way down, down, down then dropped onto her, panting. "Oh. God."

The beautiful weight of his body smashed her into the carpet. She sighed deeply as she encircled his neck with her arms, holding him tight, his lips now suckling her shoulder, her inner thighs dripping. His chest rose and fell with each ragged breath he took.

So damn satisfied drifted through her mind. *Never been like this before.*

So glad I didn't hurt you, she sent.

Those punches . . . like heaven. His body shuddered against her as though he relived the moment.

Alison wept. She hadn't meant to but her happiness knew no bounds. She hadn't hurt him. In fact, he'd taken everything she gave and he'd loved it.

Could life get any better?

She had only one thought: that she would be doing more of this with him, whether he liked it or not. She didn't understand exactly why the *breh-hedden* bothered him so much. In her opinion, the level of his desire for her was brilliant.

He drew back from her, though not breaking contact, the canyon once more between his brows. His fangs had receded. He leaned down, kissed her very gently, then slid into her mind. *You're so beautiful, but we have work to do.*

You're spoiling my buzz.

He smiled then kissed her again. "I want you safe."

She sighed. "Ten minutes? I'd really like a shower."

"Seven," he stated with a growl.

"Okay."

Kerrick lay on the carpet, his hands clasped behind his head, his cock heavy, flaccid, satisfied as it rested on his groin and thigh. He listened to Alison singing in the shower. He didn't recognize the tune but the sound of her voice made him smile.

He chuckled. He felt relaxed and content. Damn. He released a deep sigh. He still couldn't believe he'd just had the best sex of his life and that was saying something after so many centuries.

When her power had gathered then released along with her orgasm, his ascended nature had received the power as a punch in a low arc across his abdomen, which sent pleasure streaking through his groin and riding the length of his shaft. How he had kept from coming before he did, he would never know, except he'd been damn determined to make this moment last.

He felt eased as he hadn't been in centuries, the way Helena used to ease him and even his first mortal wife, Marta. He'd forgotten the joys of marriage, of this kind of union, built on deep respect and of course *crazy* attraction. And yes, he respected Alison, all that she was, all that she had proved herself to be—her courage, her kindness, that she had somehow kept herself sane when she must have felt so desperately isolated and different from everyone else she knew. Yeah, he respected the hell out of her.

Making love to her had eased him, had filled a void that had been so rarely filled given his twelve hundred years. He wanted to keep her by his side, but how could he, given the nature of his job as a warrior? How could he ever put her at that kind of risk?

The truth? He couldn't.

Yet the thought of not having her with him, not getting to be inside her the rest of his life, sliced at something deep in his chest until he started to hurt.

Okay. He really couldn't go there right now.

Instead he drew a deep breath and once more thought about what had just happened, the pleasure of making love to her. And later, with her fingers working his wing-locks, he had let go. Really let go. Damn. He'd never had an orgasm roll on and on until he wondered if it would ever end.

Damn.

The memory, so recent, jolted his body all over again. He hardened and that made him sit up.

Reminiscing was not going to help.

He jumped to his feet. He'd like a shower as well. As he reached for his clothes, his phone buzzed. Thorne. Again. He withdrew the card then left Alison's room before answering. Once past the doorway he thumbed the phone. "Give."

Thorne's voice broke over his ears, "We've just gotten word from COPASS. Can you spell *reamed*?"

Kerrick listened in disbelief. He couldn't possibly be hearing right. He made Thorne repeat it . . . twice.

In the end, he had to accept what Thorne said—Alison was slated to battle one of the Commander's top warriors in the Tolleson Two arena tomorrow at seven PM. "This is all about fucking *spectacle*, isn't it?"

"Yep. I'm headed to Endelle's palace to see if we can make this right. However, I can't say I'm hopeful. Do your best, brother."

Kerrick thumbed his phone then returned to the bedroom to his jeans, which were still sweat-soaked. He folded his clothes to his laundry on Second, folded on a fresh set of jeans and T-shirt, then put his phone away. He thought about what was coming and knew he couldn't tell Alison what was in store for her, not yet. He just couldn't. Goddammit, this was wrong. On every possible level, this . . . was . . . wrong.

Alison knew she needed to leave the shower, but the pounding of the hot water felt so good on her tired muscles.

The sex. Oh, God, the sex had been fantastic. No, *fantastic* was too small a word. *Unbelievable,* like six kinds of roller-coaster rides all in one.

A rosy sensation swelled deep inside her chest, a soft warmth and gentle vibration. When thoughts of Kerrick drifted through her head, the rose bloomed then bloomed some more until her entire body glowed.

She recognized the sensation, the beginning of love, of falling in love, of bonding, that thing females often did with men who brought them to orgasm . . . again and again.

She leaned her forehead against the tile. She smacked her forehead a couple of times.

She shouldn't even be thinking about *loving* Kerrick, of desiring a future with him, of feeling such tenderness toward him, not with the whole situation built for impermanence.

Just sex, please.

Please.

She shook her head and worked a cramp out of her neck muscle.

The truth was, she could so love this man. He could handle all her weird abilities and powers. He understood them, he admired them, he *enjoyed* them.

But deep in the back of her mind, that which nagged at her, which had lived in her since she was very young, was the fear that some of her power would get away from her and she'd hurt him, maybe even kill him. He had said her hand-blast had crossed dimensions, so, yeah, she was more powerful than even she understood. So, what if? Oh, God . . . what if?

She closed her eyes and forced herself to breathe.

After a couple of minutes of just breathing, perspective emerged. She had been forgetting one small detail. All her thoughts were focused on whether or not she would have a relationship with Kerrick *in the future* when the real question was whether or not she even *had* a future. Apparently, the Commander wanted her really dead and wouldn't stop until he got the job done.

She shifted her thoughts to the more pressing issue at hand: learning how to battle like a warrior just in case more death vamps came after her.

As she had told Kerrick more than once, *she wasn't a warrior.* The pleasure she had experienced in bonding with her own identified sword and battling Kerrick because she had his muscle memory in her body, well, all of that was one thing.

Truth? She had as much killing instinct as a dust bunny.

She left the shower, dried off, then wrapped herself in a

towel. She moved into the bedroom but Kerrick had left. She took one look at the pile of sweaty clothes she'd trained in and shuddered. She turned to the rack by the bathroom door then plucked a fresh set off the plastic hangers—jeans and a pink T-shirt this time, minus the fireworks over her cleavage.

As she dressed, she realized her triceps burned. She had worked out with weights for the last six months and she was strong, but if Kerrick had been unable to heal her throughout the training thus far, she would have been doubled over in pain.

Once dressed, and well over her seven-minute limit, she headed in the direction of the family room. Kerrick waited for her, a hard glint in his eye. Worse, he wouldn't even look at her, wouldn't meet her gaze.

A hello would be nice, she sent, the words cut with sarcasm. He turned away from her, his hands planted on his hips, his shoulders bunched and pressed low. She reached out with her empathy and there it was again, another mountain of rage, this time laced with despair.

"What is it?" she asked, every sense on sudden alert.

The way his head jerked toward her and his gaze latched onto hers, she knew she'd pushed the right button.

He released a sigh. "This damn training." He looked away, shifting his gaze off to the left.

A lie?

"What are you not telling me?"

Another sigh, forced. "I spoke with Thorne. I don't have all the details yet. He just wanted to stress with me how important it was for both of us to work hard at the training over the next several hours."

Alison knew he wasn't telling her everything. She also knew he would tell her if she pushed him. So the question was, did she really want to know?

His demeanor said enough and right now, no, she didn't want to know, not yet.

She drew her sword into her hand, her fingers tingling with recognition, her heart now slamming in her chest. Did this make her a coward, the not wanting to know? Or maybe just sensible.

One step at a time, Alison of Mortal Earth.

I don't need to know anything more, she sent. *Just train me, Warrior.*

At that he turned toward her fully. His expression lightened . . . a little. *You are a warrior, Alison. Maybe not of swords and daggers, but you have a warrior's heart and a warrior's courage.* He nodded several times. Aloud, he said, "I just want you to know this has been one of the finest nights of my life."

Alison crumbled inside. He sure knew how to get to a girl. "Ditto," she whispered. She brought her hands together on the leather-wrapped handle of her sword. She lowered her chin and shoulders. She set her gaze on his abdomen to see which direction he intended to move.

The sacrifice of hours,
Reveals the truth of character.

—*Collected Proverbs,* Beatrice of Fourth

CHAPTER 17

At dawn Kerrick stood over Alison. She was sound asleep in the guest room. He had trained her hard through the night until she simply couldn't take one more step. He'd let her shower and head to bed. The truth was, she'd need her sleep, dammit, lots of it to be ready to undergo this latest farce, which would take place in about twelve hours.

At least she had a fucking amount of power. Maybe that would get her through.

Who was he kidding? She would be fighting General Leto, former Warrior of the Blood, Greaves's second-in-command. How the hell was she supposed to defeat him? He'd been ascended for three thousand years and had fought as a warrior the entire time.

He cursed under his breath. He wanted to wake her up and keep teaching her how to use her sword, how to battle, how to size up an opponent, how to use her strengths and exploit the weaknesses of her enemy. But now he couldn't.

She needed sleep for the horror of what was about to happen to her, but oh, how he wanted more time to train her.

COPASS, that bullshit Committee of bullshit Committees, had done the Commander's bidding . . . again. As he looked down at her, resolve tightened his chest. He couldn't let the arena battle happen without putting up a fight.

Thorne had been right when he used the word *reamed*.

He thumbed his phone. "Hey, Central," he said softly, turning away from Alison.

"Hey, *duhuro*," Jeannie drawled, ready to tease as always.

"So not in the mood."

"Give." Yeah, Jeannie knew how to read the warriors, and her adjustment was swift.

"I need a lift to Second."

"You got it. Location?"

"The Cave."

He thumbed his phone and the vibration began. A moment later he stood in the middle of the rec room. Thorne was sprawled on the sofa opposite, asleep or maybe he'd passed out, probably the latter. Jean-Pierre sagged on a stool at the bar, sipping a French martini. He lifted his chin in a brief acknowledgment to Kerrick, sighed, then took another sip. He had bruises up and down both arms and shoulders. Fighting this night had gotten up close and personal for the Frenchman.

Kerrick did a double take in the direction of the pool table where Luken and Santiago were actually playing a game. Some kind of half-ass repair had been executed, which involved a lot of chicken wire and several two-by-fours. The result looked like something taken from a really run-down Mortal Earth trailer park. If they'd set up empty beer cans in a row on the rim, the picture would have been complete. At least the table was functional.

"Hey, Kerrick," Santiago called. He flipped the cue and sank three balls. He had a massive spidery bruise on the back of his left shoulder. Yeah, the boys had been out fighting.

Luken's gaze tracked the shot. "Lucky bastard," he muttered. His hair hung down his back, free of the *cadroen,* a thick mass of blond waves and stray, rebellious curls that gave him the appearance of an Olympian god.

Kerrick jerked his chin toward the sofa. "How long has he been out?"

"The last hour. He went to see Endelle."

"Is she going to protest the arena battle?"

Luken shrugged. His cue stood upright and he tapped it on the floor. "He didn't say but as soon as he returned, he started tossing back Ketel shots. You want a game?"

"No, thanks. I have to get back to Queen Creek after I make a couple of calls." His gaze drifted to Thorne.

Perfect. He'd wanted Thorne to lead the charge on this one.

What a great big fucking mess.

He left the Cave to stand just outside the doors.

He lifted his phone once more to his ear and contacted Central. "Jeannie—"

"Need a lift?"

"Not yet. I need to speak with Endelle."

A too quiet silence followed after which Jeannie drew in a breath. "She's not receiving."

"What do you mean, *she's not receiving*?" What the hell?

Jeannie sighed. "Specifically, if you called in asking for her, you were to be told, and I quote, *You got Alison into this by calling an emergency lift so go fuck yourself,* end quote."

Kerrick ground his teeth. His temper once more started pounding on the inside of his skull. He took deep breaths and tried to order his mind. If Endelle said no, then no it was.

Goddammit.

Thorne . . . Endelle . . . two strikes. Shit.

He held the phone at his back and let loose with a good long string of obscenities.

There had to be a way to fix this. He ground his teeth a little more. He hated to speak the next words, though at this point his choices were appallingly limited.

He brought the phone back to his ear. "Then I want to speak with Harding."

"You mean Chairman Harding?" He heard the disbelief in Jeannie's voice. He could hardly believe it himself.

"Get him on the com, Jeannie. Now."

"You got it but it might take a couple of minutes. He's not the most accessible ascender."

"I'll wait."

Daniel Harding chaired COPASS and as said chairman, he would have had the final approval of the upcoming mockery of a *spectacle*. Maybe, just this once, Harding would listen to reason.

Whatever.

Harding had no choice but to speak with the Warriors of the Blood. Given the Commander's access to him, Endelle had fought to retain equal rights. What the Committee allowed Greaves, by the law of the land had to be granted to the Supreme High Administrator.

At last, Harding came on the line. "I'm here to serve, *duhuro* Kerrick. How can I help?"

Complete bullshit.

"I want COPASS to reconsider its decision about ascender Wells and the arena battle. She's not a warrior."

A slight pause, then, "I'm sorry but the Committee reviewed all the data and voted unanimously. Ascendiate Wells must receive an appropriate consequence since her guardian violated a very important law, as did Madame Endelle." He enumerated their sins and ended with, "Commander Greaves had every right to submit a protest and COPASS really didn't have any other option. I shouldn't have to tell you this."

His condescending tone pushed Kerrick's temper over the edge. "What about the law the Commander broke sending a regiment to Carefree One? What about that rule?" He was pissed and couldn't stop himself.

"Now, now. Calm yourself, *duhuro*. Be reasonable. The Commander will certainly receive a severe censure from the Committee in due course. The sentence assigned to ascendiate Wells is a separate matter entirely. Endelle has thirty days to file a complaint and as you must know we take all complaints seriously."

He felt the blood rush to his face as he once more ground his teeth. "We're talking about a woman's life, an innocent," he cried. "You've basically handed her a death sentence."

"I simply do not agree. We've seen the reports on ascendiate Wells, one of which suggests her powers exceed those of Second. I'm sure she will perform admirably during the arena challenge."

"The arena *challenge*? Is that what you're calling it? A mere *challenge*? It's an old-fashioned fight-to-the-death and you fucking know it."

He paced back and forth now, his voice growing louder. He saw the doors to the Cave open and Luken, Santiago, and Jean-Pierre filed out to stand near him, a strong line of support.

Harding continued his reasonableness. "Given the gravity of the rules that you and Madame Endelle chose to break, I had no recourse. Greaves had every right to establish the contest as a fight-to-the-death event."

That did it. Kerrick's temper shot into the stratosphere.

"No recourse? Have you no conscience left, you fucking tool? And what the hell were you thinking putting yourself in the Commander's hands, anyway? What does he give you, Harding? A serum after you've drunk a human to death, you fucking piece of shit."

A brief silence followed, then Harding cleared his throat. "You are clearly agitated," he said. "I will therefore forgive these accusations so unworthy of your rank. Good night, most respected *duhuro* warrior."

Kerrick's hands shook as he thumbed his phone.

And at that moment, who should show up but Marcus yukking it up with Medichi. Marcus had cuts all over his arms, shoulders, and face.

Well, goddamnsonofabitch, the deserter had made up with the warriors.

It was the proverbial last straw, especially when the fucking vampire smirked and said, "Well, if it isn't the bastard who got my sister killed."

Kerrick's nostrils flared, his fists clenched then pumped, and the air disappeared between him and the man he hated. The feel of flesh sliding beneath the power of his right hook felt like heaven. When Marcus's fist landed square on his jaw, well, *game fucking on.*

Endelle played a cat-and-mouse game with Darian Greaves that chapped her ass up one side and down the other. She was the cat, an okay designation, and *the little peach* was the mouse, which in her opinion was way too high a lifeform for him to represent. Cat and rat worked a little better. Cat and scum-sucking amoeba made her even happier.

She had been playing this game for how many fucking centuries? Jesus H. Christ.

She was in the small rotunda off her master bedroom, deep inside her palace, a well-protected and fortified sanctuary where she performed most of her work on Second.

She spent a big part of each twenty-four hours doing voyeuristic surveillance in that mystical point of nether-space called the darkening. So far as she knew, she was the only ascender on Second Earth capable of being in the darkening, where her corporeal body reclined on her chaise longue but her spiritual self with the same external features and abilities as her body could travel through time and space. Capable of being in two places at once, she followed the bastard around the globe. Time and time again she disrupted his attempts to fold death vampire squads to his Estrella Mountain complex.

The problem was that for all her power, she didn't know how to win this game. Worse, she'd been losing ground for the past fifteen years. Of the 167 Territories of Second Earth, 50 had aligned with *the little peach.* Of course High Administrators as a lot weren't always the most ethical of ascenders. Half of them, in her opinion, were out for only one thing—power. Maybe two things—power and . . . well . . . more power.

Greaves didn't help. He'd arrived on Second loaded with persuasive abilities. He had a forked tongue and could out-slime a slug and he looked so pretty doing it. Bastard.

She didn't have his tact, his refined manners, his patience. She barked and expected everyone to fall in line, an administrative style she freely admitted had numerous flaws.

Okay, so she needed help—only where would it come from? She had a powerful ascendiate aligning with her tonight but what use could she possibly be? A thirty-plus-year-old therapist? She might as well be wearing diapers, for God's sake. The best Endelle could do was make a Militia Warrior out of her. She had enough natural power that when properly trained she'd be able to take on a squad of death vamps by herself. Big fucking whoopee.

Havily came to mind. She was still pissed about her Liaison Officer. What the hell had Havily been thinking throwing a boat on top of her desk and calling it the future? Havily didn't understand the gravity of the situation on Second Earth. A new military-admin complex wouldn't come close to resolving the broader issue, which was Greaves himself. The bastard should have ascended to Third, oh, about twenty-six hundred years ago. Instead he'd found some way to remain on Second.

She knew what she needed—help from the Upper Dimensions to stop Darian Greaves. Unfortunately, she might as well be asking for the moon.

She sighed as she continued plowing through the airwaves. In nine millennia she hadn't received even a whisper of communication from Third or any of the Upper Earths. All she knew was she was stuck on Second, she'd not been allowed to ascend, and her duty was to keep Greaves in check. But she was failing and when she thought to pray, she begged for help, on her knees, her voice splitting resonance until she sounded like two cats fighting.

At last she found the Commander's signature.

Hello. She didn't wait but dove straight at him. What do you know? He was in Kabul Two, preparing right now to fold a squad of death vamps to his compound. Bastard.

Not tonight, asshole. He stumbled as her greeting pierced his bald skull.

Ah, Endelle. Good evening, or should I say good morning.

Fuck you, little peach. She saw him standing in front of the squad, his claw twitching now. His face flamed at her appellation. She chuckled. *You might as well take off. You won't penetrate the shield I just launched around this bunch of fucking night-feeders.*

She could feel his rage as a living, writhing beast moving throughout his body, a deep blinding fury that drove his life, his actions, all those twisted unresolved *feelings* from his tortured youth. She might even have felt sorry for him except for the number of mortals he had personally dispatched.

As he dematerialized, she heard the faintest word drift through her mind, directed toward her: *Bitch.*

Endelle's eyes popped open and she sat up on her couch. In three millennia Darian Greaves had never lost his temper with her. Not once.

But he had called her a bitch and he never said things like that to her.

Holy hell!

She sucked in a deep breath and a new emotion banged around inside her chest, something very close to *hope.*

Darian Greaves was seriously rattled, which could only mean he knew something she didn't about, who else, Alison Wells.

Well, well, well, ascendiate Wells. So there was something else going on, something she didn't know about and Greaves did.

She felt a faint vibration within her mind, Thorne's signal. He was the only Second ascender who had a direct link to her mind, and his voice suddenly filled her skull. *We've got a sitch at the Cave. Marcus finally found Kerrick.*

Got it, she sent back.

Marcus and Kerrick.

She was only surprised the fight hadn't gone down sooner.

She shifted her voyeuristic powers to her warriors' off-hours rec room.

The two men went at it like apes.

Well, thank shit for preternatural voyeurism. She could see everything and how glorious her warriors were.

All of them were present, Thorne and Medichi, Luken placing bets with Santiago, Zacharius, Jean-Pierre wearing a green brocade *cadroen*, and of course the men of the hour, Kerrick now pummeling the hell out of Marcus's stomach but look out. Jesus . . . Marcus pulled away and hit Kerrick's jaw so hard his head snapped back and he actually stumbled backward.

Not for fucking long. Kerrick gave his head a shake, lowered his jaw, and moved back in. This time an old-fashioned brawl ensued that landed both men on the ground rolling, hitting, punching, grunting. Marcus got hold of Kerrick's long hair, already released from the *cadroen,* grabbed handfuls from both sides, tugged hard, and head-butted Kerrick. The crack resounded through the air.

Didn't slow Kerrick down, not even a jot. He somehow got on top and started swinging. He landed several punches, left, right, left. Endelle leaped to her feet and punched the air along with him.

She loved a good fight. Forget *spectacle*. Give her a boxing ring and two Neanderthals any day of the week.

Marcus, however, threw his hips forward and caught Kerrick about the waist with his legs. The two beasts flipped over half a dozen times, the other warriors shifting to make room for them.

Thorne shouted at them to stop, but they were two mad dogs going at each other. Only a fire hose was likely to stop the carnage.

Endelle's fist pumped more air. Her feet moved from side to side. Thorne dove in. He tried to grab Marcus's arm, which put Kerrick off balance, sending his right hook straight at Thorne's face. A subsequent crack told her that

her second-in-command had just gotten his nose busted . . .
again . . . well . . . aw, shit. She'd have to break this up now.

She sighed then folded to the Cave. She snapped her fingers, which froze both men in place, on the ground. Marcus
had his head arched back, eyes closed, and teeth gritted as
he struggled to get out of a headlock. Kerrick's face was
beet red and his eyes bulged as he squeezed.

She looked them over. "Kerrick almost has him. No . . .
I think Marcus will break out of this one."

"Tell me we get to find out," Santiago cried. "I have a
hundred bucks on Marcus."

"Lo siento, querido." She snapped her fingers again and
both men rolled away from each other then gained their
feet. "So what the fuck was this about?"

Neither Marcus nor Kerrick spoke, just stood hunched
over and tried to breathe.

"Just as I thought." She trained her gaze on Kerrick.
"Why the hell aren't you in Queen Creek? You're on fucking guardian duty or did you not get the memo?"

His face was a mess. Blood leaked everywhere and his
mouth and left eye were swelling up like he'd been stung by
a few dozen wasps. Even so, he came to attention, feet a
proper distance apart, his left hand slung behind his back.
"The shields hold, all of them, and I had to do something to
try to stop this madness."

"What madness?" Santiago asked.

Luken, who stood next to him, informed him of the upcoming arena battle.

"Madre de dios," he cried.

"No shit."

"This isn't right," Medichi said. He stepped forward and
met Endelle's gaze straight-on. "Can't something be done?"

"COPASS already approved the engagement. But all
you faithless vampires need to grow a pair. I have confidence in Alison, unlike the rest of you."

"With all due respect, we're talking about Leto," Zacharius cried, "not some squirrelly-ass death vamp." His long

curly hair hung free from the *cadroen* and in the scattered
light of the parking lot, he looked sexy as Hades. Even Endelle felt the call of his primitive nature and all those curls.
Mortal women *loved* Zach and gave up the vein without a
blink of an eye. He added, "Ascendiate Wells doesn't stand
a chance."

"Of course she does and the good news is, for a few
hours, you'll all get a break. Greaves will have his army
present at the arena to make a strong statement to the world
about his power and promises of a Coming Order, blah,
blah, blah, so there won't be any activity at the Borderlands, thank you, God.

"Besides, our girl has some serious chops." Her gaze
landed on Kerrick. "Tell them what you did last night and
why it's not so fucking hopeless."

He wiped his swollen bloody lips with the back of his
hand. "I forged minds and let her experience some of my
recent battles." The words came out thick and slurred.

Expletives rounded the group.

"No fucking way," Zach cried. "And she took it? How? I
can't even do that."

Endelle shook her head. "She's powerful, more than
even she knows, more than I suspect even I know."

Several gasps followed the last part of this statement,
which pleased her to no end because it reflected their view
of her as one approaching omniscience. *Nice.*

"We're done here. I'll see all of you at the arena tonight
and for Christ's sake arrive early in dress uniform, including you, Warrior Marcus. Alison Wells means something
as-yet-to-be-defined to Second Earth and also to this ape
over here." She jerked her thumb toward Kerrick.

"And as for you," she cried, glaring at Kerrick. "Get the
fuck back to Queen Creek and do your goddam guardian
duty. I'll send Horace to you to get you fixed up." She didn't
wait for an argument. She waved her arm and Kerrick vanished.

She then pointed to Marcus. "You, asshole. One more

word to Kerrick about Helena and I'm taking your left nut."
Just to let him know she could, she mentally gave a little
tug, which made Marcus's eyes pop, then she gave a sharp
twist. He doubled over. "What do you say?"

"Yes, Madame Endelle," he wheezed, his face turning a
pretty strawberry-red.

She inclined her head to her second-in-command.
"Thorne, get Horace. See to Kerrick first."

"Of course," he said.

"And for fuck's sake, get some sleep."

She didn't wait to hear another word. She took a breath,
turned her back on her warriors then just as she dematerialized, she smiled.

Goddamn but she loved her men, and a little roughhous-
ing now and then was a good thing. A stiff drink helped. A
good lay. Taking the vein. Without a whole variety of steam
valves for testosterone, the whole world would have exploded by now, the earth's magma along with it.

As Kerrick awaited Horace, he stood over Alison once
more, his sword drawn, the one tangible means he had of
protecting her, yet it was useless in this situation. She slept
deeply now, her lips parted. She looked even younger with
the comforter drawn partway up her cheek, her fingers curled
around the edge.

His heart ached as he looked down at her. He wanted her
in his world and he wanted her safe. In the short time they'd
been together, she'd become a litany in his head, *must protect, must protect*. He'd never been so obsessed before but
then again, Alison was like no other ascendiate he had ever
known and yeah, she was the center of the *breh-hedden* for
him. He was hooked in deep.

Making love to her had been flat-out erotic, intense, and
drive-a-car-at-two-hundred-miles-an-hour satisfying. She
matched him in power, this woman, this mortal, this ascendiate, and he was falling for her fast, an asteroid getting
close to the earth's gravitational pull and getting sucked
straight in.

He'd been inside her head. He knew she had strength. He knew she'd go the distance even if the endgame was hopeless. Still, right now, asleep in her bed, she looked incredibly vulnerable. Dammit, his chest seized, drawing into a painful knot.

I can't lose her.

Yet what chance did she have? She would be fighting the Commander's most powerful general, a former Warrior of the Blood, an ascender with incredible ability.

His phone buzzed. He folded his sword into the far corner of his bedroom, palmed his phone, then thumbed. "Give," he said, his tone flat.

Jeannie's voice, weary at the tail end of a shift, came online. "Horace begs admittance."

"Granted. Go home, Jeannie."

"I'm off in about thirty minutes. So, tell me, *duhuro,* does she have a chance?"

The soft concern in her voice wrenched the knot in his chest all over again. "I don't know."

"Aw, shit."

"You said it, but I have to go."

"You get some rest, too."

As the line went dead, Horace materialized a few feet away.

Once again Alison found herself inside a dream, flying at full-mount over White Lake. The water shimmered beneath her in the dawn's light, reflecting pink streamers of clouds. The breathtaking view sent her heart soaring.

Guardian. How the word called to her. Guardian *of Ascension.* Guardian *of the Lake.*

As though she had been flying all her life, she drew her feet perpendicular to the water then spread her arms wide, which brought her body to a position of standing in midair, the gentle flapping of her wings supporting her. She slowed the rhythm, which allowed her to descend to the calm surface of the blue-green water.

Her bare toes slid into the water and her fangs emerged.

Wings and a pair of fangs. So, she was ascended and had acquired the promised vampire traits. How at ease she felt with the lake, with flight, with her fangs. She even wore leather flight gear, like a warrior—a kilt and a weapons harness over her chest, covering her breasts and riding up to cross her shoulders then travel down her spine. The fit was perfect.

Again . . . guardian.

The lake waters were oddly warm and soothing. She sustained her position with her wings then looked up, straight up. A beacon of light, heavenly light, shone down on her and she knew she looked into Third Earth. She was overcome by a swell of love for what she saw, a deep intense and quite familiar *longing*. Tears touched her eyes. She felt the most profound need to rise into the air, to reach Third Earth. She started beating her wings as hard as she could but her body wouldn't move, as though the lake anchored her, held her in place.

She looked down and the lake once more called to her, begging for her protection.

Guardian.

Alison struggled to consciousness, picking her way through her fatigue as through a dense fog. In the distance, maybe a thousand miles away, she heard Kerrick's voice within her mind. *Time to wake up, Alison. Endelle is about to remove her protection.*

She opened her eyes and saw the vaulted twigged ceiling of Kerrick's Queen Creek home. She was in the guest bed, cocooned in the warmth of the comforter. She even wore flannel. She released a sigh, for in this moment she felt very safe.

She stretched again and felt a few leftover twinges. Nothing to complain about. Kerrick's healing had been wonderful. Her mind moved backward. The training had been intense before . . . and after.

Oh, God, how he had made love to her last night, right after she'd hurt her wrist!

The vampire had been . . . incredible. She sighed and just for a moment, before the day, or rather night, and whatever it would hold, crashed down on her, she savored the memory of being so connected to her warrior.

She closed her eyes and smiled. She sighed a few dozen times.

And what was the potion he'd put in her breast that had the ability to travel all the way to her . . .

Alison. It's time.

She heard his voice again, right in the center of her brain, less patient this time. Time for what? Dinner, maybe?

Sleep still swirled throughout her body and for just a moment she recalled the dream of wings and of flying, of feeling a profound protective drive toward the lake.

Alison. How strident he sounded. Did she really have to get up? She wanted to call him to her, to beg him to come to her bed for a few minutes, okay, maybe a day or two, and just hold her. Okay, maybe not *just hold her* but they could do that, too.

The sweetest sensations of desire began teasing her breasts and the tender place between her thighs. Now would be very nice, Kerrick and his hands. Oh, those hands. Kerrick and his . . .

Alison. The voice this time had a dagger's edge.

She sat up, sleep streaming away from her. Kerrick sounded urgent. That was right. He had trained her to fight, but he hadn't told her the why of it.

Adrenaline started punching at her. She put a hand to her chest as her heart rate increased.

She slipped from bed and made her way to the formal living room. Kerrick waited for her there and he wasn't smiling.

She looked him up and down. He had on a very strange short black leather tunic and a sleeker version of the sandals he wore when fighting in flight gear. He looked like a modern version of ancient Rome. His hair was pulled back from his face, probably contained in the *cadroen*.

The picture? So gorgeous.

She had a dozen reasons already to believe she had entered a new world, but the sight of his partially bare, muscled thighs and a purple cape flung over one shoulder put her just a little bit farther from Kansas.

She moved toward him and caught sight of a glimmer beneath the cape. When she was close enough, she pushed the cape aside. A brass breastplate, also sexy as hell and molded to his pecs, bore an insignia—a silver sword crowned with a mossy green laurel wreath, simple, beautiful, powerful.

"What is this?" she asked. A prickly sensation traveled suddenly down her spine.

"The emblem of the Warriors of the Blood."

Another question, one she didn't want to ask, slid past her lips. "Why are you dressed like this?"

His expression hardened. She felt his distance as though he had moved to another continent, Australia maybe.

Had he even made love to her last night?

She searched his eyes. "What's going on, Kerrick? Is the house surrounded? Don't I have even the smallest chance?"

He met her gaze but retained his posture, as though the soles of his leather sandals had rooted into the tiles. "Last night, what I couldn't bring myself to tell you was that COP-ASS agreed to the Commander's demand that you do battle in an arena this evening, one-on-one against his top general, the warrior called Leto."

She tilted her head. "The one at the alley? The one who used to be a Warrior of the Blood?"

He nodded.

She really couldn't have heard him right. "Let me get this straight. I'm to battle a man, a vampire, one powerful like you, in an arena, in front of thousands of people?"

He nodded.

She shook her head. "This can't be happening. How am I supposed to do battle after a single day of training?" She thought of Darian, her former client, then murmured, "He must really want me dead."

She shook her head in disbelief. She recalled the moment in the downtown alley when she had chosen, *chosen,* to demonstrate her power because she knew something momentous would happen, an action that had led to the opening of Second Earth to her. But how, *how,* had her journey brought her here, to a place where she would have to attempt something so impossible? "And I can't refuse the challenge, can I?"

This time his head did a back-and-forth wag, only very slowly. "You entered your rite of ascension when you sent the hand-blast up into the Trough. I'm sorry, Alison. No going back, not at this point. And until your ascension ceremony takes place tomorrow night, you're fair game. Again . . . I'm sorry."

She wanted to kick something. "Is this why you're so angry? Why you're as cold as ice this evening?"

His chest rose then fell. "Yes." He thawed a little, his shoulders falling. He rubbed his fist over his forehead. "I tried last night to change things but Endelle wouldn't talk to me. I even called Harding who heads the fucking Committee, but he was about as useful as rat shit."

"I can set up a field, though, right?"

He nodded. "You know my reservations. Leto has advanced powers like you, like me. Don't cast a field unless you know you can contain him."

She nodded. Okay . . . no fields unless she was certain. So how the hell was she supposed to be certain?

She turned away from him. Her eyes burned. Dammit, she did not want to cry, only how was this right or fair? What had she ever done to deserve being condemned in this way?

She thought about the despair she had sensed in Kerrick at various points during her all-too-brief acquaintance with him.

She began to understand.

"I let you sleep as long as I could, but the contest takes place in just under an hour. Endelle sent battle gear, and you'll need to eat. A meal has been prepared." He sighed. "You must ready yourself to depart."

She moved away from him intending to return to the guest room, yet her instincts wouldn't let her. She turned back to him and drew close once more. She met his gaze and reached out with her empathy. She found his familiar despair edged with, yeah, his deeply embedded guilt.

She thought of all he had done for her, all he had given her in making love to her, in being able to handle her absurd power. She put a hand on his cheek and he caught it with his, pressing hard.

"Kerrick, you're not responsible for this."

His face contorted as though she had struck him.

She cried, "Dammit, listen to me and listen good. I chose to ascend even though I'd already watched you slay a death vamp, a creature who stated very clearly that he'd come to kill me, to take my blood. I knew when I threw that hand-blast into the Trough that I wasn't going on a trip to Disneyland. Darian *chooses* to commit vile, despicable acts. Others cave to his seduction and trickery. *You* are not to blame for any of it."

His jaw worked as she had so often seen it move, as though trying to crunch marbles. His chest once more moved up and down, this time in even deeper breaths. The therapist in Alison heard a shrill clanging of bells, a warning that something needed to be addressed right here, right now. How many times had she seen this before in her clients, that stolid look that was really only a wall of glass, which a few pertinent words and some strong coaxing would shatter?

However, that sort of effort always took nimble moment-by-moment processing and she certainly didn't have the time right now to help him through. But she would wager her life that the despair living in Kerrick had been with him from the time he ascended to Second Earth. She knew this in the same way she knew that the sun rose in the east and set in the west.

Her feet began moving again, cool slaps against cold tile. When she reached the guest room, she saw black leather battle gear, as supple as velvet, hanging on the end of the rack. Only then did the tears come. Somehow a female battle costume suit, with leather boots, brought the reality of the situation home to her. She would be going against a former Warrior of the Blood. How the hell was she supposed to survive that?

Spectacle,
The lifeblood of a society,
A meager reflection,
A ribbon around the hardship of life,
The challenge of the universe.

—*Collected Poems,* Beatrice of Fourth

CHAPTER 18

Crace paraded his wife up and down the second tier aisle of the Tolleson Two arena, a long walkway around the Commander's half of the enormous building, a path designed for exhibition, for show, for demonstration, for greeting equals, for letting those beneath one's station know just how inferior they were.

He was in his element, that public place of societal ranking that most pleased his simple avaricious, power-hungry soul. Best of all, however, was Julianna, whose beauty and bearing were unequaled.

Julianna walked regally, her head held high, her neck encased in a stiff elegant ruff that spread to her shoulders and was attached to long lace sleeves. Her gown, all in white and embroidered with seed pearls, was cut very low, displaying her full perfect breasts. He had suckled them earlier and made her cry out more than once. His beloved had the most tender erotic breasts and came so easily beneath his mouth.

How he loved her.

Yet oh, how he loved more this moment of triumph. He shouldn't be gloating, but the ceiling began to withdraw and because he had worked for the past thirty hours to pull in every favor owed to him throughout the North American continent, as well as China, he knew this *spectacle* would outshine them all.

A full double orchestra played Beethoven's Fifth, a rather ostentatious choice, but then why the hell not? His future was being decided tonight and why not let the inevitable celebration begin now?

He had paid a visit to Leto in the locker room and oh, how magnificent the warrior had appeared in his black leather kilt, bare oiled chest, and determination crowding his blue eyes. Crace's heart swelled at the memory.

"The roof is fully drawn back now," Julianna cried, her gaze fixed upward. She released his arm then clapped her hands since she had a particular love of fireworks.

The distant thumping started and the night sky filled with a rainbow of sparkling color. The crowd shouted its appreciation as great bursts of light revealed mystical creatures in every bejeweled shade beneath the sun. Once fully formed in the air, the creatures began to move, to fly in vast arcs above the crowd of some fifty thousand spectators. There was only one place such fireworks existed: in imaginative Beijing Two. Yes, Crace had called in a few favors— but to great effect, for as one the crowd moaned, gasped, and squealed.

In the midst of the moving glittering lights, several squadrons of trained swans flew in organized patterns, guided by actors from the nearby live theaters, all in full-mount and in splendid swirling costumes, so that very soon the upper reaches of the arena were full of that which all ascenders adored, hell, all mortals and ascended vampires alike . . . *spectacle*.

The crowd cheered and suddenly he felt the master's presence beside him. "Well done, High Administrator Crace. An excellent beginning."

Crace turned and bowed, drawing his wife to face the Commander. This was one of the best uses he had for his beloved spouse. She dipped a very pretty curtsy, and the Commander's gaze drifted to her beautiful breasts, now peaked from the excitement of the fireworks and pushing hard at all those seed pearls.

"Julianna," his deep smooth voice flowed.

"Commander."

However, the master was never gauche and shifted his gaze to Crace. He even planted a hand on his shoulder. "You've done well."

Crace drew in a deep breath. Such bountiful praise. He felt dizzy, and visions of Geneva did an elegant Fred Astaire tap dance in his head. He could feel the soft black leather cushion beneath his ass. *The right hand of God.*

The Commander merely nodded, offered a small bow, then vanished.

"He is always so elegant," Julianna murmured.

When he glanced at his wife, he saw the flush on her cheeks and her swollen lips. He frowned suddenly. He recognized her state of arousal. She'd been exactly there not an hour ago. A quick search of her mind told him he wasn't the focus of her *interest.*

From the moment he met his wife, he had loved her, almost to the point of madness. Only one thing exceeded his devotion to her—his devotion to his master. For the first time he wondered if there was one thing after all he *would not* do for his deity.

Sweet Jesus. A shiver of fear shot straight through his heart because he didn't know if he could ever choose between his wife and Commander Greaves . . . ever.

Sometimes life, ascended or otherwise, just sucked.

Alison stood beside Kerrick in what looked like your basic locker room. She was silent, shocked out. From the corridor beyond she could hear an orchestra booming out Beethoven's Fifth.

Spectacle.

And she was the star attraction.

Great. Just great.

She shook her head. This couldn't be happening.

She glanced around trying to figure out what a dedicated therapist from regular old Mortal Earth was doing, dressed all in black leather, preparing to battle a warrior vampire from Second Earth.

Even thinking the question threatened to send her into a tailspin. She felt hysteria rising as though thick hands gripped her ribs in an attempt to force the air from her lungs. She wanted to open her mouth and scream.

Instead she drew a breath, then another, then another even though her heart pounded so hard her ears thumped.

She glanced up at Kerrick, looking for some kind of support or understanding, but he was shored up within the fortress of his own mind. And why wouldn't he be? The man lived with guilt stacked so deep in his soul he couldn't move or think straight. She knew that now. Even though he was not to blame for this ridiculous situation, he shouldered the responsibility anyway.

So, here she was . . . alone. What a familiar sensation.

The dream hadn't lasted long, the deep connection to another human being, immortal though he was, the sense of sharing, of working things out together. There was no togetherness here, just Alison trying to find the courage to take one more step down a road that still didn't make a lot of sense.

"At last, ascendiate Wells. So, let me have a look at you."

Alison heard the strong, feminine voice behind her. She whirled around and there, not ten feet away, stood Endelle, in full-mount, her wings a light golden brown. She recognized her from Kerrick's memories, although her wings had been a different color—first yellow, then black when she'd become angry with Kerrick. She was a tall and extremely beautiful woman, thick black hair, olive skin, strong features, a beauty queen from the Middle East. She wore dark brown suede, lots of it, sculpted to her body, and a cape of what looked like mink. She gave an impression of ancient and modern blended. She was also a walking PETA nightmare.

So here she was, She Who Would Live, the ruler of all of Second Earth, Her Supremeness, Madame Endelle.

In the flesh, the woman responded, inside Alison's head, just like that.

Alison reached out with her empathy, without thinking. Endelle narrowed her eyes, "Not on your life, ascendiate."

Alison retreated. "My apologies. An old habit."

Endelle nodded. "Understood." Turning to Kerrick, she said, "Make the introductions, Warrior. I'd like to formally meet the woman who's been making my life a shitfest."

At these words Kerrick took a protective step closer to Alison, the only sign he was even aware of her. "Madame Supreme High Administrator, may I present ascendiate Alison Wells, previously of Carefree, Arizona, Mortal Earth. Ascendiate Wells, Madame Endelle, Supreme High Administrator, Second Earth."

Alison held Endelle's gaze. More than anything she knew she was looking at her future in all its myriad forms. Kerrick had told her that only Endelle had ascended with the same levels of powers Alison now possessed. She also understood that Her Supremeness, as the warriors called her, should have advanced to an Upper Dimension millennia ago, remaining on Second Earth only to serve as a necessary force against the Commander.

Endelle looked her up and down. *Ponytail was a good idea,* she sent. *Black leather suits you. It's probably a good thing your man can't get past his anger right now, otherwise he'd be all over you.*

Without really thinking, Alison sent back, *I think you might have some boundary issues.*

"Boundary issues?" Endelle cried aloud, taking a step forward, the tips of every feather shimmying. "You intend to start up your psycho-crap with me, ascendiate Wells?"

Alison shook her head. "Not at all. I'm telling you I don't intend to discuss my love life with you."

"Whatever."

Endelle's wings reached all the way to the tall ceiling, while her wingspan took up at least a combined twenty feet, larger than even Kerrick's. The present configuration meant that when in full flight, with the wings extended as far as they could go, my God, the span would reach over forty feet from tip to tip.

"Let me speak plainly about today's engagement," Endelle said. "You have only one mission here—to put Leto in the ground. So do it, ascendiate. Know that I'm counting on you."

"Then you've backed the wrong horse," Alison cried. "I hate to be the one to break it to you, but the last time I checked, I was a therapist, not a warrior. I have difficulty swatting flies."

"Listen, missy, where the hell do you think you are? A vacation in St. Croix? This is Second fucking Earth and you're battling to stay alive. Get with the program and start focusing on taking the bastard out. I've seen your training and whatever you may think, you can do this. Furthermore, I expect you to." She turned to Kerrick. "You need to talk to your woman and set her straight on a few things. Now."

She lifted her arm in a theatrical sweep then vanished.

Kerrick breathed hard. He had been working to keep his temper in check, but this last completely insensitive display by the ruler of his world put him straight over the edge.

"So much for a goddamn pep talk," Kerrick cried. "Dammit, I should have warned you. Endelle gives *bitch* a bad name."

He wanted to punch something. Hard. His hands bunched into fists and stayed there. He ground his teeth. He couldn't bear what was happening to Alison, that she was being forced to battle Leto in front of tens of thousands of spectators. He felt unglued, coming apart at the seams, unraveling.

He hated this farce, this arena *contest,* which had only one end as its purpose . . . Alison's death!

"Kerrick, how am I going to do this?"

Her words, the desperation in her voice, the deep fear in her beautiful blue eyes, all did him in and he lunged for her, dragging her into his arms. He felt her sob against him as she wrapped her arms around his waist.

Kerrick. Kerrick, she wept within his mind.

He held her tight all the while stroking her back. He wanted to tell her everything would be all right, he really did. His fears, however, kept him silent.

After a minute, she drew back then looked up at him, her eyes wet. Lavender streamed over him until his senses reeled, his heart ached, and his knees turned to water.

She released his waist and drew in a ragged breath. She wiped at her face with trembling fingers.

Christ. He had to pull his shit together right now. In front of him was a novice warrior who would soon go into battle. He had to think of her in that way, not as the most precious part of his life.

He folded a tissue into his hand from Queen Creek. He dabbed at her cheeks.

"Endelle believes you can beat him," he said. "Let that be your confidence."

"She really thinks I can beat Leto?" Hope fluttered in her eyes.

"Yes. She said so last night. She told us we were a bunch of faithless vampires because you possess more power than you know. So take courage in her belief in you and let the images I gave you take over. Just remember, Leto is powerful so don't try any special tricks unless you're certain to prevail. Tell me you understand what I'm saying to you. Leto . . . Leto is a cunning vampire, a skilled warrior. I fought beside him for centuries. Be prepared for anything."

She nodded in a brisk flurry. "Yes. Yes. Be prepared for anything."

"Also, remember he has weaknesses, like any warrior.

Find his and you'll beat him, and don't doubt for a second he'll try to wear you down."

She nodded all over again.

This was better. Even some of his own fears subsided.

In a brusque movement he drew her into his arms again then kissed her hard on the lips. She met the kiss, her lips parting. He groaned as he thrust his tongue into her mouth, wishing he could take her back to Queen Creek, take her to bed and keep her there . . . forever.

He released her to settle his hands on her shoulders. "You can do this."

She nodded as if she understood even though fear still streamed from her like mist from damp earth.

He felt a displacement of air at the back of his legs. He whirled and planted himself in front of Alison, bringing his sword into his hand at the same moment in case what was arriving wasn't friendly.

But Havily materialized in front of him, looking professional as always in a navy suit, her red hair in waves over her shoulders. He shifted to return to Alison's side, folding his sword back to his weapons locker.

"Hey, Havily," he said.

She nodded. "Good evening, Warrior Kerrick, ascendiate Wells. I'm serving as Alison's Liaison Officer throughout the battle." She settled her gaze on Alison. "If you have any questions about the spectacle event, I will do my best to answer them. I'll be accompanying you onto the arena floor as well as serving you throughout the event."

"Oh, thank God," Alison whispered. "I thought I would be entirely alone."

Kerrick looked down at her, wishing like hell he could take this away from her. "Havily will take good care of you. All you have to do is ask. Right, Havily?"

"Of course, Warrior Kerrick."

"Good. I'll escort you both to the top of the ramp then I'll join the Warriors of the Blood. Havily, why don't you walk Alison through the process from the time we leave this room."

Havily's voice flowed, a soothing melodious lilt, as she explained the mechanics of what Alison could expect once she made her appearance in the arena proper.

A few minutes later an assistant appeared in the doorway, with clipboard in hand, pressing his earpiece. He waved them forward.

Showtime.

Alison's head throbbed, her heart raced like a jackrabbit running for cover, and her knees had simply disappeared. She sure as hell couldn't feel her feet.

Was this really happening?

She felt dizzy, disoriented, not exactly inside her body.

Oh, God.

Once in the corridor, Kerrick took up a place on her right and Havily on her left. The end of the hall seemed to be about ten miles away. Hey, when did she begin walking?

She struggled to breathe. She kept repeating a single line in her head: *I can do this . . . I can do this . . . I can do this . . .*

Okay.

Okay.

Suddenly the corridor was far too short and three seconds later she arrived at the arched opening to the arena proper. Havily caught her elbow and kept her from going farther. "We wait here for just a moment." Smoke from the fireworks drifted in the air and numerous robotic television cameras floated everywhere, at least four not far from her. She let her gaze drift over the impossible sight of fifty thousand spectators. Endelle's faction took up thousands of seats to the left, while the Commander's vast army, in uniforms of maroon and black, sat opposite Her Supremeness.

When Alison's face appeared all at once on the dozen or so enormous screens stationed throughout the arena, the spectators erupted into a hurricane of shouts, cheers, boos, and stomping feet.

Oh. God.

Kerrick gripped her arm. She glanced up at him. He met

her gaze, his expression fierce, but he said nothing. He just nodded once very firmly then departed, moving behind her.

I can do this.

She felt Havily's hand on her back very gently, a tender and welcome support. The comforting gesture allowed her to finally draw a deep breath.

"This looks like the Super Bowl," she cried.

Havily nodded. She leaned close and spoke into her ear. "It's time for the next leg of the journey. You ready?"

Alison glanced at her and snorted. Also leaning close, she said, "Do I have a choice?"

Havily shook her head. She straightened her spine. "Give 'em hell, ascendiate."

She guided Alison to the edge of the cordoned-off battle terrain, a lake of black matting scored with two opposing white diamonds.

Once at the rope, Havily stopped. The applause had not ceased, nor the stomping of feet, nor the boos during her entire march. Once again, on several well-placed screens she saw her face, her serious expression, as Havily leaned close and spoke into her ear.

"The area to the left belongs to Endelle's faction and the opposite, of course, to the Commander. When you hear the bell you must desist fighting of any kind and return to the white diamond on the floor nearest Endelle. I will bring you restorative drinks."

She then inclined her head and glanced in the direction of the stands. "You will want to acknowledge Madame Endelle at this time."

Alison followed her gaze and watched as the Supreme High Administrator of Second Earth nodded to her. Alison returned a formal dip of her chin. The Warriors of the Blood flanked Her Supremeness, four on her right and four on her left. They wore the same formal regalia as Kerrick. All remained seated. Beyond, thousands of Militia Warriors, both male and female, stood applauding, cheering and stomping their feet. Her gaze slid to Kerrick, seated just to the left of Endelle. He met her gaze, put a fist over his heart, then inclined his head to her. Though the gesture brought tears to her eyes, it also calmed her, eased her.

At least until Havily motioned with a sweep of her hand to the break in the ropes.

The time had come.

Her heart pounded in her chest, in her throat, in her head. Her ears rang. Once more, she couldn't feel her feet.

Before taking this last step, she glanced at Havily, who met her gaze, then sent, *I will beseech the Creator for help on your behalf.* She offered a solemn formal bow then turned and walked in her sedate manner to take up a seat in the front row among others dressed in similar formal business attire.

Alison suddenly wished she was back in her beat-up Nova, heading for the library, or Starbucks, or the nearest AMC. She wished she'd never heard of the Borderlands or the Trough or Second Earth. And why on earth had she ever sent that hand-blast into the air?

Too late now.

The moment she stepped through the opening in the ropes, the decibels of the shouting on both sides increased exponentially. She moved to take her place in the white diamond, her back to the Supreme High Administrator.

She scanned the rows opposite and her gaze came to rest on the Commander, on Darian, her former client, now her enemy. He sat on an elevated dais in a very large, tall-backed carved chair. She still wondered the why of it, the year of therapy, what he could have meant by it and why he had chosen such a public place to orchestrate her death.

His faction was surprisingly lacking in pomp and splendor, but then that wasn't really his style. His generals bore a few feathers and interesting hats, which harked back a couple of centuries. However, in the thousands of seats beyond him, his warriors, many of them death vampires, sat in quite plain black uniforms, the front-piece turned back to reveal a triangle of maroon. In stark contrast, the Commander wore one of his elegant suits, a crisp white shirt, and a maroon-and-black tie. No sash, no Roman-influenced headgear, no thick row of medals, no braiding.

He appeared, therefore, as she had always known him, the way he had come to her office in his expensive wool. His beautifully shaped bald head glimmered beneath the powerful arena lights. He leaned to one side, slightly to his left, both wrists settled on the armrests of his chair. He appeared relaxed yet wholly in command. Power rippled over him, around him, through him.

Had she ever really known him?

The answer had to be no.

Though his army continued to boo her presence, the Commander met her gaze, smiled, then inclined his head as though nothing more were at stake than the results of an egg-and-spoon race at a picnic.

Whatever.

Uncertain exactly what was expected of her, she rather thought that if she was going to fight one of the Commander's most powerful generals, she ought to be armed. As soon as the thought appeared in her mind, her identified sword appeared in her right hand, a single, swift maneuver, her fingers wrapped around the leather grip.

A tremendous cheer erupted from behind her along with a renewed vigorous stomping of feet. She took up the warrior stance, learned from Kerrick's memories, then settled the tip of the sword on the soft matting. She waited now with her left hand behind her back.

Endelle's crowd continued to cheer and stomp, another show of support, which brought her blood pressure down a little and her determination skyrocketing.

After a full minute of standing with her sword balanced next to her, Endelle's army began to boo quite suddenly.

The enemy's chosen warrior approached, though from where she stood she could not yet see him. She saw the floating cameras, though, stationed just outside the arch of a tunnel at a diagonal from her position. A moment more and his face appeared on the screen, followed once more by a sharp increase in audience response.

Alison drew in a sharp breath.

Leto. The warrior who had come down through the Trough, who had thrown the shredder bomb in the alley, who had appeared on the street flanked by death vampires while Kerrick had driven her absurd little Nova away from the downtown Phoenix Borderland.

Leto. Former Warrior of the Blood. The Commander's right-hand general. A traitor.

God help her.

For a full minute he stayed just out of her range of vision but he used the cameras to incite the crowd with a ferocity of expression, which worked the warriors behind her into a fury of more stomping feet and shouting voices, a storm of rage.

When he finally appeared, she worked hard to maintain her composure. Leto topped out easily at Kerrick's height. He was quite handsome and wore his black hair pulled back in the traditional warrior *cadroen,* which she took as a reflection of his former Warrior of the Blood status. Beyond his height, and also like Kerrick, his shoulders went on forever. He wore a black leather battle kilt and black leather gladiator-like shin guards and sandals. He had oiled his bare chest, which emphasized his enormous pecs and solid rippled abs. As he walked, he carried his sword arrogantly balanced against his shoulder. He kept his gaze pinned to her, his lips a grim line, his chin lowered.

She straightened her shoulders a little more and lifted a brow.

His lips formed a perfect sneer.

She took deep breaths as her heart set up a furious rhythm. How on earth was she going to battle this man-vampire-*whatever*?

She wondered if she could touch his mind. She sent a gentle feeler. She reached his thoughts. She watched him take a step backward, but she could go no farther. He had shields, tough shields.

He shifted his gaze away from her. He played to the crowds as he crossed the matting. He lifted his hands into the air, his sword now balanced between. He encouraged both cheers and boos as he walked. The crowd roared. Thorne's warriors taunted him the way the opposing forces had sent a tsunami of boos against her.

When he had traveled from one end to the other he made his way back to the middle then turned in her direction, plowing straight for her.

Would he attack immediately? Was this it? Did the battle begin now, no preamble, no warning, just . . . fight?

She held her ground, her sword still angled downward in a passive position. The entire arena fell silent. She reached out with her senses. She could hear the rate of Leto's breathing and the firm, confident beats of his heart. She could read his reactions and intentions one split second to the next. This at least she had the power to do.

Even as he came toward her, she kept her sword in place, the point pressed firmly against the matting.

As he closed to no more than two yards in front of her, she understood he was testing her courage as he looked down at her and met her gaze. He had blue eyes, sharp intense blue eyes. One thing about the Warriors of the Blood, traitor or not, they tended to be prime examples of the male species, ripped, powerful, and gorgeous, Leto no less so.

She never let her gaze waver from his. She sensed that in this moment he meant to challenge her mettle but not to attack, not to hurt.

She lowered her shoulders a fraction of an inch. "Bring it, Warrior," she said softly.

A faint smile curved his lips as he narrowed his gaze. He turned and brought his sword in a swift arc to within an inch of the base of her neck.

The gasp that flew up from the entire circumference of the arena sounded like a gust of wind. So fifty thousand people had expected her to die without once having lifted her sword.

Again, whatever.

For a long moment, Leto kept the blade poised at her neck, then cheering and applause erupted from a majority of the spectators, a wild sound that went on and on for at least a minute. Throughout the entire time, Leto's sword hovered at her neck, unmoving, his hands steady as a rock.

When at last the cheering died down, she said, "I'm ascendiate Wells." She could hear her voice amplified for the entire arena, a bizarre experience just in itself. However, she didn't let it deter her as she continued, "I believe you were above the Trough two nights ago. May I at least have an introduction before we begin?"

He withdrew his sword from her neck, his expression slightly confused. "I could have killed you just now." His voice, bearing an exquisite resonance, also reverberated the length, height, and width of the massive building.

She shook her head. "No. That was not your intention."

"Then you read me well." He bowed to her. "At least I face a worthy opponent. But make no mistake, Alison Wells. My name is Leto, I'm a general in the Commander's army, and given the chance I will end your life."

"Understood," she returned.

He narrowed his eyes.

He turned away.

Only as he strode fifteen feet from her did she finally raise her sword. Everything in his demeanor had shifted. She sensed it as though he had fired off a flare.

He turned then attacked in a swift deadly whirl. She knew he had expected to strike her down and finish the contest in one blow. But she had already folded behind him out of reach. He turned again and slashed toward her in a mind-bending array of slices and thrusts.

The battle was on.

For the first minute she heard the madness of the cheering, growling, stomping, screaming crowd. Not long after, however, everything disappeared from her awareness except Leto, his sword and his movements. She saw only him. She immersed herself in learning the subtlety of his signals as she made use of her real weapon—her ability to anticipate—just as Kerrick had taught her.

The only strategy she could compose at this point was defensive in nature against so seasoned a warrior. He was a powerful man, yet he could be struck down for good if she let him taste her sword. She understood the power of the blade, the burn, the sharpness of the slice of Second Earth weaponry. She didn't know how they were fashioned but she knew they cut like the infamous samurai swords.

He moved as quickly as Kerrick. He kept her hopping and folding. After a few minutes, she realized he had settled on his strategy. He was physically more powerful with profound endurance and he meant to wear her down. Simple as that.

She had no doubt he could succeed. Though she was able to match his skill, he would outlast her.

Fifteen minutes into the battle, a bell sounded.

Leto drew back and bowed to her. He turned around and headed to his white diamond, in the Commander's direction.

Alison waited before changing course. She reached out for his intention. What came back to her was only his need for water.

Assured he would not attack, she turned around to face the applause of Endelle's contingent. Havily brought her a goblet, which contained Gatorade, thank God. She drank slowly, savoring.

"Be quick, ascendiate Wells. The break is only thirty seconds long."

Oh, God.

She sucked down the remaining drink.

The bell sounded.

She felt the hairs on the nape of her neck rise. She turned and Leto was already on her. She had a fraction of a second to fold out of the way, but just before she did she touched her sword to the back of his leg. He stumbled and fell forward. Blood gushed from a long and very deep slice.

She had cut him.

She had cut him.

Her stomach rolled. She brought her sword up, preparing

for him to rise in a blur of movement and assault her again. Instead he flipped over but remained sitting, his eyes wide as he stared at her.

Now *he* waited for *her* to make the next move.

Why?

She glanced down at the mats. Blood poured from the wound, forming a glossy lake beneath his leg. He set his sword beside him and put both hands on the wound.

Holy shit! Had she just severed his hamstring? Oh, my God, she had, which meant she could finish the contest right this moment, right now.

A cheer rose up from Endelle's faction along with a cry to finish him. He continued to stare up at her, his expression intense.

Of course. He was *healing* his leg.

Finish him. Her gaze shot to Endelle, whose voice had pierced her head. *Finish him, ascendiate. You have the chance. Finish him now.*

Alison had a choice to make. She could simplify her life right now by taking out a key player in the war, by obliging Endelle, by making thousands of Militia Warriors happy.

There was just one problem.

She wasn't a warrior. She had chosen a healing profession as her life's work. She had a pacifist's soul and an antipathy toward causing pain of any kind, even if deserved. To take Leto's life went against the depths of her character.

She had therefore only one recourse. She backed away from him.

The crowd went into a frenzy of screaming, at least those who wanted Leto dead. Endelle's faction shouted vile things at her and booed her. They wanted a kill and they wanted it now. As so many times before since she began her rite of ascension, ancient Rome came to mind.

The knowledge of the crowd's gruesome expectation made her furious all over again. This was Second Earth?

She kept backing away. She shook her head back and forth. She couldn't kill him even though she knew he wouldn't show this kind of mercy toward her. The way her arm shook even now, even at the beginning of such an engagement, all he had to do was wear her down and he would succeed in his objective.

A bell sounded. Leto actually stood up and walked to his diamond amid cheers from the Commander's faction. He had healed his leg. The vampire had power.

Alison moved back to her place, her mind disordered. Given the strength of her convictions, she thought it likely she wouldn't make it out alive. That she had been able to inflict so severe a cut had been a piece of luck, nothing more. No doubt Leto knew it as well, and he wouldn't make a similar mistake.

Havily gave her the goblet. As she drank, she set her gaze on Leto. How on earth was she going to defeat him if she was unwilling to harm him?

When the bell sounded again, Leto charged forward, faster than before.

Her act of grace had awakened a demon.

He moved so fast she barely saw him. She fought with all the skill she could muster, streaming Kerrick's battle images in a constant flow through her mind so that her arms, her legs, every joint of her body knew how to respond, but truthfully what did she have left to withstand this superb, powerful warrior?

From then on, Leto pressed his advantage hard. He used his physical strength to force her into larger and larger movements. As minute piled upon minute, her breathing grew labored and her muscles grew heavy and overworked. At this rate, she wouldn't last much longer.

The bell sounded.

She received her goblet from Havily and sucked the Gatorade down as though she had been walking through the desert for hours. Sweat poured off her body and she cursed the person who had put her in all this leather.

She was barely refreshed and her breathing hadn't calmed at all before Leto was on her again. As her ankles grew heavy, Alison's courage faltered.

Kerrick's voice and words shot into her head. *Use your wits. Think. You can beat him.*

His presence had an effect, strengthening her weakened muscles and reflexes as well as her spirit.

Watch him. See how anxious he is to defeat you? Use it against him.

A light went on and her courage returned.

From that moment forward, she began to plan. Though she had an aversion to hurting the man so willing to kill her, there might be another way to finish the battle. She knew humiliation fired him and perhaps would also make him reckless.

"Leto," she said quietly. Again she could hear her voice amplified throughout the arena.

He scowled and struck harder.

She lifted her sword in answering blows. "You must know by now I won't take your life."

"Then you're a fool!" he shouted, his voice also echoing to the rafters, his sword slashing.

"You must tell me which you prefer, to end this civilly or to be humiliated in front of the Commander and his army."

These words enraged him. He thrust hard and wild. She had her answer.

She dodged, folded, leaped into the air. His ire overtook his sense. She saw her opportunity.

She leaped again, rolled over his shoulders, caught his sword arm with a deadly slice, and removed it at the elbow. He fell on his stomach, his sword sliding with his arm. He tried to regain his feet, but she laid a shield over his body and set her foot on his neck. Blood pumped from the wound with every quick beat of his heart. He pinched his lips together in a taut line. His face paled.

She glared at the opposition. Silence and horror returned to her. From Endelle's ranks behind her, a "death" chant began. She felt the blood of the combined warriors rise up. She heard their shouts of triumph as they called for Leto's death, the traitor's death.

She knew they had lost innumerable comrades in the many battles they had endured. She understood their hatred of the enemy. Regardless, she couldn't take this warrior's life. Everything within her rebelled at the idea.

She was not a warrior.

She touched Leto's mind. *I know you wish for your death, but I refuse to give it to you.*

I am proud to die as a warrior. Nothing less will answer. Finish this.

She sank deeper into his mind, doing what Kerrick had called mind-diving, the deep form of engagement that would allow her inside his head, to see his thoughts, his memories. She expected resistance only to find he had released his shields . . . *as though he wanted her to know.*

She saw his life. She saw the family he had lost to a squad of death vampires, night-feeders who had been stalking ascenders instead of pillaging humans on Mortal Earth. She saw his level of rage, something she had seen in Kerrick before the battle. She found another smaller shield, a very powerful shield, and pressed. In slow stages, the shield gave way and she saw the truth that could not be told. Oh, God, Leto was a double agent! She forged an instant mental shield around Leto's mind and her own. She felt other entities pummeling to get in, and knew she had a mere second to absorb this truth. She gasped.

Oh, God, Leto. What am I to do now?

Keep your silence.

Done.

She released him, tears in her eyes.

She took her foot off his neck but kept the pinning shield in place. Blood pumped steadily from the vein of his arm. He would die soon anyway from blood loss if she didn't do something. She moved swiftly, knowing that if she saved him, he would still be forced to attack her, despite what she had just learned about him.

Too bad.

She lifted her hand and stared into Leto's eyes. *Hold on . . . we're going for a ride.*

You can't fold out of here. Shields everywhere.
Not gonna fold.

She thought the thought. She snatched this small pocket of time and the two of them went through a whirlwind until she rolled back over his shoulder the opposite direction and stood on the other side of him, his sword raised, though frozen in place high overhead. "What the fuck?" he cried, his voice sounding through the arena.

The resulting power rippled in a circle outward, and just as had happened in her office, a sonic boom sounded. Again, in slow waves, the majority of the arena spectators began to cheer and applaud, wild cries that grew louder and louder at her unexpected exhibition.

Endelle's voice entered her head once more. *Well, now you've shown me something, ascendiate.*

Leto scowled at her. "What did you just do?"

Alison shrugged. "Pocket of time reversal."

He stared in return. "Who the hell are you?"

"A therapist, not a warrior, still hoping to ascend."

He grimaced. "We're battling here." But she saw the chagrin in his eyes.

She shook her head. "Not anymore."

"Like hell," he said. To her mind, he sent, *Don't have a choice, ascendiate. I'm sorry.*

She felt his intention like a ball of fire in her stomach. For her, however, everything had just changed. She knew what she had now and she didn't hold back. She sent a devastating hand-blast, threw him on his back, cast a shield, and once more put her foot on his neck.

"I'm not a warrior," she stated in a clear voice. She looked up at the nearest floating camera. "I'm. Not. A. Warrior."

She released the shield. Leto was on his feet in a split second.

He sent his own hand-blast. She felt it coming, swiped her hand through the air, sending the blast in the direction of the ceiling. She waved her hand again and all that power turned into an enormous display of fireworks in every color of the rainbow.

Applause thundered now except from among the opposing armies. Silence filled those sections of the arena. Each was losing the hoped-for victory.

She sent her own hand-blast this time and dislodged Leto's sword from his hand. She brought the sword toward her, which pulled another enormous shared gasp from every direction. Endelle's faction behind her cried out warning after warning. She wasn't afraid because at the exact moment of touch she reconfigured the molecular identification of the sword, rendering the weapon harmless.

She held the sword aloft for all to see, turning in a wide circle.

When she didn't fall over dead, another great cry rose up in astonishment all around the arena. She eased into a slow smile and relief replaced all her tension.

Well, what do you know. She'd done it and Leto wasn't dead. She faced him once more.

"I will not fight you," she cried. She tossed the sword to him.

He caught it easily, but stared at it. With a change of configuration the grip had to feel different to him. Regardless, he shifted his attention back to her, lowered his chin, and once more blurred in her direction, fast. "Then die," he shouted. Behind him, the Commander's army raged. Almost as one they screamed at him, urging him to continue the fight, to take Alison's life.

She cast a new shield, this time around herself. He struck but could not penetrate. He struck a dozen times, twenty, thirty, but to no effect.

She waited.

Continuous applause resounded from all over the arena.

Finally, Leto was breathing hard. Sweat dripped down his body. "My God. Who are you?" he asked again. He leaned over at the waist to catch his breath.

After a long tense moment, in which both armies fell silent, he finally dropped to one knee in front of her and laid his sword at her feet.

"I concede," he stated in a loud clear voice.

Silence fell on every spectator present.

She released her shield.

He stood up, his complexion pale, his gaze for one split second full of agony. She reached out with her empathy and read him. Dammit, he wanted out. Of course he wanted out. Just like the Warriors of the Blood, his role had taken its toll. He was on the razor's edge of disintegration, his vulnerable position at risk of discovery.

She approved of this warrior. He had honor and character and he had lived a double life for eight decades, serving as a spy. *A spy!* But for whom? She had seen the name *James* deep within Leto's head but not Endelle's, which meant that Endelle knew nothing about his activities, of that she was sure. Worse, when Leto defected, Darian had forced him to take dying blood as proof of his loyalty. At the same time, he was given an antidote to nullify the effects. Leto did not have the paling, beautifying, and faint bluing of the skin that most death vampires exhibited. No one would ever know he was, essentially, a death vampire. But all these years, he'd had to continue taking both the tainted blood and the antidote to sustain his mission. What a horrible mess.

Darian, her Darian, had forced him down this path. Either he took the dying blood or he would be killed. There had been no choice.

He bowed once to her, turned on his heel, brought his sword into his hand, then headed back in the direction of his lockers. She tested her internal mental shields. Could she keep Leto's secret from Endelle, from the Commander, from Kerrick?

She wondered just how deep this hole could get.

The crowds had already begun to disperse except for the attendant armies and administrative corps. Apparently, the entertainment was over.

The Warriors of the Blood stood in sober array in front of thousands of Militia Warriors. Her decision pleased no one.

To Kerrick, she sent, *I couldn't do it.*

I know. A pause followed. *I treasure your heart more than anything else in the world.*

Her eyes filled with tears as she blew him a kiss.

She could not, however, look in Madame Endelle's direction. She suspected the Supreme High Administrator of Second Earth would have a few choice words for her as soon as the cameras disappeared.

CHAPTER 19

Crace could do little more than stare at General Leto's retreating back as the warrior disappeared into the archway leading to the underground rooms of the arena. He couldn't even blink. The fucking vampire had failed.

He shook his head over and over.

"My darling?" Julianna whispered.

He glanced at his wife, who winced. "He should have won," Crace said. "He should have beat her, killed her."

"Darling, please?"

Please, what? What the hell was she begging for now? Didn't she understand the magnitude of what had just happened? Couldn't she see that the dream of a seat at the Geneva Round Table was fading, turning to a brilliant shade of *dirt brown*?

"My darling, *please*?" The latter word was spoken aloud and in his mind at the same time, which caused a burst of pain to explode inside his skull.

"What?" he shouted.

"My hand," she whispered, tears rolling down her cheeks. "You're crushing my hand."

He looked down and realized he was close to cracking several bones. He released her at once but he couldn't even apologize. He couldn't speak. He watched tears fall onto the swell of her breasts as she held her hand in her lap.

As the cameras shut down, as Alison's face disappeared from the now blank arena screens, as the spectators began to stream through the exit tunnels, Kerrick stared at Alison and marveled. One question surfaced above every other thought—could he have a life with this woman whose powers exceeded even Second abilities? Would she be able to stay alive on Second when Helena could not? Would she be able to cast her shields and keep a thousand death vampires from slaughtering her? *Could he have a fucking life with her?*

His heart thundered in his chest at the possibility. A woman in his life, permanent, *bonded,* treasured. Did Alison's arrival on Second Earth actually mean a change for him, a different life, that which he had vowed never to have again so long as he made war?

Moving at lightning speed, he reached the hall leading to the arena floor. Another dash and he breached the tall arched opening to the arena. He rushed toward the black mats, his gaze centered on Alison's blond ponytail. Just as she turned in his direction, as though sensing his presence, he was on her. He caught her in his arms and spun her around and around, her feet dangling off the floor. He kissed her hard. *You were magnificent.*

"It's over," she whispered, her arms wrapped around his neck.

"You were brilliant."

He kissed her again. He stroked her damp hair. He held her tight against him.

She drew back and smoothed her hand over his cheek. "We're okay . . . you and me?"

He nodded.

"Maybe we have a chance?" she asked.

His heart melted, a big puddle in his chest. "We just might."

He planted his lips once more against hers and penetrated her mouth with his tongue. She took him willingly and suckled. He arched over her and deepened the kiss, settling her booted feet back on the mats. She moaned softly.

"Okay, you two, knock it off," Endelle cried, joining them.

He released her but didn't let her get far as he slung an arm around her waist, drawing her flush against his side.

Havily crossed the black mats as well and addressed Alison. "Congratulations. You were absolutely amazing. That was beautifully done—and to think you had several Third Earth abilities, though I shouldn't be surprised. Imagine, a reversal of time. I had heard of it but I've never seen it done. And the wave of resulting power! It passed through me like a cool breeze. Exhilarating."

Alison broke free of Kerrick's clasp and embraced the Liaison Officer. "Thank you for being with me tonight, Havily. You are my first friend on Second and I will always be grateful for your help and support."

"It was my pleasure. If you need anything, you have only to ask. And now"—here she glanced at Madame Endelle—"I have a new military-admin mock-up to recreate, something I do in my spare time, something that would help *someone* to defeat the Commander if only that *someone* would spare me a few minutes of her time."

Endelle offered a snort in response and a roll of her eyes. Havily in turn bowed to her, shifted to face Kerrick, smiled at him, pinched his cheek, lifted her arm, then vanished.

Kerrick moved in and once more took possession of his woman. She melded to his side, this time sliding her arm around his waist. He held her close since directly across, the Commander waited with his army. Alison's ascension was by no means complete, which meant she was still fair game. When Darian fixed his gaze on her, a growl erupted from Kerrick's throat.

A moment later the Commander levitated from his black regal chair and floated, without wings or any other visible means of support, across the black matting. Bastard.

Never once, however, did he shift his gaze away from Alison. She was his object, his mark, his reason for the arena contest, his goal in now crossing the battling mats. He paused four feet in front of her, his large brown eyes fixed to her, unblinking, searching. He floated down to settle his Italian footwear on the mats.

Kerrick touched Alison's mind and found her erecting shield after shield against the Commander's deft probes. Kerrick couldn't control yet another growl or the thrumming of his wing-locks.

A slight blink indicated that Greaves may have sensed the threat that Kerrick was ready to mount his wings in defense of Alison.

Endelle broke the tension. "Well," she said, her tone lustrous with sarcasm, "look what the goddamn cat dragged in."

Kerrick wanted to hustle Alison behind him. He wanted her safe and away from the Commander even though he didn't sense an attack coming. After all, Greaves could hardly act against Alison in this setting. As much as COPASS tended to defer to him, the Committee wouldn't be able to ignore a direct assault. Neither Greaves nor Endelle was permitted to attack anyone directly and there were some rules even Greaves had to obey, at least when he was in the open. Like now.

Alison had not been so close to Darian since she stood beside him at the railing of the medical complex staring down at her first very pale, very beautiful death vampire. But here he was, in the flesh, one of the most powerful beings on Second Earth, her former client. He had sent Leto to the downtown Borderland in pursuit of her. He had sent a regiment to Carefree. He had arranged the arena battle just for her, all with one intention.

Yet she had counseled him. She had heard his story. She knew him, at least to the extent anyone could know a man without a conscience, a sociopath. She knew the pain he had suffered as a child, the cause of his mental disorder.

Still. He had intended for her to die.

He held her gaze, his large child-like eyes beckoning. "You surprised me tonight, my dear. Imagine, a reversal of time and sword re-identification and the final shield. So much power. I know of only two beings on Second who can do these three things, and we're both right here. Was that how you repaired the window in your office? Of course it was."

She heard Kerrick hiss softly, and another split-resonant growl rumbled through the air. Her vampire-warrior-guardian was in full protective mode.

The Commander's gaze drifted to Kerrick. "Easy, boy. I'm offering compliments. Your woman did quite well."

"No shit." The words shot past Alison's ear. Kerrick's body was on fire, a shield of raging heat against her side. She felt his warrior fury rising but for some reason it eased her and she leaned her head against his shoulder. They were together. They were a team, like Joy and Ryan. She sighed. Yes, like her sister and her brother-in-law.

The Commander shifted his gaze back to her. "I *learned* so very much while watching you battle General Leto. Overall, I consider the evening a very instructive experience."

So that was it. That was the game. Darian, *the Commander,* was a man of strategy, so of course he had more than one purpose in the spectacle battle. If she didn't die, then he would learn more about her strengths and her weaknesses. She was his enemy now.

"I can see I am disturbing what should be an evening of celebration so I will bid you good night. I wish you every happiness, my dear. And do take care."

He didn't wait for her to respond but turned in the direction of his army. He lifted an arm and in the blink of an eye, he and the great mass of his contingency simply vanished.

Alison stared dumbstruck at all the empty seats, the

vacant dais, the solitary ornate chair from which he had observed the battle.

"Holy shit," Kerrick muttered. "He sent his entire army away with one thought."

"How did he do that?" Alison whispered. She couldn't imagine the level of power required to perform such a feat.

"Poser," Endelle muttered.

Alison glanced up at her and laughed outright. "Poser?"

Endelle rolled her eyes. "A fucking parlor trick. Don't let him get to you." She huffed a sigh, turned slightly to her right, then nodded in the direction of the stands, dismissing her army. In contrast with the Commander's army, Endelle's contingency simply started heading to the various exits.

She turned back to Alison. "You, on the other hand, ascendiate Wells, are goddamn useless. All you had to do was finish Leto off. You had him in the palm of your hand and you let him go. What the fuck were you thinking and by the way, what was that little private party you had with him and don't tell me you didn't do anything of the sort, because I know you did. Did you do a little mind-diving with Leto?"

Alison felt Kerrick's body stiffen against her. "Alison," Kerrick's deep voice rumbled against her ear. "What the hell is Endelle talking about?"

She pulled away from him, far enough to meet his emerald gaze. His eyes flashed with warning. "I can't tell you."

"What?" he cried, his brow sinking low. Another growl erupted from his throat, this time directed at her. "Don't tell me you went inside that traitor's head. Tell me you fucking didn't!"

"Back off, Fido," Endelle said. "So she was in his head. Big-fucking-deal. It's not like she had her legs wrapped around his waist." She shifted her attention back to Alison. "I just want to know what the hell you talked about. The fact you set up a shield even I couldn't penetrate tells me you weren't discussing the weather."

Alison glanced from one daunting ascender to the other. Each was bent toward her in outright aggression. For a split second she wondered if battling Leto would be the easy part of the night.

She drew in a deep breath and decided to deal with the larger of the two problems first. She stared into Endelle's striated brown eyes. She chose carefully the words she sent. *Though I can't relay everything I saw, I can tell you Leto wants out.*

A little late for that.

Alison shook her head very slowly.

What are you not telling me? She narrowed her eyes and tried to break through Alison's shields, a pressure that got harder and harder to withstand.

Alison lifted a hand. "Don't press against my shields," she cried.

"I'll do what I want."

"If you're wise, you won't."

Endelle cocked her head. "What the hell is going on, ascendiate?"

This time Alison set up a shield that encompassed Endelle. Alison communicated telepathically, *Leto requests that I do not share with anyone, including you, what he shared with me, except for one piece of information. He wants you to contact an ascender by the name of James, resident of Sixth Earth and gatekeeper of Third.*

How the hell am I supposed to contact Third or Sixth? Endelle sent. *I haven't had one fucking whisper from the Upper Dimensions in millennia, not since the time I agreed to serve as Supreme High Administrator nine thousand years ago.*

These words slammed through Alison's head, a powerful sensation caused equally by Endelle's astonishment and her frustration. *You've been flying blind,* she sent. *All these years?*

Endelle stared at her. After a long moment, she sighed heavily then nodded.

"I don't know what to tell you," Alison said, releasing the shield. "But I think you've gotten a raw deal."

"I find the understatement really annoying. But, yeah. *Raw deal* sums it up."

Alison didn't know what else to tell Her Supremeness. She had no idea what a gatekeeper was and as far as communicating with Sixth Earth, well, Alison was still trying to get used to Second. The information Leto had shared with her while she'd been in his head was now cloaked behind as powerful a shield as Alison could create within a pocket of her mind.

"Fine," Endelle muttered. "I'll take it from here."

Alison took another deep breath then turned back to her caveman of a boyfriend. She was about to explain to him what had happened, but he stepped close to her and with his nose about an inch away from hers, he cried, "My woman stays out of the heads of other men."

"What?" she cried.

"Just stay the fuck out of Leto's head or anyone else's. Are we clear?"

"No, Kerrick, we're not *clear.* Who do you think you are telling me what I can and cannot do?"

Endelle whistled. "You go, girl!"

Kerrick knew he'd drifted into some kind of Neanderthal overdrive, which wasn't helping at all, but his body, his mind, his blood rebelled at the thought that Alison had been in Leto's head. She wasn't to go into the minds of other men . . . ever. EVER. He growled. He glared. *I want an explanation,* he sent. *What the hell were you doing in his mind? How much did you see? Was he in yours? Did you like being in there? Does he have intentions toward you now? You do know he's the enemy, right? A goddamn traitor?*

Alison's eyes opened wide; then she had the audacity to actually smile. *You are so jealous.*

He growled all over again and narrowed his eyes. *If*

wanting to tear Leto's limbs off one by one means I'm jealous, yeah, I'm jealous. But it was more than that. *Jealousy* was a very small word compared with what he was feeling right now. Jealousy was a breeze when what he felt carried hurricane-force winds.

You know, all your cardamom is starting to get to me. I feel like I walked into a Moroccan café. Her voice had a soft quality, seductive, not what he expected right now.

This isn't over.

Then we'll talk later.

Just don't ever go into the mind of another man again. Have you got that?

She put her hands on her hips, those hips covered in a whole lot of tight clinging leather. His gaze drifted down then back up.

I'll do what I please, she responded, but her blue eyes had taken on a challenging glint, which had less to do with her will in the matter and more to do with wanting to get him worked up.

He caught her buttocks and pulled her right up against him. Despite the fact that Endelle stood by grinning at the new kind of spectacle he was making, he ground into her and let her feel exactly how worked up he was.

Much to his pleasure, Alison's pupils dilated. Her lips parted. She took breaths like she'd forgotten how to breathe.

Endelle made a series of gagging sounds. "Okay, now you've gone too far. Jesus H. Christ, a pair of vampires in heat."

Alison looked at Endelle. "I need a shower," she said and with that, without another word of explanation or of apology or begging of permission, she lifted her hand and vanished.

"Holy shit," Endelle cried. "She just folded between dimensions!"

Kerrick knew the tunic he wore was not the best outfit to have on for what he was feeling. He was about to beg a fold from Her Supremeness, but Endelle held him back with a slight pressure on his arm. "Hold up, Warrior. I should let

you know that we're not having a public ascension ceremony for Alison."

"Makes sense." He really needed to get the hell out of
there.

"*The little peach* isn't finished yet, so I'm not making it
easy on him. We'll have the ceremony at my palace and a
dinner afterward. Got it?"

Kerrick could hardly hear her. He was picturing Alison
stripping off all that leather, turning on the faucet, steaming
up the shower. And he really needed to teach her a thing or
two about warrior-vampires and what they expected from
their women.

But Endelle could rattle on. "I want all the warriors
present and whether you like it or not, I want Marcus there
as well as Havily and no, you don't need to know the fuck
why. Beyond that, it'll be a closed ceremony."

He really didn't give a good goddamn about Marcus.
Especially since his mind was full of Alison, water streaming down her hair, over the curves of her body. He wanted
to lick those dimples just above her buttocks.

"I've told Thorne to put a twenty-four-hour guard on
the Queen Creek house. The warriors will work a rotation
through the rest of tonight and all day tomorrow."

Images of having an entire night with Alison and maybe
an entire day did little to calm him down. He nodded once
more. "Good. That's good."

"All right, horn-dog. Get going." Endelle lifted her arm
and the next moment Kerrick landed ass-first on the granite
island in the kitchen.

He didn't care. His thoughts were all for Alison and her
trip inside Leto's head. He slid off the island, clenched his
fists then lowered his chin. He really needed to give her a
lesson about inappropriate mind-diving.

He growled low.

His fangs emerged and lengthened.

He listened. He heard the shower running, not in the
guest bath but in the master bath.

Oh, yeah. She'd gone to his bedroom this time.

His body shuddered. He got very firm, possessively hard. He needed to make sure she understood that her mind, her body, her blood were not to be shared with anyone except him.

The *breh-hedden* had returned with a howling vengeance.

He sent her a little message. *You are to stay the hell out of Leto's mind or any other man so long as we're joined.*

Alison nearly fell on the wet tile as Kerrick's words punched into her head. She caught herself with one hand by gripping the showerhead just above her. She returned the soap to the inset in the wall behind her then rinsed.

Her heart banged around in her chest, although it wasn't fear beating at her this time. Kerrick's voice in her head, laced with jealousy and possessiveness, drove through her body like a fast car on a salt flat and nothing but air in the way.

She knew what was coming and her body screamed for it—full-on sex with her warrior vampire. She pressed her back up against the tile, hardly able to breathe, her hands to either side of her.

Water flowed on her from several different directions, from several different heads.

There would be no preamble this time, or soft touching of her breasts or feathery wet kisses over her abdomen or between her thighs, no teasing sensual fangs probing gently or releasing a seductive potion into her skin.

When he appeared, stripped naked, chin dipped low, fangs distended, expression determined, she was ready. His thick sex was hard as a missile and her knees struggled to work at all. However, she knew in about a nanosecond that would *so* not be a problem.

He entered the shower growling, his shoulders hunched, his thighs tensed. He slid one arm around her waist, pulled one of her legs up, angled his hips, and drove into her. She threw her head back and cried out, the pleasure so intense she was already close to orgasm. He pounded into her and with just a handful of strokes sent her over the edge. She came so fast and so hard that she doubled over him and bit his shoulder. At the same time, the resulting wave of power struck him and he grunted his pleasure. How much she loved that she couldn't hurt him.

He kept growling and driving. The man had a point he intended to make and he took his time. She came again, clenching around his rock-hard cock. Each time, waves of her power hit him, and each time he grunted in response. *So sexy,* he whispered in her mind. *All that power. Now tell me you'll keep clear of other men.*

I'll keep clear.

When she returned to earth, he still drove hard.

"Give me your neck," he commanded. His split resonance nearly caused her to come again. She tilted her head back and to the side. She would deny him nothing right now. She closed her eyes. He sank his fangs in a quick thrust that stung like hell at first. As soon as he took heavy pulls, desire flared over her neck, over her breasts, and down her abdomen to once again tighten her internal muscles.

She panted in agonizing gasps.

Open your mind, he barked within her head.

Won't that complete the breh-hedden? she sent.

No. You won't be taking my blood while I take yours. Full communion requires a simultaneous taking of blood.

Alison was relieved. She wanted this moment with Kerrick, but the thought of the *breh-hedden* still freaked her out.

Despite her nerves, she opened her mind wide. When he plowed through, his hips still pistoning into her, his fangs drawing blood, she came again and again and again, his body absorbing each attending hit of power. He owned her body right now, her mind, her blood, and the orgasm went on and on. She cried out, her back and buttocks sliding against the tile, the water spraying his back and her face.

When she clenched around him again, she touched his mind that was still in her mind and whispered, *Come for me, Warrior. Give me all you've got.*

He growled loud and low even through the pulls at her neck. She rippled her fingers over his wing-locks. *Oh, God,* he cried, his voice pummeling her mind.

His body sped up but time slowed. She was so tight around him that she felt every sensation as he slammed into her core then jettisoned his seed into her. He withdrew his fangs at the same moment and shouted in a new split resonance, which echoed around the bath. Euphoria filled her mind, his and hers combined. How strange to feel his pleasure, yet it amplified her own. She screamed as another orgasm caught her. Another jolt of power. She released a plaintive cry, the high keening of a bird in flight.

This would be the right time to die, caught in such an exquisite tangle of sensation, of feeling him in her mind, of hearing his triumphant cry, of having so much pleasure searing her veins.

The tension in her body lessened as each second passed. The rock of his hips slowed and finally stopped, but he remained within, connected to her.

He withdrew from her mind, a sensation she was getting used to, and settled his head on her shoulder. She gently drifted the tips of her fingers up and down his wing-locks. He released a deep sigh, the rise of his chest lifting her once more up and down the tile.

Something new touched her as he pressed his hips in a slow, soft undulation against her, his cock still connected deep, though not nearly as hard. He groaned against her neck.

Deep within, her female organs began to contract and release. She felt the path of his seed and now in her mind she could see a golden trail. How was this even possible? Dear God, how was any of it possible?

Now she could see the chrysalis of her genetic material, a bright burning light at the end of a tunnel. The imagery made her smile then laugh. She could see his sperm, like lightning. She leaned against him, her hand stroking his thick pec. It was all too absurd, too wonderful, and why wouldn't it be like this? Kerrick was known for his preternatural speed. If his DNA wanted to make a child, why wouldn't it move at an accelerated rate?

She felt the moment when her egg received his sperm and their child began all the fantastic portentous crazy cell replications.

The whole thing couldn't really be happening. Maybe she was just fertile and her imagination had gone into hyperdrive. But then she could feel Kerrick's wing-locks beneath her fingers, and hadn't his fangs just penetrated her throat?

She *knew* they had just created life. She wanted to tell him, yet somehow this wasn't the right time. A frightening premonition jolted her mind. In this limited way, she could see the future or at least sense it. There would be a moment, a critical hour when Kerrick would need to know she carried his child. She understood this as surely as a child grew within her.

Did I hurt you? he asked, touching her mind gently.

Of course not, she returned. She wanted to say more, to tell him how wonderful the moment had been, but she just couldn't find the right words. *Splendor* seemed shallow and *magnificent* really inadequate.

Alison? Are you sure you're okay? I was kind of rough.

She hugged him. She drew back and met his gaze. She spoke quietly, both aloud and in his head at the same time so that he could feel her sincerity. *"How about you do that again every day for the next ten thousand years?"*

He smiled. He frowned. He grimaced and growled. He kissed her hard, so hard. He took her mouth with his tongue, the way he'd taken her body with his cock, only this time she got to suckle.

Since he was still inside her, he didn't have far to go at all when he firmed up. He rocked into her again and as though he'd been as starved for the experience as she was he took her in the shower over and over, until the water ran cold and she really was too exhausted to move one more centimeter any direction.

He rinsed off her legs, toweled her dry, and carried her to his bed. He spooned her. He told her about the dinner party Endelle was giving as part of her ascension ceremony. All very private. She smiled, so content. "Good. I want to meet your warrior brothers."

"And they want to meet you."

She squeezed his arm as tears tracked down the side of her face and onto the pillow. What had Joy said? *Why don't you find a bodybuilder, someone who could handle all that power?* She smiled and wept some more.

She breathed deeply, her heart so very full.

Kerrick and a child. And one more day of her rite of ascension and she would be in the clear, no longer at the mercy of Greaves's plans to annihilate her.

All her dreams seemed to be coming true. How grateful she was that she had chosen to ascend, despite the battle with Leto.

And how far away all her old fears had drifted. She belonged on Second Earth. Her powers could be used for good in this new world. Hadn't she proven her worth during the arena battle? She was so happy. To think she had done the impossible and yet her powers had made the impossible possible. She had vanquished Leto without harming him.

This was who she was in the deepest parts of body, mind, spirit. She was a giver of life, not a taker.

Her hand slid over her abdomen.

A giver of life.

Crace had returned to the Commander's office. He felt blanked out and empty.

He sat in the laid-back, slanted chair in front of his deity's battleship desk, his gaze fixed to the bank of Italian cypresses. Another whirring. Another quarter turn. The lights blazed to keep the shrubs healthy.

He reverted his gaze to Greaves.

The Commander sat very quietly, his tall-backed executive chair swiveled away from Crace. Given the position,

Crace had a side view of Greaves. He had his elbows on the arms of the chair, his hands brought together, the fingers of his right hand steepled with the claws of his left.

He had no expectations at this point. He knew the failure of the arena battle was not his fault just as he had known that the failure of the regiment to off Kerrick and Alison in Carefree had not been his fault.

But what the hell did that matter? Alison still lived and there didn't seem to be any way around so critical a point. Jesus. Reversal of time. Re-identification of hard metals. Impenetrable shields.

His mind swam. Crace was very powerful, but he couldn't do these things. These were not even powers typical of Second. These were *Third* abilities.

An ascendiate with Third abilities.

Geneva seemed as remote as the moon right now. Lake Michigan would dry up before he ever won a seat at the Round Table.

"You despair too easily, my friend," came the silky voice.

"I failed you, master. Why would I not despair? I came to Phoenix with such hope of truly being of use to you."

The Commander turned in his direction, leaning his bald head against the cushioned high back of his leather chair. He had the cleanest nails, at least on his right hand, and the onyx ring winked beneath the recessed lights. "What makes you think you have not been of use to me?"

Crace shrugged. He had no fear in this moment. How could he, when he was a dead man? "Alison lives."

The Commander held his gaze, his dark eyes unreadable as he nodded faintly. "Yes, she does. But have you no other suggestions for me?"

Crace blinked. The Commander wanted a suggestion?

"We have one more day," Greaves said. "Surely we can accomplish something in a day."

Crace drew in a sharp breath. "And you wish me to continue on?"

Greaves nodded. "Of course. However, I do have a requirement at this juncture in our intimate association, a gesture I'd like you to make as a symbol of your fealty and devotion to the Coming Order."

Greaves held out his palm and a flagon appeared, an ornate ceramic goblet with purple grapes clinging to the sides, a green vine forming the stem and base. He set the flagon on the dark wood of the desk.

Crace could hear his heart thrumming in his ears. He stretched his nostrils and smelled the most delicious bouquet of human blood, laced with something so fine, a delicate flower-like fragrance, a hint of gardenia perhaps. His heart rate increased. The scent aroused him. He needed the contents of the flagon. Whatever it was, he had to have it. Now.

Then he knew.

"Why?" he asked, his heart thudding heavily, a cross between absolute panic and intense desire.

"I must be assured of your loyalties at every step of the way from this point forward." He held out his right hand again, and a small crystal goblet appeared bearing a swirl of gold liquid.

The antidote.

Crace had heard rumors for decades. He thought of Harding, who had trimmed down in the past ten years and whose face had grown more pleasing. Even his heavy jowls had shrunk. Harding. The Commander's devoted pawn.

He stared at the flagon. Of course. He was not being given a choice. He was not so stupid as to think otherwise. He hoisted himself from the chair and rose unsteadily. He felt dizzy, sick to his stomach. He'd heard accounts over the years from death vampires about the unimaginable thrill of taking dying blood for the first time.

So this was to be his life, his future.

He confessed he had always wanted to try . . .

He didn't look at the Commander. There was no point.

He put a shaking hand about the bowl of the goblet, drawing it close. He swirled the blood, which moved sluggishly. The movement once more released the faint flowery bouquet. He closed his eyes. He had fantasized about doing this.

What man hadn't since the erotic properties of such blood was widely known?

He put the flagon to his lips.

"Yes," the Commander whispered, the thinnest hiss across the desk.

Crace breathed and tipped the flagon. A flow of blood hit his lips, his tongue, the sensitive pockets of his mouth. He groaned. Gardenia, spice, blood flowed into his throat and ran in a river down, down, down. He had never tasted anything so divine. He grew hard as a rock, throbbed now and wept. The small of his back tightened and without warning an orgasm surged through him, powerful, direct, a stunning surprise. He resisted the urge to pump with his hand. However, *touching* wasn't at all necessary as the climax rolled through him and filled his briefs.

Euphoria hit, a sense that all was right with the world and would be forevermore. He had never known such peace, such well-being, such pleasure still riding his cock, racing through his veins, invading his mind. He loved the universe and the universe loved him back. Life would never be more perfect.

Without warning his mind speckled black and white until he found himself stretched out on the carpet, flat on his back, the flagon gone.

He had only one thought. He should have done this a long, long time ago and couldn't think why he had ever resisted the best experience of his life.

"Feeling better?" Greaves had moved to stand over him.

Crace looked up at his master. Yes, he felt better, stronger, more powerful than ever. Unbelievably. He rose to his feet with ease. He stared at the Commander and understood. This was the source of Greaves's advanced power. He knew it without having to be told.

The Commander merely laughed. "Now let us discuss what we can accomplish where our troublesome ascendiate is concerned."

Crace's mind had never been so clear, his energy so strong,

his abilities so at the fore. "I recommend subterfuge, something unexpected."

At that, the Commander's left brow rose. "An idea so soon?"

"Tell me what you know of ascendiate Wells. Tell me what she fears."

Greaves told Crace and Crace smiled. "Then we will use her power against her chosen clan. Many will die and she will be broken . . . forever."

The Commander smiled, a warm easy curve of his lips. "Now you have shown me something."

"The only difficulty I foresee is Madame Endelle."

"I will manage the Supreme High Administrator at the time of the attack." He cast his arm in the direction of the massive ebony desk. "When you are ready, make use of the antidote. Just don't wait too long. Waiting allows dying blood to act on the features, to create excessive beauty as well as the paling and bluing of the skin. Do you understand?"

"Yes, master." He nodded.

"I have matters to attend to. Once again, put your plans together. When I return, we'll march through the details."

"Very good, master."

The Commander lifted an arm and vanished.

Crace remained in the same position for a long time, staring at nothing, savoring the bliss in his stomach, his veins, his head. He had never felt so alive, but he wanted to hold to this exhilarating sense of power as long as he could. The antidote could wait a little while longer, maybe long enough to get to his wife and make use of her exquisite body.

Arousal returned in a flame of sensation. He thought the thought and returned to the Bredstone, to his wife. He folded the antidote to him as well. Still, he didn't want to mar this first experience. Yes, the antidote could wait.

Leaving a world behind,
Slays the heart.

—*Collected Proverbs*, Beatrice of Fourth

CHAPTER 20

Alison awoke naked and on her side, a heavy, muscled arm draped over her. She had never experienced this in the course of her life. She had never dared to. Yet here she was waking up with a man wrapped around her. He was fully erect, his hard length pressed against her buttocks, not a surprise since he'd been asleep for some time.

The room, his bedroom, was full of morning light. The dark wood blinds were open, a blue sky visible beyond, as well as desert for miles. Mist covered and protected the Queen Creek home and, oh, Medichi strolled by, his sword balanced on his shoulder, weapons harness beneath. The warriors had guarded the property through the night and would continue to do so, taking turns the rest of the day. Nothing was being left to chance.

She sighed, savoring, working hard not to take anything for granted in this moment. She was with her man, her vampire, in bed, waking up with him, both naked. Her skin tingled all over and tears started to her eyes. She had never thought to experience this kind of connection with a man . . . ever.

She slowly slid her hand over his forearm and pressed gently. He was all muscle and warm skin, his cardamom scent wafting to her nostrils. She took deep breaths, one after the other. She didn't want him to awaken. She just wanted to take in that heavenly spice, part him, part cardamom. Her breasts swelled at the erotic scent, she grew wickedly wet, yet still she didn't want to disturb the moment.

She smiled. She had prevailed and she had won the pleasure of being with Kerrick. She had a child growing within. She had a completely naked man at her back. Life could not get better.

He stirred behind her, his thick cock gliding up her backside. Desire rose again, a whirling sensation inside her body, tightening her abdominals, which caused her hips to rock against him.

He groaned. "Lavender. I'm smelling lavender. Please tell me you're awake?"

"I am."

"Thank God," he groaned. His arm snaked around her, over her breasts. He pulled her close, his hands roaming. "You feel like heaven."

"I love that you're in bed with me."

He leaned over her, pushed her hair aside, and kissed her neck. "I want you."

"I want you more."

"Not fucking possible."

She still had yet to get used to warrior-speak. At the same time the profanity grounded the experience for her, made it real when so much of this new life had thrust her into the center of a tornado.

He kissed a line up her cheek, arching over her body, sliding his lips up to her lips, then he kissed her. Even her mouth felt well used from the night's pleasures.

She drew back and met his gaze. "Why is it I've only known you half a minute, but I feel as though it's been several lifetimes?"

"It's the call of the *breh-hedden*. I feel the same way."

"Kerrick, I want in," she said, knowing this was exactly what she needed.

He nodded and smiled. He growled. He rolled over onto his back then pulled her on top of him. She settled herself over his hips, his erection a length of thick rope against her. "To do this, you'll want me inside you."

She had to laugh. "Spoken like a man. You sure that's necessary?"

"You think I'm joking but you'll see. Now climb on board."

Her body shuddered at the invitation. She rose up then positioned her core over the head of his cock. She was so ready for him as she eased him inside. Her body wept for him, even more when he groaned and arched, his hips thrusting as if he couldn't help himself. He pushed and filled her.

Heaven, she murmured within his mind.

He sighed and arched again, stretching her then moving in a slow, sensual rhythm. He pulled her down onto his broad, muscled chest, tucking her beneath his chin. His heavy ripped arms engulfed her. She was in a perfect cage of his body, encased, protected, pleasured.

When she had said she wanted in, she hadn't meant for sex to happen, but as soon as he opened his mind and she fell inside, sex for the first minute was all that *could* happen. She was aroused like nothing she'd ever experienced before and she understood, in a sudden flash, what it was to be a man when he entered a woman, the strange power, the erotic nature of penetration, the full-on stimulation—because right now, she had penetrated him. His mind was laid out for her, a banquet on which to gorge, and she was so aroused.

The sensation of control grabbed her and before she could think the thought, she arched away from him and orgasmed hard, her power punching at him as it always did. He caught her with his muscular arms, holding her in place. *I love it when you do that. So damn sexy. Now take the real ride.*

He worked her body, slow erotic undulations, as her mind began to descend within his. It was like sinking into a warm pool and floating, the water just easing out of the way. When she was merged completely, his life, flashes of remembered events, all twelve hundred years of it, began to stream through her, shared and experienced, savored and hated, all his hopes and fears, all the love, sex, and battle, the loss of his two wives, the leaving of an infant son behind on his ascension—the baby, Evan—then the deaths of his two children all those centuries later.

The most surprising element, however, was that she saw and experienced the depth of his devotion to the Warriors of the Blood, a true Brotherhood of men, powerful men, vampires dedicated to a better world, a safer world.

Within the body of the stream, she got to know them all through his eyes and through thousands of interactions, the peculiar bond he shared with Thorne, their leader, with Medichi and his love of wine, with Jean-Pierre and his love of women, Santiago and his ability with weapons, Zacharius and his vanity, Luken and his gentle soul, even Marcus before the terrible breach tore them apart at Helena's death.

My turn whipped through her mind. She felt a great wave rise up as he moved her out of his head and started to penetrate hers. He turned her bodily at the same time, so that when he crashed fully inside her mind, he was pounding her hard. She let him but couldn't lift even a finger to touch him. She was overwhelmed with his presence in a way that set every nerve in her body on fire. She shared her life with him, her history as he had, holding back only the new life within and her strange telepathic conversation with Leto.

Otherwise, he filled every hidden cache of her memories. Rapture once more approached, spearing her deep between her legs where he had taken possession of her body, where his cock thrust. The sensation of intense pleasure spread upward through her torso, engaged her heart, swept into her head and cast fireworks around until she screamed the orgasm over and over and over. The resulting roll of power took him into the air, her hips with him since he refused to lose the connection. Landing back on the bed, he spun her out, thrust, retreated, thrust harder, rolled his hips, and sucked on her neck.

Come for me, she sent as her own orgasm barreled down on her once more. *Now. I need all of you.*

She cried out as pleasure took hold of her, a great fire in the well of her body. As the sensation increased, she cried out over and over, another wave of power punching at him.

He shouted, groaned, cursed, then with a final cry spent himself hard into her, thrusting until completely sated.

At last, he lowered himself back onto her.

Now her arms could move . . . well, a little. She wrapped them around his broad shoulders and drew in a ragged breath.

"Awesome," she murmured. "Let's do it all over again in about fifteen minutes."

He laughed, bouncing on her chest. "I love you, Alison. I'm so in love with you. There, I've said it. *I love you.*"

Alison's heart swelled. To hear him speak of love—! And yet there was something in his tone, an edge of desperation that caused her a ripple of concern. She had been inside his head. She had seen his grief after Helena and the children died, she had felt the impact of two hundred years of keeping his vows so he wouldn't be a threat to another woman ever again.

She breathed in and out, struggling to find the right words, but nothing came to her, no gentle ease-into phrasing, just four words and she said them aloud now: "Tell me what happened."

Kerrick lifted up and looked at her. He knew exactly what she meant, what she wanted to know.

Christ. He drew out of her, breaking the erotic connection.

He slid his hips to the edge of the mattress, his legs following. When she turned on her side away from him, he stroked the back of her neck. Right now he wanted to bolt, to leap out of bed, to run hard, away from the house, away from her, away from the subject. He didn't want to talk about Helena or his children, not with Alison, especially not Alison, because this was his failure, his greatest failure.

He had let her inside his mind, let her romp around, and he'd loved it but it also meant she had seen his past, especially the nature of his grief. She was also a therapist so of course she would want him to talk. This far down the road, he saw no point in trying to evade the subject.

He summoned a breath then another. He let the words flow. "I was fighting. It wasn't very late, maybe eight o'clock. I was at the north end of the White Tank Mountains on Second. That night Greaves hammered us with pretty-boys at every Borderland, which was unusual at the time.

"Thorne suspected something big was going down. We all did. We just couldn't imagine what, which meant we didn't know what to prepare for.

"Helena wasn't powerful like you although she had a few fully developed gifts. Her telepathy was perfect. If she had been more powerful, if she had been able to sense something was coming, if she'd had even a small piece of the clairvoyance I know you have she could have summoned me and together we could have done something. At least, I think we could have. I don't know because I wasn't there when it happened. Maybe I would have misread the situation as well." He paused. He didn't want to speak the words.

To her credit, she remained silent, letting him find his way.

"Helena and I engaged in full communion—body, blood, mind—so we were very close, as close at two ascenders can be just short of the *breh-hedden,* but it wasn't enough to help us that night."

She put a hand on his shoulder. "What was the difference,

then? I mean why wasn't your full communion with Helena the same as the *breh-hedden*? I don't understand."

He frowned. Shit, this hurt because it went to the central issue, the reason he should never have married Helena in the first place. "Because of the difference between telepathy and mind-engagement. Helena didn't have your power. I couldn't be in her mind the way I can be in yours, because I would have hurt her. Nor could Helena be in my mind, because she didn't have the capacity. We were able to communicate telepathically, but that is still very different from mind-engagement.

"All ascenders can take part in some level of full communion by making use of telepathy, but most ascenders can't get into the head of another. Some believe mind-diving is more a Third Earth ability than a Second Earth power, which is why the *breh-hedden* is extremely rare and occurs only among the Warriors of the Blood . . . and powerful women." His throat felt choked and raw. "Helena just wasn't advanced, not like you. Other than Endelle, there is no one like you in our world."

He squeezed his eyes shut and forced himself to breathe. His chest was tight and his heart pounded at the memories. He took another deep breath and continued. "As for Helena and what happened that night, because of her telepathic abilities and because there had been a lull in the battle, we were talking back and forth within our minds. It was wonderful. She and the children had just come back from town. They'd unhitched the horses. She was very big on making sure our kids learned those kinds of skills early. Kerr and Christine always complained, of course, but at nine and seven those two knew how to care for any of the horses we had on the property and how to keep the wagons and carriages in good shape even if they couldn't yet do the work themselves.

"God, I was proud of them, all of them. Helena was a wonderful mother, patient, kind." A new weight descended on his chest and his throat grew tight, the memory pulling hard now. "So, she was in my head, telepathically telling me about some fabric she had just purchased, a recent import from Mortal France, a very fine silk, when the communication was suddenly disrupted." He remembered the moment as though it were yesterday. "I was standing and before I knew what had happened I was sitting, my head in my hands, tears rushing out of my eyes for no apparent reason . . . except I knew, I knew they were gone, all of them.

"The stable had been rigged with enough gunpowder to blow a hole through a mountain. The Commander wasn't leaving anything to chance. In addition to my family, two of the servants died as well. They'd been in the stable helping out, as they always did."

He felt Alison release a deep breath. "Was the Commander ever charged with the crime?"

"There was no proof of his complicity but he offered up a pair of death vamps for trial. They were convicted and hanged on the flimsiest evidence. Were they guilty? Who knows. I will always lay the crime at the Commander's feet. He was the one with the motivation."

He took a breath in, shoved one out. He ached into the pit of his stomach. This was why he didn't like to talk about what happened. The memories were as fresh as yesterday. The pain as real.

"So you believe he killed your family to hurt you."

"Demoralizing an enemy is a legitimate tactic of war."

She turned toward him and looked into his eyes. She kissed him. She kissed him over and over, her hands on his face, her fingers gliding into his hair. She kissed his lips, again and again, pushing at him, her tongue driving into his mouth, her arms snaking around his neck, her body lush, warm, and *alive* against his.

He drew back and looked into her eyes once more, wet blue eyes, rimmed in gold, sparkling, telling him things she neither spoke aloud nor into his mind, desperate things made up of hopes and dreams.

She kissed him again, those insistent pushing kisses,

working his mouth, her body writhing against his. She was here, she was now, she was alive, all for him, to comfort him, to listen to his pain, to hear it, to feel it, to accept all that he was, even his profound failure.

He rolled her onto her back, hard once more, ready for her. When he drove into her, he looked into her eyes and never stopped looking; nor did she shift her gaze away from him even for one passion-drenched moment. Instead the frenzy became about the now of his life and the now of her life, her ascension that would mean everything to him, that would herald a new, shared future, God help them both.

When her climax took hold of her, and her power punched against his abdomen, blue eyes still locked to his, he spent himself in a wicked blur of movement.

As his body settled down, she kept nodding then finally said what was in his heart as well: "Tonight, at my ascension ceremony, our life together begins. I'll be free of the Commander. The death vamps won't be hunting me anymore."

He nodded.

"Yes," he whispered, but he kissed her hard and ignored the desperate feeling of the moment. Would they truly begin a new life or was this just one big massive lie?

Alison stood in the middle of the marble floor beneath the enormous central rotunda of Endelle's palace with Havily just off to her left side and behind her a foot. She was almost home free. She could feel it. Once she completed the ascension ceremony, Darian—the Commander—would have no legal right to continue his attack on her. According to everything she understood about ascending, he would turn his efforts in another direction, perhaps to another ascension-in-progress, who knew?

What she didn't understand and what made her nervous right now was why Greaves hadn't attempted another attack. She didn't know what to make of it, a circumstance that caused her to look over her shoulder more than once, and the fresh air from the open walls did little to calm her nerves.

Despite her concerns, however, this was the moment she had been waiting for, the completion of her process of ascension, the point at which she would become . . . an ascender . . . a vampire . . . an immortal.

She weaved on her feet. She ordered her mind, or tried to.

Endelle stood in front of her, nearly ten feet away. She wore a formal black robe, which just barely touched the top straps of her stilettos. She held out her right hand and a book appeared. She grimaced, flipped through several pages, put her forefinger on a paragraph, and started reading.

The words spoke of the beauty of the dimensional worlds, the exalted nature of ascension, of the community Alison was entering, and of the depth of responsibility each ascender bore to the future of Second Earth. Service was hailed as the greatest privilege and chief duty of every resident of Second. Alison tried to take in what was being said, but Endelle's frequent sighs and rather bored voice dominated the meaning of the text.

Kerrick stood in guardian position behind Alison and just to her right, his mind never far, a calming, hovering presence with a gentle touch against her thoughts.

The Warriors of the Blood were stationed behind both Kerrick and Havily, in formal regalia—minus the heavy brass breastplates—all seven warriors, including Marcus. Warrior Marcus's acceptance among the warriors had apparently increased with each successive night of battling.

She could feel the heat of so many large male bodies behind her. But they shifted on their feet, cleared throats, and released breaths. The Commander had been quiet since the Tolleson arena battle, which made all of them uneasy, like that old expression about waiting for the other shoe to drop, only it wouldn't be a shoe, it would be a sword, a lot of swords.

A cool breeze flowed over Alison from the open walls. The absence of doors, walls, and windows gave an impression of an Olympian dwelling, especially since the palace had been built out from the side of the McDowell Mountains.

Yes, Olympus came to mind. Alison smiled for if she

could have made a comparison, Juno suited Madame Endelle quite well. The goddesses of Olympus were remarkably self-involved, unsympathetic in nature, demanding, and of course very beautiful. Yes, very much *Juno*.

Endelle's voice broke through Alison's thoughts. "Do you agree to serve Second Earth with a mind and heart dedicated to service?"

Alison nodded. "I do."

"Do you agree to abide by the laws of Second Earth, especially as they apply to the limitations of involvement with Mortal Earth?"

"I do."

"And do you solemnly pledge your loyalty to me, as Supreme High Administrator of Second Earth?"

"I do."

"You may approach."

Alison moved forward to stand three feet in front of her.

"Closer," Endelle commanded.

Alison took two steps to position herself within a foot of her. Endelle folded the large ceremonial book away. She placed her hands on Alison's face over both cheeks, her fingers spreading to cup her jaws as well. Endelle's skin felt warm against hers and soon grew warmer.

"I hereby imbue you with Second immortality, all the qualities that will allow for long life and the sharing of blood and potions. May you bring peace to our world."

As power flowed from Endelle, Alison closed her eyes and parted her lips. She took deep breaths, absorbing the sensations with some difficulty though she wasn't certain why.

"Dammit, Alison," Endelle cried. "Release your shields! So damn stubborn. So ridiculously powerful!"

She let go and a warm wave flowed through her body. The sensation was like swimming in tropical waters. She felt covered, surrounded, filled, oddly complete, as though until this moment something unknown had been missing from her life. Her eyes filled with tears.

So this was ascension, the true gift of ascended life, a

wonderful ease, a sense of belonging and oneness. Was this what everyone felt?

Every ascension is different. Kerrick had told her that.

She opened her eyes and met Endelle's gaze. For once, the leader of Second didn't seem so hardened. Even the wooded appearance of her eyes had softened and she actually smiled. "Congratulations. You have completed your rite of ascension. From this moment forward, should Commander Greaves or any of his minions have the temerity to attack you, any or all will be held accountable under the full weight of the law. I say this to assure you that none of us expect further aggression. With that said, welcome, vampire ascender Wells."

"Thank you," Alison responded. She nodded several times. "Thank you." Her mouth felt strange, her gums achy. Huh. The presence of fangs? Her heart skipped a beat as she thought of what she might do with her fangs and how Kerrick had used his when pleasuring her. Her body responded improperly and she took more deep breaths to compose herself.

"Turn around, ascender Wells, and greet your fellow countrymen."

She turned slowly, her heart so full she couldn't speak. The warriors set up a loud applause coupled with whistles and shouts. Havily grinned.

Kerrick smiled his crooked, off-center smile. He nodded and a blast of cardamom hit her square in the chest.

She staggered beneath the blow, but she smiled. She was like him now, truly his equal, and she couldn't wait to be with him again.

He crossed to her quickly then gathered her into his arms and embraced her. "I didn't know," she murmured into his neck. "To think, I might have refused this." He held her for a good long moment. She could feel the tension in every limb, in the way he held her so tight, a combination of fear and love.

He caught her chin with his fingers and placed a soft kiss on her lips. "Welcome to Second."

When she met his gaze, she got lost, thinking of all they'd been through and all the ways he had made love to her, and should life be even a little fair, all the beautiful centuries they would have together. God willing.

But even then, as the warriors congratulated her, she watched them always checking over their shoulders, gazes shifting about, prowling, always on guard, fists bunching as though preparing any moment to bring swords into their hands.

Doubt ripped through her suddenly.

Would Kerrick and she truly have a life together or were they kidding themselves?

A servant arrived in the doorway and announced that dinner was served. Endelle's stilettos clicked across the marble as she led the way into the dining hall.

Kerrick offered his arm, and together they fell in behind Her Supremeness.

Alison glanced behind her. Havily had taken Luken's arm. The rest of the warriors also followed, except two. As she crossed the threshold she had a final glimpse of both Marcus and Santiago standing near the open wall, staring deep into the landscape beyond, hunting, searching. Santiago lifted his gaze to the skies.

She knew what they were searching for—death vamps.

A chill traveled down her spine, gripping her skin in a tight ripple of fear. No matter the assurances, this was her life now that she had ascended.

Marcus took up last place in line to go into dinner, waiting until Santiago completed his visual sweep of the exterior. His hand itched for his sword. He didn't like the setup even though Thorne insisted the palace had a state-of-the-art security system. He hated the open walls.

What the hell was Endelle thinking? An attack could come from so many directions, through the various connected rotundas, all of which, by the way, were large enough for death vamps to take to the air.

As the party moved into the dining room, once more he

looked up. The ceilings were tall motherfuckers and would allow for anything in flight to climb high then descend at will like a rocket.

The dining room was vast and would no doubt accommodate more than a dozen large round tables for a sit-down dinner of a hundred. So yeah, the space could easily shelter a small war. Especially tonight, with only one table set for the celebration dinner.

In the round. Fuck. He'd be able to see Kerrick easily and the sonofabitch could see him.

He shouldn't even be here and resented the hell out of the fact that Endelle had insisted. What was the point? Alison had just completed her ascension ceremony. She was safe now—or at least as safe as she would ever be—and he could go back to his life on Mortal Earth, his real life. He ought to just leave but taking off would only piss Her Supremeness off, which was never a good thing. He wasn't dismissed until she let him go. No questions or complaints allowed.

He avoided eye contact with Kerrick. Ever since they'd gone head-to-head, a silent truce had characterized their subsequent interactions. Of course he had one major distraction on hand, which kept him occupied most of the time anyway . . . Havily.

She looked incredibly tempting in a simple black dress and somewhat boxy black shoes. All that black coupled with her peachy-red hair, which hung in glossy waves to the center of her back, made him ache.

Thank God she'd gone in just after Alison and Kerrick. Luken had offered his arm and she'd taken it. Night had fallen and somehow her honeysuckle scent had gotten heavier and thicker as the hours wore on. He had a hard-on he just couldn't seem to get rid of.

As he strolled behind Medichi, he had to admit one damn thing—Havily was his fucking *breh*. Four thousand years, one wife divorced, two wives buried, and at the dawn of all-hell-is-about-to-break-loose the woman meant for him shows up in the Sonoran Desert Two, looking like heaven and smelling like sin. Never had he been so drawn to a woman, so enthralled by her presence and by her scent. And he knew, *he knew,* she was equally attracted to him. She was also pissed off about it, since the disdain in her expression when she glanced his way was full of fire and brimstone.

He was a deserter and she despised him.

EOS.

So what the hell did any of it matter? He could give an armadillo's spleen what she thought of him and the hell he would ever take a *breh,* a real *breh.*

Goddammit. He just wished to hell she wasn't touching Luken. Her hand on his arm made him want to mount his wings, draw his sword, then slice the bastard all to hell.

Shit, he needed to get back to his life, to his numerous corporations, to his empire building. He could forget all about the woman if he no longer had to be around sniffing her and throwing wood one minute out of every two. Jesus. Four millennia and he might as well have been sixteen years old again.

As he took a seat two away from Kerrick so he wouldn't be opposite him, he glanced at Endelle. She sat in a throne-like chair to emphasize her rank. He narrowed his eyes. Had she orchestrated this? All the centuries he'd been battling death vamps on her behalf, since the year 1997 BC, only one other warrior had ever found a true *breh.* Even Kerrick had admitted Helena hadn't fallen into that category. Helena hadn't been powerful enough, which had been one half of the problem, one half of the reason she had died. She hadn't been able to sense the future, to get herself or her children out of harm's way.

But those thoughts were a black hole and he wouldn't go there. Otherwise he'd find some excuse to provoke Kerrick and once more beat the shit out of him, or at least try to.

He sucked in a breath. He just had to wait this evening out, maybe make war tonight if the pretty-boys showed up, then get permission to get the fuck out. He settled his shoulders back and as soon as the wait staff started pouring wine, he started drinking.

After two full glasses, he looked up to find Alison's gaze on his. Compassion rested in those blue eyes of hers. Jesus H. Christ. So the bastard had told her what happened to Helena. Fuck. She inclined her head then looked away, thank God.

He caught a waiter's eye, lifted his glass, and watched the white wine climb up the bowl.

He still couldn't believe the Third Earth powers she'd demonstrated while fighting Leto. Jesus, talk about power. She had all of Second's abilities, like Endelle on her ascension, plus a few of Third's. That was one boatload of ability. Hell, maybe she'd stay alive for the bastard.

A nerve on his cheek twitched. He sucked back more of the white wine. So Alison Wells was Kerrick's *breh,* when Helena hadn't been. A flood of expletives sloshed through his head all over again. And Alison was here and now, which meant Kerrick got to be happy, that goddamn motherfucker.

He swallowed hard and forced himself to calm down all over again.

The salad arrived, which he ignored.

He kept drinking, wishing like hell he had Scotch to the rim instead of Sauvignon Blanc.

He felt a bump on his arm. Medichi lowered his head, "Hey. Pass the rolls, asshole."

Marcus took the damn basket then shoved it at Zach to his left. Unfortunately, somewhere in that movement, his gaze landed on Havily. He would have looked away but she met his gaze head-on. Her cheeks turned pink and a sudden wave of honeysuckle had him swallowing the white wine like he was dying of thirst.

Havily wished herself gone, long gone.

Being in the same room with Warrior Marcus had become a physical torture, the kind she craved and despised all at the same time.

The lovely beet and walnut salad, which she had been unable to touch, was removed and a savory entrée placed in front of her. But all she could do was pick at the sage and rosemary chicken breast, sautéed green beans, and garlic mashed potatoes. The tastes might have pleased her enormously had it not been for one thing—all she could smell was that ridiculous fennel scent, which now puffed at her in great clouds from across the table. She wished Warrior Marcus would stop doing whatever it was he was doing. Her nose was clogged with his smell, which in turn kept her achy deep into her abdomen.

She stretched her back.

She felt like she was ovulating and now she struggled to breathe. Her breasts were swollen and her bra was way too tight. Luken, who towered over her, could see down the bodice of her dress and his gaze fell there often. He'd had a thing for her over the past few decades, since he'd served as her guardian. She wished she hadn't sat beside him. He kept leaning close and asking her tender questions. Of course they were tender, he was Luken, the giant with the beautiful heart.

She just wasn't interested in him, not romantically. She ought to be, though. He was sweet and kind and honorable. But that was always the difficulty with attraction, with love—the choice was not always the most sensible, rational, or realistic.

Not that she was *choosing* anyone! She wasn't. She would *never* choose Warrior Marcus.

She was, however, grateful that after tonight, she wouldn't be seeing any of the warriors for a good long while. They'd go back to making war, Marcus would undoubtedly return to Mortal Earth, and she would begin rebuilding her architectural rendering of the new military-admin complex.

She cut a slice of chicken, stacked it with a cut green bean, and bathed it in mashed potatoes—the perfect bite. She opened her mouth but all she could smell was fennel. Oh, for God's sake. She glared at Marcus. Why wouldn't he stop doing whatever it was he was doing? And why didn't anyone else complain of the smell, the luscious, erotic fennel he kept casting at her as though he wanted her buried in the stuff.

His eyes narrowed as he met her gaze but he looked away then picked up his wineglass . . . *again.*

She had to do something to get her mind off of his absurd scent. She glanced at Santiago, who sat between Jean-Pierre and Medichi. "Anything new on the weapons front?" she asked. He was incredibly handsome in a Latin way, sensual lips, an interesting nose with a few traceable curves. Even his nose was sexy.

He nodded. "A woman after my own *corazón.* Now, why can't I meet a woman who will talk metals with me?"

Jean-Pierre elbowed him. "You always bite first and never ask questions later, that's why."

"Fuck you, *amigo,*" Santiago responded.

Jean-Pierre laughed, his long elegant fingers pulling meat off a bone. Jean-Pierre had a faint French accent and very sexy, really beautiful hands.

Havily just shook her head and laughed. How would she ever get a straight answer when the warriors were in a group like this? They always cut one another down, in a friendly way, of course, like brothers.

She gave up on enjoying her dinner, picked up her wineglass, and leaned back in her seat. "Well, what are you working on right now? You always have something on the design table."

He leaned forward, his brows together. He chewed in his slow measured way. He never seemed to do anything in haste. He showed care and thoroughness, even while eating. "Zach and I keep talking about how we want a weapon halfway between a sword and a dagger. Daggers are good. But I'd like something that throws like a dagger but is more effective, does more damage in a combat situation, something bigger."

Havily nodded. "What length would work the best, do you think?" It was so the wrong question to ask. She knew it as soon as the words left her mouth and she could feel the heat rise on her cheeks even before he answered.

Santiago chuckled, leaned back, then with just a hint of fangs offered his sexiest vampire grin, an easy thing to do with all his beauty. "I have a way to measure that would be *perfection*," he said, casting his arms on the back of Jean-Pierre's chair and Medichi's to his left. She had no doubt exactly what he was referring to.

She might have drowned in embarrassment if she hadn't at one time been engaged to a Militia Warrior. Instead she rolled her eyes.

The men guffawed.

"You're dreaming again," Jean-Pierre said.

"You're jealous."

"Of that?" He glanced at Santiago's lap. "Bah."

Havily sipped her wine then shook her head.

Men.

Warriors.

Whatever.

Death comes.

—*Collected Proverbs*, Beatrice of Fourth

CHAPTER 21

A little after ten o'clock Kerrick held Alison in his arms and moved in a slow circle on one of the smaller rotunda floors in Endelle's palace. "As Time Goes By" played on a top-of-the-line audio system, a classic song from an old movie he'd seen when it first came out, *Casablanca*, during Hollywood's heyday.

He wished he had known Alison then. He would have taken her on a date to a theater, maybe even to Mortal Earth for the premiere. He knew she loved old movies. He'd been inside her head.

Endelle had provided a perfect dinner, an excellent celebration for Alison's ascension, although Her Supremeness had not stayed long. After the dessert course, she had excused herself.

"All right, lame-asses," she had said. "I'm back to work."

She had withdrawn to her meditation room, where she mentally followed Greaves all over the planet preventing him from sending death vamps back to his Estrella Mountain compound. Word had it she did this by way of the darkening, that region of nether-space that allowed a person to be two places at once. Kerrick couldn't begin to imagine either the power or the mental energy required to police the sonofabitch the way she did.

The rest of the warriors, with the exception of Marcus and Luken, were not far, just a few yards away, sitting on the terrace, smoking cigars, laughing, drinking. Marcus sulked by the bar. Luken danced with Havily. He had such a crush on her, poor bastard, but she wasn't the least bit interested.

As he danced Alison in a slow circle, his gaze fell once more on Thorne. He sat turned away from the others, his phone to his ear—probably talking to Central. He swirled a glass of Ketel in his left hand.

Thorne, the one they all relied on.

Kerrick looked away. No doubt Central had just called. Of course. The warriors would have to go out anytime now. These were stolen hours, the hours of Alison's ascension. Kerrick frowned. Usually the Commander would have sent squadrons to every Borderland long before this.

As far as that went, why hadn't he made another attempt on Alison's life? Well, too late now. Where Alison was concerned, the Commander was out of time. She'd completed her rite of ascension, which meant she had the same protection under the law as all Second Earth ascenders. Of course, that didn't mean he wouldn't attack the palace just as a general *fuck you* to Endelle and the Warriors of the Blood. Still, Alison was off limits now, unless Greaves wanted to face the courts again as well as the wrath of the warriors.

He glanced at all the open walls and doorways. The palace had a kick-ass security system that would scorch anything trying to fly in. As for materializing, he wasn't so sure, but he knew Central kept a tight watch on the place.

"Something wrong?" Alison asked. "You just tensed up."

He forced himself to relax. "By now I'd usually be out

fighting. I'm not used to the quiet." He released a sigh. "I'll adjust."

He slid his arms even tighter around Alison. She gave a murmur of approval. God, she felt so good against him, her arms around his waist, her head tilted against his shoulder, her lips lifted to him, teasing his neck. He loved that she was tall. She really did fit him, in every possible way.

And she had fangs now. He shuddered, anticipation sending little fireworks through his veins.

What? she sent.

You can take my blood now.

He felt a similar tremor pass through her. A resulting whorl of lavender rose up to torment him.

He would leave the basement now and she would share his bed. He'd even begun to think that maybe they should talk about completing the *breh-hedden*. She was powerful and her abilities could make a difference. Maybe.

She was pressed up flush against him and he was sure she could feel just how much he enjoyed this dance. When she shifted just a little so that her abdomen glided over his erection then at the same time she kissed his neck, yeah, she knew exactly where he wanted to be right now.

At the same time, he didn't want the dance to end.

Was this really happening? He hadn't had a woman in his life in so long, in two centuries. Would he be able to keep her safe? Would her proximity to him make her a new kind of target? Of course, the rules were different now and Greaves couldn't go after her, not without repercussions. But would that stop Greaves at this point? What he didn't know, what he couldn't know, was just how much of a threat the Commander believed Alison to be. After all, he hadn't made another attempt on her life within the allotted three days. He drew in a deep breath, his throat closing up. "Alison," he whispered.

She drew back and looked up at him. His chest rose and fell. Her fingers worked the hair at his nape.

"I'm so glad you're here," he whispered.

She smiled. "So how soon can we leave?"

His answer reached the tip of his tongue until an unexpected frown entered her eyes. "What is it?" he asked.

"Not sure. I just feel . . . uneasy." She stopped moving.

"Oh, shit. This cannot be good."

"No, it isn't."

He looked around but saw nothing out of the ordinary.

"Would the Commander attack me now?" she asked, her eyes wide.

Kerrick shook his head. "He would be a fool to try it. You've completed your rite of ascension. If an attack were aimed at you, he'd be held accountable."

"So he won't attack?"

Kerrick looked down at her and an old fear hit him like a blast to the chest. When he considered the present gathering, he had a sudden awareness that this would be a perfect time for an attack, with all the warriors gathered under the same roof. "It wouldn't be aimed at you," he said, more to himself than to her. "*We* would be the target, the Warriors of the Blood." He remembered the *why* of Helena's death. She'd been married to a warrior. A chill went through him.

Marcus sipped a fine brandy, one of his favorite drinks, more than even Scotch. He sat alone not far from the bar. The warriors were out on the patio, smoking, telling jokes, the usual male-bonding bullshit. He didn't belong with them. Besides, sitting by himself and sipping the rich fortified wine suited his current temper.

He watched the Liaison Officer dancing with Luken. The warrior was really into her, the bastard.

Marcus uncurled his fingers for the hundredth time from around the glass. He had a habit of crushing tumblers, among other glass things.

He should have left the same time Endelle retreated to her cave. Instead he hung around. His instincts were firing off missiles right now and he couldn't ignore them. His need to protect Havily kept him pinned to the bar stool, watching her in her short dress, which grew even shorter with Luken's arm around her waist as he moved her into a couple of turns.

He was still hard as a rock and he couldn't tear his gaze from the back of her legs, the tops of her thighs, hoping for a glimpse of her ass, the thought of which forced him to sit well forward. And all he could smell was a powerful drift of honeysuckle. Goddammit.

He took another sip. He forced himself to look away. His gaze landed on Alison and Kerrick. They'd stopped dancing and she was looking around the rotunda with a frown between her brows.

A frisson traveled down his spine. He didn't wait to second-guess what he felt. With a wave of his hand, he changed from tunic to flight gear. He drew his sword into his hand.

He wasn't alone.

The blur around each of the warriors indicated the same call to arms had been registered in lifted hairs on neck and arms.

"Central just called," Thorne shouted. "We've got incoming."

Marcus crossed to Havily in a few brisk strides. With Luken on the other side, they'd work to keep her safe.

"Oh, shit," squeaked from her usually prim mouth.

"Don't move away from either of us," he cried.

"How are they going to get through Endelle's security?"

"There's only one way. Greaves must be here."

"An attack on the palace?" Luken shouted. "This is so fucking illegal."

"When did the Commander ever give a shit about that?" Marcus gripped his sword in both hands, his instincts clanging like a fire alarm. His back muscles thickened, his winglocks hummed.

Death vamps shimmered into the rotunda, directly to the space in which the warriors had just geared up. Marcus swept his gaze over the group. Goddammit, there were too fucking many. Twenty, twenty-one. He stopped counting.

"Mounting," he cried. His wings flew through his wing-locks, as did Luken's, one more layer of protection for Havily.

The first attack came as three launched near him, rocketing high into the air, flying into the enormous height of the rotunda, trying to draw him away. He had never felt so focused in his life with *his woman* at his back and her existence depending on how deftly he and Luken maneuvered through the next few minutes.

"How we doin'?" he cried.

Luken responded, "I got four and they're goin' down."

"Good. Keep Havily between us. Havily, don't even think of folding. They'll follow you."

"I'm not going anywhere."

"Good. That's good." He heard Luken grunt and his sword ring as he engaged his pretty-boys.

Marcus's own trio gave up the airspace but drew their wings back to close-mount and fired toward him like missiles. He took a deep breath, lowered his shoulders, dipped his chin. "Here they come."

He plucked the dagger from his breastpiece and let it fly. It struck home, straight into the heart of the vamp to the left. At almost the same time, his sword met metal and he moved at preternatural speed to fend off each pair of thrusts again and again. The whole time he could sense Havily moving with him, completely in sync. He knew exactly where she was and only as he severed a head, leaving him but one death vamp to contend with, did he realize she was in his mind delivering a warning, very quietly.

Three on your left, she sent as a new wave of enemies flew in through the open walls. So yeah, the security system was down and there was only one ascender who could have done it. Greaves. Shit.

He also heard Havily on the phone. "Jeannie, we need cleanup. Is there anything you can do?" Pause. "There have to be at least two dozen bad guys here. But there's . . . blood and other things all over the floor."

In small increments, lights flashed and death vamp debris got cleaned up, thank you, God.

Havily, Marcus sent, *you've got one helluva cool head on your shoulders.*

Just keep fighting, Warrior.

More death vamps flew in, so this was a full-blown attack. Fortunately, Greaves couldn't enter the battle himself. From what Medichi had told him, COPASS had only a handful of rules that they enforced the hell out of. Endelle and Greaves staying out of the fray happened to be, thank God, one of those rules.

Alison couldn't believe her ascension celebration had turned into a full-on battle. She was tempted to bring her sword into her hand and engage but the combat was ridiculously close and there were so many death vamps. She didn't have this kind of experience at all. It would be far too easy to accidentally wound one of the warriors.

She stuck close to Kerrick. He'd told her to stay at his back and had called Medichi over to guard her on the other side. Her heart beat heavily. She had never seen such a flurry of wings, and every kill meant that a terrible spray of blood landed . . . everywhere.

Havily's voice rang out. "Major cleanup coming."

A light flashed bright, like the one at the medical complex, blinding her for a second. Her stomach boiled as bodies, feathers, and body parts disappeared. She felt lightheaded, especially since the clash of metal sounded in her ears. Between Medichi and Kerrick, the fighting was fast, furious, and deadly.

She measured the movements of both warriors and stayed within a couple of yards of each of them. Medichi didn't mount his wings, but Kerrick's white feathers flurried around her, sometimes stinging, sometimes soft flutters.

Over the next few minutes the death vamps kept coming. But eventually the numbers began to diminish and it seemed clear to Alison that the attack would soon be over—until she saw blurred movement near Luken, Havily, and Marcus.

A different kind of attack.

The blur solidified. Darian the Commander stood near them. He didn't engage but watched her, a satisfied smile curving his lips. He must have created an intricate powerful mist to disguise his arrival, which prevented those nearest him from detecting his presence. However, she had no problem seeing through all the cobweb-like filaments that crisscrossed his face and body

What do you intend to do, ascender? Darian's voice was in her head!

She fortified her shields and effectively pushed him out. *The Commander,* she whispered into Kerrick's mind.
Where?
By Marcus.
I don't see him. Kerrick wielded his sword against two opponents now. Sweat dripped from his body.
I see him, Alison sent. *I can kill him. I know it.*
I still don't see him. Are you sure?
There. By Marcus. This will be simple. Move to the left, Kerrick. I can end all of this, right now, here, tonight. Adrenaline flooded her. One powerful hand-blast and she could take him out, forever. Maybe this was her purpose, the reason Darian had so feared her ascension. Maybe she was destined to end the war by taking his life.

He moved closer to Marcus but he began to fade. He must have been shoring up his mist. She wouldn't have much time at this rate. She had to make a decision and she had to make it quick.

Her heart pounded in her chest. She had been unable to take Leto's life even before she learned he was working as a double agent. She was a therapist and believed in the redemption of the soul. However, Darian Greaves fell into an entirely different category, and though taking life was repugnant to her, if she had the chance to stop him, to destroy the greatest force of evil on Second Earth, shouldn't she do it? Her conscience spoke for her: The monster across the room had to be stopped.

Darian's arms vanished from view, then his legs. *Kerrick, I'm going to take him out.*

Wait. Just wait. I don't see him. I'm almost finished here. One last pretty-boy to go.

Alison held back a few moments more, but Darian's head and most of his shoulders were no longer visible; she had barely a torso to aim at.

As Kerrick finished off the last death vamp and moved to the left, she saw her opening. She lifted her hand and gathered power into her palm. A blast that could pass through a dimension could also dispatch an enemy of Second Earth.

Good-bye, Darian, she sent. Just as she fired, Kerrick's voice rang out, *"No!"*

What happened next occurred in slow motion. The blast left her hand and she stumbled backward. At the same moment Darian's image disappeared as well as all the cobweb-like signatures of his mist. Beyond, Marcus, Luken, and Havily all stared in horror, facing certain death from her hand. Then, in preternatural speed and at the very last split second, Kerrick moved in front of them and took the full force of the blast in his abdomen and chest.

He kept flying at the same angle he'd been moving. He glanced off Luken to land another twenty feet away into an adjoining rotunda.

Alison stood transfixed at what had just happened, at what she had just done. So Darian hadn't been there at all—or had he moved at the last second? Oh, God, had she just killed the man she loved?

The Commander stood beside her now and murmured, "Oh, how unfortunate. I had meant for the other three to die, but well done, my dear. You've taken out a warrior I've been wanting to be rid of for, oh, twelve hundred years."

Alison lowered her arm and turned to her right to look into the Commander's eyes. Comprehension struck. "You tricked me?"

He shrugged, stroked her cheek with his finger. "This is war, my dear. Welcome to Second." He lifted an arm then vanished.

Alison folded straight to Kerrick and dropped down beside him. Swords still clanged, the occasional bright flash of light blinded her, voices called across the rotunda floor. What did any of it matter when her beloved lay on the floor, his eyes rolling in his head, his body shaking, and the black leather of his weapons harness peeled back from his abdomen? She couldn't look at the destruction of his flesh.

She had to do something, fast. Surely, she could change what had just happened, what she had just done.

Pocket of time reversal!

Yes, of course.

She thought the thought but nothing happened. She stood up and reached out with her hands but nothing happened. She tried to latch onto the sequence, tried to find a rope of time, but couldn't. Why? *Why?* Why not this time, when she really needed it? But no matter how hard she tried she couldn't find the key.

When she suddenly heard the Commander's laughter, however, she knew exactly why.

"Someone get the healer," she cried.

More blinding flashes of light, but metal no longer clashed against metal. Large bodies gathered around her. She clasped Kerrick's hand and begged him to hold on.

"Get Horace," she cried.

She glanced at Thorne, who dropped down beside Kerrick's head. He slid his arm beneath his shoulders and lifted him to rest on his lap. He kept a hand pressed to Kerrick's forehead.

"Too late," he whispered. Tears shed from his eyes.

Alison shook her head. No. No! *No!* This couldn't be happening.

"Why did you fire at us?" Luken asked.

"I was deceived. I thought I saw the Commander in front of you. He tricked me."

Kerrick could not die. She would not let him die.

Kerrick stared up and watched as the painted ceiling of the rotunda melted away and the black night sky appeared, a death vision. He lay on his back, life draining from him. He saw the drift of galaxies as his dying brain reached up and out.

He had less than a minute now. He could no longer feel what had a moment earlier been his ice-cold limbs. He barely had an awareness of his body—only a deep sense of regret.

Alison, he called again.

Kerrick?

Relief flooded what was left of his conscious mind. He shifted his gaze and there she was.

Drink from me, my love. You must take my blood. Now.

Too late. Love you so much. He closed his eyes. He faded into a very dark place.

"Thorne," Alison cried. "Get Endelle back here. She can heal him."

"I've tried. She doesn't respond."

Darian had thought of everything. Of course. No wonder she couldn't use her powers.

"Then you must hold him to my throat. He's got to have my blood."

Thorne didn't move. "He's gone."

"No." She saw the despair in Thorne's face. "Listen to me, Thorne. You must help me. He's not gone yet. I would know. Please. Trust me."

Thorne finally met her gaze. His eyes cleared. He nodded. "Medichi! Get Horace here. Now!"

"On it."

Thorne pinned Kerrick in his arms, lifted him high onto his lap, and supported his chin. Alison took him to her neck, positioning his fangs. His face was slack but she had new ascended physical power now. She drove his fangs into her vein and because he was completely powerless, she directed her blood into his mouth. She used her hand on his neck to direct the flow down his throat.

Horace appeared a moment later. "Oh, dear merciful Creator," he cried. Despite the severity of the wounds, he settled in immediately and laid his hands over the shredded abdomen. "He'll need surgery as well . . . if we can bring him back."

Alison merely nodded then closed her eyes.

Kerrick, she whispered over his mind. *Come back to me. Do you feel my blood within you now? The power singing through your veins? Come back to me. I need you. Please, Kerrick. You must try. Horace is here tending you.*

She eased the flow. *Talk to me, Kerrick.*

Silence returned.

She entered his mind and traveled very deep but found only darkness.

Panic seized her.

You must try, my darling, she sent deep into his mind, into his soul, into the remnant of his consciousness.

Then she knew what she had to do and the timing now made complete sense. *There's something you must know. We're having a daughter, you and I. She will have such power but she will need her father to help order her mind and to train her. You must come back to me, to us. We can do this . . . together . . . you and I . . . for our daughter.*

She drew out of his mind. She pressed her hand to his chest and sent gentle pulses into his lifeless heart.

She couldn't lose him.

"Darling," she said aloud and in his mind, quietly so she wouldn't hurt the men around her. *"You must return to me. Please, Kerrick, come back to me. Can you feel my blood in you now, making you strong, renewing your life?"*

She could sense the Warriors of the Blood weighing in, Thorne, Medichi and Luken, Santiago and Zacharius, Jean-Pierre. *"Your brothers are here. We're with you, Kerrick. Thorne holds you against me."* She smiled suddenly. *"How powerful Thorne is and so incredibly handsome. He has a real aura of command. He would make a terrific breh for me, don't you think?"*

The gasp all around her could no doubt be heard a mile away.

But from a great distance, from so deep within her own

mind that she doubted what she was hearing, she heard him. *Thorne? Never. You're mine. Mine.* Suddenly she felt a deep draw at her neck, and then another and another.

Joy rose up, a fountain within her heart, higher and higher. Tears flowed, her hands shook.

"He lives," Thorne cried, still holding him firmly against Alison. "He lives." Tears now fell from Thorne's eyes. "Jean-Pierre. Get an ambulance. He won't survive dematerialization, not in this state."

"*Oui,* boss."

The warriors gave a shout. After several minutes, Kerrick's eyes opened and he pulled away from Alison's vein. He looked at her. *I love you,* he sent then winced.

She could barely see him for the tears that swam over her eyes. She nodded, smiled, and found his lips. She tasted her blood on him and kissed him hard.

"Welcome back," she whispered.

Another shout rang out.

Horace kept his hands above the wounds, the powerful glow from his efforts spreading light over Kerrick's face.

Alison could see the pain in his eyes as he struggled to breathe. "We're . . . having a daughter?" he whispered.

She nodded as she wiped the tears from her face. "How's that for ascension?"

He held her hand but suddenly his face twisted in pain.

Thorne cried, "How we doin' on the ambulance, Jean-Pierre?"

"Five minutes."

"Hold on, brother," Thorne said, his hand on Kerrick's shoulder.

Kerrick nodded, but his breaths were shallow, his skin clammy, so very pale.

Alison glanced at Horace. The healer's face dripped with perspiration.

The sound of a distant siren allowed Alison to take her first real breath.

* * *

Marcus still held his bloodied sword at the ready. His gaze swept the rotunda, back and forth, back and forth. If a new attack came, he would be prepared and he could alert the others. His free arm was flexed, tight, tense, and he held it in back of Havily, protectively. Luken had long since joined the mass around Kerrick.

He glanced down at Havily, who stood next to him, one arm wrapped around her stomach. She held her fingers against her mouth as she looked at Kerrick. Tears drenched her eyes. "He saved us," she said, her voice trembling. "All three of us."

"Yes, he did." Bastard. Now he owed him one.

Emergency techs entered the building on a run, a gurney with them, even a doctor in tow who shot orders left and right. Kerrick's arms were hooked up in lightning speed to bags of blood and clear bags that contained who the hell knew what. Again with preternatural speed the team streaked in the direction of the ramps leading outside. Alison and Thorne both went with them.

Havily turned toward him. "I wanted to thank you, Warrior Marcus. I would have died here tonight without your protection. I am . . . most grateful."

Marcus looked into light green eyes and felt his soul drift into dangerous territory. He had been avoiding this moment from the first time he arrived on Second and caught her honeysuckle scent in Endelle's office. He had never wanted to be this close to her but here she was addressing him, her lips parted, her eyes shimmering with tears. She shook and he did the only thing that made sense—he folded his sword to the bedroom he used in Thorne's house then slid an arm around her shoulders. He pulled her against him, letting the warmth of his large male body comfort her.

He had kept her safe. Just as Luken had, but she hadn't turned to Luken. She had turned to him.

Oh, shit, she felt incredibly right in his arms. His bold vampire nature lit up, like a switch thrown at a baseball stadium. This was his *breh*. She belonged to him, to no one else.

No one else.

He felt her fingers slide just beneath the front of his weapons harness, curling around the leather, holding on. She trembled. She drew back and looked into his eyes. His gaze fell to her lips and a completely improper idea took shape, one he couldn't seem to resist.

He leaned closer to her until his lips found her mouth. When she didn't retreat, he pressed and licked, he pushed seeking possession, demanding admittance.

He pushed again.

Her lips parted. He thrust his tongue deep, staking out the territory of her mouth.

His arm snaked farther around her waist and conscious thought, choices, decisions began to disappear. His ascended nature and his vampire aggression took over. The beast in him awoke, slowly at first but gaining speed in quick measures.

Growls poured from his throat. Soft moans returned from the woman, hungry sounds that cranked him up. He started forcing her back, through a doorway leading to another rotunda, this one dark and private.

Back and back he pushed her. A soft mewling sound bled from her throat. Deeper into the room he shoved her. With his right thigh between her legs, he lifted her up with each step he took until at last her back hit a solid surface, a wall.

Once he pressed his body up against hers, a wild frenzy took hold of him with only one thought in his brain—he had to get inside her, push his cock in deep, make her his.

She panted against his neck, willing, so willing. Her fingers tore at his harness. His hands tugged at her dress. He caught the fabric up around her waist. He ripped her thong to pieces. He reached for her leg. Oh, God, he was almost there.

Suddenly he flew away from her and fists pummeled him. She screamed. Oh, God, his woman must be in trouble. He had to get to her, to protect her.

He fought hard, punching at whatever body got close and he had just enough awareness to know that more than one warrior pulled at him and hit him.

"No, Luken, don't!" she shouted. "Medichi, stop!"

Luken must be hurting her and what the hell was Medichi doing? Growls erupted from his throat. He saw only red.

Distant phrases flew over his hearing: *What the hell happened? Keep him away from her! He's out of his mind.*

He pushed at the arms and legs now pinning him. He had to get to Havily, to keep her safe, to take her back to his home, to Bainbridge, to his bedroom. He had to keep her there, with him, guard her, protect her.

He shoved a body off him. He caught sight of her, a wildness in her eyes as Jean-Pierre held her back. He would kill Jean-Pierre for touching her. He had to get to her. He crawled toward her now, dragging a massive body along with him. The creature on his back was so heavy. He tried to push him off but couldn't. He crawled a little more, his knees scraping over the marble, probably bleeding by now.

Something flipped him over then the last thing he saw was Luken's ham-like fist flying at his face. The last thing he heard was Medichi's voice crying out, "It must be the goddamn *breh-hedden*. Again. Holy shit! It's a fucking epidemic!"

Crace stood in the center of the Commander's peach orchard, his heart shriveled in his chest. Small moon-like lamps floated in the air, illuminating the freestanding patio. What had begun as a great adventure upon his initial arrival in Phoenix Two—indeed, what he had believed would be the most significant moment of his life—had essentially turned into a fucking nightmare, one that seemingly would never end . . . except perhaps now.

As he met his deity's gaze, he felt nothing, just a vast cold emptiness in his chest. He didn't even sweat.

"Why so despondent, brother ascender?" the Commander asked, a faint smile on his lips.

Yes, he supposed despondency had layered ice over his

sweat glands and emptied his heart and lungs of all sensation. So why the fuck did the Commander smile?

"Warrior Kerrick lives," he stated, reminding his deity why it was that a smile made no sense right now.

"Damn shame, of course. But look how close we got. I haven't been able to get that close . . . ever. Just once successfully, to Kerrick's wife and children, but that hardly counts."

Crace sighed. He knew he was going to die. He'd failed his deity time after time over the past three days. His execution stood in the wings, waiting for the Commander's pleasure.

"I must say," the Commander said, his hands clasped behind his back, his eyes narrowed. "I believe this experience has been very good for you. I think you've grown. When you arrived, you were so glib, so sure the task would be simple. Frankly, I thought you a fool. But right now your mind has a proper attitude. Yes, I believe you've grown."

Crace held back another weighty sigh. "These are very kind words, master."

The Commander released his hands, turned, then sat down on one of the stone benches. "You must learn patience, my dear Crace, as I told you from the beginning. You must learn to take the long view of such things. I strive to remind myself that you are not even two centuries on Second Earth yet. A few more centuries, given the level of your powers, will do much to sharpen your abilities and give you a sense of peace within your life."

Much chance of a long view of anything.

"You are not sweating as you usually do."

"A man does not sweat when he's certain of death."

"Then you should always remain *certain of death,* my friend."

Crace now stood dead center of the orchard and of the patio. Commander Greaves was a man of subtlety and not easily read. However, Crace understood something right now. "You mean to keep me alive." He was absolutely shocked.

"You are still of much use to me. I would be foolish to dispense with so much acquired knowledge." He narrowed his eyes. "I had intended to end your *service* to me but I was and still am rather impressed with this last scheme you concocted. It should have worked. I believed it would. We were neither of us prepared for Kerrick's ability to survive. He shouldn't have but then Alison was involved and she is far too powerful." He shook his head. "You see, even I am surprised. And I am never surprised."

Hope floated to the surface of Crace's heart and eased the tight knot in his chest. He drew a real breath, the first since the ambulance had departed from Madame Endelle's palace. He'd been in the wings, waiting and watching, protected by the Commander's superior mist as he observed the work of the death vampires. When the most insidious part of his plan unfolded, when the newly created ascender actually fired on Warriors Luken and Marcus, he couldn't believe his luck. Even when Warrior Kerrick intervened and took the blast instead of the other three, he'd nearly revealed his position by shouting with triumph and joy. Then the worst had happened. Alison had brought Warrior Kerrick back to life. He still couldn't believe the bastard lived. The blast should have taken out all four ascenders. So much power among the warriors. No wonder the Commander aimed most of his effort at trying to bring down the Warriors of the Blood.

He offered a simple bow. "I am yours to command, my master, now and forever."

The Commander rose. "Ah, I simply adore your manners, quite perfection. I believe Julianna has taught you well." He took Crace's arm and wrapped it about his own. "But come, we have plans to make. Unfortunately, it would seem the gods have for the moment favored the Guardians of Ascension—but the tide always turns, and that, my dear Crace, is the real nature of life—the tide always turns. We just need to give it a loving nudge. In the meantime, I fear we have another ascension to prepare for. My Seers have been very busy. This time a mortal with wings."

Crace stopped walking. "A mortal with wings? But . . . that's impossible."

Greaves fell still. "The very same thing I said about Alison when I learned of the extent of her abilities. But come, let us see Harding. He will desire sustenance by now as well as a reason to overlook our little invasion of Endelle's palace. And if you like, you shall have sustenance as well."

Crace shuddered.

Yes, he would like sustenance.

Yes, indeed.

A good friend speaks what no one dares to say.

—*Collected Proverbs*, Beatrice of Fourth

CHAPTER 22

Alison cut the tags off a new silk blouse, a green blouse she had purchased earlier at a pricey Scottsdale Two shop. She had worn a similar blouse the night she had first met Kerrick, the night she had been introduced to the world of ascension, to the world of the vampire.

A sob caught in her chest. She willed away the spasms yet the tears remained. They fell, streamed, ran down her face. Her nose was a mess. She kept blowing her nose, shaking her head, cutting off tags.

She had erred and she didn't know how to make things right, how to move forward.

Havily had let her stay in her town house, in the spare room, just as she had once promised. Alison had needed new clothes, so she had gone shopping. Such a normal thing to do, especially after she had almost killed her boyfriend.

Her throat hurt. More tears splashed all around the bedroom.

Three days had passed. She had spent three days at the hospital, chained to Kerrick's bed, willing him to get better hour by hour, even after the chance of his dying had long since passed. She had willed his healing to improve, she had begged Horace to come to the hospital and use his healing powers, she had consulted with the surgeons, she had gone to the hospital chapel and begged the Creator to speed his healing, to make him well, to make things right, to erase the past, demolish the night of her ascension celebration, to forgive her, forgive her, forgive her.

Kerrick would live. After taking a hand-blast to the abdomen, he had come back from the dead. He'd survived surgery. He would live to fight another day.

Now she bent over a pair of DKNY jeans, her favorite. Tears plopped, darkening the denim in grief-stricken polka dots. She cut off more tags. She hiccuped as she straightened. She folded the jeans over a hanger. She shoved the hanger into the closet. Looked at all the new clothes. She whipped around and folded more tissues from the box in the bathroom. She sounded a horn with her nose and wiped. She wiped some more.

Kerrick had almost died.

The thought broke her. She dropped to the carpet between a double bed and mirrored closet doors. Great rolling sobs charged out of her body. Heavy waves of grief and regret punched the air.

What a fool she had been to have thought Second Earth would be different for her.

Havily appeared in the doorway. She rushed forward and called to her in a sweet repetitive flow of words, "No, no, no, no, no." She dropped beside her and surrounded her with her arms. "Don't cry, ascender. Don't cry. He lives."

"I almost killed him. I almost killed him."

"He lives."

"He died."

"You brought him back."

Alison rocked.

Havily rocked with her, whispering tender words in her ear, "He lives, he lives, he lives."

Alison hiccuped again. She honked into the tissues. She rocked a little more. She shifted toward Havily and met her gaze. "I can't be with him, can I?"

"Of course you can."

"No, I can't. I have too much power. I should have known. I should have known."

Havily folded a fresh tissue from the bathroom and wiped Alison's cheeks. She thought, *I feel this way, too, like I could fall on my face and sob like a baby.*

She shouldn't feel so desolate, not after what happened, not after Marcus had morphed into a crazed beast, not after he'd tried to have his way with her against the wall of the third rotunda of Madame Endelle's palace, right in front of the Creator and everyone.

She didn't understand her attraction to the man at all. He was the antithesis of what she desired for her life. She wanted a man who felt as passionately about Second Earth as she did, about desiring to make a significant contribution to the improvement of society and certainly to the ending of the war.

Warrior Marcus—and surely he didn't deserve the appellation *warrior*—knew little of selflessness. He had only aided the warriors by order of the Supreme High Administrator.

No. Warrior Marcus was not worth even one thought, let alone the thousand she had spent on him since she had first caught his fennel scent at the Cave.

Now he was gone. He'd returned to Mortal Earth for good.

Tears fell from her eyes, soft streams of incomprehension.

"I've made you cry," Alison wailed, her sobs coming harder.

Maybe weeping was infectious. The trouble was, Havily

didn't understand the source of her anguish except she kept remembering Marcus, weighed down by Luken's mountain of a warrior body, his arms shaking as he crawled toward her, trying to get to her. He kept calling out, *Havily, I'm coming. I'll protect you.*

The tears flowed faster, harder.

Marcus had left late that night, after Horace had healed him, after he had begged the warriors to forgive him for his unconscionable behavior. He hadn't even come to see her, not even to apologize . . . although, she hadn't wanted, expected, or needed an apology because she had been an oh-so-willing participant in his I-must-have-you-now assault.

She folded more tissues from the bathroom. She handed over a little stack but kept a similar thick wad for herself. She blew her nose.

When Marcus had pinned her against the wall, she hadn't been frightened, not in the least. Surprised, maybe. Hungry for him . . . oh, God, *yes,* so hungry.

Maybe she'd been celibate too long. After all, she hadn't looked at another man, hadn't been remotely interested, in fifteen years. Her mission had consumed her waking hours. The belief she could make a difference in the war through administrative restructuring had replaced romantic love, had become her raison d'être, her purpose, her lifeblood. She didn't need love. She didn't want love. Truly.

Then Marcus had come and in three days, he had shattered the simplicity of her life and all because *she wanted him.* She wanted him with a ferocity that now commanded even her dreams.

So she wept.

Kerrick reclined in his hospital bed. He detested being stuck in the sterile environment because it spoke of weakness and vulnerability, two things a warrior could never be. Worse, he'd had time to think.

His abdomen still caused him tremendous pain even though surgery as well as Horace's help had speeded up what on Mortal Earth would have been months of recovery and a plethora of scarring. Ascended vampire healing would allow him to leave the hospital in three or four more days almost good as new.

He lifted his left hand carefully and shoved it through his long loose hair. He took a careful breath. Damn. Even breathing caused him trouble. He had never been wounded like this before.

Alison had been with him every day. Her presence had been necessary, even critical for his recovery. This morning, however, he'd awakened with new thoughts, horrifying thoughts, the revisiting of past tragedies, of deep painful regrets, deeds he still wished undone.

Former wives came to mind, former children. He hurt all over again as though life had just strapped a band around his chest and kept tightening it as the hours progressed.

As for Alison, his thoughts weren't focused on the mistake she had made, on the hand-blast she had sent that had almost cost him his life. No, when he thought back to her celebration, all he could recall was the terrible sensation of battling in full-mount with his *breh* at his back and knowing how one wrong slip of his sword would take her life, that if he didn't make every right move, if he took one wrong step to the right or to the left while battling the death vamps, she would be struck down and most likely killed.

He didn't blame Alison for what happened after that. He knew who to blame, that bastard who had styled himself *the Commander* simply because he wished it so.

As attacks went, this one had been damn clever. Greaves had fed Alison a vision and she'd bought it. Clearly his intention hadn't been to harm her but to use her, which once more forced the issue of proximity. Since she was ascended and had completed her rite, she was now safe from direct attack, but not from collateral damage should she remain connected to him or to any of the Warriors of the Blood.

The oh-so-logical conclusion barreled down on him

Ever since COPASS had been created and the rule of law was established over the ongoing conflict between Endelle and Greaves, no ascendiate, however powerful, had been attacked after an ascension ceremony. So this attack hadn't been about Alison. She'd merely been the tool Greaves had chosen to use to once more take up arms against the Warriors of the Blood.

What had he been thinking? The truth was, his thoughts had been selfish, focused on his pleasure, his need for Alison, his desire for her. Bottom line? He'd been keeping himself in a powerful state of denial about his current position as a Warrior of the Blood.

And now they were having a daughter.

He closed his eyes and drew in a deep breath. The near-fatal accident, Alison's hand-blast to his chest, had become a huge awakening to the folly he had almost committed with her.

He'd been living in a dream, pretending Second Earth was something other than what it was, as though his life as a warrior, his place of service, wasn't the difficult dangerous task it was.

Yes, being in the hospital, bedridden so his internal organs could continue repairing at light speed, had given him time to think, to plan, and that plan didn't include Alison being anywhere near him.

There was only one reason he didn't embrace the idea fully—the thought of living without her plunged a knife straight through his heart. How was he to live in a world in which he couldn't be with her, touch her, possess the well of her body?

From this point forward, however, her safety, as well as the safety of their child, could be the only consideration. And they would never be safe near him.

A knock on the door, then Alison entered his room. She wore a light green silk blouse. She had worn something similar the evening he had first met her at the medical complex and, yeah, her hair was bound up again, wrapped into that tight twist. How long ago was that? Years ago . . .

She looked so beautiful yet so sad. Her eyes were red-rimmed and her nose looked a little swollen. The pressure on his chest increased incrementally with each step she took toward him.

"Hi," she said, her voice little more than a breathy whisper. She drew close, leaned over him, and kissed him . . . *on the forehead*.

He shifted his head and met her gaze. Dammit, she had tears swimming over her blue, gold-rimmed eyes. "What's wrong? The baby okay?"

She touched her abdomen. "Baby's fine."

He released a sigh. "Good. That's good."

She drew a chair forward, close to the bed, as was her habit. She sat down and took hold of his right hand. Tears now pelted her cheeks. She kept wiping them away with her free hand but more followed.

"Alison, what's wrong?" He thought he knew. Well, they were like-minded. He knew her mind. She knew his. Yeah, he knew.

She lifted her gaze to his. "We can't do this, can we?"

So she'd reached the same damn conclusion. He shook his head back and forth, back and forth. His throat tightened. "I don't see how."

She nodded and a sob escaped her as she put her forehead on the back of his hand.

"Don't cry." Stupid words, especially since his eyes burned and his jaw cramped.

He let her be and worked hard to unknot his throat. After a while, she rose and plucked several of the very thin hospital tissues from the box by his bed then blew her nose. Even with her eyes leaking and a cloud of tissue pressed to her face she looked so damn beautiful.

Once recovered, she said, "I've been thinking that perhaps I should go somewhere else, not stay here in Phoenix, maybe live in a different city."

"Another city?"

She turned toward him and huffed a breath. "Just how easy do you think it would be to stay apart if we lived in the same place?"

He looked away from her. "It would be impossible. But where would you go?" Would he ever get to see his daughter? If so, how often? How the hell could this work? Yet he knew she was right. From this point forward, he was the real danger to their safety, just as he had been to Helena.

Still, the thought of Alison anywhere but next to him made his biceps crunch into boulders. His instincts where she was concerned were alive, painfully so.

"What the fuck are you talking about?" a hard feminine voice bellowed into the room. "Another city, Alison? Don't be a saphead."

Kerrick turned toward the door. Endelle materialized wearing a very strange cape made of peacock feathers and a short spotted hide dress. Add a few strands of beads and she would have looked as though she'd just returned from Mardi Gras. Christ.

She waved a sheaf of papers in the air. "Alison, you are to report to the Militia Warrior Training Camps, Female Division. Your CO will expect you tomorrow at eight o'clock sharp. All the information is here."

"What?" Alison cried.

"She's not a warrior!" Kerrick shouted. He had moved, jerking forward, but oh dear God that was so the wrong thing to do given his recent surgery. He settled back against the pillows and groaned . . . loud. Sweat broke out all over his body. He struggled to breathe as pain shot through his stitched-up organs and muscles as though someone had fired up a flamethrower and turned it on high. Christ almighty. Obscenities a mile long flowed through his head.

"You were saying?" Endelle murmured. She even laughed.

The bitch was back and apparently full of plans.

Endelle cut her gaze to Alison. "Your exceptional powers must be put to the best possible use. When properly trained, I know you'll be able to battle death vamps one-on-one, and with experience over the next several decades you might even be in charge of the facility; certainly you'll be training warriors by then. You do know about our Militia Warriors."

Alison's voice sounded faint, disbelieving. "They're sort of like the National Guard and a police force combined. But—"

Endelle cut her off. "Yeah, that's about right and you'll be one of them so no more discussion about leaving Phoenix Two. And for God's sake, no fucking whining! Oh, and congratulations on the baby. Good luck, ascender Wells." As she dematerialized, she tossed the papers in the air. They floated every which way, a couple of them landing on Kerrick's bed.

Alison gestured in the direction of Endelle's recent appearance. "What on earth was she wearing? The fur was bristled, kind of stiff. What was that?"

Kerrick shook his head. "I don't know. Hyena?"

Alison laughed but shortly afterward her expression fell. She planted her hands on her hips and shook her head over and over. Meeting his gaze, she said, "I can't believe she expects me to be a warrior. I'm about as fit to be a warrior as you are a . . . a . . . well, a hairdresser, for God's sake."

He let loose a bark of laughter, gasped as pain ignited once more, then clawed for air. "Don't . . . make me . . . laugh," he sputtered.

"Sorry. That wasn't meant to be funny but it kind of is." When she started to laugh again, he put a pillow over his abdomen and took more deep breaths.

Yeah, a woman—now a vampire—who could make him laugh. How the hell was he supposed to let her go?

The shared amusement didn't last long, however, and for the next hour, she sat beside the bed just holding his hand, not speaking, and once more making a serious effort to empty the tissue box.

Alison flew over White Lake. Euphoria kept her mind in a state of bliss, her heart fluttering in her chest, her fingertips tingling. She stretched out on the wind, her wings propelling her forward in deep pulls.

Flight. Best creation ever.

As before, she dipped in the direction of the lake, dropped her legs, fluffed her wings into an almost parachute-like position, and slowly descended to the water. Her toes dipped in. The lake anchored her.

A tremendous yearning filled her chest, a longing so fierce she wanted to weep and shout and cry out. She looked up, straight up, and this time she saw a swirling blue vortex and beyond . . . oh, she could see beyond to a new world of white marble villas, some hanging among the clouds, a beautiful world.

Third Earth. Same geography. Different dimension.

The yearning increased. She tried to fly upward, but the lake had its hold on her, a powerful grip, which she could not break no matter how hard she tried.

The presence of others encouraged her, strengthened her. She took their hands. Together they formed a powerful chain until at last she began to rise. The hands dropped away. She flew straight up, into the swirling blue vortex, faster and faster.

"Not yet," a man's voice cried out, an unfamiliar voice. "You must wait a little while longer but you will be the instrument of breaking that which must be broken. In the fullness of time, all will be revealed."

Alison awoke, her eyes flipping open to the sight of another ceiling. Oh, the ceiling in Havily's spare room. She pressed a hand to her chest. The yearning remained, the longing for Third Earth. She had just arrived on Second. How could she already be feeling such things, all over again, for a different dimension?

Guardian drifted through her mind, in almost the same masculine voice as she had heard speaking in her dream.

She squeezed her eyes shut and took deep breaths. The dream had advanced. Others, though indistinguishable, had been in the dream, and this time she had flown toward the Trough, toward the blue spinning vortex that led to Third Earth. *To break that which must be broken.*

Here she was headed to the Female Militia Warrior Training Camp and still dreaming, even more forcefully, about Third Earth.

Just what the hell was she supposed to do with that?

"Fuck off." Kerrick glared at Jean-Pierre. Six days in the hospital had worn on his nerves and now his brother lounged in one of the chairs, his words designed to torment.

Jean-Pierre shrugged. "But if you do not want her, Kerrick"—his name sounded like *Karreek*—"I wish to court her. She's lovely and smells of the sea."

She smells of lavender you fucking idiot and there's no way in hell I'll let you near her.

He looked away from Jean-Pierre. "Why the fuck are you here?"

"To open your eyes, you motherless piece of shit." Again . . . *sheet.* But the women loved his accent. Would Alison?

He shuddered. He threw back the light covers then flipped his legs over the side of the hospital bed. He ached over his abdomen but he was well enough to get the hell out of bed and out of this sterile environment. He folded off the gown and with enough speed to keep Jean-Pierre from going blind, folded on a pair of jeans and a T-shirt.

He stood up, but staggered.

Jean-Pierre caught his arm. Kerrick shook it off. "So you came here to bust my balls over . . . ascender Wells."

"I came," he said, easing his voice over the English words, "to talk sense into that fat head of yours, *mon ami.*"

"Her decision as much as mine."

"She belongs to you, you must see that. She is your *breh* and she carries your child. Don't be so fucking stupid." *Stoopeed. "Très stupide. Idiot.* You love her, *non*?"

"Yes." Like rain to earth.

"But she will find someone else, *non*?"

"She should."

"Somone to raise *your* daughter, yes?"

"Again, fuck off, Jean-Pierre. You think I haven't had these thoughts?"

"I think you have not accepted your death, or hers. We all die, even in these ascended worlds. You have a chance to be happy. You should take it."

Kerrick turned toward him. "So why the fuck haven't *you* taken a wife, O wise French asshole?"

He shrugged. "I love all women. I could never love just one. I am not like you." He tossed a negligent arm as though that finished the discussion.

"You're so full of shit. You just wait, J.P. *She'll* come along and then you'll discover for yourself exactly what kind of hell this is and why you won't be able to be with her."

He braced his feet apart and started to walk. He pushed the door to his room open and ventured into the hall. The more steps he took, the stronger he felt. A squadron of nurses came running at him, squawking the whole time, but he moved past them. He had to get out of the hospital.

Jean-Pierre caught up with the gaggle of women in scrubs and before he knew it, the Gallic warrior had enthralled them all and led them away. He might in this moment hate J.P., but his brother still had his back.

He left by the front sliders and located his phone, then brought it without a thought into his hand. He called Central. "Hey, Jeannie."

"There's my man," she cried. "How the hell are you, *duhuro*?"

He smiled and his chest eased a little. "Couldn't be fucking better. Give me a lift to my house in Scottsdale Two."

"You got it. How's your spaghetti stomach?"

He looked down at his abdomen and patted the achy flesh, crisscrossed with fading scars. "More like lasagna now."

She laughed, which made him laugh, which made him grimace.

"Here ya go, Warrior Kerrick. Feel better."

He felt the vibration, that brief winking out then flashing back in, and he stood in the entry of his home gasping in pain.

Oh, fuck. He shouldn't have dematerialized so soon. *Holy mother of God.* He struggled to breathe as his cells settled back down, but again it was like someone was holding a blowtorch to the inside of his body. Shit. Only after several minutes did he dare move, and he still hadn't taken a deep breath.

He remained in place and looked around, at the expansive living room off to the right, full of oversized furniture, the kind meant to fit warrior bodies. He glanced to his left, to the massive library he'd built book by book for centuries. In front of him the formal, curved, wood-paneled staircase, which led to his bedroom, the one he hadn't used in two centuries.

He glanced at the door leading to his basement. He repressed a sigh.

Without thinking too much, he moved forward and one step at a time, climbed the stairs, his abdomen screaming by the time he reached the landing at the top. He turned to the right, moved down the hall to the double doors, left wide. Beyond was the master suite where he had lived with Helena all those years ago.

Once in the bedroom, everything was as he remembered: the enormous, four-poster bed, also built for his supersized body and meant for maneuverability. He'd maneuvered over Helena's body and she'd loved it. His heart ached now, as much for her as for the absence of Alison at his side.

He passed by the bed, moving to the tall arched window at least fifteen feet in height. The rolling mansion grounds stretched a good quarter mile beyond. He looked down. Lawn traveled forever, trees brought in from all over the world, and flowers everywhere. Toward the back, mounds of honeysuckle covered a ten-foot wall, both sides. He could hear the chattering of the shrub birds from where he stood.

Helena had insisted on a garden. *If we must live in the desert, we will transform the desert.* She had been a trouper, a real warrior's wife. But then her brother was a warrior, so she understood their world well, she knew the dangers, she had accepted them, she had laughed at Kerrick's concerns.

Then she had died.

He drew in a deep breath, one hand planted on his abdomen to keep things from moving while he breathed. Helena had never made promises, had she? She'd never spoken in terms of years. She had adhered to what became AA's watchphrase, *One day at a time.* She had asked for nothing more.

But he had never believed her. Yet now, as he thought of her, he knew she truly hadn't asked more than *one day* of him, ever, that she'd understood from the beginning the risk, accepted the risk, and lived full-throttle despite the terrible reality of his job.

And she'd paid for it. So had his children.

Now he had another child on the way, a daughter this time. What would Alison name her? he wondered. Would he ever get to see her? Would she have Alison's blue eyes? Her soft blond hair? Her deep empathy? Her ability to throw a hand-blast that could cross dimensions, or shred a warrior's abdomen?

He wanted to know. He needed to know.

His chest felt crushed now as he stared out at the quiet property.

A singular question surfaced. He hadn't been in this bedroom for almost two centuries. Now he was here.

Why?

Two weeks into her training program, Alison entered the showers at her barracks. She rinsed off the two inches of dust she'd accumulated in the course of the day's field training. Her lungs felt clogged. She blew her nose a dozen times trying to get rid of all the powdery dirt lodged in her sinuses.

She wished more than anything she could call her sister and talk everything over with her. Joy had been her friend, her confidante, yes, even her counselor, for well over a decade despite the fact that six years separated them. However, phone calls to Mortal Earth weren't allowed without special permission and right now her CO wouldn't see her. For some reason the woman was tense, even anxious about her presence at the camps, but she didn't know why. In time Alison was certain she could work everything out, but right now that meant she couldn't talk to Joy and get the comfort and relief she really needed. Besides, if much more time passed, her sister would start to get worried that maybe she'd gotten kidnapped during her made-up trip to Mexico.

Whatever.

At least the shower eased her. Though she had entered the program physically fit, the rigors of the military training left her muscles on fire at the end of each day.

She had stayed on the field an hour past the time the last trainee headed to the showers. She needed some alone time, away from the jockeying-for-toughest-bitch-position that went on constantly. She hated the strife, and her nerves had reached a snapping point. She feared she'd end up on overload, release too much of her power, and send one of these macho females to perdition.

The water beat on her head and neck, all across her shoulders in a blissful pounding. As some of her tension disappeared, she became aware of a dragging sensation in her chest, as though gravity had doubled its hold on her heart.

She missed Kerrick so much, more than she had thought possible. Only fourteen days had passed, but her loneliness had become a series of tsunamis that kept swamping her. She wept silent tears into her pillow at night. She smelled cardamom in her dreams.

How was she going to endure this separation?

She turned into the water and let it stream down on her head. Tears joined the flow. She pressed a hand to her lower abdomen, aware, as she always was now, of the life inside her. She wanted her baby to have a father, to grow up as she had grown up beneath the love, care, and affection of two parents. The tears flowed harder, faster for a long time, until at last she could draw breath and not want to fall to the wet tiles and sob her heart out.

Shutting off the water, she toweled dry then dressed in clean green fatigues and socks. She stretched out on her cot and put her hands behind her head. It felt so good to lie down, and she had a lot to think about, to process.

She knew one thing. She couldn't continue as she was, so painfully heartbroken every night. Something had to change.

As she considered her situation, a seed of resistance began to grow, built of anger and grief, forged perhaps in memories of having fought Leto in the Tolleson arena. What was the point of having endured such a tremendous contest only to end up alone, at the training camps, and weeping?

Somehow the two concepts did not mix.

What was the point of so much power, of having ascended with the same level of ability Endelle had possessed upon her ascension, but to be trapped in a training program for which she knew she was fundamentally unsuited?

Was this truly all her ascended life would be? How was this any better than her cloistered existence on Mortal Earth? The result was exactly the same—she was essentially alone, as she had been all her life. She was still holding back her powers and trying not to hurt anyone, just as she had on Mortal Earth, and she was still living a constrained, frustrating, not-built-for-her existence, dammit.

What was she doing training to be a warrior anyway? She had no heart for this form of service. She never would. In this profession she would be a shade-loving fern expected to thrive beneath a desert sun.

Worse than that, however, she was sick at heart. She hadn't seen Kerrick for two weeks now but instead of the separation getting easier, it had gotten harder.

When she had split from Kerrick at the hospital, she hadn't expected to feel so much, to feel as though her heart had been torn in the process and just continued to bleed, refusing to be healed. She loved him, yes. She'd slept with him, well, a lot. He'd gotten her very pregnant. But she'd only known him three days. Surely she wasn't that attached.

Hah.

Her love for him possessed her, and the deep sharing of minds possible only on Second had changed everything because she knew Kerrick.

She *knew* him.

She. Knew. Him.

Mind-diving had given her so much understanding of his essential noble warrior character as well as knowledge of his life. For that reason half the pain she felt when she thought of him was also a projected pain based on how she knew he would be feeling right now, separated as he was from her.

Kerrick had known what it was to love well and to love deeply. He fit the model of a man or woman who had been happily married once and was much more likely to want to marry again. He'd known two fine marriages. She'd lived those marriages with him when she'd been within his mind. Even now when she thought of his first wife, Marta, and his second wife, Helena, she had great affection and appreciation for these women because they had each given Kerrick great pleasure, deep satisfaction, and tremendous relief from the struggles and pressures of life.

Knowing especially of Helena's sacrifices, she kept asking herself the tough question: Was she doing the right thing in separating herself from Kerrick?

Part of her, the old part, the part that had grown up on Mortal Earth essentially separated from society, felt certain this was the right path, because it was how she had always lived. But there was another part, a new part, a new inner eye, that kept nagging at her, kept asking the question—*Do you still intend to live through your fears alone?*

But the consequence of making a mistake—like the one she had made at Endelle's palace—was, simply, death. So how could she justify being close to Kerrick, ever, when she had so much power, which had already once almost taken his life?

The answer was—she couldn't!

Her thoughts turned to Kerrick's second wife, Helena. She had seen this woman through Kerrick's eyes, the love he had for her, his devotion to her, and his admiration of her.

She smiled when she thought of Helena. She could see the arguments she'd had with Kerrick. She played them through her mind, how he had refused for years to be wedded to her, but how Helena in the end had prevailed. *A stalwart woman, a woman unafraid of life.* Though she understood the risks of marriage to a Warrior of the Blood, she had insisted on marrying him anyway.

In all those arguments, Helena had never once said something like, *Our love will prevail.* Her arguments instead had addressed the reality of his situation: *I refuse to live in fear, not now, not ever. You are what I want and I accept all the risks inherent in your warrior life.*

What would it be like to live with such courage, such fearlessness?

The arena battle once more came to mind. If she could survive something so horrendous as battling Leto *mano a mano,* why couldn't she survive whatever else Darian threw at her?

But maybe that was the wrong question to ask.

And in that moment, the heavens parted and Alison finally understood the real question she needed to ask herself. No one knew the number of their days, but wouldn't it be better to live full-out, to ride the hurricane, however frightening, than to continue to retreat into a pit of despair?

Her heart rate sped up. She rose to a sitting position. She drew a deep breath and the fatigue of the day's workout fled her.

Wouldn't it be better to ride the hurricane?

The imagery shot adrenaline full-blast through her system—but at almost the same moment, a strange sensation gripped her as the hairs at the nape of her neck stood up. She recalled the same prickling awareness at Endelle's palace right before the attack.

Like the warriors, she didn't wait for further enlightenment. She leaped to a standing position and drew her identified sword into her hand, all the way from the guest room in Kerrick's Queen Creek house, right where she had left it.

She felt a quickening down both sides of her back and instinctively knew she felt what would one day be her winglocks, although Kerrick had assured her she probably wouldn't be able to mount wings for at least a year.

A moment more and three death vamps, all in full-mount glossy black wings, blurred into the long-empty barracks.

Alison folded to a distant corner of the ceiling. She couldn't fly yet, but she could levitate.

At first the pretty-boys were confused, but when they saw her location, they launched as one. She was unsure of her ability to fight them all, so without dwelling on the why of it too much she folded directly to the Cave, straight into the middle of the room. Fortunately, three of the warriors were present—Luken, Medichi, and Santiago.

She called out, "Death vamps," in a loud voice. She took up her position, assuming the warrior's stance, legs apart, hands together on the leather-wrapped grip, sword upright.

Surprise registered first, then a quick gathering of wits and weapons.

A few seconds later, as the death vamps followed her trace, she simply moved out of the way and let the men get down to business.

The battle lasted only a matter of seconds. Three seasoned powerful warriors against three pretty-boys gave the death vampires odds of about a million-to-one they'd live.

They didn't.

Medichi called Central for cleanup.

Alison stood nearby, shaking. She was officially AWOL, and though she should return and even prepared to fold, Medichi caught her arm and shook his head. "Stay, ascender

Wells. Tell us what happened. My guess is you'll be in danger if you return."

She nodded because she suspected he was right. Who knew what waited for her back at the barracks? She had been assured that once she ascended the attacks would end. Both Kerrick and Endelle had been wrong.

She related that she'd stayed behind to be alone for a while. She touched her stomach absently. "Then I got that *feeling,* that creepy sensation that a spider was on my neck."

All three warriors grumbled their understanding.

"The next thing I knew, there they were."

"In the barracks?" Medichi cried. "Armed?"

"And in full-mount. I knew I couldn't fight them myself and I didn't know what else to do so I folded here. I was afraid if I led them anywhere else on the base I'd be putting a lot of women in jeopardy. I'm so sorry."

"Goddammit, don't apologize," Medichi cried. "You did the right thing, but shit this is so fucked up. Death vamps hunting down an ascender at a training facility . . ."

Alison frowned. "So I'm right in that they shouldn't have been attacking me at the barracks—that this isn't *normal.*"

"Not even a little. You're an ascender now, and this attack is highly illegal. Endelle can take this to COPASS and the Committee will be forced to act against Greaves. The bastard doesn't own all of them yet." He started pacing then muttered, "Although it doesn't mean you won't be attacked again. Shit, we've gotta get Kerrick in on this, and Thorne. Hell, all the brothers should be here. Let's give Jean-Pierre and Zach a shout as well."

Kerrick. Oh, no. "Are you sure this is necessary? Do you really need to bring Kerrick here?" Oh, God, how much she wanted to see him.

If her heart was pounding before, now it slammed around in her chest.

Medichi drew close, his eyes full of compassion. "I'm sorry, Alison, but he'd have our balls if we didn't. So take pity on the three of us."

She glanced from Medichi to Luken to Santiago. She

nodded. She released her sword back to Kerrick's guest room. The memories from her time in his house flowed over her in sudden painful waves. Her throat tightened.

She waited, her heart hammering away. She smoothed back her still-damp hair. She had no idea what she looked like. What would she do if she saw him again? More importantly, if she had more courage, like Helena, could she have a life with him? Would her daughter then be able to really know her father?

Change comes,
But only when the heart has been shaped by suffering.

—*Collected Proverbs,* Beatrice of Fourth

CHAPTER 23

Kerrick hadn't seen Alison in two long fucking weeks and he swore he felt like he'd had his heart ripped out of his chest. Instead of getting easier, staying away from her had become an exercise in masochism. He knew where she was—the training camps. He received reports from her CO daily. He'd insisted on at least that much. She was carrying his child. He needed to be sure she was safe despite the fact they could not be together.

So why did he feel like a bastard, like he'd let her down?

He sat in his library, a tumbler of Maker's in his hand. He stared at nothing in particular. He had a couple of hours before the night's fighting took up his time—and thank God for the fighting. He would have gone insane otherwise.

Two weeks had passed since he had last seen her and he just couldn't seem to find his feet. He recalled the last time he'd sat in this chair, reading that pretentious book about the history of ascension in hopes of finding some way to withstand the onslaught of the *breh-hedden*.

His phone buzzed. He reached out with his senses—Medichi. The brothers were at the Cave, and he'd already refused to join them there. He'd be at the Blood and Bite for the usual, but right now he needed to be alone.

Since returning from the hospital, he'd moved out of the basement, using it only to do his daily workout. For reasons he didn't understand, he'd been sleeping in the master bedroom. He still wasn't sure why he'd made that leap. After all, nothing had changed materially in his world.

Except Alison.

But she wasn't in his world anymore, was she?

And his baby grew inside her.

But what did that matter? They'd both decided they couldn't be together, a joint decision.

Fine.

His phone buzzed again. Once more—Medichi.

Once more, he didn't respond.

But when the phone buzzed a third time, he felt Thorne's summons. He stood up and answered. The few brief sentences that struck his ear sent blood rushing to his head, his heart thumping. "Fold me there now."

He felt the vibration then landed hard, two bare feet on the Cave floor. He ignored all six warriors, spinning around until he found the only person right now who mattered.

"Alison! What the hell happened?"

She stared at him and her lips parted but she couldn't seem to speak. Then a wave of lavender hit him full in the chest and he took a step back. Oh, shit. He squeezed his eyes shut and rubbed a hand down his face, holding back his body's quick response as much as he could. He barked, "Tell me what happened."

She spoke slowly at first as she recounted the attack at the barracks then gathered speed and finished with, "I thought it might be sensible to lead them here, believing of course they would follow, and sure enough—"

"Goddammit." He turned to Thorne and met his wrecked gaze. "Has Endelle been informed?"

"She's coming."

"Good. Because this can't happen again." His voice had split into three resonances and all the warriors shifted around, staring at him.

"I won't let it happen again." He gave a frustrated shout and punched at the air. "This is such fucking bullshit."

A mumbled agreement rippled through the brothers.

He paced now and breathed hard. He couldn't look at Alison but her smell was intoxicating; if he didn't keep moving he'd throw a whole lot of wood and probably attack her. If her scent was any indication, she'd welcome it. Goddamn *breh-hedden*.

Alison could barely draw breath as she stared at *her* warrior. He walked around like a madman but looked so damn sexy in jeans, a snug dark blue tee, and, oh, God, his gorgeous bare feet again. It had to be the pregnancy hormones because the way she felt looking at him was like everything she'd ever felt for him, multiplied by ten. No. By a thousand.

Her body wept and she knew she had to be flooding him with her designed-just-for-him lavender pheromones, but she couldn't help it.

Her lips felt swollen and her breasts, which were already bigger because of the pregnancy, were tight in her bra. At least the loose fatigues couldn't reveal anything of that nature to the other warriors around her, thank God.

The air blurred near Kerrick and he stopped pacing. Endelle appeared, a hard look in her ancient, lined eyes. She wore a strange bodysuit in some kind of shiny gray material, not quite leather. "What the hell is going on?" She caught sight of Alison. "Ascender Wells, why the fuck aren't you at the training camps as ordered?"

Thorne, however, cut in and told her about the death vamps, then added, "You know what this means—she can't go back. They've obviously made the decision to *remove* her. This won't be the last attack. Her ascension was just the beginning, not the end."

Kerrick moved to stand beside Thorne, his gaze fixed anywhere but on Alison.

This time Endelle paced. She let fly a long string of expletives, then started over. She repeated the exercise several times. "He's never gone this far before. Why this rule? Why now? Why Alison? Shit. He must know I'll take the complaint to COPASS. Shit."

Alison, however, barely paid her the smallest bit of attention. Instead she couldn't keep from staring at Kerrick. She was struck all over again by how handsome he was, how tall, how muscular. His warrior hair was unbound and she wanted to weave thick bunches through her fingers. And she knew those muscles, every last inch of them, stem-to-stern, upside down, downside up. Oh. God.

"Ascender Wells," Endelle snapped. "Look at me."

The strength of Endelle's voice forced Alison to tear her gaze away from Kerrick and focus on the Supreme High Administrator.

Endelle narrowed her eyes. "We'll put a guard on you at the training camps. The next time death vamps show up, don't go running to my elite group. We have a chain of command in the military. Use it."

A general disapproval and protest erupted from every warrior present.

Alison cried, "But how many Militia Warriors will die trying to protect me? The situation is untenable and I won't have it."

A collective intake of breath joined another shuffling of feet. "*You* won't have it?" Madame Endelle shouted.

Alison was about to state her case, this time in definitely more respectful terms, but she found herself facedown on the Cave floor, never a good place to be, and a foot, encased in a stiletto, on her neck. "Learn your place, ascender Wells. Learn it quick. I have a very short fuse."

Alison felt the vibration and found herself in the CO's office at the training base. She was still facedown but the pressure on her neck was gone.

She looked up. She was alone. Oh. God. Still on her knees, she leaned back. She reached out to Queen Creek and once more drew her sword into her hand. She listened and waited. She knew exactly what was going to happen next and not because of her clairvoyance.

By the time the CO and Madame Endelle appeared, maybe thirty seconds later, so did three more pretty-boys. They didn't stay long, however. One look at Madame Endelle and all three vanished.

"Fuck," Endelle said. She looked at Alison. "Looks like Thorne was right. Well, isn't this a new kind of shitfest. I guess the fun with you is just beginning."

As soon as Alison dematerialized from the Cave, Kerrick had Thorne fold him back to his home. He headed straight for his bedroom and with a thought removed his clothes. Making a beeline to the shower, he hopped in and flipped the levers, all eight of them, and took an incredibly cold shower. He felt as though lavender had been imprinted on his sinuses and brain and he couldn't get rid of the scent. And he was hard as a rock.

Shit.

What the hell was he going to do?

The cold water beat at him, but his skin was on fire. He wondered why steam didn't rise out of the shower despite the water's arctic temp. If only he hadn't been in the same room with Alison. Desire just kept spreading through his body and all he could smell was lavender, lavender, and more lavender.

When at long last, some of his painful desire had diminished, he turned off the shower, then ran his towel over the two million goose bumps afflicting his skin. Goddamn that water was cold. He let loose one full-body shiver then folded on flight gear for the night's work, adjusting the weapons harness.

He looked around the bedroom. He stared at the bed. He planted his hands on his hips. He narrowed his eyes.

He shook his head back and forth over and over.

He had made a mistake, goddammit. He had thought he could go back to the way things were before Alison had come into his life. He had thought he could simply renew his vows and ignore the desire he felt for her as well as the primitive protective urges that twisted his thoughts in her direction one minute out of two.

But something had changed in him beginning from the time he'd first seen her at the medical complex. Yes, the *breh-hedden* had hit him hard, taken him to his knees, but that wasn't what snagged him now. Something incomprehensible had hold of him. He knew he had erred in turning away from Alison but he couldn't figure out why.

He thought of Helena again. She had given her life to be with him. *I've chosen to be with you,* she had said. *It is my privilege, my pleasure, even my honor to be with you and bring peace to your life as you do to mine. You are my choice, for better or worse, come life or death.*

Come life or death.

Endelle had said, *Give Helena a little credit.*

When he had taken Alison's hand-blast to his chest and abdomen and begun recovering in the hospital, his natural instinct had been to retreat. After all, that was how he had lived for the past two hundred years. But throughout those centuries, he'd been a shell of a man, flying on nerves and Maker's, holding the line at the cost of dying a little each day.

He would always feel responsible for Helena's death. That was the nature of being a man, the inherent sense of responsibility to keep everyone alive, to keep everyone happy, satisfied.

He released a heavy sigh, the kind weighted with guilt, lots of it.

The question seemed to be: Was he thinking of Alison right now or thinking of himself? Did he truly fear that his proximity to her would cause her death or did he merely fear the agony of losing her should she die as a result of the Commander's aggression? Some of both, he supposed, but what was the right path in this situation? He longed to be with her, a longing that kept her in his dreams when he slept and in his thoughts when he was awake.

Now she faced a new situation. Against one of the prime laws of the land, Greaves had sent death vampires against her. Holy shit.

Thorne was right, the attacks on her would never stop. Her ascension was a beginning, not an ending, and Endelle was wrong to think three squads of Militia Warriors would do anything except cost lives, possibly even Alison's.

What came to him was his present need to let go of his guilt over what had happened in the past to both Marta and Helena and to all three of his children. Life was hard and had been from the beginning of time. Choices were made and, yeah, like Endelle had said, *Death happens.* One day in the future, he would die as well as Alison, even their daughter.

But no longer would he deny the simple truth, good or bad—that he belonged with Alison and he belonged with his daughter.

Alison's presence in his life had done this for him, forced him to take that extra step out of the confines of his present life and into . . . the future.

He laughed and shook his head. Goddammit, just seeing her had made him feel like more of a man, more powerful. How the hell was that possible? The *breh-hedden,* of course, calling to him in wild shouts from the edge of his tightly held life.

Only this time he didn't stop the sensation. He let it fill him, the physical intention, the pure sexual need, the whir-rings of his mind begging for Alison's presence inside his head.

He stood at the foot of his bed and pictured her lying naked right there, her long blond hair spread out over his pillows and sheets. He wanted her in his bed, in this bed, the bed he now slept in. He wanted her with him now and always.

Then he knew, then he understood that his life had changed completely, not just a little but in every possible way. He saw the future, how this was going to go down from this point forward, and why he intended to complete the *breh-hedden* with Alison. No way was his lovely therapist, built to help others, going to be subjected to fighting. Some women were built for war. She was built to save lives. He felt stronger in his spirit than ever before, determined, full of purpose.

Come hell or high water, come good times or bad, come life or death, he would be with Alison, he would love her, he would protect her to the extent he could, she would be his *breh* and he would serve her as he had from the moment he first met her, as her Guardian of Ascension.

He smiled, he laughed, he punched the air a few times, he gave one powerful shout to the heavens. No longer would he look back, but he would set his face to the future and live, really live.

He felt a strange low-level vibration in his body, something he had never felt before. He drew in a deep breath. *Holy shit.* Was it possible?

Hell, yeah, it was possible.

Tonight he began a new life, and sure as hell this was the way to start it.

He calmed himself down and pictured the library. He thought the goddamn righteous fucking thought. *The journey between lasted a rough second, maybe two, a dark ride through nether-space, a blanking-out then sudden hard awareness, a blinding rush of adrenaline followed by a blast of endorphins.*

He had folded himself to the library.

Praise be to the Creator, at long last he could fold.

He shook his head. He closed his eyes, thought another thought. He experienced another vibration of blood and bone. He opened his eyes. He was back in the master bedroom.

He laughed and shouted. He dematerialized about a dozen times. His fist pumped the air.

He could fold.

He. Could. Fold.

Goddammit, he could fold!

One last trip back to the master bedroom and his body stilled. The *why* of it became a big question in his mind, but somehow he already knew.

Alison was the *why* of it, the *why* of everything.

Now, how to tackle the problem that was Endelle?

Alison listened to her CO arguing with Madame Endelle about how many guards she would need to post, twenty-four/seven, to ward off a constant stream of tag-attacks like the one that had just taken place. Alison had risen from her kneeling position, her sword still in hand. She kept up a constant surveillance even though it was unlikely the death vamps would return, not with Her Supremeness around.

When the CO, a tall woman with broad shoulders, dipped her square chin, placed the tips of her fingers on the desk, and leaned toward Madame Endelle, Alison could have chewed the sudden tension streaking through the air. She half expected to find the CO on the floor, a stiletto at her neck, but for some reason Endelle allowed the aggression.

"But Madame Supreme High Administrator, what you suggest would mean suicide for those involved. With all due respect, ascender Wells is the only warrior I have on the entire base capable of battling even one death vampire, let alone three. You know the ratios required for regular Militia Warriors to defeat death vamps? Four-to-one in order to prevent a mortality rate at point of combat of less than twenty-five percent. Four of our soldiers to one death vamp . . . and some would still die. Ascender Wells would require a twelve-warrior detail around her at all times, and that's assuming only three pretty-boys show up. She is unmanageable for us. At the very least, she requires the protection of the Warriors of the Blood."

These facts, presented as they were by a woman of reason and authority, forced Alison to confront her situation in an entirely different light. Until this moment, she had assumed she could create a life for herself, *by herself,* on Second Earth. But that simply wasn't true.

Whether she liked it or not, she needed a lot of protection, not just for herself but for her daughter. She had no doubt that creating a child from Kerrick's DNA would also pose a threat to the Commander. From this point forward, she would need to live in a completely secure home and have access not just to Kerrick but to all the warriors just to stay alive.

She also pondered her earlier thoughts about a pressing need to live life full-out, to *ride the hurricane* instead of *retreating into a pit of despair.* She smiled as visions of a life with Kerrick suddenly shot through her mind.

She also thought of her repetitive dreams about White Lake, which had continued to present themselves every night since she had arrived at the barracks. They always ended the same, her toes in the water, her gaze fixed toward the Trough leading to Third Earth. This time a man's voice had entered the dream, an unfamiliar voice. She had wanted to open the Trough to Third but he had restrained her, telling her the time had not yet arrived.

The word *guardian* once more whispered through her mind in that same masculine voice.

Guardian.

Kerrick was a Guardian of Ascension, as were all the Warriors of the Blood.

"What the hell is the matter with you?"

Alison shifted her gaze to Endelle. "I'm sorry?"

"I can see inside your head. Why is the word *guardian* playing over and over like a stuck record?"

"I'm not sure."

"You know, you have a fucking active mind and it's bugging the shit out of me."

"Sorry to disturb," she said, but she smiled.

"And would you kindly take that dumb-ass look off your face?"

Alison shook her head. "This, training to be a warrior, is not the right path for me."

"And you think you know what the right path is?"

Alison nodded. "Yes." She spoke the word with such certainty that Endelle stared at her. Alison pressed, "I think we should return to the Cave, and if you would summon the Warriors of the Blood, I will explain myself. Please hear me out in the presence of the warriors, and if after you've listened to all that I have to say and you still want me back at the barracks, I'll return willingly."

"Fine. Whatever."

Endelle folded her phone into her hand and whipped it to her ear. "Thorne. Are the warriors with you?" She rolled her eyes. "Well, get everyone back to the Cave. Now."

The card phone disappeared.

Endelle slid her hand to the nape of Alison's neck, squeezed, then folded them both to the warriors' rec room. Alison stumbled when her feet touched down, the result of Endelle's frustrated touch.

Medichi, Jean-Pierre, and Santiago were still there along with Thorne. Santiago sat on a stool this time and with his right hand held a huge sub to his mouth. He took a big bite, his eyes wide. In his left hand he flipped a dagger, a piece that glinted with red jewels on the hilt. Luken and Zacharius returned next, both in flight gear. The warriors would be on duty all night as it was.

Thorne put his phone to his ear, spoke in a low voice, nodded a couple of times, and a moment later Kerrick blurred into the room. His gaze skated in Alison's direction, caught, and held. This time he let loose a wave of cardamom that hit her in a full-frontal assault and knocked her flat on her ass.

He smiled, crossed his arms over his chest, and stared down at her. He wore his black leather kilt, weapons harness, heavy battle sandals, really hot studded wrist guards, and a moment later mounted his enormous white wings, something she knew, *she knew,* he had done just for her. He looked sexy as hell, exactly the way he had looked when she had first met him. Even his hair was free of the *cadroen*.

She picked herself up and dusted off her fatigues. She met his gaze, unwavering this time, his expression intense as though he was trying to tell her something without saying it either aloud or in her mind.

Something had changed.

Her breath caught. She blinked or tried to.

What is it? she sent.

But he offered only a shake of his head and a faint smile, a familiar crooked curve of his lips. Her heartbeat sped up.

What had changed?

Oh, God, everything. *Everything.* She felt it in the air between them.

She stepped away from Endelle and moved to a position in which she could address both the Supreme High Administrator and the Warriors of the Blood.

The warriors stood in a broad arc in front of her, some of the most powerful ascenders on Second Earth.

Thorne, with his bleary red eyes, stood near the chicken coop of a pool table.

Luken ranged next to him almost protectively like a guard dog, his thick muscles on display since he already sported flight gear.

Medichi carried his regal height at the apex of this warrior mountain, the tallest among the men, but the one who never mounted his wings.

Zacharius stood next to him, all that thick curly hair trapped in the *cadroen,* but fanning out down his back, his blue eyes narrowed, waiting.

Santiago sat on a stool beside Zacharius, his long wavy black Latin hair hanging loose, shiny, gorgeous. He lifted his hand and the sub disappeared, sent somewhere. He shifted his knees in order to face her.

Jean-Pierre drew up next to Santiago. He held a cue stick in his hand, his long elegant fingers wrapped around the narrow wood. He was an aristocrat in even the grace of his hands.

Endelle stood a foot from him, her wooded eyes dark, her arched brows sitting low, a restlessness to the air surrounding her, impatient as always. *We haven't got all day* screamed from every pore of her body.

Kerrick stood to the left of the pool table, his enormous wings fluttering slightly at the tips, his gaze never leaving her face.

Alison had the strangest feeling, a familiar odd déjà vu sense that she had been here before and would be here again and again, that her destiny, which had been birthed at the medical complex, was being thrown into the stratosphere right here, right now. She had thought that to ascend was everything, the be-all and end-all. She had been wrong. She had only understood her place a few minutes ago in her CO's office, which also meant she was beginning to understand that her arrival on Second Earth had ramped up the war.

She squared her shoulders. "I know now why the Commander wants me dead."

Endelle snorted. "We all know why. You have too much fucking power."

"Yes, but what purpose does that power serve?"

She saw it all so clearly. The revelation came from her dreams, from the deepest parts of her subconscious, from the mysteries well beyond the human rational mind.

She recalled the beauty of staring up into the Third Dimension, of seeing that world open to her, of being painfully drawn to Third Earth but unable to get there. She recalled the pull of the lake, the need to protect the lake.

She stared at Madame Endelle, drew in a long deep breath, moved to the edge of the pool table, and dove straight in: "One day, a few years from now, I open the Trough to Third Earth."

First, a long combined intake of breath, and then silence—heavy, weighted, fearsome silence. A tomb, sealed for a thousand years, could not have been quieter than the Cave.

Endelle's jaw went slack.

Kerrick's green eyes shone with admiration.

The rest of the warriors stared, first at her then at one another; then almost as a unit they turned to look at Endelle. Waiting.

Alison shifted her gaze to Kerrick to see how her announcement had affected him, wondering if he would think she'd suddenly gone insane. How shocked she was to see the certainty in his eye as he nodded once to her. He showed a level of trust and confidence that she had not seen in him before.

She felt buoyed to continue, to explain her meaning, and faced Madame Endelle once more. "I've dreamed repeatedly of White Lake, as well as the Trough and Third Earth, every night since my rite of ascension began. When I dream, I'm always dressed in warrior flight gear and I'm flying over the lake at full-mount. Though I can't explain how I know my purpose, I just do." She pressed a fist to her chest. "Here. And this is why Darian, the Commander, wants me dead."

Endelle blinked only once as she stared at Alison. She finally looked away and started to pace. Her brow had dipped low, and sparks flew from her body as though she could not contain the energy of her thoughts. Back and forth she paced in front of the mountain of her Warriors of the Blood.

"Passage to Third Earth. Shit. Holy shit. Holy, holy shit." She stopped in front of Alison. "Don't fuck with me, ascender. You'd better be damn certain about this. No doubts, questions, not even a glimmer of *What the hell am I saying?*"

Alison shook her head. "Not even a little" came as a whisper from her throat.

But the moment the words left her lips, a deep sinking sensation invaded her heart, forged not from doubt but rather from certainty, profound, raw, overwhelming certainty. She was the instrument by which the pathway to Third would be opened and her life had just gotten harder, a lot harder. She dropped to her knees then buried her face in her hands. She was overcome, and tears flooded through her fingers.

How long she remained there, she didn't know, but to her surprise she felt cool hands take hold of hers. She lifted her gaze and met Endelle's ancient wooded eyes. The Supreme High Administrator of Second Earth folded a dry cloth into her hand and wiped Alison's cheeks, nose, and chin.

Alison looked into Endelle's face, so full of miraculous understanding and compassion, those qualities that ordinarily escaped Her Supremeness.

Endelle nodded. "The responsibility just ground you into the dust, didn't it?"

Alison's lip quivered. "Yes," she whispered.

"I remember this day in my own life some nine thousand years ago. I thought about slitting my wrists."

"Oh, God."

"If you had been flippant, I would have put my foot on your neck again. But this, seeing the devastation in your eyes? Yeah, you've convinced me of the truth of the situation. But holy shit, Alison, opening the Trough to fucking Third. That's major shit."

Endelle, the toughest, meanest bitch ever born, gathered her into her arms and held her. *Welcome to my world,* she sent.

Thorne couldn't keep his feet from moving backward. He didn't stop until his ass hit the pool table. He stared at a fucking nightmare, Endelle on her knees and the newly created ascender proclaiming that she was the vessel by which Third Earth would be opened to Second.

He wanted his Ketel ice-cold and burning down his throat.

Did no one understand, like he did, what this meant? That a new log, the size of an eighteen-wheeler, had just been dumped on top of this burning heap of a bonfire called war?

He scrubbed his hand down his face. He had hoped that Alison's powers would have brought an alignment meant to ease the stress on the warriors, on Endelle, on him, but didn't anyone else get that Darian Greaves would escalate, not fall back?

Thorne needed to get to the Convent, to get to his refuge, but new pain beat at him, for he knew, *he knew,* that the woman he protected would soon be dragged into the war.

Goddammit.

Kerrick took deep breaths, expanding his lungs to their fullest. Pride flowed through him, admiration, full-on lust. God, he loved this woman, and love held him in a state of euphoria, of a decision made, of hope wrestled to the ground, of possibilities, of a future with Alison.

The tide carried the past out to sea. He turned his face to the shore for the first time in two hundred years. Alison was a new land, a new life, a promise of the future.

So she would, in time, be *the one* to bust through the Trough to Third.

Holy hell. His wings shimmied, a fluttering at the tips, a shiver down his spine.

He watched her with Endelle. He couldn't remember seeing Her Supremeness show such tenderness before. Ever. What did this suggest for the future? One glance at his brothers told him they had the same thought. Wonder lit each face like they were looking at a flying pig.

Understanding whirled around him, a cyclone moving faster and faster. Alison had spoken the word *guardian* the first time she had told him of her dreams about White Lake. Had she been a man, he would have concluded she was meant to serve as a Warrior of the Blood. Certainly she had the power. She just didn't have the heart. Besides, only males were guardians.

He frowned and crossed his arms over his chest. His biceps twitched.

Guardian.

What if the concept needed to be expanded? But that would be such a break with tradition.

And yet, from the time Alison had answered her call to ascension, she had been an anomaly, the unexpected. She was his *breh,* something he had never expected to come to him, not when the *breh-hedden* was so rare. Yet here she was.

He drew in another deep breath because what he was about to propose went completely against all Second Earth traditions.

Dreams of White Lake? Now he would deliver the interpretation.

"Madame Endelle," he said, the strength of his voice hitting the walls then bouncing back.

Endelle rose to her feet, Alison with her, both turning to look at him. Endelle planted her hands on her hips and scowled at him.

He moved to stand beside Alison. He took a couple of deep breaths. Endelle had the power to kick him from one end of the earth to the other without moving an inch. Needless to say, he was reluctant to open the door.

"Well, Warrior, what the fuck do you want?"

He prepared to get his ass kicked as he said, "I believe ascender Wells may be a Guardian of Ascension."

She rolled her eyes and spoke in a voice that had *idiot* written all over it. "What the hell are you talking about? Or have you forgotten that guardians are both male and warriors, neither of which ascender Wells professes to be."

Kerrick nodded. "She has dreamed of herself as a guardian, which is a primary indication that she should be granted a special dispensation." He dipped his chin. "Consider. If you granted her guardian status, then COPASS would be honor-bound to bestow on her the rights of guardianship."

Endelle's brow puckered. "The rights of guardianship, which means Alison would have full protection from personal attack. Goddammit, Kerrick, you might actually have something here." She shoved her hands into her long black hair at the temples. She blew the air from her cheeks and shook her head.

"What does this mean?" Alison asked.

"When COPASS was created at the turn of the twentieth century, one of the rules we put into place and to which

Greaves agreed was that all private property held by either
party could not be attacked. All the Guardians of Ascension as well as Greaves's generals have this same right. We
don't attack their estates and they leave ours alone. In addition, the rule extends to personal attack. We stay away from
them and except for conflicts at a Borderland or on Mortal
Earth they stay the hell away from us. Any attack on a
guardian, apart from conflict at a Borderland or on Mortal
Earth, must be prosecuted to the full extent of the law. Even
Greaves doesn't cross this line."

"So wherever I am, on Second," she said, "I would be
safe?"

"As safe as is possible in this world and a thousand
times safer than without the designation."

Alison drew in a quick breath. She turned to Kerrick
and sent, *Then I have a chance, our daughter has a chance.*

Kerrick nodded. He even smiled. *Exactly,* he sent.

"Well," Endelle cried. "I have to say, Warrior Kerrick,
that this is a goddamn brilliant strategy. Fucking brilliant. I
congratulate you and I will see to this. COPASS owes me
because of the attack on the palace and the Commander
can just stick his dick in a meat grinder! Hah!"

Kerrick recoiled at the imagery, and more than one warrior hissed. On the other hand, for all the trouble Greaves
had caused . . . well . . .

As hope soared, Alison trembled. She saw in Kerrick's eyes
a determination that had not been there before. She wanted
to leave the rec room with him right now, and tell him of
her change of heart, but there was still one more matter to
be settled.

She turned to Her Supremeness. "Madame Endelle.
Will you rescind my orders to train as a Militia Warrior?"

"And what would you suggest, ascender? With guardian
status you could still serve as a Militia Warrior, since you'd
be safe from attacks at the barracks."

Alison met Endelle's gaze. She saw the striated brown

eyes and she had experienced the woman's compassion. For nine thousand years, Endelle had carried her burden of authority and command *alone*. The woman needed a lot of help. She also needed to work on her anger management skills. Mostly, however, she thought it likely Endelle could use a friend.

Though she felt certain that the suggestion she was about to let fly was akin to inviting a scorpion to ride around on her shoulder, she said, "If it would please you, I would serve as your assistant." Oh, God, had the words really left her mouth? She had a powerful prescience she would regret this most profoundly in the coming days, weeks, months, years, hell, decades . . . oh, God.

A slow smile spread over Endelle's face as though she had also read Alison's thoughts. Of course she had. Endelle said, "I think the punishment in this case fits the crime. I'll let your CO know she can get back to business as usual while you, my lovely ascender, can show up to my fucking office tomorrow at eight AM sharp." She glanced past her to Kerrick and looked him up and down, a lascivious light in her eyes. "If you can even walk by then."

Alison kept the blush from her cheeks, but just barely. She had very much entered a new world, of warriors and vampires, of the ascended and flight-ready, of violence, profanity, and all sorts of sideways references to sex. Time to embrace it all, so she shrugged then said, "When was *walking* a significant problem on Second anyway?"

At that, the warriors burst out laughing.

Endelle nodded. "Well, well. There might be hope for you yet." She lifted an arm then vanished.

The Cave remained silent for a long moment after she left.

Finally, Zacharius offered the most pertinent comment. "Was she wearing snakeskin?"

> *The myth of the* breh-hedden
> *Alive in the hearts of lovers*
> *Behold what is most precious*
>
> —*Collected Poems,* Beatrice of Fourth

CHAPTER 24

Kerrick took a deep breath and drew his wings back into his wing-locks. He knew one thing as he leveled his gaze on Alison—he'd be taking her to bed and completing the goddamn *breh-hedden* . . . tonight.

He was about to suggest they depart when Thorne caught his arm.

The leader of the Warriors of the Blood looked him square in the eye, nodded, and even managed a rough smile. "So this is it, man."

Kerrick returned the smile. "Yeah." He doubted his voice could get lower.

Thorne punched him in the arm then laughed. "We won't be needing you tonight, just so you know."

Kerrick started to protest since he could always join up later, but Thorne split his resonance. "No," he stated in his I'm-the-fucking-boss voice, the one he rarely used, especially with Kerrick. "See you tomorrow."

For some reason, Kerrick's throat seized. He was headed down a new path, and Thorne would go to the Blood and Bite for one last drink before Central started burning his ear with death vamp movement. He didn't know what possessed him, but he grabbed Thorne in a hard embrace and Thorne responded, holding on tight.

"You lucky sonofabitch," Thorne shot over his ear.

Kerrick's throat tightened up a little more and his eyes burned.

Christ.

Of course the moment ended about as fast as it began. Kerrick released him. Both men started clearing throats and nodding their heads in quick flurries.

Thorne's gravel voice rattled the air between them. "You want a lift back to Scottsdale Two?"

Alison drew near, sliding her arm around Kerrick's waist. He wrapped his arm around her shoulders and squeezed.

"I've got it," she said.

"Actually," Kerrick said, looking from one to the other. "*I've* got it."

They both stared at him. Thorne's eyes popped. "What the fuck? You can fold?" Of course this brought all the brothers' attention in his direction, and within two seconds they'd formed a new arc around him.

"You can fold now?" Alison cried.

He nodded. He couldn't stop grinning. He felt like a kid at a T-ball game who'd scored his first home run.

All the brothers pounded his back, his arms, his shoulders.

"That's amazing," Alison cried. "How? When did this happen?"

The warriors stopped to listen but his eyes were for her. "About the time that I decided I wasn't going to live my life without you."

He heard her quick intake of breath and saw her eyes shimmer with tears. "No crying," he said, kissing her forehead. "There's no crying in ascension." Would she get the reference?

She chuckled. "*A League of Their Own.* I love that movie."

His gaze locked with hers and he could smell a sudden gust of lavender. He breathed in, his nostrils flaring, his eyes closing. Oh. God.

Thorne took the cue without having to be told. He ordered a full-scale assault on the Blood and Bite. The brothers cheered as they folded one after the other, each casting a raised fist of triumph in Kerrick's direction before vanishing.

The sudden emptiness, the quiet in the room affected him. He loved the Brotherhood, the jibes, the cheers, the solid comfort of male bonding. He felt their presence even when gone. He looked around the beat-up hovel of a rec room, the flat-screen smashed and hanging at an angle, the ragged leather sofas, spit wads on the ceiling, the pool table that looked like roosting chickens would show up any minute, new bottles of Ketel One and Maker's and all the other preferred drinks of the warriors, now spread out on the bar.

His brothers.

As he glanced down at Alison, he knew all that would change, from this moment forward. He would have two loyalties now, but the greater would be to this woman, to their child, to his family.

"So you can fold now," Alison said once more.

He nodded. He eased her from his side to gather her into his arms. She rested her hands against his weapons harness and smiled up into his face. He searched her gaze. They were together and his heart was so full. "I want you to know I meant what I said—I won't live my life without you, without our daughter. But those are *my* feelings, *my* wishes, *my* intentions. What are yours? Because as much as I long to be with you, I won't force my will on you. I would never do that."

As she put her hand on his cheek, her eyes glistened. "I want to be with you more than life itself and I refuse to live apart from you. So I have only one question I need to ask you."

"And that would be?"

"Can you take me with you when you fold?"

He laughed. "I don't know but I'm sure as hell willing to give it a try."

"Then do it, Warrior."

He nodded and with both arms holding Alison tight, he thought the thought.

He materialized a couple of seconds later next to his bed with Alison still in his arms. She sniffed twice then threw her arms around his neck and wept.

He wasn't sure why she was crying so he waited. He stroked her hair, her shoulders, her back. His neck grew wet. "I just thought," she said at last, dragging a breath into her lungs, "this would never happen." She sighed and sniffed a little more. He felt a slight movement of air—oh, she'd folded a tissue—then she blew her nose. "But I didn't mean to cry. I'm just so happy."

"I know," he said, savoring her body pressed up against his. "I love you so much. I didn't think we'd get to be together, either. It seemed impossible but I'm so glad you're with me. Here. Now. You feel so damn good in my arms . . . guardian. My wonderful therapist guardian."

She chuckled. He slid his arms around her a little more then squeezed. With her arms still wrapped around his neck she hugged him back.

He had his woman where he wanted her, in his bedroom, right next to his oh-so-massive bed. He wanted her naked and between the sheets.

"Kerrick," she murmured, drawing back, her hands now fondling his biceps. "What changed . . . for you, I mean? Why are you okay with our being together now? I mean I could see that something was different the moment you returned to the Cave, but what?"

He looked into her eyes, her beautiful blue eyes rimmed with gold and still wet with tears. He slid his hand behind her nape and with his thumb stroked her cheek. He loved her so much. "About the time you went to the training camps, I moved into this room, the bedroom I'd shared with

Helena all those decades ago." She shifted slightly and glanced at the bed. She sighed and returned her gaze to him. He continued, "I kept thinking about her, about Helena, about the kinds of things she used to say to me, the arguments she'd used to persuade me to marry her. She was fearless, Alison. But more than that, she had accepted her death, a lesson I needed to learn, especially if I wanted to be with you as well as to have a shared life with our daughter.

"I need you to understand that the warrior drive to protect is like—well, it's as powerful as the shield you set up to defeat Leto. With that drive comes both guilt and an unwillingness to accept failure."

She swallowed hard. "So, for you, Helena's death, and the deaths of your children, was a failure."

His heart sank. "An enormous one."

"But Kerrick—"

"No. Don't try to soothe the pain. You can't and I'm good with it, I really am, but I won't pretend that their deaths didn't create a chasm between you and me." He huffed a sigh, his hands now gliding up and down her back. "The truth is, I could not have taken this step with anyone other than you, because of the powers and abilities you possess. I could never have married an ascender like Helena again because I know in my heart the results would have been the same. She would have died.

"Which is why our being together seems so miraculous to me and why the *breh-hedden,* arriving as it did *with you,* frames that miracle. Who you are, with your powers and abilities, is the reason I can take this step today, the only reason. Nothing less would have made any sense or made our life together possible.

"So I find myself grateful beyond words for you. For. You."

Here he paused and took in a shaky breath. "Even with all that, however, I still had to take one more step because I know, regardless of your powers or mine, should either you or I err one degree to the right or left, if either of us should commit a miscalculation or misinterpretation like the one at the palace, then that is how swiftly our time together ends. Which means that *the other*—or God help us, our daughter—would have to bear the results of death and separation.

"So what I chose, instead of losing you, was to let my failure go, as much as I was able, and to embrace what has been given to me today. What I'm trying to say is that I've accepted my death, as well as yours and our daughter's, and that despite my fear of future sadness and suffering, I want to be with you today, to know you, to love you, to have you in my bed, sharing my life and raising our daughter together."

He looked down at her, willing her to know just how sincere he was. She rose up and kissed him. He thumbed her cheek again and kissed her back. "So what of you?" he said. "What changed for you?"

Alison struggled to find the words. For one thing, she was still wrapped up in everything he had just said, his words a blanket of comfort yet composed of such startling fear and confession and acceptance that she was overwhelmed. She wondered just how carefully she had thought her own situation through. More tears tracked down her cheeks, for him and for her.

She wiped them away with the tissue that had practically become a lump of clay in her hand. With a quick fold, she got rid of the lump and brought a fresh tissue to her. Once more she blew her nose and wiped her cheeks. Her forearms rested on his massive chest, her arms pressed against the ridges of his weapons harness, the hilt of his dagger between them. She looked up at him. "I don't suppose you could lose the harness."

"Absolutely." A vibration touched her arms and the next moment she landed on skin. She slid her arms up around his neck once more and pressed her chest against his.

He murmured his approval, his arms surrounding her again, a blessed cage of solace and reassurance.

She searched for the words to explain. At last, she began. "The reality of having destroyed your chest and abdomen wrecked me, tore my confidence to shreds. The last day I was with you in the hospital, I was convinced I could never be with you because I could never again trust myself.

"Being at the training camps was a blessing because all those field exercises, the hours in the gym, the grueling marathon runs tended to block my grief at being separated from you. But once on my cot, for those few minutes I had before sleep plowed over me like a tank, my heart would turn to you and all the longings and despair returned in full force. I would break into a sweat and tears would pour from my eyes. My need for you, to be as close to you as I am now, tensed every muscle of my body. I can't even begin to explain how hard it was.

"Then sleep would come and I would begin a new day. But night brought the same suffering, the same struggle, and ended the same as each day before, my body sweating, shaking, my pillow damp.

"This evening, however, before the death vamps showed up at the barracks, I'd been asking myself a host of really tough questions, like wouldn't it be better to live full-out than to retreat into a pit of despair, and retreating was what I'd been doing my whole life. And yes, I'll cut myself some slack and say it was necessary on Mortal Earth, but here, on Second, ever since I was forced to battle Leto, something inside me changed. In that moment I saw what I had, what I had been given, the breadth of my powers—but more than that, I loved that I could just be myself.

"Then later, after I'd wounded you, I thought I had only one choice . . . to retreat into myself, to live a quiet, relatively obscure life as I had on Mortal Earth, in order to protect everyone around me.

"Kerrick, I can't live that life anymore. That life is done. That's what's changed. I want to live fearlessly, like Helena. I know I have a lot to learn about my powers, but I'm done *retreating in despair*. On the other hand, I have to ask, aren't you afraid I'll hurt you again?"

He shook his head, his emerald eyes glowing with love.

"What I've been trying to tell you is that even if you become, through no fault of your own, the instrument of my death, I'm okay with it. We're at war and I have no doubt the enemy is already plotting the next round of fun for you, for me, for my brothers, and for Endelle." He paused and kissed her forehead. "We'll do our best, you and me. The rest we'll leave in the Creator's hands."

Alison felt the peace now dominating Kerrick's thoughts, his acceptance of what he could never change, that death happened, even the possibility that death could come through her powers.

For herself, she surrendered to the same possibility but grew determined to become a student of her abilities. At least in that way she could gain more confidence in the future.

She felt his chest rise as he took in a deep breath. She also felt his anxiety spike. "What is it?" she asked.

"Are you ready for this—the *breh-hedden* I mean—and all that it might entail, known or otherwise?"

She took a deep breath. "After all that we've been through, I have no doubt that this is the right path for both of us. At the same time, yeah, I'm a little nervous."

"You want to walk through it?"

She nodded and put her hand to her throat. "So, you'll take me here."

He took a deep breath. "Oh, yeah." His eyelids fell to half-mast as his gaze slid over her throat. Cardamom suddenly drenched the air between them.

The heady spice sent sudden shivers over every inch of her skin. "Then what do I do?"

He nodded and gave himself a shake. "Well, you'll take my wrist at the same time. The *breh-hedden* can only occur if we take blood at the same time."

She touched her lip and felt the incisors lengthen with a mere thought. "I'll take you with my fangs," she murmured. "Wow."

"Exactly."

Another flow of shivers and desire struck low.

"Sweet lavender," he murmured, leaning close and sucking in a quick breath as he kissed her forehead again.

"Then we'll join our minds while we're joined physically and that completes the *breh-hedden*?"

"Yep. And if the historical anecdotes hold true, once we complete the process, you and I will be able to find each other even without telepathy. We'll be able to fold to each other's positions any time, any place."

She smiled and kissed him once, a gentle touch to his lips. "Well, that would be something."

Kerrick looked into blue eyes, rimmed with gold, that had the power to hold him in thrall without once invoking a preternatural power. She was the woman for him. He loved her. He desired her. He needed her. The thought of communing with her caused his wing-locks to thrum. He always felt out of control when she was near, like if he really let go, his wings would mount when he didn't want them to.

"I'm smelling cardamom," she said. "Lots of it." A dewy blush crept over her cheeks. Her lips grew swollen then parted. "So are you going to do anything about it, Warrior?"

The challenge in her words awoke the beast. He narrowed his eyes and growled, a low sound that vibrated heavily in his throat. He wrapped his arms around her a little more then kissed her, a forceful, don't-mess-with-me kiss that had her moaning. He thrust his tongue between her lips. She suckled, which brought another growl rumbling in his throat.

He released her but her body had a boneless quality that made him smile. In a quick movement he lifted her in his arms then mentally rolled the comforter and sheet to the foot of the oversized bed. He settled her on the bed, the way he'd wanted her from the first, her long blond hair feathered out over the dark sheet.

He pushed aside one of her legs, making room so that he could move between. He leaned over her then planted his hands on either side of her shoulders. He looked into her eyes. "So, you ready for this, ascender?"

She drew in a deep breath and nodded. "Yes," she whispered, her hands once more riding his biceps, stroking up and down.

Supporting himself with one hand, he slid the other under her stiff green shirt and made gentle circles on the bare flesh of her stomach. She arched, writhing beneath his touch. Lavender swirled up from her body, from every pore, even from her sweet breath as he leaned down and put his lips on hers once more. He kissed her in a teasing drift that brought soft moans from her throat.

He drew back and looked into her eyes, the blue eyes that had tempted him from the first, exquisite eyes with just a hint of gold around the rim of the iris, her eyes, his *breh*'s eyes. "I love you so much."

Her hand slid to the nape of his neck. "Kiss me again."

He obliged her and for a long time he savored her lips then the moist recesses of her mouth as his tongue drove deep. She slid her fingers through his hair.

He kissed her cheek, her neck, then moved lower to lick her in a long glide up her throat. "I want your blood," he whispered, his voice little more than a deep hoarse rumble.

Once more she palmed the back of his neck, pressing. "My vein throbs for you."

He licked and kissed the skin above her vein. He could feel the powerful pulses against his lips, the invitation so erotic. He was already hard but the thought of sinking his fangs and taking what he wanted shot desire through him like a bolt of lightning. The head of his cock ached for release. The arms poised above her shook with need. And they'd barely gotten started.

Jesus. How the hell was he going to last when he swore that with only two deft tugs he'd be gone?

He took a deep breath, his fingers still teasing her stomach. She moaned and arched, her hips pressing back into the bed then up toward him.

"Kerrick," she whispered. "I want you. How about you get me naked."

He hissed as he leaned back. "So good," he whispered.

He groaned as his hands slipped to the top button of her shirt. He could have folded her clothes off, but dammit, he needed every precious second of this time with her, even though he thought the waiting might just blow the top of his head off.

He took a couple of deep raspy breaths as he undid her shirt. He followed the release of each button with his lips, one hot inch at a time. She panted and writhed beneath the lingering swipes of his tongue.

Once he had her bra exposed, he used a fang and sliced the damn thing in two, savoring the cry that broke past her lips.

As he pushed the lace away from her breasts, his hips jerked in a single hard pump and once more his wing-locks sent a vibration through his body. He put a hand to her lower abdomen and this time folded off her olive-green pants. He looked down. Oh, God. She wore a black lace thong and he groaned.

"Spread your legs."

Your voice, Kerrick, she sent. *Oh, God, your voice, so deep.*

At the same time she parted her legs wide. He settled his thighs low so that he didn't make too much contact. He'd lose it if he did, and he needed to take his time.

He leaned over her, moving his forearms lower. He drew her left breast into his mouth and suckled. She cried out, flinging her arms wide. She wrapped her legs over his buttocks. He suckled until she was writhing beneath him and begging for more. Her hands once more found his hair. She tugged, pulled, and wrapped her fingers in his thick locks, her hips gyrating against his abdomen.

He tended to her other breast, sucking, laving with his tongue. She panted softly, her chest rising and falling in erotic pulses, moans flowing out of her throat as he continued to tend to each breast in turn.

She kept calling his name within his head, *Kerrick, Kerrick,* which again drove him crazy.

He released her breast and drew back. He couldn't get

far since her hands were buried in his long warrior hair and she didn't seem to want to let go. Her face was turned to the side, her eyelids closed, her back arching, her hips undulating, her breath punctuating the air. Goddammit, his wing-locks surged and thrummed. He could feel familiar oil glistening at the apertures, weeping. How the hell was he going to hold on to his wings?

Shit. This whole experience might just kill him.

He settled his mouth on her other breast once more. The feel of her beaded nipple against his tongue . . . oh, God.

Her lavender scent now flooded the room. She was already close to orgasm and his erection throbbed.

He closed his eyes and focused once more on each breath he took. He swore that if his heart were any weaker the damn thing would give one hard jerk and stop pumping altogether.

Without losing contact with her breast, he folded off his kilt, wrist guards, and sandals. The briefs disappeared as well. Her legs, still wrapped around his buttocks, now connected skin-to-skin.

"That's nice," she murmured. "So nice." She moaned now, deep moans from the bottom of her throat. He released her breast and moved down her body, her legs releasing their hold on his buttocks. When he'd reached the juncture of her thighs, he leaned close then carefully slid his fang beneath the left side of her thong and sliced, then the right. With each tug, she gave a little cry.

He peeled back the triangle of lace to reveal her beautiful light curls. His cock twitched. His wing-locks surged. He stroked her gently with the back of his finger. She groaned. Lavender rose to him in heady waves now until his brain was drunk with the scent.

He had to taste her. He slid his tongue down her cleft, dipped low, and dragged over the entrance to her core.

She cried out. "Oh, God, Kerrick." He knew what she wanted.

"Patience," he murmured, his voice hoarse.

"Please." She was begging for contact, *hard* contact.

I just have to have one more taste, he sent, laying his thoughts over her mind. He licked deep this time. *Your honey is like heaven.*

Kerrick. Please.

Her breathing came in long gulps now, her fingers still working through his hair.

He drew himself upright and made eye contact, his knees between her spread legs. Her lips were parted, her breaths quick, full of gasps and uneven. She watched him, her gaze skating over his face, his shoulders, his chest, then falling to his groin.

He took his heavy cock in his hand. She licked her lips. He stroked himself. "Is this what you want?"

She nodded. "God, yes."

He stroked again. "You want me to give it to you?"

Her eyelashes fluttered. "Please. Now. Hard."

He stretched out and poised the head of his cock at her wet swollen entrance. When she moaned and her hips rocked, he plunged into her. She cried out, clutching at his shoulders, his back, his waist. He leaned over her, his forearms resting on the bed.

He moved inside her, his cock at hair-trigger. He pulled back, thrust forward. Once more he concentrated on his breathing. He set up a rhythm.

She looked into his eyes, her hands having found purchase on his shoulders. Tears streamed down the sides of her face and into her hair. "I love you so much."

"I love you, too," he whispered. "Oh, God. You're so tight." She arched her neck, which caused her hips to rock, which in turned stroked him and dammit, he almost came. He hissed and took more deep breaths.

She turned her neck to the side. "Take my vein," she cried, releasing his shoulders.

He didn't hesitate. He crashed down on her neck and bit her hard, sinking his fangs deep. She cried out.

Now take my wrist, he sent.

"Yes," she moaned, her hips meeting his with each thrust of his cock.

His arm felt weighted, heavy, hard to move as he positioned his forearm over her mouth. She grabbed hold with one hand, brought him against her mouth then bit. The feel of her fangs making a virgin strike made his cock jerk all over again and his wing-locks vibrate. Dammit. He was being pulled apart at a thousand different points of his body.

But he would hold himself back. More deep breathing as he drew on her vein, pulling hard. He surged in her now as she suckled his wrist.

Your blood, Kerrick, like an exotic wine.

He groaned, surged, pulled back, breathed, then thrust.

Her blood, flavored of lavender, slid down his throat and power burgeoned in his body. He was a machine over her now, his cock working her deep, his throat swallowing her blood, the muscles all across his shoulders, arms, and back engorged, his wing-locks on fire. So much fucking power.

Alison, I'm going to enter your mind and afterward you'll possess mine. Just be prepared . . . this will complete the breh-hedden.

He heard her breathe through her nose in one long breath as she continued to pull at his wrist.

Do it! her mind called to him.

As he pumped into her, as he took her blood, he pressed his mind against hers and felt her give way. He tumbled inside her, invading her thoughts, seeing instantly just how close to orgasm she was. A tornado of sensation moved around him, whipping his body into a frenzy.

Alison felt the orgasm sitting at the knife-edge of her consciousness. The big body pounding into her, drinking from her vein, penetrating her mind, whose blood flowed down her throat, now possessed her in every possible way.

She wept for release yet held it at bay, holding back, restraining, wanting the moment to last. She panted over his wrist, her mouth still suckling as though she had always known how to take blood in this way. She longed for the moment she could take Kerrick at his neck, and the thought sent new blistering sensations straight up her core.

She felt the seizing begin, deep inside, around his thick hard presence. She could no longer restrain what had to be released.

You're going to come, he whispered within her mind. *I can feel it.*

Deep guttural groans poured from her throat even as she continued to take his blood. She tried to warn him, but the orgasm swamped her, filling her with pleasure that spread like fire from her tender cleft up through her core to rise like a powerful geyser through her body. She screamed against his wrist, but kept drawing his blood into her mouth. At the same time, power rolled from her and struck Kerrick, who groaned heavily in return.

Oh, God, Alison. I'm so close. His hips thrust harder and deeper as she held him with tightened muscles. He kept taking her blood at her neck, groaning, then grunting. A jumble of words moved through her mind, *beautiful, fuck, hard, like-a-fist, touch me, oh, God . . . Alison.*

Yes.

Move into my mind. Now. This is it.

She obeyed the command, still panting over his wrist, his blood like small explosions in her throat. But as he retreated from her mind and she moved into his, as she saw the height of his pleasure, as she saw his love for her, a second orgasm barreled down on her, streaking like lightning over all her sensitive flesh. She screamed. Her power rolled from her and once more beat at him.

Then everything changed, shifted. The sudden *oneness* she experienced with Kerrick in the middle of this profound moment stunned her. She felt all her pleasure. She felt his. She felt him taking in her pleasure at the exact same moment.

As one, each released the vein, the retreat of the fangs sealing the wounds. His gaze locked with hers as pleasure flooded his body, her body, his, hers. Theirs.

Holy shit, he murmured inside her head.

No kidding.

He kept thrusting, hard and fast. She couldn't look away. She orgasmed, power released, and his mouth opened. *I felt your pleasure,* he said.

I know. I can feel what you feel. Unbelievable.

She felt the tensing of his back.

I'm going to come, he sent.

She could feel the intense rush of fluid through his cock, the tremendous pleasure of his orgasm as he pumped into her and filled her. His orgasm continued on igniting hers. Fireworks lit inside her brain. She laughed. She cried.

He laughed with her, his body still surging. *Oh, shit.*

What?

Again, he cried within her mind. *I don't know how but I'm going to come again.* She could feel it as well, that he was readying, which in turn fired her up all over again.

At the same time she could feel the thrumming and weeping of his wing-locks. She also saw the connection and she knew exactly what she wanted to do.

No, he protested.

"Yes," she whispered. She teased the sensitive apertures, her fingers gliding between the hypersensitive ridges between each engorged lock.

"Oh, God," he moaned.

"Just let it go, Kerrick, because I can feel it, too." She started writhing as his pleasure rose, which sent her pleasure skyrocketing. His pleasure, her pleasure, theirs. Jesus.

Within her mind she felt his lower back tense, the tightness of his balls, the pleasure riding the length of his cock, then the pleasure riding once more along the tender flesh of her cleft and streaking up her core.

"I can feel your orgasm." *Holy shit.*

She felt his wings begin to mount as he continued to plunge into her.

Can't help it.

The pleasure of wings mounting, of his orgasm, hers, theirs.

Oh. God.

She screamed. He cried out as he filled her with his seed. Stars exploded in her mind. In his. She levitated as his wings took them off the bed, into the air. She held his neck, his buttocks. He held her back and her buttocks. He grunted with each thrust, her fingers gentler now on the ridges. He managed, still surging, though slower now, a loving rock of his hips while he sustained them in midair, the practiced flight of centuries.

Slowly, he drew his wings closer to his body until she felt the bed once more beneath her back. He took several deep breaths and since she was still so deeply connected to him, she felt his body calling the feathers back, one by one, absorbing the intricate mesh-like filaments that created the superstructure. Flight hormones, like sex hormones, drifted through his body. She felt it all.

He looked into her eyes. "How strange is this? I can feel my lips and your lips. I feel my pleasure and yours."

"Ours."

He shook his head back and forth. "The oneness." He slid his hands down her arms until he locked their hands together.

She sighed. He kissed her. She sighed again.

"I love you," he said. "I love being this close to you, feeling you from the inside out. I knew the *breh-hedden* would be wonderful, but I sure as hell didn't expect this. The moment you moved into my mind, I felt everything you felt while feeling everything I felt." His lids lowered, and his voice was husky. "And can I just say, your orgasms are amazing."

"Ditto."

He kissed her hard. Drew back. "I love being inside you." He rocked into her.

She moaned. "I love you being there." She moved her hips to feel him better. He groaned, and why wouldn't he since she could feel the pressure of her body stroking his cock and just how good it felt to him.

She kissed him, suckled at his swollen lips, breathed in the fierce cardamom scent that suffused the room. "I love how you smell." She put her nose to his thick muscled shoulder and breathed in then licked his skin.

He stroked her cheek and gazed into her eyes. He sighed. "I'm going to remove my mind now. Okay?"

She nodded. He withdrew slowly until his mind separated from hers, but she didn't feel bereft as she had before.

An odd sensation traveled around her head, a strange kind of awareness. Even though he was no longer in her head, she could feel his location, the way his stomach felt pressed into her hips, the way his forearms dipped into the mattress supporting his torso, the way his lips felt as he smiled his crooked smile. She touched his lips with her fingertips. She kissed him and could feel his lips kissing back.

"This is weird. I can still *feel* you, even though you're no longer in my mind."

He cocked his head. "You're right. Huh." He leaned down and kissed her then drew back. "I can feel you as well, but just the exterior of you, your head against the mattress, your fingers in my hair—you like my hair, don't you?"

"I love your hair."

He kissed her again. "Yeah, I can feel you."

"Right now the toes on your left foot are rubbing the sheet back and forth very slowly."

He lifted his brows. "So they are." He frowned then smiled. "And I can feel what the pads of your thumbs feel as you stroke my biceps."

He took her hand and lifted her fingers to his mouth. He kissed each one. "I love your smell. Mm. Lavender."

"Cardamom." She smiled.

He remained inside her for a long time, his weight pinning her to the mattress, anchoring her to her new life. She slid one arm around his massive shoulders, and with the other buried her hand in his long hair.

He nuzzled her neck. He stroked her arms gently.

You're mine, he whispered softly through the euphoric pathways of her brain. *I'll fight with everything I've got to stay alive and to keep you safe. You know that, right?*

With all my heart.

Later, wrapped up in his arms, in a warm cocoon of love, a great love, a profound love, she fell into a deep sleep.

The dream came again. She wafted her wings as she flew over White Lake, her lake, the lake she now protected as a Guardian of Ascension. She sensed a presence, an evil warning, that plucked on the hairs at the nape of her neck.

She drew up and in the distance she saw squadrons of death vampires heading toward her. She was about to fold, her thoughts full of her need to reach Kerrick, but before she thought the thought, Kerrick appeared in front of her, in flight gear and in full-mount, a sword in each hand, his white feathers gilded by the early-morning sun. The brilliance of his presence rendered her speechless. She could no longer see the approach of the death vampires; nor did she fear them. Her warrior flew as her vanguard.

The lake once more called to her, and she lowered her toes into the water and looked up to see the blue swirling brilliance of Third Dimension above her, calling, calling, calling. She felt a tug on her hand and when she looked to her left to see who it was, Havily was there, smiling at her.

The longing returned in full force. She turned her gaze back up to the blue vortex. She tried to rise, but she couldn't, even though she felt Havily encouraging her to try.

Not yet, but soon, the man's voice spoke within her head.

When she awoke with Kerrick's arm surrounding her, she thought of the dream and what it would mean for the future. She didn't know exactly but trusted that time would reveal what she needed to know. She drew his arm tighter across her chest and hugged him. He shifted slightly in his sleep, his big warrior body a shield around her, now and forever.

Soft words came to her, a whisper from deep in her soul, so deep she didn't at first hear them, but they repeated, spoken in that same masculine voice, *Tend to Havily's dreams.*

The future gains peace,
In the resolution of the past.

—*Collected Proverbs,* Beatrice of Fourth

CHAPTER 25

The next morning Alison folded to Endelle's office complex and at first stood stunned outside the massive pyramid-like buildings, each structure embellished with lush hanging gardens on every floor. This truly was a new world, one she hoped she'd be able to explore, one that valued horticulture as an art form.

She entered the building along with a variety of administrative and executive types. She rode the elevator to the top floor.

SWWL SUPREME HIGH ADMINISTRATOR OF SECOND EARTH was printed in absurdly tall gold lettering on a long bank of plate-glass windows.

Tacky, Alison thought.

But quite typical.

The doors swished open, and as she crossed the threshold she was aware of tremendous chaos. A sea of desks spread out in front of her, all occupied, all weighed down with paper. There were no plants in sight, no color on the walls, no pictures of family members. She thought of the classic film *Nine to Five*.

Toward the back, bundles of papers were stacked everywhere, giving the environment the look of a recycling plant doing a very poor job.

Even so, she could feel an electric excitement in the air and wondered what was going on.

Almost as one, the brigade of administrative assistants, male and female, rose in a sudden wave and applauded in her direction. She turned around to see what kind of dignitary had arrived, perhaps even one of the warriors, but no one was there. She turned back around and found all eyes on her. Oh. The applause was meant for her. She could not have been more astonished. Nor could she keep a blush from warming her cheeks.

She put a hand to her chest and drew in a deep breath. She worked to keep tears from flooding her eyes. She gave a little wave and smiled, not certain what else to do.

Whistles followed. The applause grew louder. Executives from various offices opened doors and also put their hands together.

An assistant, a female, with curly brown hair, approached her. The young woman quieted everyone with two raised hands. She turned to face Alison. "We have been anticipating your arrival, ascender Wells. We welcome you to Second Earth and to our offices. We wish you every blessing as you serve Madame Supreme High Administrator. Again, welcome."

"Thank you so much."

The applause once again thundered through the long crammed space and only stopped when Madame Endelle appeared at the end of the corridor off to the left. The slight bristling of her enormous wings, gold this time, sent everyone back to work.

Once she had managed her staff, she addressed Alison, "Well, I sure as hell hope you're ready for this." She drew her wings abruptly into her wing-locks, a movement that caused a breeze to flow over Alison as well as a slight scent of animal. Oh, she wore a skirt bearing stripes, similar pelts of some sort, all stitched together, made up of . . . raccoon, maybe?

"We might as well get started. Take these."

She waved her hand and an old-fashioned stenographer's pad and pen appeared in the air in front of Alison. She grabbed them as they started to fall, then she laughed. Had Her Supremeness not heard of a laptop?

She led her down a long hall of offices to a massive executive suite at the very end. With zebra hides scattered over the floor, the room reflected an essential part of Endelle's unique persona. A massive slab of white marble formed the top of her desk and was supported by . . . elephant tusks?

"Woolly mammoth," Endelle said. She dropped into her black chair draped with what looked like an Appaloosa horsehide. She narrowed her eyes at Alison. "Now, let's get one thing straight. I'm in charge and there will be a lot of paperwork and legal issues to resolve before you are granted guardian status. So don't even think about taking a high tone with me or making any more fucking demands. You will do as you are told for a good long while."

"Yes, Madame Endelle."

Alison couldn't repine. She had what she desired most, a place in a society that accepted her bizarre range of powers, and a real hottie of a vampire for a boyfriend who adored making love to her, taking her blood, and exploring her mind. She still reeled from waking up this morning to his body stroking hers then his tongue doing such things . . . okay, better to stay focused on the business at hand.

"No. Go right ahead," Endelle said, having clearly dipped into her mind. "I think you just made my day."

Alison guarded her thoughts, blanking out in order to keep her private life private. She set her mind to a mundane recollection of other things she had done, like putting cups in the dishwasher this morning. *Top row. Right side.*

Endelle rolled her eyes. "You are no fun at all."

Plates stacked on the bottom. We need more coffee since Kerrick prefers his like mud. Maybe purchase a second coffeemaker for me. I wonder what the grocery stores on Second look like. I think I'll bring flowers home tonight.

"Enough," Endelle cried. "You will bore me into the grave if you keep going."

Alison smiled. She was grateful, brim-full of thanksgiving for her new life. She was happy to be across from She Who Would Live. No, she could not repine, and right now, if Endelle asked her, she'd drop down and kiss the woman's feet.

Endelle's laughter chimed through the room. "That won't be necessary," she said. She trilled her laughter anew. "All right, let's talk about what I expect of you."

Alison sat down opposite her and listened. She Who Would Live spoke long and eloquently about the nature of her duties, which covered everything from fetching Starbucks from Mortal Earth to visiting High Administrators around the globe. "And I want you to teach those idiots at the training camps how to throw a proper hand-blast.

"All in all, I'm glad you've come, Alison. I trust I don't have to tell you how important it is that nothing I say to you from this moment on leaves either this room or your mind. Do you understand?"

"Of course," Alison said.

Endelle formed a shield around them both then clasped her hands together on the desk. "Now, let's talk about Leto."

That night, Kerrick sat at the bar at the Blood and Bite, the music off for the moment, the strobes quiet. Only a few couples moved around on the dance floor pretending the music still played.

He wore flight gear ready for the night's work. He had shared dinner with Alison then shared her body but before he knew it, he was back to his duties as a Warrior of the Blood.

He'd barely touched his Maker's. All his brothers had gathered around him but no one had asked the question that burned in the air, all but sending smoke rings to the rafters.

Words weren't sufficient anyway, so he extended his right arm and turned it over so that the bruising on his wrist was visible.

"Holy shit," Luken murmured.

"So you did it," Zacharius cried.

Santiago slapped Kerrick on the shoulder. "Fuck."

"Yeah," he responded. He nodded. He tried to think what the hell to say to them. Even now, he knew exactly where Alison was . . . in the kitchen emptying the dishwasher, and . . . she was singing.

He sighed.

A ripple of tension passed through the men. Bodies shifted, glasses got plunked down on the bar. Sam moved bottles back and forth, refilling as needed. Fire went down throats.

Still, the warriors didn't move away from him so he knew he needed to say something to relieve the intense curiosity. He opened his mouth to speak, but words failed. He gestured with a palm up and brows raised. He frowned, he grimaced, he shook his head. He felt compelled to tell them something, but what?

Heaven, however, seemed like too small a word. *Rapture* fell flat. *Extraordinary* was . . . well . . . just *ordinary.*

Finally, he said the only thing that made any kind of sense or could explain how complete the experience had been for him. "For the first time in about two hundred years, I slept . . . for eight hours straight."

Bodies shifted once more, soft curses broke the air, shoulders fell, and breathing recommenced.

"Sleep," Thorne murmured. "Well, that would be something."

"No shit," Medichi echoed.

"Merde," Jean-Pierre stated succinctly. "I'd kill for so many hours of sleep all at one time."

Two mornings later, just after dawn, after Kerrick had been home from a night of battling for a full *twenty minutes,* Alison reclined in bed, her fingers caught yet again in his hair. He had made passionate love to her and she was beyond satiated. He had not been patient enough to allow for the entire *breh-hedden,* but she suspected fulfilling the breadth of the ritual would be saved for special occasions or at the very least when time, urgency, or fatigue wasn't a factor.

She giggled since he kissed her stomach, ribs, and belly while at the same time talking to their daughter.

He looked up at her. "What about *Lucy*? We could call her Lucy."

"Why are you thinking about names when she is still just a ball of replicating cells?"

"Because she's *my* ball of replicating cells and of course I'm thinking about names." He kissed her stomach then bit at one of her ribs, which made her squirm and giggle some more. He kept palming her naked breasts and occasionally shifted position to kiss her deep between her thighs, so she suspected, *hoped,* he would make love to her again before he fell asleep for the day.

"So what do you think about Lucy?" he pressed again.

Alison smiled. "It's a thought." She twisted her fingers a little more through his long warrior hair.

"How can you not like Lucy?"

"Lucy is a perfectly lovely name," she stated.

"But you aren't really into it."

She sighed. For some reason he wanted the matter of his daughter's name settled right now.

Alison had a different idea entirely, but she felt nervous about bringing it up since she had no idea how he would receive it. She was afraid the name she really wanted for their daughter would open old wounds instead of giving the respect and honor, the legacy, she intended.

He turned back to her stomach and got very close. She thought he meant to kiss her again and prepared to enjoy his lips on her abdomen once more. Instead he addressed the fiery ball of cells.

"Lucy," he said, deepening his voice in a really wretched imitation of Darth Vader. "I am your *father.*"

Alison groaned. Her *breh* was such a ham. A terrible, wonderful, sexy, ascended, vampire ham. Who'd've thought?

He kissed her stomach then looked up at her. "So you're not going for Lucy."

Since he wouldn't let the subject go, she said, "Actually, I have another idea."

He narrowed his eyes. "What's going on? Your heart rate has increased. Are you worried about telling me?"

She nodded then took the leap. "What if we called our daughter Helena?"

He blinked. His lips parted. "You want our daughter to be named for my second wife?"

She had caused him distress. She could feel it. She reached toward him then cupped his face with both hands. "Let me explain. Helena gave her life to be with you, to ease you. Knowing what you, what all your warrior brothers go through, I'm so grateful to her for being with you those ten years of your life. I would like our daughter to have that kind of heart, that kind of enormous courage."

He took her hand and kissed her palm, a long lingering kiss. He looked up at her, his emerald eyes shimmering. "You amaze me," he whispered. *So generous* traveled from his mind to hers. "Naming our daughter for Helena would honor her, and nothing would please me more. Thank you, Alison. I'm so grateful. So very very grateful."

Again, he kissed her palm.

She looked down at the warrior head bent over her hand. She loved him with all of her heart, her mind, her soul.

She was his *breh*.

She would forever be his *breh*.

Later, when Kerrick had fallen asleep, Alison left the beautiful warmth of her warrior's bed, now her bed, picked up her new iPhone, then moved onto the balcony, which overlooked a vast rolling lawn. At the far end, beneath the shade of dozens of trees, enormous mounds of honeysuckle were alive with sparrows flitting everywhere and chattering like mad. Dawn had broken over the Valley of the Sun.

Her heart beat in little irregular bursts as she punched in the number that dialed her sister.

Joy's melodic voice demanded to know if she was still in Mexico.

Mexico?

Not exactly.

Alison wrapped her arm around her stomach as tears flooded her eyes. She turned slightly to look in the direction of the bed.

Kerrick was on his back, one massive arm, bunched with muscle, thrown over his head, his thick torso bared to the waist. His neck was raw where she had taken him at the vein the day before. She definitely needed more practice but he wasn't complaining.

"Joy," she whispered, not wanting to wake him. "I had to call to let you know . . ."

"What?" Joy breathed, her voice low as well. "Tell me, tell me."

"I've met someone."

Squeals erupted from the other end of the phone. "And . . . and you've done it? I mean you've had sex and it was okay? Nobody got hurt?"

"No one got hurt," she echoed. "And you were so right. He's strong, *very* strong, and he can handle all my weird power and abilities."

Joy squealed again. Ryan's muffled voice sounded in the background. "Everything okay?"

"Lissy met a man."

"That's good but oh, thank God. I thought the pipe broke in the bathroom again."

"Hush. Go back to sleep." Returning to the phone, Joy once more spoke in a quiet voice. "So is he a bodybuilder or what?"

Or what, was the answer.

"Not *exactly* a bodybuilder."

Now . . . now to explain about vampires, wings, and the dimensional world of ascension.

ASCENSION
TERMINOLOGY

ascender n. A mortal human of earth who has moved permanently to the second dimension.

>**answering the call to ascension n.** The mortal human who experiences the hallmarks of the *call to ascension* will at some point feel compelled to answer the call to ascension, usually by demonstrating significant preternatural power.

>**ascendiate n.** A mortal human who has answered the *call to ascension* and thereby commences his or her *rite of ascension*.

>**ascension n.** The act of moving permanently from one dimension to a higher dimension.

>**ascension ceremony n.** Upon the completion of the *rite*

of ascension, the mortal undergoes a ceremony in which loyalty to the laws of Second Society are professed and the attributes of the vampire mantle along with immortality are bestowed.

call to ascension n. A period of time, usually several weeks, in which the mortal human has experienced some or all of, but not limited to, the following: specific dreams about the next dimension, deep yearnings and longings of a soulful and inexplicable nature, visions of and possibly visits to any of the dimensional Borderlands, etc. See *Borderlands.*

rite of ascension n. A three-day period during which an *ascendiate* contemplates *ascending* to the next highest dimension.

the Borderlands pr. n. Those geographic areas that form dimensional borders at both ends of a dimensional pathway. The dimensional pathway is an access point through which travel can take place from one dimension to the next. See *Trough.*

breh-hedden n. A mate-bonding ritual that can only be experienced by the most powerful warriors and the most powerful preternaturally gifted women. Effects of the *breh-hedden* can include but are not limited to: specific scent experience, extreme physical/sexual attraction, loss of rational thought, primal sexual drives, inexplicable need to bond, powerful need to experience deep *mind-engagement,* etc.

cadroen n. (Term from an ancient language.) The name for the hair clasp that holds back the ritual long hair of a *Warrior of the Blood.*

Central pr. n. The office of the current administration that tracks movement of *death vampires* in both the second dimension and on *Mortal Earth* for the purpose of alerting the *Warriors of the Blood* and the *Militia Warriors* to illegal activities.

the darkening n. An area of *nether-space* that can be found during meditations and/or with strong preternatural darkening capabilities. Such abilities enable the *ascender* to move into nether-space and remain there or to use nether-space in order to be in two places at once.

death vampire n. Any *vampire,* male or female, who partakes of *dying blood* automatically becomes a death vampire. Death vampires can have, but are not limited to, the following characteristics: remarkably increased physical strength, an increasingly porcelain complexion true of all ethnicities so that death vampires have a long-term reputation of looking very similar, a faint bluing of the porcelain complexion, increasing beauty of face, the ability to enthrall, the blackening of *wings* over a period of time. Though death vampires are not gender-specific, most are male.

dimensional worlds n. Eleven thousand years ago the first *ascender,* Luchianne, made the difficult transition from *Mortal Earth* to what became known as Second Earth. In the early millennia four more dimensions were discovered, Luchianne always leading the way. Each dimension's ascenders exhibited expanding preternatural power before ascension. Upper dimensions are generally closed off to the dimension below.

duhuro **n.** (Term from an ancient language.) A word of respect that in the old language combines the spiritual offices of both servant and master. To call someone *duhuro* is to offer a profound compliment suggesting great worth.

dying blood n. Blood extracted from a mortal or an *ascender* at the point of death. This blood is highly addictive in nature. There is no known treatment for anyone who partakes of dying blood. The results of ingesting dying blood include but are not limited to: increased physical, mental, or preternatural power, a sense of extreme euphoria, a deep sense of well-being, a sense of omnipotence and fearlessness, the taking in of the preternatural powers of the host body, etc. If dying blood is not taken on a regular basis, extreme abdominal cramps result without ceasing. Note: Currently there is an antidote not for the addiction to dying blood itself but for the various results of ingesting dying blood. This means that a *death vampire* who drinks dying blood then partakes of the antidote will not show the usual physical side effects of ingesting dying blood; no whitening or faint bluing of the skin, no beautifying of features, no blackening of the *wings,* etc.

folding v. Slang for dematerialization, since some believe that one does not actually dematerialize self or objects but rather one "folds space" to move self or objects from one place to another. There is much scientific debate on this subject since at present neither theory can be proved.

grid n. The technology used by Central that allows for the tracking of *death vampires* primarily at the *Borderlands* on both *Mortal Earth* and Second Earth. Death vampires by nature carry a strong, trackable signal, unlike normal *vampires.* See *Central.*

Guardian of Ascension pr. n. A prestigious title and rank at present given only to those *Warriors of the Blood* who also serve to guard powerful *ascendiates* during their *rite of ascension.* In millennia past Guardians of Ascension were also those powerful ascenders who offered themselves in unique and powerful service to Second Society.

High Administrator pr. n. The designation given to a leader of a Second Earth *Territory.*

identified sword n. A sword made by Second Earth metallurgy that has the preternatural capacity to become identified to a single ascender. The identification process involves holding the sword by the grip for several continuous seconds. The identification of a sword to a single ascender means that only that person can touch or hold the sword. If anyone else tries to take possession of the sword, other than the owner, that person will die.

Militia Warrior pr. n. One of hundreds of thousands of warriors who serve Second Earth society as a policing force for the usual civic crimes and as a battling force, in squads only, to fight against the continual depredations of *death vampires* on both *Mortal Earth* and Second Earth.

mind-engagement n. The ability to penetrate another mind and experience the thoughts and memories of the other person. The ability to receive another mind and allow that person to experience one's thoughts and memories. These abilities must be present in order to complete the *breh-hedden*.

mist n. A preternatural creation designed to confuse the mind and thereby hide things or people. Most mortals and ascenders are unable to see mist. The powerful ascender, however, is capable of seeing mist, which generally appears like an intricate mesh, or a cloud, or a web-like covering.

Mortal Earth pr. n. The name for First Earth or the current modern world known simply as earth.

nether-space n. The unknowable, unmappable regions of space. The space between dimensions is considered nether-space as well as the space found in *the darkening*.

pretty-boy n. Slang for *death vampire,* since most death vampires are male.

Seer n. An *ascender* gifted with the preternatural ability to ride the future streams and report on future events.

Seers Fortress pr. n. *Seers* have traditionally been gathered into compounds designed to provide a highly peaceful environment, thereby enhancing the Seer's ability to ride the future streams. The information gathered at a Seers Fortress benefits the local *High Administrator.* Some believe that the term *fortress* emerged as a protest against the prison-like conditions the Seers often have to endure.

split-resonance n. Split-resonance is a state of vocal expression, including speech, in which the resonance has been split into two or more resonances. Resonance, when split, has a profound impact on the listener. Split-resonance can be used to enthrall, create emphasis in conversation, express a variety of emotions, and arouse during sex. When used with telepathy, split-resonance can cause severe pain within the mind of the listener.

split-resonance v. To split resonance is to craft any vocal expression, including speech, into several resonances at once. See *split-resonance n.*

Supreme High Administrator pr. n. The ruler of Second Earth. See *High Administrator.*

Territory pr. n. For the purpose of governance, Second Earth is divided up into groups of countries called Territories. Because the total population of Second Earth is only one percent of that of *Mortal Earth,* Territories were established as a simpler means of administering Second Society law. See *High Administrator.*

Trough pr. n. A slang term for a dimensional pathway. See *Borderlands.*

Twoling n. Anyone born on Second Earth is a Twoling.

vampire n. The natural state of the *ascended* human. Every ascender is a vampire. The qualities of being a vampire include but are not limited to: immortality, the use of fangs to take blood, the use of fangs to release potent chemicals, increased physical power, increased preternatural ability, etc. Luchianne created the word *vampire* upon her *ascension* to Second Earth to identify in one word the totality of the changes she experienced upon that ascension. From the first, the taking of blood was viewed as an act of reverence and bonding, not as a means of death. The *Mortal Earth* myths surrounding the word *vampire* for the most part personify the Second Earth death vampire. See *death vampire*.

Warriors of the Blood pr. n. An elite fighting unit of usually seven powerful warriors, each with phenomenal preternatural ability and capable of battling several *death vampires* at any one time.

wings n. All *ascenders* eventually produce wings from wing-locks. *Wing-lock* is the term used to describe the apertures on the ascender's back from which the feathers and attending mesh-like superstructure emerge. Mounting wings involves a hormonal rush that some liken to sexual release. Flight is one of the finest experiences of ascended life. Wings can be held in a variety of positions, including but not limited to: full-mount, close-mount, aggressive-mount, etc. Wings emerge over a period of time from one year to several hundred years. Wings can, but do not always, begin small in the first decade then grow larger in later decades.